THE
GOD
MACHINE

✦ Book 2 ✦

THE GOD MACHINE

✦ Book 2 ✦

EMERGENCYCOMPLAINTS

Podium

Cover design by Iromonik

ISBN: 978-1-0394-5053-0

Published in 2024 by Podium Publishing
www.podiumaudio.com

THE
GOD
MACHINE

✦ *Book 2* ✦

CHAPTER 1

Luke woke up a little bit stiff, sort of cold, and ravenously hungry. Zea was practically lying on top of him with both her own cloak and his pulled over top of her. Their legs were tangled up, and she had one of his arms firmly anchored around her, his hand grasped with hers. Her hair tickled his nose with each breath she took.

It was a good way to wake up.

After a few minutes of just sort of existing and enjoying the moment, Luke disentangled himself and left Zea wrapped in both cloaks while he went to relieve himself and see about finding something to eat. Game was surprisingly scarce, considering how easy it normally was to find something meaty and aggressive to kill, but **[Survivalist]** was quick to point out various nuts, berries, and roots that were edible.

"I guess we're going vegan today," he said as he gathered them up in his pockets, then used the hem of his shirt as a basket when he ran out of space.

He didn't have a clue how to prepare them, and they would probably taste like shit raw, but Luke was hungry enough that he didn't care. His only regret was that he'd completely demolished all the food they had last night while they were walking. Zea hadn't said anything about it, but he could feel her judging him.

He found her awake at their campsite and hard at work rebuilding the fire that had burned low throughout the night. Wordlessly, he deposited his haul into a pile nearby. She gave it a look, then arched an eyebrow at Luke.

"Sorry, it was all I could find. I don't have anything to cook them with."

"I'm not surprised." Zea reached into her bag and pulled out a small, long-handled metal pan. She sorted through what he'd brought back and separated out the fruit, then tossed the roots into the pan and held it over the new fire.

"Here, take over for me while I finish this," she said, gesturing for him to hold the pan. "Just keep it at that height and give it a shake a few times a minute."

He watched, bemused, as she started cracking shells and peeling things and doing other stuff that he didn't even have the words to describe. "How do you know how to do all of this?" he asked.

"This is basic [Cooking] stuff. Do you not have that skill?"

"I don't, no."

"That's weirdly impressive that you managed to go this long . . . Oh, right . . . I'm sorry. You probably don't have a lot of the skills people normally pick up just from living life."

"It can't be that bad, can it?"

"I have twenty-eight skills," Zea told him.

"Oh . . . wow." Luke called up his own status and skimmed his list. "I have . . . sixteen."

"And how many of those are combat skills?"

"Eight . . ."

Zea sighed and shook her head. "This is what I mean. Since you got here, you've done nothing but fight. And that sucks. There should be more to your life than just fighting to keep it."

"I mean . . . it's not all bad. And besides, it's not like I didn't have a life before I got here. My whole existence hasn't been just running headlong into the next disaster."

"Still—Oh, hey, give that another shake and pull it off the heat. Still, it's not fair to you, and it's not fair that you got pulled into this whole shit show. Thousands of people want you dead for something that's not your fault."

Luke did as instructed, though it was a mystery to him how she knew it was done. It all looked the same to him, which was probably why most of what he cooked for himself ended up burnt. If this ended up not tasting like crap, he would have to consider picking up [Cooking] for himself.

"Do you think we'll run into more people looking for me?" Luke asked. There were no cell phones, no internet, not even a postal service as far as he could tell. They didn't have cameras, so he doubted anyone really knew what he looked like unless they'd personally interacted with him, though he did find the idea that someone had made some big oil painting of him from memory to use for a wanted poster sort of funny.

"If we're quick enough, we might stay ahead of it," Zea said. "But I'm not that quick. You might beat it, but I won't."

"So the next city we get to, we could expect trouble from the church?"

"It's probably best to plan as if we should. We'll be better off sticking to small villages and towns for resupplying and sleeping, maybe staying off the main road completely. You need a new set of clothes, too. You can't just go walking into town wearing a shirt covered in bloodstains."

"That's true," Luke said. "Uh . . . I don't have anything else to wear though, and I don't think we're going to find a pants tree anywhere on the road."

"Yeah. It's going to be an issue. No matter what we do, people are going to remember it if anyone from the church comes around asking questions. A dwifkin buying human-sized clothing is weird. A human covered in dried blood is probably worse. Maybe we could steal something."

"Um, not to change the subject, but, Zea, I'm sorry you got caught up in all of this. You don't have to come with me. You can take the money and go somewhere else. I'm sure they won't look for you all that hard if I'm still out there running around."

Zea just rolled her eyes. "You're an idiot. Of course I'm coming with you. But I have some stuff I need to tell you first. I don't want you to be surprised later if shit goes wrong because of my past."

Luke had figured she'd had something going on, but it hadn't felt polite to bring it up. She'd been homeless and hanging onto life by her fingernails, no family, no real friends, no belongings. When they'd met, she'd been wearing literal rags. People didn't fall that low for no reason.

"I'm an escaped slave," she said. "So, you know . . . a fugitive, kind of like you. Fun, right?"

"Slave?" he echoed. "What the fuck. This world allows slavery? Why? That's like the evilest shit."

"Your world doesn't?" she asked, surprised.

"Well . . . not most of it. Not where I lived, at least. So . . . Yeah, that's super fucked up."

"I'm glad to hear you're not on the slavers' side, but technically speaking, I'm runaway property. There are people who make their living hunting for slaves, and we're all marked magically to make it easier to recover us. That's why I live so far north. You noticed there weren't many dwifkin in Valtira, right?"

"That's true," Luke said. "I guess, practically speaking, my only concerns are the chances that someone will recognize you and try to capture you, and where we can get warmer clothes in your size."

"So that's the other part. The reason I'm a slave. You know how most people don't level up as high as you have, and AP is scarce for them? Well, one of the ways rich people get around that is by making slaves level up and get support skills for them. I'm an enchanter. I've got a whole bunch of skills related to it, but they're mostly rank 1 since I wasn't there long enough to start merging them. If I hadn't run, they would have forced me to level up a bunch more, set me to work enchanting anything and everything they wanted, then killed me in a decade or two as soon as I started showing signs of XP madness."

Luke just sat there, speechless. He'd never given much thought to how exactly a society that existed under the system functioned, or the ways in which the rich would abuse the poor, but it seemed there were shitty people everywhere. Exploiting others for profit was a tale as old as time, and the fact that people who leveled too high regularly went insane and had to be put down was no reason to slow down the collection of money.

He made a mental note to come back to the idea of merging skills. Curt's build notes had given him the impression that the skills had to be at max rank to do that, which would require a ton of AP, so either he was misunderstanding something or slave owners regularly pushed their slaves up to level 35 or 40 so they could afford to do that. Neither would surprise him.

"Anyway, yeah . . . I escaped by suppressing the slave runes. That's the danger of training an enchanter; we know exactly how we're being controlled and how to fix it. It's costly to get what I need to keep them from reactivating, and the only way to permanently drain them is to let them run for a few years, more than long enough for a slave hunter to follow the trail to me."

"That's why you're so poor," Luke realized. "I knew there had to be something. You're too smart to not be successful."

Zea rolled her eyes, but he caught a smile on her face. "So I'm going to be an ongoing financial drain to keep around, in addition to slowing you down. I was going to talk to you about all of this before but . . . Well, it didn't work out that way. You sure you still want me to come with you?"

"Yep. You're the brains of this outfit. I couldn't do it without you. Plus, maybe I can help?"

"Maybe," she said. "This thing you have . . . Can you change anything? Could you take away all the skills they forced me to take, lower my level back down?"

"I don't know," Luke said. "Probably, if I can purify the bloodline more? Or when I get to the God Machine and do it manually? Uh, System, can I do that?"

"It is within the realm of possibilities, though you are not currently able to make these kinds of changes."

"System?" Zea echoed. Her eyes widened as she caught on. "It's . . . here? Right now?"

"Sure," Luke said. "As much as it ever is, I guess. Thanks, System."

"You are quite welcome. If you'd like your companion to be able to see and speak with me as well, you should be able to manage that if you are able to reach the next stage of purification."

"That's cool, I guess." Luke turned to Zea and added, "System says if I can purify my bloodline, I can make it so you can see and talk to it too."

"Good luck with that. A ritual master who specializes in bloodline purification is going to be attached to a noble house, and they do not freelance. You would need permission from the head of house to borrow their services, which, even if they're willing to give it, is going to cost you. I can't really see us pulling that off."

"Shit. I guess maybe I can do it myself? I'm not going to stop leveling, so I could spend the AP and buy it myself?"

"That's a terrible idea," Zea said bluntly. "You already stick out with all the XP you have, which, by the way, did you level up again?"

"I did," Luke admitted. "I knew I needed some more stats to keep up with Myla. I was hoping to get a few more under my belt before she caught up with us, but that didn't happen. Good thing you were here."

"You're lucky you threw away that monster core and I stumbled across it. That feather you gave me wouldn't have lasted more than twenty seconds without the extra power I fed into it."

"That reminds me, what did you do at the end? Something blew up."

"Let's just say that enchanting is a delicate art, and if the mana flows aren't properly managed, you might find yourself with a bomb in your hands." Zea gave an evil little laugh, but then she sobered up and added, "Aldrick, you need to reconsider this whole leveling thing. If this doesn't work out like you think it will, you'll be putting yourself into an early grave. Even if you can reverse it, people aren't just going to ignore a level 50 walking around."

"Oh, I'm going to take a skill for that. It's called **[XP Mask]**. It makes it so that no one can sense my XP, but I can't sense anything else's either. I've been holding off because I don't want to attack something way above my level."

"What the fuck? There's no skill like that!"

"Uh . . . Yes? There is? System? Is there something I should know about this skill?"

Name	Luke Bennet	Zea Stenter
Level	23	12
XP	43801/44653	6047/6597
AP	0	23
Bloodline	SysAdmin	None
Strength	42	3
Agility	40	5
Stamina	36	4
Perception	39	10
Skills	Mace Mastery (2)	Dagger Mastery (1)
	Sword Mastery (1)	Stealth (2)
	Unarmed Martialist (3)	Keen Instincts (1)
	Power Strike (1)	Lock Picking (1)
	Life Surge (1)	Disguise (2)
	Peripheral Awareness (2)	Deception (1)
	Counter (2)	Bartering (2)
	Twitch Reflexes (2)	Streetwise (2)
	Stealth (1)	Cooking (1)
	Survivalist (2)	Mending (1)
	First Aid (1)	First Aid (1)
	Wood Carving (1)	Thalian (3)
	Leatherworking (2)	Neyardic (3)
	Thalian (2)	Ostari (1)
	Disguise (2)	Mana Manipulation (1)
	Deception (1)	Mana Sight (1)
		Metallurgy (1)
		Whitesmithing (1)
		Goldsmithing (2)
		Gem Cutting (1)
		Engraving (2)
		Rune Forging (1)
		Painting (1)
		Arcano Dynamics (1)
		Sleight of Hand (1)
		Steady Hands (2)
		Cold Reading (1)
		Temperature Acclimation (2)

CHAPTER 2

X P Mask] is a unique bloodline skill," System said.

"Why the hell didn't you tell me that?"

"You never asked."

"Aldrick," Zea cut in. "You've got a vein in your forehead that's looking like it's about ready to burst."

"I . . . It. Just sometimes, it. So. Mad."

He was hardly intelligible, but that was as much as Luke cared to say on the subject. He took a deep, deep breath, counted to ten, counted to ten a second time, and said through clenched teeth, "Are there any other unique bloodline skills?"

"Quite a few, but they are currently locked."

"Can you show them to me anyway?"

"Certainly."

A window popped up in front of Luke detailing several skills. The first one was something called **[Analyze]**, which he could use to peek at the statuses of other living creatures. That would be fantastic once he took **[XP Mask]**. It wouldn't replace being able to feel the XP of other creatures, but if his perception was high enough, he figured it wouldn't make much difference.

Another one was called **[Stat Assignment]**, which seemed to do nothing more than let him rearrange where he'd allocated his AP. He supposed it might be a nice reset button, or if he needed to pump one particular stat for something and then change things back. The description said it took a few minutes to adjust the total, so he doubted it would be useful in combat.

They started getting wilder after that. There were skills to adjust other people's stats too, or to remove or add skills to their status. He found one that would inflict status conditions at any duration, even permanently, and another one that would fabricate raw materials out of nothing. "This is like having debug mode," he said. "Why does this even exist?"

"The SysAdmin abilities were implemented as skills as a way to reconcile them with the system as a whole. They are generally used only by the gods themselves, and only sparingly."

"And if my bloodline was purified enough, I could do that? Just look at someone and tell them, 'No, you don't get to have agility anymore,' and set it to 1? Or take away skills from them?"

"That is correct."

"Why the hell am I going on this long-ass road trip then?"

"Some commands cannot be executed except at the console."

"So what you're saying is, if I ever want to get home, I'm going there one way or another. But theoretically, I could still bring back my family even if I never made it that far."

"Um, Aldrick," Zea said. "I'm sure you sound a lot less crazy to yourself than you do to me, but can we maybe get this campsite broken down and get going while you talk to yourself?"

"Oh! Shit, yeah. Right."

While they cleaned everything up, and Luke snacked on some of the food they'd made, he told her about what he'd discovered. "So you really could reset me," she said. "But that would mean finding a ritual master to do the bloodline-purification ritual on you. Or . . ."

"Or what?" Luke asked, pausing in his work.

"I could do it."

"You could do . . . the ritual?"

"Well not yet, but I could spend AP on it. It'd be temporary, right? I'd have to gain a few levels to take the first rank, maybe a few ranks even, but then after your bloodline is pure, you could just wave your hand and reset it."

"That might work, but if something goes wrong, you could be heading into an early grave."

It was a better plan than anything he'd come up with, and he could help her level up too. The system didn't seem to factor contribution much into XP. It just divided it in half and doled it out. That meant that he could fight things that were level 20 or 25, get her a sling or a crossbow or something, and as long as he was helping, she should level quickly.

He tried to remember how much AP the skill needed but couldn't. Then he shook his head and laughed at himself before opening the skill store and checking. Rank 1 was 50 AP, and it would surely go up insanely fast from there.

"Um, so this is kind of rude to ask, but what level are you? I'm not sure how much AP this skill needs to max it out, but it's going to be a lot."

"We . . . We could trade statuses," Zea said. "I trust you."

"We can?" Luke blinked in surprise. "How do we do that?"

"You have only to will it to her," System said.

"Just kind of think about sharing it with the person you want to see it," Zea said at the same time.

"Oh, that seems easy."

Luke did that, though he wasn't sure if it worked. Before he could ask, a new status window opened up in front of him with Zea's information on it. She was level 12, but with 23 unspent AP. He was guessing those were new levels from killing the inquisitors last night. Her stats were low, but that wasn't surprising. Perception was the highest at 10.

She hadn't been kidding about her skills though. There were eighteen of them at rank 1, and he wasn't even sure what most of them did. "What the fuck is **[Arcano Dynamics]**?" he asked.

Zea wasn't listening though. Her mouth hung open, but she didn't look impressed, just horrified. "Oh gods, this is awful," she whispered. "It's all just . . . fighting and surviving. I'm sorry. So sorry."

"Huh?"

Zea crossed the camp and hugged him tightly. "It's not fair what they did to you," she whispered, her face buried in his side. "You're like one of those gladiator slaves, nothing but pain and blood and struggles."

"Hey now," Luke said, gently pushing her back to look at her. "I told you, it's not like that. I've only been here for two months, and yeah, they've been kind of shitty here and there, but it's not all bad. Plus I got to meet you. You're pretty flexible for a girl with only 5 agility."

Zea sniffed, then gave him a shove and said, "Oh, shut it. You jerk. See what I get for trying to show you some sympathy."

Her eyes unfocused for a moment, and she said, "Luke. So that's your name."

"That's me. I guess we should probably both come up with new identities moving forward."

"That's a good idea," she said, still not looking at him.

Luke waved a hand in front of Zea's face to get her attention. "Hey, it's really not that big of a deal, okay? Yes, it was kind of scary, and it sucked to live through, but I'm fine. Everything is okay. I'm going to do this thing, and I'm going to revive all my family members that this world killed, and then . . . I don't know. They're all going to go home, maybe? Or we'll stay here. I haven't figured that part out. I thought I knew, but . . . Things change."

"Let's think a little less long-term for right now. We need to start walking. You need new clothes. And I am damn certainly not planning on spending another night sleeping outside."

At Zea's prodding, they started moving again. She fed him a hundred questions to ask System, almost all of them things he never would have even thought to ask about, and though she had a lot more luck than Luke did, by the end, she was just as sick of talking to it as he was.

"Why did you ask about evernight deposits?" Luke asked. "Also, what's evernight?"

"It's an enchanter thing," she said. "I need some help keeping up with your stats. I'm fucking wiped out over here, and you haven't even broken a sweat."

Luke looked down at her in surprise. "Do you want to take a break? Or . . . I could carry you?"

She scowled up at him, but said, "A break would be fine."

They found a little glen with a few big rocks in it and sat next to one. Luke used it at a backrest, though he didn't really need it, and Zea laid next to him with her head on his lap. "Maybe I should put some points into my stats," she said. "It would push back the ritual skills, but I know you could go faster if you weren't waiting for me."

Luke hid a wince, but it was true. Zea moved a lot like a regular person from Earth, both in terms of speed and how well she made it across rough terrain. Luke would move at least five times faster and without the need for a break. They were also going to lose a significant portion of their travel time while she slept. If he got four hours in a night, that was more than enough. Zea wanted at least eight, and preferably ten or eleven.

"You know I'm not going to leave you behind, right?"

"Yeah, I know," Zea said. "I still feel bad about slowing you down."

"So, I had some thoughts about that. You're going to need to level up quickly, which means killing monsters, but your stats are so low I don't really feel like it's safe for you to even get near the kind of monsters I fight. A stray hit could kill you."

"Yeah, but . . . every point I waste on stats is that much further away from getting you the good bloodline skills."

"It won't matter if you're 1 AP away from getting the skill if you die," he said. "Besides, you know . . . I don't want you to die, regardless. You're kind of important to me."

"Yeah, I'm pretty awesome."

"Awesome pain in the ass sometimes, but yeah, I think I'll keep you around for a while."

Zea jabbed him in the ribs with a finger. "Please. Least you could do. So, stats first?"

"Some, definitely. You should consider a few combat skills too. I'm planning on doing most of the killing, but you're going to have to do at least a little so the system will give you half the XP, right?"

"How am I supposed to do that?"

"Maybe a crossbow," he suggested, thinking of all the goblins that had carried them. Luke thought he might be able to make one sized for Zea, but it would probably be better if they bought it from somebody a bit more capable than him.

"Okay, stats first. Then skills next time. Can't believe I'm doing this, but . . . here goes."

Her whole body stiffened as she boosted up her stats, and he could visibly see muscle swelling in her arms. She'd been in good shape before, but now she looked lean, and maybe a bit too toned for her clothes. It wasn't a bad look by any means; they just weren't as loose as before.

"How you feeling?" he asked.

"Holy shit, that feels amazing. It's no wonder you've bumped yours up so high. I can't even imagine what 36 stamina must feel like."

"It's pretty cool to be able to run all day and never run out of breath," he said. "You need a minute to adjust?"

"Yeah, just let me soak it in for a bit before we get going."

That was reasonable, he supposed, but he remembered his first few big stat increases and how much energy he'd had right after.

"Hey," Luke said.

"Hmm?"

"Come here."

"What?"

"Just come here," he repeated.

"I'm already here."

"Yeah, but it's hard to kiss you all the way down there."

She smirked up at him. "Don't see how that's my probleeee—Eaaaah!"

Luke scooped her up into his arms and pulled her onto his lap, where she received a thorough kissing, one that she returned quite vigorously. "This was not how I planned to spend my break," she protested weakly.

"Plans are for changing," he told her.

"Is that a fact?"

"It is."

Their break ended up lasting a lot longer than they'd planned, but neither of them minded.

Name	Luke Bennet	Zea Stenter
Level	23	12
XP	43801/44653	6047/6597
AP	0	0
Bloodline	SysAdmin	None
Strength	42	7
Agility	40	12
Stamina	36	12
Perception	39	14
Skills	Mace Mastery (2)	Dagger Mastery (1)
	Sword Mastery (1)	Stealth (2)
	Unarmed Martialist (3)	Keen Instincts (1)
	Power Strike (1)	Lock Picking (1)
	Life Surge (1)	Disguise (2)
	Peripheral Awareness (2)	Deception (1)
	Counter (2)	Bartering (2)
	Twitch Reflexes (2)	Streetwise (2)
	Stealth (1)	Cooking (1)
	Survivalist (2)	Mending (1)
	First Aid (1)	First Aid (1)
	Wood Carving (1)	Thalian (3)
	Leatherworking (2)	Neyardic (3)
	Thalian (2)	Ostari (1)
	Disguise (2)	Mana Manipulation (1)
	Deception (1)	Mana Sight (1)
		Metallurgy (1)
		Whitesmithing (1)
		Goldsmithing (2)
		Gem Cutting (1)
		Engraving (2)
		Rune Forging (1)
		Painting (1)
		Arcano Dynamics (1)
		Sleight of Hand (1)
		Steady Hands (2)
		Cold Reading (1)
		Temperature Acclimation (2)

CHAPTER 3

W hat's this place called?" Luke asked. They stood on a hill east of the town, big enough that he couldn't easily count all the houses, never mind the dozens of farms dotting the landscape. The forest had thinned out considerably after a day of travel and had practically disappeared by the second. That was good for their travel speed, but bad for hunting new monsters to kill.

They had found a few monsters, just barely enough to level them since they were both less than 1000 XP to the next level. Luke saved his AP to take rank 4 of **[Unarmed Martialist]** and **[Tactical Foresight]** next level as planned. Zea spent 5 AP on **[Cadence]** as a tie-in skill to her planned new job as a ritual master and banked the rest to start saving up the 50 AP needed for **[Bloodline Purification Ritual]**.

"I have no clue," she said. "It might be best if I go in alone. You draw too much attention."

"Maybe," he said, remembering the first small village he'd wandered into. "Oh, that reminds me. One place I went to, everyone kept calling me Guardian and treating me like a war vet. What's that about?"

"Someone made some assumptions based on your level and your age. It's not a bad cover actually. We might be able to make it work if you get some more ranks in **[Disguise]** and **[Deception]**. Guardians are people who defend the borders against the endless hordes, such as they are. Basically they repel monsters, and it's not really that unusual for a young person to have a lot of XP from that before they retire from the front lines."

"What would I need to do?" Luke asked.

"You need a lot more knowledge about just about everything in general so people aren't suspicious of you, and to get rid of your accent. Then you'd need to pick up at least a few mannerisms that indicate you're accustomed to a military lifestyle. We don't have time for any of that right this minute though, so I want you to stay here while I go try to figure out how I'm going to find you some new clothes that don't have extra holes and a lot of blood-stains on them."

Luke handed over the money he had on him and said, "You should get some new shoes if there's a cobbler in town. Maybe pick up some road supplies, more than just you need, and say that they're for the whole group?"

"Could work," Zea agreed. "I'll play it by ear. You'll wait here for me?"

"As long as nothing happens."

Once Zea left, Luke settled down and made himself comfortable. "System, can you tell me about history?"

"Yes," System replied. "I may not be able to answer all your questions, but I can share the general shape of events."

"Great, let's start with this Guardian thing. They're some sort of national guard, from the sounds of it?"

"That is essentially correct. The area you are currently in, Thalasa, isn't considered a country so much as a collection of city-states bordering one another. Each city controls the surrounding area to whatever extent they are able, and they have a loose set of agreements for trading purposes and to supply resources to the cities that field military forces in order to patrol the borders between civilized areas and the wilderness.

"In about one hundred miles, you'll leave Valtira's sphere of influence. From there, if you continue north for another two hundred miles, you will reach the city of Kazos, where the Guardians have a heavy presence. Kazos is surrounded on west and north sides by unsettled land, and the average level of its populace is 16. A period of work serving the Guardians is required of all locals when they become adults, and most are retired from service around level 20."

"That seems like the worst place to pretend to be a Guardian," Luke said. "If anyone would know I'm a fake, it would be the actual, real Guardians."

"I am not able to speculate on that," System told him. "Would you like to hear more about the history of the Guardians locally?"

"Not really, but I guess I should."

Luke spent the next three hours trying to focus on System's lecture and occasionally asking questions. He learned about some of the larger battles the Guardians had engaged in, about the time Kazos had been invaded when an entire army of hobgoblins had marched south out of the mountains, or about the time the city had to field a dozen warriors over level 50 to halt the advance of something called an alabaster doganaut. Apparently, those were scary as shit, and there was a big memorial in the city to honor the sacrifices of the people who'd pushed their levels so high and had to be killed afterward.

By the time Zea showed back up, his head was so stuffed full of history and geography that he was sure it would explode. Luke hadn't enjoyed his time in the public-education system and had never had any plans to continue that with higher learning. He liked to do things and learn new skills as needed. Learning for the sake of knowing wasn't something he enjoyed.

He did recognize the need to know all of this, at least as long as he was still a low enough level that other people could conceivably take him out. That was a temporary problem, and he could justify skipping the lectures to just go grind enough bloody weeks and months so as to be untouchable, but that would still leave Zea vulnerable. Any heat he brought on himself would also affect her, and that wasn't something he was willing to do.

So Zea found him massaging his forehead when she marched back up the hill, a large burlap sack held in both hands. "What are you doing?" she asked.

"Getting a lesson on local history, geography, monster ecology, culture, and traditions from System so that my disguise will be better." He eyed the bag she was holding and added, "Is there a change of clothes in there?"

"You're in luck. I did manage to get new pants and a shirt. There's also a river a mile north of town you can bathe in first before you put them on. I even got a bar of soap."

"Yeah, I see it," Luke said, pointing toward a line of trees. "And I actually know how to make soap. One of my skills told me."

"How the hell do you see it from here?" Zea asked, frowning as she peered north. "There's no way. It doesn't matter how high your perception is; there's too much between us and the river."

"There are plenty of small gaps you just can't see," he explained. "You can trace the path of the river from a whole bunch of little slices. There are also a lot of people gathered at one spot where it bends. I'm guessing that's the laundering bank, so maybe we'll avoid that."

They left together, Zea muttering under her breath about his bullshit perception stat and him pretending he couldn't hear her. When they got to the river and found a relatively slow spot, he stripped down and jumped in while she sat at the edge and cleaned herself more carefully. "Try not to get anything bitten off while you're in there," she called out to him when he resurfaced.

"Is that a real possibility?" he asked, swimming against the current to remain in place. It was a lot faster than he'd expected, but it wasn't really all that hard to hold his position with his enhanced strength. He didn't really get tired anymore either, at least not from this little amount of exertion.

"I don't know what kind of fish live in this river. Why do you think I'm over here out of the water?"

"Because you'd have to get naked otherwise, and then we'd end up losing another half an hour of daylight once we start making out?"

"No! I mean, maybe a little, but it's mostly because of the fish, and also because this water is fucking cold."

Those were both good reasons, though Luke found he wasn't much bothered by the cold anymore. He still felt it, but it was more like he was aware of it than that he felt any sort of biting pain from it. Between that and his experiences in the bathhouse, he could only assume that increasing his stamina gave him some built-in resistance to temperature changes.

On the off chance that something with fins and teeth did come along and go after his sensitive bits, Luke scrubbed himself off as quickly as he could with the soap and climbed back out. He then took some time to launder his old clothes while he air-dried and pretended not to notice Zea checking out his butt.

It was hard to keep that up when she leaned over and slapped it, and if he hadn't caught her going in for the slap with **[Peripheral Awareness]**, he probably would have tumbled face-first into the river. "It's like you're trying to delay me with these antics," he said. "Maybe you're working for the church after all."

"Is that the kind of girl who catches your eye? You're just lucky I'm not the jealous type, or I'd be wondering what went on during those lunch dates."

"The second one was a lot more exciting than the first. I got poisoned and had to run for my life. The first one was just a bit of meat and bread and casual conversation."

"Oh, is that all?"

"Everything I'm willing to admit to," Luke said with a smirk.

Once he was dry enough, Luke got dressed while Zea made exaggerated noises of disappointment. He wrung out his old clothes as best he could, which was pretty damn good, all things considered. Then he spread out them on a rock for twenty minutes while he helped Zea finish up her chores. They collected their things and left.

"Oh hey, you got new shoes after all," Luke said. "How are they?"

"Expensive is how they were. Bastard knew I was in a hurry and wouldn't give me even a copper for the old ones."

"The old ones were basically scrap leather," Luke pointed out.

"Don't you take his side!"

Luke laughed. "How much do we have left?"

"Nine gold, six and a half silver."

"I guess we'll have to find work again soon. Maybe the next city. Hell, maybe I could do Guardian work for real. What do you think that pays?"

"No idea," Zea said. She didn't sound happy. "A month ago I would have thought this was an amazing amount of money. I could have lived stress free for months off this."

"The bills always catch up eventually. Speaking of which, what do our expenses look like?"

"Well, about that . . . I've got about a month before I need to renew the blocking enchantment on my slave mark. So I need to find an enchanting lab I can borrow equipment from and get a vial of bellwine ink. If I can get some syrocho leaves and a bit of eucanthrum, that would be even better. More expensive up front, but the enchantment would last for a year instead of a few months."

"I don't know what any of those things are," Luke said. "Do you think we can get them in the next city we pass through?"

"Probably. That's going to be Kazos, less than a week from here if we take the roads. Luke, you know this stuff is going to take almost all your money, right? We'll be starting over from nothing."

"Our money," he corrected her. "And that's fine. We'll figure something out."

"I hope so."

They walked in silence, but Luke could see her mind working to figure out what to do. He didn't know what she was going to come up with, but he trusted it would be good. She was smart that way. He was lucky to have her with him, but he wished it had come about under better circumstances.

Name	Luke Bennet	Zea Stenter
Level	24	13
XP	45005/50687	7261/8325
AP	24	8
Bloodline	SysAdmin	None
Strength	42	7
Agility	40	12
Stamina	36	12
Perception	39	14
Skills	Mace Mastery (2)	Dagger Mastery (1)
	Sword Mastery (1)	Stealth (2)
	Unarmed Martialist (3)	Keen Instincts (1)
	Power Strike (1)	Lock Picking (1)
	Life Surge (1)	Disguise (2)
	Peripheral Awareness (2)	Deception (1)
	Counter (2)	Bartering (2)
	Twitch Reflexes (2)	Streetwise (2)
	Stealth (1)	Cooking (1)
	Survivalist (2)	Mending (1)
	First Aid (1)	First Aid (1)
	Wood Carving (1)	Thalian (3)
	Leatherworking (2)	Neyardic (3)
	Thalian (2)	Ostari (1)
	Disguise (2)	Mana Manipulation (1)
	Deception (1)	Mana Sight (1)
		Metallurgy (1)
		Whitesmithing (1)
		Goldsmithing (2)
		Gem Cutting (1)
		Engraving (2)
		Rune Forging (1)
		Painting (1)
		Arcano Dynamics (1)
		Sleight of Hand (1)
		Steady Hands (2)
		Cold Reading (1)
		Temperature Acclimation (2)
		Cadence (1)

CHAPTER 4

It only took a few hours of traveling before they left the grasslands behind and found themselves once again heading into the forests. Luke considered that to be good news, since they hadn't found anything worth any real XP around the town, and they needed a lot of XP if they were going to execute their plan to turn Zea into a ritual master.

Zea was less than impressed with the idea, not only because it was hard to overcome a lifetime of conditioning that too much XP was bad, but also because it likely meant another night of sleeping outdoors. She'd had enough of that over the last few years to last her the rest of her life, but unfortunately, it didn't look like they'd be regularly sleeping indoors anytime soon.

They stuck close to the road when they could, if only to make sure they kept going in the right direction. Occasionally, Luke would detour into the deeper woods in search of some walking XP. Once, that backfired on him and he ran into some sort of giant lizard thing with six legs that was at least level 30. He thought he might have been able to kill it, but there were plenty of softer targets around, so he simply scooped Zea up in his arms and fled.

"That? That thing right there! That's why people stay on the roads and why we have Guardians," she said after he set her down on her feet about five miles away from the lizard.

"I'll be sure to let them know where to go about finding it," he said. "Whew, scary fucker though, wasn't he? Did you see all those teeth?"

"Yeah, I saw the fucking teeth!" Zea said. "Wouldn't even need to open his mouth all the way to eat me in one bite."

"Another good reason not to tangle with that guy. We'll find something a little smaller to pick on."

Zea huffed and crossed her arms. "I must have been crazy to follow you out here."

Luke sighed and flopped down onto a nearby log. "I'm sorry," he said. "I wish it could have been different."

"Hey, no, come on. I'm just joking. I know you didn't want this to happen, that you're trying your best."

She sat down next to him and leaned over to put an arm around his lower back. Luke shifted in place and put his arm around her too. "I know, and I know it's not my fault, but I'm still sorry. You had enough on your plate without dealing with my problems."

"I am an adult, you know? I could have walked away. I could have turned you in and maybe collected a little reward money if they didn't kill me too. I made a decision to keep working with you. And honestly? I don't really regret that. I'm not thrilled with sleeping in the woods. I'm not thrilled with grinding out more XP, even though I know why and that we can fix it at the end. It's the worry about whether we actually get to the end that weighs on me. But I don't regret spending my time with you. I like you."

"I like you too, even if you are getting all sappy on me."

"Oh, fuck all the way off." Zea gave him a shove. Luke blinked down at her, and she scowled back up when he didn't move. She shoved again, then muttered, "Stupid high stats. What'dya need them to be that high for anyway?"

"So I can do this!" Luke shouted, sweeping her up in one arm while she shrieked in mock surprise. Luke spun them both around several times before leaping ten feet straight into the air. He kissed her at the apex of the jump, then landed on the ground so smoothly that their lips didn't even break contact. Luke's legs flexed to absorb the shock, and when he let her go, her own feet easily reached the ground.

"Okay, that's a pretty good reason," she admitted. "But come on, let's get going. I keep thinking that lizard is going to come crashing through the trees and attack us."

"I won't let it eat you," Luke promised.

"What if it eats you instead? What do I do then?"

Luke shrugged. "Tell it off?"

"Oh, sure, that'll definitely work. Come on, let's go. Maybe we can find a small town and rent a room for the night. It looks like it's going to rain."

Luke regarded the clouds overhead and shrugged. "Yeah, maybe. Okay, let's go."

Zea was a bit nervous about waiting in the forest for Luke to get back, but on the other hand, she'd been right about the rain. He was the one out there getting soaked while she stayed relatively dry huddled under a tree. Her cloak had been worked over with an oil that made it shed water, which also helped a lot.

Suddenly the branches were pulled aside and a man was standing there. She kept herself from shrieking by dint of sheer willpower, and after a second, she recognized Luke. "Holy crap, knock or something," she said.

"Sorry. It's . . . It's bad. Pretty much what I thought," Luke said as he slipped between the branches and let them settle back around them.

"How many?"

"At least ten. Maybe twenty? They've got a camp a few miles from the road, but I think there's another bigger one somewhere farther back. Their trail leads deeper into the woods, and there are four other trails that run between the base camp and the road. They're watching at least a three- or four-mile stretch for travelers to rob."

That was less than ideal. Bandits weren't all that common around here, if only because the powers that be took a dim view on a bunch of people leveling up that high. The welfare of locals and merchants might or might not have been a concern, but an armed force pushing up into the 30s or 40s was definitely something that would get stamped out.

"It's not the end of the world. We'll just bypass that section of the road and let people know in the next town. Somebody will send out some soldiers to take care of them quickly."

"Yeah, um, about that. I may have sort of gotten caught by a few of them while I was snooping around."

Zea's eye twitched. "What did you do?"

"Look, it's not my fault! They must have sensed my XP. **[Stealth]** told me I was completely hidden."

"Isn't that only at rank 1?" Zea asked.

"Well, yeah, but like . . . I had other things I needed to spend the AP on."

"Okay, well, obviously you got away someh—Ah fuck, you killed them, didn't you?"

"Yeah." Luke didn't sound happy about it, which was honestly one of the things she liked about him. He was very willing to resort to violence when the situation called for it, but it wasn't his go-to response when dealing with other people. He always seemed to feel bad about it later too. Even those church inquisitors who'd been after him weighed on him.

Sometimes she wished she still felt like that when she had to kill someone.

"So we need to either stand our ground or make a run for it then. What are you thinking?"

"I'm thinking that I could get away clean just by outrunning them, but you can't. So if we run, there's a chance they'll catch up to us, or even get ahead and lay out an ambush. I also don't think there's anything we could do to build a fortified position before they find us, not one that will hold against that many people."

"You want to take the fight back to them?" she asked, surprised.

"Someone is going to kill them sooner or later anyway, and we need the XP. We could save some poor guy from pushing himself closer to an early grave, not to mention all the people they're going to attack before anyone shows up to deal with them. Besides, they've got a lot of stuff, and we could use some of it."

Those were valid points, she supposed. She certainly wouldn't shed any tears if a bandit group met a grisly end. They might have good reasons for what they were doing, but she doubted it. The last few years had been relatively peaceful, with good harvests. It didn't seem likely that there were any starving-farmer types among the bandits. They were probably more along the lines of bored and lazy soldiers who'd decided they'd make more money killing people than they did fighting off monsters.

What she objected to was the recklessness of it. If Luke was right and there were twenty more bandits out there, that was not a fight she thought he could win. Even if they were all under level 10, she'd be concerned about him. More than that, even if he came back alive, he would almost certainly be injured, and she wasn't sure how hard it would be for him to cope with the fact that not only had he killed more people, but this time he'd gone out of his way to do it.

"This isn't a fight you have to take on," she told him. "We can make a run for it. I'm sure we'll get away. Let other people handle it."

Luke's head snapped around, and he stared out through the tree branches. "Might not have much of a choice," he whispered harshly. "Stay here."

Then he slipped out through the branches into the rain. Zea tried to snag his shirt and stop him, but he was gone before she even raised her hand. "Damn it," she said. "You idiot. Don't you dare fucking die on me."

Luke could hear them approaching, following the trail he'd left when he'd rushed off after killing the first three bandits. It didn't really surprise him that they'd found his trail. No doubt anyone willing to perform banditry for fun and profit would have excellent outdoorsman skills. He just hadn't expected them to catch up to him so fast.

There were five of them in this group, fully half of what he'd guessed at based on the number of tents in that little camp of theirs. Five bad people who were capable of killing others for the chance at some pocket change, who had probably already done it many times. Hell, they'd tried to kill him once already.

His grip tightened on his mace, and he closed his eyes. They were about two hundred feet in front of him, the noise of their approach partially covered by the rain. Otherwise he would have heard them coming from a lot farther off. Well, that worked both ways. They'd have an instant's warning when they felt his XP coming at them.

Before he moved to attack though, he wanted to make sure there weren't other bandits coming in from behind. Zea wasn't strong enough for a fight like this yet, and she didn't have a magic feather to keep her hidden while she fought anymore.

Nothing. All he could hear was the rain drizzling down through the treetops, the sounds of the bandits breathing, the occasional scuff of their clothes or shoes rubbing against something. All he could smell was water and mud and a patch of nearby flowers. Luke opened his eyes.

The bandits weren't visible through the trees yet. They would be soon, he was sure, but by then it would be too late. He plotted out his route, left first to avoid a bramble patch, and then a straight jump up a small chest-high ridge. They'd see him at that point, but there were plenty of trees for him to weave through, and the underbrush was light there. They wouldn't get more than two or three seconds of warning, and he'd be behind cover for most of that.

It was time to do some work.

Name	Luke Bennet	Zea Stenter
Level	24	13
XP	46042/50687	7987/8325
AP	24	8
Bloodline	SysAdmin	None
Strength	42	7
Agility	40	12
Stamina	36	12
Perception	39	14
Skills	Mace Mastery (2)	Dagger Mastery (1)
	Sword Mastery (1)	Stealth (2)
	Unarmed Martialist (3)	Keen Instincts (1)
	Power Strike (1)	Lock Picking (1)
	Life Surge (1)	Disguise (2)
	Peripheral Awareness (2)	Deception (1)
	Counter (2)	Bartering (2)
	Twitch Reflexes (2)	Streetwise (2)
	Stealth (1)	Cooking (1)
	Survivalist (2)	Mending (1)
	First Aid (1)	First Aid (1)
	Wood Carving (1)	Thalian (3)
	Leatherworking (2)	Neyardic (3)
	Thalian (2)	Ostari (1)
	Disguise (2)	Mana Manipulation (1)
	Deception (1)	Mana Sight (1)
		Metallurgy (1)
		Whitesmithing (1)
		Goldsmithing (2)
		Gem Cutting (1)
		Engraving (2)
		Rune Forging (1)
		Painting (1)
		Arcano Dynamics (1)
		Sleight of Hand (1)
		Steady Hands (2)
		Cold Reading (1)
		Temperature Acclimation (2)
		Cadence (1)

CHAPTER 5

The bandits weren't prepared for Luke in any way, shape, or form. They probably should have been, considering he'd already killed a few of them, but he caught them by surprise. Two of them died in the first second of combat, one of them without ever even so much as turning around and seeing Luke's approach.

After that, the forest became a noisy place. Screams and curses filled the air, punctuated by the sound of crunching wood and bodies slamming into the ground. The bandits were furious and panicked in equal measure, and Luke tore through them like paper. Precisely one of them managed to do anything besides run, and even then, the only reason he lived that long was that he was wearing a nice, sturdy breastplate that somewhat protected him from Luke's first blow.

The bandit, wheezing in pain, tried to stab Luke with a long, thin sword that looked like it would snap if it was jabbed at anything harder than soft pine. Luke easily swatted it aside and killed the man.

[You have slain 5 creatures between levels 8 and 12. 482 XP awarded.]

Luke dismissed the notification and eyed up the breastplate. It was damaged from being struck, and the guy who'd been wearing it was a lot smaller than him. It might have fit, just barely, before he'd hit it, but he didn't think it was worth much to him now. He made a mental note to keep an eye out for anyone closer to his size wearing armor, so that he could kill them without damaging it.

He made his way back to the tree Zea was sheltering under and pulled aside the branches hiding her from sight. "It's safe now," he said. "For a little bit, at least."

She didn't look happy with him, and that was an understatement. "Why didn't you just stay here?" she demanded, springing on him and pulling him all the way under the tree.

"They were too close. Couldn't risk them finding you."

"But it's fine to risk yourself?"

Luke shrugged. It wasn't much of a risk, not really. He could feel their XP, and all of them had been relatively weak. There was a level 15 bandit Luke had spotted when he was scouting the camp, and that guy was by far the strongest. The only thing Luke wasn't sure about was the location of a second camp. He hadn't seen anything that looked like it might be loot, so either these bandits sucked at their jobs, or they were stashing that somewhere else. Considering how much road they were apparently trying to cover, his guess was that there were more of them in a more permanent base deeper in the woods.

"The bandits need to go. It's low risk for me, and we could use the supplies and hopefully money from raiding their camp. Wouldn't it be nice to be able to sleep at an inn every night? To just buy passage on a ship when we finally get there and not have to worry about scraping together coin? To get you some equipment and supplies for your enchanting?"

"Sure, that would all be great, but I'm not keen on you risking your life fighting ten or twelve people at a time."

"There are maybe half that left at the camp I found, and I just fought five-on-one and finished the battle without a scratch in less than thirty seconds. I appreciate the concern, but you're worrying too much."

"No, you idiot! You're not worrying enough! Earlier this week you got captured by inquisitors and almost died, or worse. You have no idea how close that was. If you hadn't had that feather—which, by the way, where even the fuck did that come from?—and they hadn't sent that monster after you, then you threw the core away, where I found it! Do you have any idea how lucky you were?"

"I mean, yeah, you're right. In my defense though, if not for that monster blindsiding me, I wouldn't have been in that predicament to begin with. So I kind of feel like it's a wash."

"Okay, but what if I hadn't been there? What if I didn't know how to modify enchantments? Then what?"

Luke sighed and sat down. "You're right. I know it was close. I know you saved my ass, okay? I'm not doing this on a whim. We need the resources these bandits have, and I have to figure karma's got my back on this one. Has there ever been a group of assholes that deserved to get robbed more than a bunch of bandits?"

"Probably. Have you ever met a nobleman?" Zea said dryly. "I'm not arguing that they don't deserve it. I'm worried that you're overextending yourself. We should at least go together."

Luke sucked in a breath and said, "Yeah . . . Um. I don't know how to say this nicely, so I'll just say it. You're not there yet. You don't have a combat build, your raw stats are low, you don't have any way to heal from injuries, and you're not well equipped. I'm sorry, but you're a liability in this scenario."

"I, that is, you—I mean, it's not like—"

Luke let her sputter for a bit before he cut her off. "You are an amazing woman with many amazing talents. You're smarter than I am, by a lot. But you're being kind of dumb right now. This right here is what I'm good at. I'm a big, dumb thug with a big, heavy metal stick."

"Come on, that's . . . not true."

"It is a little bit," Luke said. "I know I'm not that smart. I made peace with that a long time ago. Stuff doesn't usually come easy to me, and it seems like everyone else is always running past me to the answers while I'm still trying to figure out what the problem is. That's just how it is. This though? This I'm good at. This I can do. So, I'm going to go do it. And when I come back, I'm going to have money and supplies, and this is one stretch of the road that won't have bandit problems for a little while."

Zea tried to hug him, but Luke held her back. "Come on, I'm already soaked. No reason for you to be all wet too." She just stared at him, so Luke grinned and said, "Not going to make the obvious joke?"

"No. No, I'm not. Go on then. But you'd better not die and leave me all alone out here."

"I won't. I promise."

Luke decided that the rain was a good thing. He was a lot better at spotting things than he was at hiding, and the weather helped him hide from the bandits. They were all huddled up in their tents in the camp, two men to a tent except for the big one in the middle. There were seven of them, all within twenty feet of each other, and none visible thanks to the heavy oil-treated canvas.

It felt like someone making a living by finding and murdering travelers for their stuff would have a high perception, but that did not seem to be the case. Then again, it only took one spotter to alert the rest of the crew that they had a victim coming down the road. The ones he'd run into so far were better at tracking than anything, which could be explained by a few different skills, and the fact that it was raining so hard made footprints really obvious in the mud.

He thought he could accurately target all of them even without being able to see them, but it did put a damper on his plans to loot some new armor, and he was less than confident in his ability to kill a bandit in one hit when he had a rough guess of where to aim. He'd just have to do the best he could.

There probably wasn't much point in trying to use **[Stealth]** when it did fuck all to hide his XP from the bandits, but it didn't hurt anything to try anyway, and it might let him get a few steps closer before someone noticed him. The only decision he had left to make was which tent he wanted to strike first, and it was a toss-up between the closest one where he thought he had good odds of taking out two bandits before anyone reacted, or going for the leader's tent, where he could both get rid of the highest-level enemy and possibly leave them without any group cohesion if they didn't already have any procedures in place for what to do without any orders from a commanding officer. Somehow, he doubted they were that disciplined.

Luke stalked around the perimeter of the camp to line himself up with the big tent's backside. Whoever was in there was about as far from the entrance as he could get, though admittedly with it only being about seven feet across, that wasn't that far. Once he had his course set, he dashed forward, mace raised. Mud splattered with each step while **[Stealth]** screamed at him to slow down, keep a measured pace, and stay behind cover. Luke ignored that.

His mace connected with the canvas and tore the tent stakes out of the ground. An instant later, it hit the body on the other side of that canvas and blasted the bandit leader off his feet. Luke tore himself free of the collapsing tent and leaped sideways to attack the next closest one. His mace came down twice and struck both people inside. One of them spasmed and then fell still, but the other fought his way free, cursing and screaming the whole time.

Luke caught a glimpse of a man with a shattered leg dragging himself upright and hopping toward the trees before the other four bandits ran out into the rain, weapons drawn and ready to fight. The captain wasn't among them, but Luke also hadn't gotten any notification dings to let him know that anyone was dead yet.

Fighting in the mud and rain was difficult, but the bandits had far more troubles with it than he did. Just judging by some of the things they yelled back and forth, some of them were having a hard time even keeping track of where he was. Luke circled the camp and finished off the one trying to limp away, which in hindsight might have been the wrong move.

It gave the rest of them a bit of time to organize around their leader, who'd finally clawed his way free of his tent and was bellowing orders. The remaining bandits were lining up, grabbing bows, and trying to sight Luke down. Once again, the rain and the darkness combined with his overall speed helped keep him safe. Luke darted forward, arrows and crossbow bolts went flying in various directions, none of them close to hitting him, and he crashed into the line like a wrecking ball.

In short order, three more bandits were dead, one was on his back wheezing and gasping out his last breaths, and it was just the lamed captain and a single bandit who'd abandoned his bow to draw a sword left. Both were eyeing him warily, neither willing to make the first move.

"You take the left side, I got right," the leader growled out.

"No problem," the bandit said, his eyes never leaving Luke.

Luke raised an eyebrow at them. He supposed in their shoes, he would have tried some sort of strategy too, but that didn't seem too likely to work. All it really did was give some cover to the leader's lamed leg, which would maybe buy them an extra few seconds. The whole fight kind of felt like bullying little kids. They just couldn't keep up with him.

They advanced together and struck at the same time. Some sort of skill activated between the two of them, and Luke found himself on the back foot as their attacks played off each other. Unfortunately for them, it was relatively easy to simply step off to the side and break their formation. If they'd been a bit farther spread apart, it might have been more of a problem, but as it was, he charged up a **[Power Strike]**, drove the captain straight into the mud, then finished off the swordsman with an almost casual backhanded strike.

"Yeah, so, I have some questions," Luke said, leaning over the captain and pinning his hand down with his foot.

Name	Luke Bennet	Zea Stenter
Level	24	13
XP	47166/50687	7987/8325
AP	24	8
Bloodline	SysAdmin	None
Strength	42	7
Agility	40	12
Stamina	36	12
Perception	39	14
Skills	Mace Mastery (2)	Dagger Mastery (1)
	Sword Mastery (1)	Stealth (2)
	Unarmed Martialist (3)	Keen Instincts (1)
	Power Strike (1)	Lock Picking (1)
	Life Surge (1)	Disguise (2)
	Peripheral Awareness (2)	Deception (1)
	Counter (2)	Bartering (2)
	Twitch Reflexes (2)	Streetwise (2)
	Stealth (1)	Cooking (1)
	Survivalist (2)	Mending (1)
	First Aid (1)	First Aid (1)
	Wood Carving (1)	Thalian (3)
	Leatherworking (2)	Neyardic (3)
	Thalian (2)	Ostari (1)
	Disguise (2)	Mana Manipulation (1)
	Deception (1)	Mana Sight (1)
		Metallurgy (1)
		Whitesmithing (1)
		Goldsmithing (2)
		Gem Cutting (1)
		Engraving (2)
		Rune Forging (1)
		Painting (1)
		Arcano Dynamics (1)
		Sleight of Hand (1)
		Steady Hands (2)
		Cold Reading (1)
		Temperature Acclimation (2)
		Cadence (1)

CHAPTER 6

The bandit snarled and tried to punch the side of Luke's knee, but he was too injured and at too awkward of an angle to take a serious swing. Luke smacked the fist away with his mace anyway, shattering the bones in the bandit's hand in the process.

"Like I was saying, this camp seems kind of half-assed to me. I was thinking maybe you guys had some base farther away from the road where you keep all the shit you stole. I mean, it's either that or you all suck ass as bandits because it can't be worth sharing a tent with another dude for . . . what?"

He looked around the camp. The bandits weren't wearing fancy clothes. They didn't have expensive gear. The tents were serviceable but not extravagant. Not even the leader's tent was anything special. There were no crates full of loot to be found. The firepit had a single wooden box next to it, left open and exposed to the elements, that had some wooden plates and cutlery in it. Luke could have whittled better with his rank 1 **[Wood Carving]** skill using any random piece of wood he found lying around.

"Zixin take you," the bandit said. "You ain't walking away from this just because you got the drop on a few of us out here."

"Well, duh. I'm not trying to walk away. I am literally asking you where the rest of your band of merry men are hiding."

"You'll never see them coming," the bandit told him.

"Look, I'm going to find them anyway. You've got a trail leading deeper into the woods right there." Luke gestured toward a spot on the west side of the clearing that had been worn down and led farther away from the road. "I'm pretty sure the rest of your buddies are at the end of it. So, am I right? How many are there?"

The bandit didn't answer, didn't do anything but glare at him despite being belly down in the mud. His leg was fucked up, his arm was fucked up, his hand was broken, and Luke was pretty sure all he needed to do was grind his heel down on the other hand to break a few more fingers there. The guy either had some sort of pain-suppression skill or he was a complete masochist because he just looked pissed.

"Alright, I get it. You don't want to betray the other bandits. It's kind of a surprising show of loyalty, but okay." Luke brought his mace around and considered the angle of his next strike. The bandit had on some sort of leather armor, not really what Luke wanted, but the right size. It was a start, if he could avoid splattering it with brains, blood, and bone chunks.

[Twitch Reflexes] pinged on the palm-sized knife the bandit had somehow pulled and was holding in his broken hand. That must have hurt like a bitch, but the bandit was determined to stick Luke with it and was already driving it toward Luke's calf when the skill pulled his leg out of the way. That of course freed up the bandit's other hand, and he promptly rolled onto his back. The knife flashed in the rain as he threw it to his good hand and slashed at Luke again.

The mace came down and struck the bandit's face, kind of like a golf club swung with one hand. It tore through skin and bone and left a stained smear across three feet of mud next to the corpse. A moment later, Luke got the kill notification ding.

[You have slain Human Bandit (level 15). 231 XP awarded.]

"So much for answers," he muttered. Then he set about looting the bodies and piling anything useful up in the leader's tent. There wasn't a lot of use in the small camp, just a few coppers between them, a couple of blankets and bedrolls, most of which smelled awful, and the various weapons. The bows were a bit too big for Zea to use, he thought, but maybe she'd surprise him. The other weapons weren't in the best of shape, but they might be worth something to sell.

While he was working, Luke asked, "System, who is Zixin again? I've heard that name before."

"The goddess of death," System replied. "She oversees the disposition of all souls when they depart from Aros and reach the afterlife. In human society, she is worshipped primarily as part of the Pantheon, but not usually in everyday life, other than to ask for blessings to ward off death."

"Oh, sure. That makes sense. So basically that guy was wishing that I'd keel over dead of a heart attack or something. What a prick."

They'd attacked him first, and then sent more bandits out to find him after he'd killed the first group. It was hardly his fault the rest hadn't been prepared for him to strike back. It wasn't like their camp was hard to find. If they were all too scared of getting wet to keep a proper watch, especially when they knew there was someone out there, that was on them.

Inside the tent itself was a crate that was partially covered under the collapsed canvas wall. Luke frowned at the sight, mostly because he'd kind of planned on stealing that tent since it was the biggest, but now it had a big hole ripped in the canvas from where he'd hit the bandit through it. The crate itself was stuffed full of clay jugs of what he quickly discovered was eye-wateringly powerful alcohol. Just the smell alone from uncorking the first one burned.

Whatever the hell that was, he was sure it was deadly to his liver. The hooch might be worth something, but the crate itself was so big that it was going to be awkward to carry. Luke was hoping to find something smaller and more valuable elsewhere. For now, the tent's sole purpose would be to protect what little he'd been able to scrounge up from the weather until he got back.

The leader's armor was the last piece of loot he was interested in. It was a bit uncomfortable, too wide around the chest and not as flexible as he'd like, but it didn't cut his range of movements as much as the old metal armor he'd briefly worn before finding out exactly what the rainbow circle on it meant. He wasn't sure how much it would help, but it didn't seem like it would hurt, plus if he threw on someone's cloak, it might help sell the disguise.

His preparations complete, Luke started up the trail.

He had to admit, he'd been expecting a larger version of the first camp, or maybe some crude log huts or something. Even some old stone houses that had been retaken by nature and were falling apart wouldn't have surprised him. He was not expecting a Goddamn walled fort.

Admittedly, it wasn't in good shape. The wall was mostly for appearances, since it had collapsed in eight different places. Chunks of the fort were missing too, and the whole back half had kind of fallen over, but it was still a bit of a shock to come across a four-story building with a twenty-foot-high wall circling it. There could be a hundred bandits living in there with room to spare.

Just because it *could* fit a hundred bandits didn't mean there were that many. Luke was no expert on banditry, but it just seemed like way too many people for a few miles of road. If they had to divide the spoils of the work up that many ways, nobody would get anything. He didn't know exactly how many bandits were there, but he was betting it wasn't much more than the first group he'd dealt with.

That was no reason to get sloppy, since ten or twenty bandits were still more than enough to kill him. He proceeded slowly, relying strongly on the rain and **[Stealth]** to keep him safe. No one was on the walls, at least not that he could see, and he approached them without issue. Twenty feet wasn't all that high to jump for him anymore, and he easily got his hands on the lip of the wall to pull himself up. As he'd expected, there was no one there.

Considering the weather and that he assumed bandits were lazy and undisciplined, he wasn't that surprised. These ones were off duty or whatever, so there was no reason to be sitting out in the rain getting sick. Luke spent a few minutes making sure he was right about that, even going so far as to drop back down off the wall and scour the grounds around the fort for any spotters or guards.

It was obvious at least what parts of the fort were in use. Most of the grass was overgrown, up past his knees in most places, but the bandits had stamped down a few clear paths from the front gate to the trail or a few of the outbuildings not connected to the main keep. Luke considered checking those buildings, but he had to figure that considering how much room the main building had, there wasn't likely to be anything valuable kept in an outdoor area.

He decided to investigate those buildings later, if he didn't find the loot in the big building first. Luke's eyes flicked from window to window, looking for motion or shadows that might indicate someone standing there. It would have been laughably impossible a month ago, but now that he was inside the ring of the stone wall and only a hundred feet away from the keep itself, it was easy to confirm no one was watching. **[Stealth]** only served to reinforce that when it let him sneak up to the side of the building without complaining.

A quick lap around the outside and some careful peeking inside confirmed Luke's suspicions. Almost the entire fort was empty. Only at the main gate did he hear anybody at all, and even though he had to make sure to stand far enough back that his XP didn't give him away, he was still able to count the voices. There were five people, three talking while they played some gambling game with dice, one huddled up near a fireplace and sniffling constantly, and one that had come to check on them and bring them some food, but who'd never left.

Much like the other bandits, they were all somewhere around level 10. Luke's biggest hurdle would be the door itself, which he assumed was locked or barred in some way. The windows were too narrow for a person to go through, but if he wanted to break down the door, he probably could. It was only a question of whether he could do it fast enough.

Alternatively, there were plenty of ways in on the backside of the fort. He circled around and climbed up a pile of rubble, then hopped up to a second-floor hallway, one that had a layer of moss growing on the stone and several creeping vines taking over the walls. The door leading deeper into the fort was closed and rusted shut, but it was easy enough to break the handle off and let it creak open under its own weight.

Luke prowled through the fort until he found a flight of stairs that would take him back to the ground level, then started working his way forward. Most of the space was empty and covered in grime, debris, or cobwebs. Sometimes, it was all three. That made it very easy for him to figure out when he'd reached the part the bandits were living in, as things got noticeably cleaner. Not clean by any measure, but the difference was night and day.

He didn't find that group of five bandits first. Instead, Luke stumbled across the kitchen. A middle-aged man with arms as thick around as Luke's thighs and a potbelly so huge Luke had to wonder how the man aimed when he took a piss stood at a table, ladling out something thick and gritty looking from a cauldron into individual bowls.

As soon as Luke passed by the door, the man's head snapped up. With a smooth motion, he pulled a cleaver out of a wooden block and said, "Come on out. You're not fooling anyone."

Name	Luke Bennet	Zea Stenter
Level	24	13
XP	47397/50687	7987/8325
AP	24	8
Bloodline	SysAdmin	None
Strength	42	7
Agility	40	12
Stamina	36	12
Perception	39	14
Skills	Mace Mastery (2)	Dagger Mastery (1)
	Sword Mastery (1)	Stealth (2)
	Unarmed Martialist (3)	Keen Instincts (1)
	Power Strike (1)	Lock Picking (1)
	Life Surge (1)	Disguise (2)
	Peripheral Awareness (2)	Deception (1)
	Counter (2)	Bartering (2)
	Twitch Reflexes (2)	Streetwise (2)
	Stealth (1)	Cooking (1)
	Survivalist (2)	Mending (1)
	First Aid (1)	First Aid (1)
	Wood Carving (1)	Thalian (3)
	Leatherworking (2)	Neyardic (3)
	Thalian (2)	Ostari (1)
	Disguise (2)	Mana Manipulation (1)
	Deception (1)	Mana Sight (1)
		Metallurgy (1)
		Whitesmithing (1)
		Goldsmithing (2)
		Gem Cutting (1)
		Engraving (2)
		Rune Forging (1)
		Painting (1)
		Arcano Dynamics (1)
		Sleight of Hand (1)
		Steady Hands (2)
		Cold Reading (1)
		Temperature Acclimation (2)
		Cadence (1)

CHAPTER 7

Luke knew he sucked at sneaking around, that he lacked the skills to hide his XP, and there was only so much agility and **[Stealth]** could do to help. His current strategy was just to get as close as he could and then close the distance without giving a target more than a second to react. But that didn't mean he was going to shy away from a new opponent just because they'd seen him coming.

The cook stood there, cleaver in one hand and his other hand empty and held out to the side, and his feet solidly set beneath his bulk. It kind of reminded Luke of a wrestling stance, like the cook was expecting someone to come charging in and that he was going to get a good grab on them. Even without considering stats, the man's arms were enormous, and though they jiggled as he moved, it was obvious it wasn't all fat.

Perhaps most importantly, the cook was obviously there of his own free will. He was just as much a bandit as any of the rest Luke had killed, even if he didn't personally drag himself down to the road to ambush travelers. Luke liked to think he was nothing if not thorough, and it was just dumb to leave an enemy alive behind him, especially one who knew he was there.

He walked into the kitchen, mace in hand.

"Who're you?" the cook asked.

"Traveler who got jumped by some dumbasses who thought they'd win because there were more of them."

The cook snorted. "I fucking told him not to put all the idiots in one group. Does he listen?"

"Yeah, I'd love to have a word with whoever's running this place," Luke said. "You think you could take me to him?"

"I can do that. Course, you'll be tied up, and I'll have to beat the piss out of you first."

"You can try."

The cook lumbered forward, the cleaver coming around in a wide arc and aimed at Luke's shoulder. He stepped backward out of the way and brought his mace up to smack against the man's enormous belly. To his surprise, the cook took the blow without flinching, barely even letting out a grunt as his fat rippled. "Oh," Luke said, blinking in surprise. "That's new."

The cook flashed him a gap-toothed grin, grabbed hold of the mace just below the head, and jerked the weapon up and back. Luke tried to resist the pull, found himself getting dragged forward, and needed to release his hold on the weapon in order to avoid having his face split open by the cleaver.

Luke slipped backward outside the cook's range and scowled as the man casually tossed his mace deeper into the kitchen. He mentally kicked himself for being cocky; he hadn't expected anyone to match his strength and felt extra stupid because he'd even noted how big the man's arms were before the fight had started.

The cook felt like he was level 13 or so, maybe just a bit weaker than the guy in charge of the first camp Luke had hit. There was more to it than simple level of course, but that did introduce hard limits to how much AP a person had, how high their stats could go, and how strong their skills were. So either something funky was going on, or Luke was way off in his estimate of the cook's level.

Whatever it was, the man knew how to fight. He pushed Luke continuously and worked hard to control their brawl. Luke found himself being forced into a corner, his mobility options sharply limited within seconds, and nothing but his knife left to use as a weapon. That was more of a tool than something he fought with, and he felt more comfortable allowing **[Unarmed Martialist]** to work its magic than he did trying to engage in a knife fight.

Luke ducked, dodged, and weaved his way around the slashing cleaver. He threw punches at the cook, focusing on vulnerable joints in the man's arm when he could in an attempt to disarm his opponent. The cook was too canny though, and he recognized when he could turn his arm to take a hit on the meaty part of it and when he needed to pull back.

The fight came to something of a standstill, with the cook unable to match Luke's agility and variety of combat skills, and Luke having problems landing a solid hit in return. He kept looking for the opportunity to put a **[Power Strike]**–infused punch between the cook's eyes, but the man was too aggressive in his own attacks for Luke to get in.

The amount of sheer power in the cook's arms was unbelievable. Luke had fought literal giants and felt less overwhelmed. The man took punishment like it was nothing too. He'd ignored every shot Luke had managed to tag him with and just kept coming back for more. If the cook managed to grab hold of Luke, the fight would turn against him very, very quickly.

"Come on, hold still!" the cook growled as he tried to clamp his free hand down on Luke's arm. Luke jerked backward, and his back bumped up against the wall. The cook sneered at him and added, "Nowhere left to run now, you little shit."

That was true. He'd been backed into a corner, and the cook's arms were thrown wide to block him from darting either way. Fortunately, a fort had higher ceilings than the average home, and when the cook lunged forward to pin Luke down, he simply jumped straight up and over. He sent a **[Power Strike]** through his leg and let his foot crack down hard on the top of the cook's skull, then pushed off to land in the middle of the kitchen near his mace.

Luke scooped it up and spun in place, expecting to see the somehow indestructible man already coming at him, but was surprised to find the cook's back to him still, one hand on the wall to brace himself while he swayed on his feet. Whatever durability he'd displayed in his arms and torso didn't seem to extend to his skull.

There wasn't a chance in hell that Luke was going to give the cook time to recover. This wasn't an arena match with spectators where he had to fight fair, and this guy had been a tougher fight than just about anything else he'd ever faced. While the cook was dazed and trying to recover, Luke unleashed a second **[Power Strike]** through his mace and caved in the man's skull.

[You have slain Ogrimun Bandit (level 12). 147 XP awarded.]

Luke's brow furrowed as he read the notification. "System, what is an ogrimun?"

"That is the term for a crossbreed of an ogre and another species."

"Well, that explains why the bastard was so damn strong, at least." Luke couldn't imagine the logistics of exactly how that particular pairing happened. Hopefully the ogre was the mother, otherwise there had to be a lot of tearing involved.

The cook had been an ugly bastard, and he was pretty tall, but Luke would not have put him at nonhuman levels of physical stature. Maybe ogres were smaller than he thought. "Is there any way to tell if someone is an ogrimun just by looking?"

"They are universally large. The smallest of them push the upper boundaries of what the other parent's species is capable of growing to. They generally have more jagged teeth, and it is not unusual for the skin and hair coloring to tend toward dark greens, browns, and other earth tones."

Other than the cook's size, Luke didn't think any of those other signs were present. He just looked like a big, fat, burly guy who'd been crazy strong.

Hopefully there weren't any other bandits like that, or if there were, they looked more obviously nonhuman so he could pick them out of the crowd.

More importantly, that fight felt way harder than a level 12 should have been. The system giving him the same XP as he would have gotten from a random goblin or earth elemental, or any of the weak bandits he'd crushed in a single blow, did not feel fair to him. It needed a rules update to account for more values than just level.

"Could I change how XP is calculated?" Luke asked.

"Theoretically, you might be able to someday. Right now, that is beyond your abilities."

"Well . . . Theoretically, good. The system does not give out fair rewards."

"No," System agreed. "It was not designed to be fair. The Pantheon structured it to suit their need: to cycle XP quickly and prevent too much of it from building up in any individual being."

"Of course, right. Because fuck all the mortals. The only thing that matters is what the gods want."

"I am not able to speculate on—"

"Yeah, yeah, I know," Luke cut it off. "It wasn't a question."

He was wasting time now. Luke had learned what he needed to know: what to look out for in future ogrimuns. "Is there anything else that might help me spot someone who's not fully human just by looking at them?"

"Of course. It would depend what the other parent's species was though."

"And is it likely that there will be anyone like that here?"

"I can't give you that information at your current access level."

"Whatever. No surprise there. Okay, back to work."

The fight hadn't been particularly quiet, but nobody had showed up to investigate. Luke counted himself lucky that the keep was so big and that the bandits didn't feel the need to huddle up in a few rooms right next to one another. It made it harder to search for them, but easier to take them out in small groups once he found them.

Someone would show up eventually, if for no other reason than to find out what was taking so long with their dinner. If Luke had gotten lucky and come through five minutes later, he might have missed the cook entirely. Now he had an unknown deadline before the alarm was raised and nothing he could do about it. Removing the body wouldn't clean up the bloodstains, and besides, the cook would still be missing.

Speed was the name of the game now. He needed to find and take out the rest of the bandits before they started clumping together. If nothing else, he was at least going to take out that group near the front door and get that opened up. Luke knew roughly which direction he needed to move, and if he encountered any roaming bandits, he'd have to silence them quickly.

His build really wasn't designed for this kind of work. A tracking skill would help. More ranks in **[Stealth]** would help. Whatever skill the church agents all used to reduce their XP presence would help most of all. None of them had ever felt like they were anything other than an average, unremarkable level for the populace. System, of course, wouldn't tell him what the skill was, but he was guessing they had at least three ranks in it to get coverage that good.

It took longer than he thought it would, mostly on account of getting lost a few times, but eventually Luke found his way to the front of the keep. There were only four bandits there now, but that was fine. It would be easier to take them out quickly and hopefully silently. That was probably wishful thinking on his part, but he'd do his best.

The three that were playing dice would go first. They were closest to where he'd enter the room. Then he'd go for the one remaining guy by the fire, get the door open, reevaluate his position depending on how much noise the fight made.

Plan of attack decided, he sprinted down the hall and burst into the room.

Name	Luke Bennet	Zea Stenter
Level	24	13
XP	47544/50687	7987/8325
AP	24	8
Bloodline	SysAdmin	None
Strength	42	7
Agility	40	12
Stamina	36	12
Perception	39	14
Skills	Mace Mastery (2)	Dagger Mastery (1)
	Sword Mastery (1)	Stealth (2)
	Unarmed Martialist (3)	Keen Instincts (1)
	Power Strike (1)	Lock Picking (1)
	Life Surge (1)	Disguise (2)
	Peripheral Awareness (2)	Deception (1)
	Counter (2)	Bartering (2)
	Twitch Reflexes (2)	Streetwise (2)
	Stealth (1)	Cooking (1)
	Survivalist (2)	Mending (1)
	First Aid (1)	First Aid (1)
	Wood Carving (1)	Thalian (3)
	Leatherworking (2)	Neyardic (3)
	Thalian (2)	Ostari (1)
	Disguise (2)	Mana Manipulation (1)
	Deception (1)	Mana Sight (1)
		Metallurgy (1)
		Whitesmithing (1)
		Goldsmithing (2)
		Gem Cutting (1)
		Engraving (2)
		Rune Forging (1)
		Painting (1)
		Arcano Dynamics (1)
		Sleight of Hand (1)
		Steady Hands (2)
		Cold Reading (1)
		Temperature Acclimation (2)
		Cadence (1)

CHAPTER 8

The bandits were already scrambling to their feet before Luke showed up, but he buried them before they could organize any sort of defense. The first bandit took a mace to his ribs and was smashed backward into the wall. The second one got kicked in the knee hard enough to cave the joint in and make his knee bend the wrong way. He fell away, howling in pain, and Luke blasted through the pitiful defense his friend put up to put a fist into the man's face.

[Twitch Reflexes] caught a crossbow bolt coming at him and let him smoothly pivot out of the way. The bolt streaked past him and took the guy with a busted knee right in the chest, just close enough to the heart that Luke was surprised the guy stayed on his feet. Regardless, those three weren't going to be running any time soon, and he took the second to kill them before turning to the last one.

The fourth bandit was an older man, perhaps in his late fifties judging by the head full of shaggy gray hair, thick beard, and weather-worn face. He reloaded the crossbow in a smooth, steady motion and brought it back up to fire.

Luke crossed the distance before he could, and by the time the old bandit was ready to shoot at him again, it was far too late. He threw himself to the side in a desperate attempt to save himself, but Luke's range was too great for him to overcome, and the mace cracked down on his arm. The crossbow tumbled across the floor, and Luke struck the man down with his next swing.

[You have slain 4 creatures between levels 10 and 13. 545 XP awarded.]

With the enemies cleared out, he went over and unbarred the front entrance before venturing deeper into the fort. The crossbow got left behind, but he made a mental note to go back for it later. Luke didn't trust his own skills with it, but it might be a good weapon for Zea. She could use it to help him kill monsters from a distance, even if it was a little bit too big for her to wield comfortably. As far as he was concerned though, it was nothing but a hindrance for him to carry it into a close quarters fight right now.

There was at least one more bandit that he knew about from his earlier spying, but he was betting there were more than that somewhere else. If there were more than ten left, he'd be surprised, but stranger things had happened. For now at least, the size of the fort was working in his favor. The bandits were so spread out that he'd gone through two fights without reinforcements showing up.

Luke prowled through the old fort, his senses trained for noise, movement, anything that would give away a bandit's position. For about twenty minutes, he went up and down old, dusty hallways, empty except for broken furniture and rubble. When he finally did catch a noise, he had to stop and shake his head. It was the sound of snoring.

Luke followed it and found a hallway of rooms, perhaps some sort of servant quarters originally. Half of them had nothing but the rotted remains of doors left and were empty. Of the remaining ones that had escaped the ravages of time and the elements, Luke guessed six of them were occupied. He heard snores coming from three of them, so he targeted those first.

The first door wasn't locked. Luke opened it and went in, where he found a man snoozing on a straw-stuffed pallet. It would be the work of a moment to kill him, but Luke was hesitant to do it. Killing someone who was attacking him was one thing, but killing someone that he'd attacked was a different story. He'd kind of justified it in his mind because the initial group had attacked him first, and their buddies were obviously hostile.

This guy though . . . He wasn't even awake. The smart thing to do, the logical thing to do, was to pull his knife and slit the bandit's throat. If Luke gave him the chance, the bandit would try to kill him just like every other person in the place. It was hard though to just do it cold like that. He stood there for close to a minute, his fingers flexing around the hilt of his knife, telling himself if he couldn't do it, he might as well leave the fort right now.

He hardened his heart and slashed the blade across the sleeping man's throat. Blood splattered across the wall, and the man's eyes flew open. He stared at Luke, confused and in pain, but only for a moment. Then he died.

Of all the kills Luke had made since arriving on Aros, that one was by far the worst. He turned away, took a moment to compose himself, and walked out of the room. When he opened the door to the next one, it was easier to take two long steps up to the pallet and repeat the process.

In a way, it was a relief when the bandits who were still awake noticed him and started making noise. He didn't feel so guilty about killing them that way.

* * *

He probably shouldn't have been surprised that the bandits stored all their loot in the jail cells. The metal was still holding strong after however many years, it was in a portion of the fort that hadn't collapsed and wasn't showing any signs that it was going to, and probably most importantly, there was a locked door leading to the jail in a room that the bandit captain had taken over.

As far as Luke was aware, there wasn't another way in or out of the wing with all the cells, and whatever the room had been used for originally, it held a bed with an actual mattress now. The captain had a wardrobe with different outfits in it, a rack that had five different types of swords mounted on it, and a surprisingly detailed ledger of the loot. Apparently, the man believed in fair distribution of wealth to his fellow outlaws.

The bandit captain also believed in keeping his keys on his person, which was probably a smart move, but which Luke found incredibly annoying. Unlike the rest of the keep, the jail was in good condition. Luke had battered the door down, only to find stone and steel blocking him from accessing the goods. He could get through, given enough time and effort, but it would be much, much easier to just unlock the cell doors.

Unfortunately, he had no idea where the captain was. Luke was confident that he'd gone over the entire fort, but there was no sign of the man. Either he wasn't there, or he was well hidden. The cook had been the only real challenge, even compared to when he'd been fighting five or six bandits at a time.

"I bet there's some sort of lock-picking skill that would make this easy," Luke muttered to himself. Now that he thought about it, he was pretty sure Zea had that skill already. Technically, he had some spare AP still. He was sure he could afford it, but it just didn't seem worth it for this one specific use, not when he knew he could get through those bars on sheer strength alone.

The only question was whether it would be better to smash the locks with his mace and hope that broke the doors open or if he should just skip straight to trying to bend the bars. He had the time to experiment, so he found an empty cell with a closed door and smashed it as hard as he could. The metal deformed but held.

Two more blows broke the locking mechanism, and the cell rolled open, albeit with a lot of muscle power on his end. Nothing really fit right anymore, and he had to fight to get it to slide over, but it wasn't too terribly difficult. Experiment complete, he went back to the cells that had the good stuff behind them and repeated his attacks against the locks.

Luke wasn't sure what he was going to find inside all the boxes, chests, crates, and trunks piled up in the cell, but he was eager to find out. He cracked open the first one, then stopped, confused. It was . . . dresses? Frowning, he pulled them out one at a time until he'd emptied the whole trunk and held eight dresses in his arms.

"What?" he asked. Shrugging, he stuffed them back into the trunk and slid it to the side. They were probably worth something, or maybe the bandits had just taken them as part of the luggage of some travelers they'd robbed.

The next box had a bunch of wooden masks in it. He even recognized a few of them, like the goblin mask on the top and a boar mask he found near the bottom. After that was a crate with a small army of taxidermied squirrels and the remains of a broken mop, followed quickly by another trunk of clothes, men's this time, and a box that was literally filled with rocks. And not the good, shiny rocks either! Boring, plain, flat river rocks.

"What kind of shit-tier loot is this?" Luke demanded.

There were more containers to open, and Luke stubbornly sorted through them, trying to find something that wasn't garbage. There was nothing to be found though, and he eventually gave up in disgust. Why anyone would bother to lock up this kind of stuff was utterly beyond him.

Hoping against hope that the next cell would have something a bit more valuable, Luke busted the lock and started sorting through it. His mood brightened immediately when he found a set of pewter goblets with silver rims. Those weren't all that valuable, but at least they weren't worthless. There was a small case with several sets of earrings, bracelets, and rings, all copper or silver, and a few books packed tightly in a leather satchel.

Luke took his time going through it all. He didn't have a keen eye for value, and he knew there was too much stuff to take it all. He needed to decide what he was going to take and what would get left behind, with an emphasis on small and lightweight high-value goods. The jewelry was a good start. There was some silverware that he figured was worth something as well in another chest. After that, it got harder to figure out what was worth the effort.

He spent nearly an hour in the cells, tearing apart the accumulated spoils of banditry, all the while desperate to find something that would cover the expenses he expected to take on. And then he found the holy grail, buried all the way in the back, hidden under at least a thousand pounds of other stuff.

It was a little metal lockbox, about a foot wide and half that deep. The lock was broken on it already, and it opened easily. Inside were a hundred or more coins, mostly silver, but with a few gold mixed in. "Ka-ching," Luke said. That went right into the win pile.

If he never found anything else, that one box alone made it worth all the effort. He was still going to go through the rest of it, but he'd been gone long enough that he probably needed to haul what he'd already found back to Zea. No doubt, she'd cycled right past worried and gone on to being pissed at him.

"What in the fuck happened here?" a voice said from down the hall. Luke's head snapped up and he saw a human-shaped shadow flicker across the floor as something filled the doorway leading from the captain's room into the prison area itself.

"Ah, I see," the voice continued. "That's annoying. It'll take me months to rebuild all this, but at least I get to kill the son of a bitch who fucked up my operation."

If Luke had learned anything in his time on Aros, it was that the guys who had no XP at all were the most dangerous. He scrambled to his feet and grabbed his mace.

Name	Luke Bennet	Zea Stenter
Level	24	13
XP	48089/50687	7987/8325
AP	24	8
Bloodline	SysAdmin	None
Strength	42	7
Agility	40	12
Stamina	36	12
Perception	39	14
Skills	Mace Mastery (2)	Dagger Mastery (1)
	Sword Mastery (1)	Stealth (2)
	Unarmed Martialist (3)	Keen Instincts (1)
	Power Strike (1)	Lock Picking (1)
	Life Surge (1)	Disguise (2)
	Peripheral Awareness (2)	Deception (1)
	Counter (2)	Bartering (2)
	Twitch Reflexes (2)	Streetwise (2)
	Stealth (1)	Cooking (1)
	Survivalist (2)	Mending (1)
	First Aid (1)	First Aid (1)
	Wood Carving (1)	Thalian (3)
	Leatherworking (2)	Neyardic (3)
	Thalian (2)	Ostari (1)
	Disguise (2)	Mana Manipulation (1)
	Deception (1)	Mana Sight (1)
		Metallurgy (1)
		Whitesmithing (1)
		Goldsmithing (2)
		Gem Cutting (1)
		Engraving (2)
		Rune Forging (1)
		Painting (1)
		Arcano Dynamics (1)
		Sleight of Hand (1)
		Steady Hands (2)
		Cold Reading (1)
		Temperature Acclimation (2)
		Cadence (1)

CHAPTER 9

The guy in charge of the bandits wasn't physically imposing. He was a few inches shorter than Luke with a slim build and a thin, dark mustache over his lip that matched equally thin, dark hair. If Luke had to describe the feeling of the XP coming off him, he would have said it reminded him of some of the children he'd seen in towns and villages on Aros. Sometimes it was so low that even looking for it, he couldn't find anything. In this case though, Luke was betting the guy was a lot more like Myla, with multiple overlapping skills hiding it all.

"I suppose it wouldn't hurt me too much to build up a little more XP," the bandit leader said, drawing a slender sword from its sheath at his hip. "Or maybe I'll keep you alive for now and sell you to some noble twat who wants to level his kid up quickly."

"That's a lot of shit talking coming from a guy who used to run a whole bandit camp until I killed them all."

"That's because the key to successful banditry is quantity over quality. Your minions have to know that even if they all jumped you at once, you'd kill them easily. Otherwise that's exactly what they'll do once they start getting stupid ideas."

The bandit stepped into the prison area and closed the door behind him, cutting them both off from the light. Luke supposed both their perceptions were high enough to make out fine details even without light, but the bandit wouldn't know that. He might get a surprise hit off if he acted like he couldn't see very well. Luckily for Luke, he had just the right skill for that.

Pulling on **[Deception]** to fuel the idea that he was partially blinded, Luke shuffled backward a step and turned his head a bit, his eyes squinted like he was searching for something he couldn't quite see. The bandit was all arrogance; he'd see what he was expecting. If he was as good as he thought he was though, Luke would only get one surprise attack off. It would need to count.

"You should know something about me," the bandit said, stepping to the left as he spoke. Luke's head snapped around to face the noise, and he shifted in place to square himself up with the bandit. "I spent a lot of years running a confessional for the Inquisition Department after I retired from fieldwork. When I say that I might capture you and sell you off, I want you to know that I mean you'll be kept weak through torture, but you won't die. I am a professional, after all."

He advanced while he taunted Luke, but then silently swept back to the right. Luke kept his eyes trained on where the bandit wanted to pretend he was and shuffled backward another step. The bandit reached out with his sword when he was about eight feet away and tapped the metal bars on the opposite side of the hall, just to bait Luke in.

Luke took the bait and stepped forward with a wide swipe that looked like he was trying to clear as much of the hallway as possible. It would have been a fair play to make if he really couldn't see anything, and the bandit bought the ruse. He slipped forward after Luke's swing and drove his blade downward in an attempt to stab Luke through the thigh, only to miss completely when Luke shifted his weight and pulled his leg out of the way.

The bandit was quick though, and he skittered backward, perhaps already sensing he'd been tricked. It was too late by then, and Luke reversed the direction of his mace, charged it with a **[Power Strike]**, and bounced the bandit off the bars of a cell. Against any of the other bandits, except maybe that cook, that would have meant a lot of broken ribs and a man who wasn't getting back up off the ground again.

The bandit took the blow with a grunt, landed lightly on his feet, and dodged Luke's follow-up attack. He didn't even have the decency to lose his weapon. "Well played," he said with a smirk. "I underestimated you, and you took advantage of it."

Then he came back in, this time with a blazing-fast series of thrusts delivered from seemingly impossible angles. It had to be some sort of skill; the only other explanation was that his agility was just that high, and if that had been the case, Luke wouldn't have tagged him with that first hit. The stabs came at him too fast for him to even attempt to parry, so he relied on **[Twitch Reflexes]** and **[Unarmed Martialist]** to keep him safe.

By the time the bandit slowed down from his flurry of attacks, Luke was bleeding in five different places, and they were thirty feet deeper down the hall. Unsure of how often he'd have to face an attack like that and unwilling to let his enemy take the initiative to do it again, Luke surged forward. His mace swished through empty air as the bandit dodged backward, under, and in one case that involved stepping off the wall and backflipping to land on his feet, over the attacks.

Luke's agility was almost as high as his strength, and he couldn't touch the bandit even after landing that solid first blow. Mixing in elbow strikes, kicks, and other attacks from **[Unarmed Martialist]** helped, but mostly in forcing the bandit back whenever he tried to exploit an opening in Luke's slower attacks.

Neither of them were getting tired, despite their wounds. The bleeding had already stopped from the original stab wounds, and the longer he fought, the less they hurt. That wasn't all adrenaline either; his stamina was helping to repair the injuries. The bandit had fully recovered from the one solid hit Luke had managed to land on him as well.

The fight had lasted a solid two or three minutes already, a kind of Zen experience that left him completely in the moment with no room for other thoughts. The hallway was covered in a screen of rubble from Luke's attacks hitting stone walls, but neither of them were bothered by the hazard, not enough to let it slow them down at least. Luke wasn't going to win the way things were going, but he still had a trick up his sleeve, not to mention his trump card.

If possible, he wanted to avoid using **[Life Surge]**. The aftereffects sucked, and it put him on a strict clock to overwhelm his opponent before the skill ran out. Against someone with a high stamina like the bandit leader, he didn't think that was the best call. So instead, he let the bandit take the lead, get a feel for how Luke moved, how he thought. The fight was starting to go against Luke, the older man's experience in combat helping him predict Luke's every attack.

Then Luke spent 15 AP and bought rank 3 **[Mace Mastery]**.

The fight looked completely different. Instead of blinding attacks that Luke was struggling to keep up with, his mace moved without even needing to think about it. He intercepted a sharp thrust from the bandit's sword, managed to catch it between two of the flanges on the mace, and twisted sharply to pull the weapon to the side.

That wasn't enough to disarm the bandit, of course, but if there was any single area Luke had an advantage in, it was his strength. He slammed the blade down to the ground and lashed out with a front-facing kick that forced the bandit to either abandon his grip or have his knee caved in. Or, as Luke quickly found out, there was a third option.

The bandit twisted in place and threw himself into the air, upside down, and did a sort of cartwheel move that kept his hand on the hilt of his sword. It looked fancy as hell, something some kind of gymnast at the Olympics would have done to show off. It also left him incredibly vulnerable since his entire body was off the ground and not forcing Luke to fend off an attack of some sort.

Luke heaved the mace back up, aiming for the bandit's skull. He missed, but only by an inch or so, and the mace slammed into the bandit's shoulder. He was blown sideways into the wall, and Luke was on him before he could recover. Luke slammed his weapon into the other man's body twice more before the bandit scrambled away.

Those last few hits must have knocked the fight out of him because the bandit fled back down the hall. He was still surprisingly nimble for a man who'd just gotten the shit beaten out of him, but not so quick that Luke couldn't keep up with him. He got the door open and got three steps into the bedroom before Luke caught up.

After that, the fight quickly went Luke's way. The bandit tried to pull out another skill that increased his speed, but he'd held on to it until too late in the fight, and with his injuries, it wasn't enough to save him. Luke pulped the man's hip, then crushed his chest, and was about to bring the mace down again when he heard the kill notification ding.

[You have slain Human Bandit (level 27). 769 XP awarded.]

"Holy shit, why was this guy so much stronger than the rest of them?" Luke asked. "I mean, I know why. But, like, the fuck."

Now that the fight was over, his hands shook, and it was a struggle to keep his breathing steady. That had been by far the most stressful fight he'd been in to date, even including that duel with that goblin. Myla might have been worse, but considering how he'd been taken out by an ambush there, he didn't really consider it much of a fight. Zea was the one who'd fought that battle.

Speaking of which, she was going to be pissed. He would just have to hope that the loot he brought back mitigated that because he was definitely going to get shit about running off to fight bandits for the next week. He resolved not to tell her that he'd almost died to some random no-name who'd been tougher than anyone else he'd ever met. That would have been the shittiest ending to his journey.

Luke took a few minutes to put himself back together, stole the dead man's sword and his purse, then gathered up the jewelry case and the broken money box. There were definitely other valuables in the pile, but he didn't see a good way to travel with them. If they'd had a cart or a wagon, that might have been a different story, but that also would have required them to stay on the road.

Maybe someday he'd come back to pick through the rest of it, when things weren't so dire. Or maybe he'd just sell the location and a description of the loot to someone else. Either way, there wasn't much more he could do at the moment. He made his way back through the keep, scooped up the crossbow and the quiver of bolts near the front door, and headed back out into the rain.

He kept his eyes and ears open, but he was pretty sure at this point that he'd either killed all the bandits or that the ones he'd missed had run for the hills. Either way, he didn't see any between the keep and the campsite, where he paused once again to break down one of the tents and collect the loot he'd piled up there, what little of it was travel sized.

There was only one last thing left to do: face the wrath of a pissed-off short lady who very well might punch him in the balls as soon as she saw him.

Name	Luke Bennet	Zea Stenter
Level	24	13
XP	48858/50687	7987/8325
AP	9	8
Bloodline	SysAdmin	None
Strength	42	7
Agility	40	12
Stamina	36	12
Perception	39	14
Skills	Mace Mastery (3)	Dagger Mastery (1)
	Sword Mastery (1)	Stealth (2)
	Unarmed Martialist (3)	Keen Instincts (1)
	Power Strike (1)	Lock Picking (1)
	Life Surge (1)	Disguise (2)
	Peripheral Awareness (2)	Deception (1)
	Counter (2)	Bartering (2)
	Twitch Reflexes (2)	Streetwise (2)
	Stealth (1)	Cooking (1)
	Survivalist (2)	Mending (1)
	First Aid (1)	First Aid (1)
	Wood Carving (1)	Thalian (3)
	Leatherworking (2)	Neyardic (3)
	Thalian (2)	Ostari (1)
	Disguise (2)	Mana Manipulation (1)
	Deception (1)	Mana Sight (1)
		Metallurgy (1)
		Whitesmithing (1)
		Goldsmithing (2)
		Gem Cutting (1)
		Engraving (2)
		Rune Forging (1)
		Painting (1)
		Arcano Dynamics (1)
		Sleight of Hand (1)
		Steady Hands (2)
		Cold Reading (1)
		Temperature Acclimation (2)
		Cadence (1)

CHAPTER 10

"I. Thought. You. Were. Dead," Zea said, punctuating each word by throwing handfuls of the gold and silver coins at Luke.

"Hey, stop that. Stop! You're making a mess."

Luke caught as many as he could, but he couldn't snatch dozens of coins out of the air in only a few seconds. Coins bounced off of him and rolled into the dirt, hopefully to be reclaimed and not lost under loose leaves or in the tall grass.

"I don't give a fuck about the money! You ran off and left me alone in the woods! You were supposed to come right back."

"Well . . . Yeah, but . . . It's not like I was abandoning you."

"We didn't need to fight all the bandits, and you definitely didn't need to fight them alone."

Luke sat there, scratching the back of his head. "We had to get the money some way," he said. "Robbing thieves seemed like a good way to do it. And they were . . . mostly all low level."

"What does *mostly* mean?" Zea asked, her eyes narrowed into a suspicious glare. "Because it sounds like that means some of them weren't low level at all."

"There was one guy who was much stronger than he should have been. I guess he was part ogre. It wasn't really a hard fight, just kind of unusual."

He decided he wasn't going to mention the last fight if he didn't have to. That had been unexpected, completely at odds with everything else he'd found in the old fort. The way Zea was looking at him though, he suspected his **[Deception]** skill wasn't strong enough to get him through the conversation on its own.

"Hey," he said softly. "Look, there was always going to be some element of risk, no matter how we got the money. We need to be higher level anyway if this plan is going to work, and the world is better off without a bunch of bandits. Plus, they had way more money than the average monster. This was a win all the way around."

"That's not the point," Zea said. "I shouldn't have to spell this out for you, but you're not getting it. We didn't make a decision. You made a decision by yourself after you left me behind. If we're going to be a team, you can't do that. I get that there are risks, a lot of risks, big risks sometimes, but they're supposed to be our risks, not just yours."

"I . . . Fuck. You're right. I'm sorry."

Luke had spent so much of his time on Aros on his own that he hadn't really thought about including Zea in the decision-making process now that they were out of the city again. He'd just kind of assumed she would follow his lead, the same way he followed hers around people. It was now glaringly obvious to him that this had not been a good assumption to make.

Thankfully, Zea seemed to feel she'd gotten her point across. She sighed and set the lockbox down between them. "Here, you get those ones over there and I'll pick up the ones on this side."

Together they refilled the box. Luke wasn't entirely sure they recovered all of them, but if they missed one or two, it wasn't the end of the world. Between that and the jewelry they'd pawn in the next city, he figured that was probably enough for two people to take a boat across the ocean. All they needed to do now was find a seaside city and book passage.

Maybe, if he was lucky, there'd be enough left over to commission some armor for the both of them. Luke had really been hoping for good armor, but the best he'd gotten was what amounted to a leather muscle shirt. It wasn't really all that surprising, and he honestly wasn't even sure he needed armor anymore. Between the defensive skills and the healing he got from **[Life Surge]**, he was doing fine without it.

He still wanted it, of course. Not getting hurt at all was much better than recovering from it, and as long as it was flexible, it would take a lot more than thirty or forty pounds of steel to slow him down. But if it came down to it, Zea was a higher priority for armor than him, and unless something changed drastically, getting the boat tickets was the highest priority of all.

Before that, they needed to get there, and they needed to level up some more. Zea needed three more levels to have the 50 AP to spare, and Luke had pushed his own plans back by another level when he ranked up **[Mace Mastery]** midfight to throw that bandit off his rhythm. After that, he wasn't entirely sure. Depending on which bloodline skills unlocked after they completed their plan to obtain **[Bloodline Purification Ritual]**, he might start putting AP toward those. The costs were outrageously expensive, but the things some of them could do were completely broken.

Being able to just tell the system that someone was paralyzed wasn't all that different than being able to tell the system to kill that person. Fabricating objects was basically the same as unlimited wealth. Messing with stats and skills completely destroyed any need for a build. Why settle for having holes in his capabilities when he could be excellent at literally everything?

He might even look into learning how to do magic, even though it sounded like a complicated pain in the ass. It wasn't like he wouldn't have the AP to waste on it at that point. Nobody really seemed to be interested in using it, but he suspected that was because of the high number of support skills required to even work with mana, let alone shape it into a spell itself. Then each individual spell cost even more AP. It was a real point sink. The average person would have to spend every single AP they had just to get access to a handful of weak spells.

Considering how much a person could do with even 20 or 30 AP invested directly into stats, Luke wasn't surprised that anything to do with magic ended up being highly specialized. He certainly didn't regret the path he'd taken, even if he had deviated significantly from the build notes Curt had laid out for him. But someday, maybe soon, he would have a chance to expand in new directions.

"Do you think the rain will let up soon?" Zea asked, breaking Luke out of his contemplations.

"Hard to say. I don't think it matters much. It's been coming down so long, it's not like it's any drier here." Luke looked down at his still-soaked clothing. "Or maybe that's just me."

"No, it's been pretty miserable for me too," she said. "I guess we might as well start walking? Road's probably clear. We could make good progress."

"Yeah. It'll keep us warm too. Going to be a muddy mess though."

They collected their things, including the new supplies and weapons Luke had taken from the bandits, bundled everything up, and left the dubious shelter of the pines.

As much as she still wanted to wring his neck, Zea thought Luke at least understood what he'd done wrong. She felt kind of bad about throwing the money at him, but she was so pissed at the time that he'd run off and left her to risk his life by himself, and then doubled down on that to go hunt even more bandits. She regretted losing her temper after, even if he did deserve it.

The fact that he'd come back with what likely amounted to several months' worth of money was a mitigating factor. He hadn't been wrong to raid the bandit fort, but it should have been a decision they made together. Either way, it was over and done with. As long as he didn't do something stupid like that again, they'd be alright.

A large part of her was wondering what the fuck she was doing out there with him. She'd taken an enormous risk just going with him, and now she was pumping herself with XP, every monster they killed shortening her life span, just to pick up a skill that would help him. If he was wrong about how this all worked, she was literally killing herself for a guy she'd only known for a few weeks.

And then the big lump was so oblivious to it all that he just blundered forward, acting on every random thought that popped into his head without even a moment's consideration for the consequences. He shouldn't have trusted her at all, let alone so completely, but he did. It was kind of cute, she supposed. A smile tugged at the corner of her lips.

He'd come back with a lot of holes in his new clothes though, something she didn't think would have happened if the bandits were all as weak as he'd said. She'd avoided commenting on it since he didn't seem to want to talk about it, but it was somewhat exasperating that he'd need new clothes again. On the other hand, they were modestly rich now, and he hadn't had any dumb ideas like trying to give the money away. They could afford some nice clothes.

She wasn't sure about pawning the jewelry though. Some of it was pretty unique, and she wasn't confident about finding a pawnbroker that would keep their mouth shut about where they got something hot if anyone came around asking questions when she wasn't a city native. Hell, she was barely confident about the broker they'd used last time. She wouldn't have gone to him at all if it had been anything other than temple gear, but he was the only one who'd take it.

Come to think of it, they never had figured out how Myla had latched on to Luke so quickly. It was obvious that he was foreign just looking at him. His mannerisms, his accent, and even his skin color were all off. But Valtira was a big city, and it was stretching things to think an inquisitor had run into him after a few days by sheer chance.

That didn't necessarily mean it was the broker, of course. It was possible someone friendly with the church might have reported Luke. It was possible that it truly was just bad luck. Hell, he was a fucking off-worlder apostate. It was even possible the gods themselves had told someone where to look for him. If there was ever anyone that would warrant personal attention from a higher power, it was Luke.

All the same, she didn't think she'd be trusting a pawnshop anytime soon. If they sold the jewelry at all, she'd do it when they were on their way out of town so there was no chance of someone hunting them down while they were there. Even that was a risk. It was probably best to just throw them out, but she'd keep them tucked in the bottom of the bag just in case they found themselves in a desperate situation that only a few more coins would solve, however unlikely that seemed.

Plus, well, it hurt her soul to throw money away. Throwing it at Luke was one thing; abandoning it was something else altogether. Zea didn't have it in her to throw them out, and besides, Luke had mentioned something about melting the jewelry down. It wouldn't be as valuable that way, but it would be safer to unload.

The clouds drifted away as they walked, and by the time they settled down for the night, things had started to dry out. Even better, they came across a medium-sized town with a population of about a thousand, large enough to have two inns. They got a room for the night, or rather, she got a room by herself and had Luke come in through the second-story window later so that no one would notice a human-dwifkin couple traveling together. The last thing they needed was to leave a trail of witnesses for the church to follow.

Fortunately, Luke barely needed to sleep, and he was gone again before the sun came up with a promise to meet her on the road north of town. Unfortunately, that meant the bed was far colder than she preferred for the second half of the night. It might have been necessary, but she sure as hell didn't appreciate it.

Name	Luke Bennet	Zea Stenter
Level	24	13
XP	48858/50687	7987/8325
AP	9	8
Bloodline	SysAdmin	None
Strength	42	7
Agility	40	12
Stamina	36	12
Perception	39	14
Skills	Mace Mastery (3)	Dagger Mastery (1)
	Sword Mastery (1)	Stealth (2)
	Unarmed Martialist (3)	Keen Instincts (1)
	Power Strike (1)	Lock Picking (1)
	Life Surge (1)	Disguise (2)
	Peripheral Awareness (2)	Deception (1)
	Counter (2)	Bartering (2)
	Twitch Reflexes (2)	Streetwise (2)
	Stealth (1)	Cooking (1)
	Survivalist (2)	Mending (1)
	First Aid (1)	First Aid (1)
	Wood Carving (1)	Thalian (3)
	Leatherworking (2)	Neyardic (3)
	Thalian (2)	Ostari (1)
	Disguise (2)	Mana Manipulation (1)
	Deception (1)	Mana Sight (1)
		Metallurgy (1)
		Whitesmithing (1)
		Goldsmithing (2)
		Gem Cutting (1)
		Engraving (2)
		Rune Forging (1)
		Painting (1)
		Arcano Dynamics (1)
		Sleight of Hand (1)
		Steady Hands (2)
		Cold Reading (1)
		Temperature Acclimation (2)
		Cadence (1)

CHAPTER 11

Luke had gotten a look at a map before he'd left Valtira when he was preparing to walk, and he hadn't much cared for what he'd seen. There was a giant blob of mountains blocking off a chunk of the coast, which limited access to the sea so much that Valtira was the northernmost port on the southern side of those mountains.

According to Zea, it also meant that every ship going north was going to stop there for the last resupply before they continued up the coast almost a thousand miles to Sicanti, which was their destination. It functioned as the gateway between the western and eastern continents, and the only ways to get there were a boat that was going to stop in Valtira, or by walking. For obvious reasons, they'd chosen to walk.

The pair quickly settled into a routine, traveling a few miles away from the road and on the lookout for monsters. They foraged for supplies, camped out in their new-to-them tent, and hunted for XP. It wasn't until a few days that they started to get closer to the mountains, the woods got thick again, and they started finding monsters . . .

"Don't stand there!" Luke yelled as he swatted some sort of hybrid bear-baboon monster in the face. It was midcharge at Zea when he intercepted it, and she smoothly trained the crossbow over to release a bolt into its gut.

"I couldn't get a better angle," she called back.

"Yeah, but there might be more in the cave."

"Oh shit, yeah. That's a good point." She hopped off the rock shelf leading up to the cave and walked over to Luke. "Is that thing going to get back up?"

"I don't know. It's not dead yet," Luke said, eyeing up the monster. It was face down, ass up in the dirt and bleeding from a nasty head wound. He took a long step over toward it and finished it off. "Nope, now it's dead."

[You have assisted in slaying Bearboonikan (level 17). 149 XP awarded.]

"Oh, that did it," Zea said. "Level 14 and 22 AP waiting to be used."

"Nice! I'm still about 1500 XP short."

Zea peered up at the cave. "Do you want to go poke around in there?"

"Not really," Luke said. "It would be harder for you to get a clean shot in a tunnel."

He left unsaid his bad experience with getting hopelessly lost the last time he went underground. That wasn't something Zea needed to know about. That thing about having a clear line of sight was totally true anyway, even if it wasn't exactly a difficult problem to work around.

"Okay, if you're sure."

Luke could feel her staring at the back of his head. He might have resolved to say nothing at all, but he caved almost immediately. "I have a bad sense of direction," he admitted. "It's best to stay topside."

Zea snorted. "I knew it. You're just as human as the rest of them. If that's all you're worried about, I can navigate. But I'm also okay with moving on if it's a deep cave. We might as well end the day a couple miles closer to Kazos if we're going to be walking that far anyway."

"I guess. Well, let's take a quick peek inside and see if there's anything near the front, then we'll leave?"

There was not in fact anything of note in the first few hundred feet, at least not counting the leavings of the bearboonikan and signs that there might possibly be as many as four or five more, judging by the strange nest-like beds they found scattered around the cave. That little bit of trivia was all it took for them to decide not to explore further.

"Come on, this place stinks, and there's nothing worth seeing here," Luke said.

"Zea."

"Yeah?"

"Do you think that bear-monkey thing could climb trees?"

"I dunno. Maybe, why?"

"There are four more of them coming our way right now. It's going to be hard to keep you safe."

Zea scrambled to her feet and scooped up the loaded crossbow next to her. She kind of hated it just because of the size, but it was what she had. There was no arguing that she was safer standing back and taking free shots at monsters while Luke got in their faces and kept them busy. Four at once could be a problem though. If even one decided to ignore him, he'd have a hard time breaking away from the other three to intercept it.

"We knew there were risks," she said. "Here, help me up into the branches."

Luke held out his hands in a cup that she stepped into, and he boosted her upward. It was a constant source of amazement to her how much easier everything was to do with her stats so much higher, even though they were a fraction of Luke's. She couldn't even imagine a world seen through 39 perception.

Once she was settled in place about ten feet up, she said, "Which direction are they coming from?"

Luke pointed off to her right. "Just past those trees. They're studying us now and circling around. I'm going to go over there to make things noisy. I'll try to get them out in the open for you to tag, but don't worry about it if you don't get a shot. There's always another monster next time."

"Are you sure you should be fighting them four at a time?" Zea asked. Rationally, she knew how strong he was. She'd seen his status, and it was all hard stats and combat skills.

"It'll be fine," Luke told her. "None of them feel that strong, and I don't think they've got any skills to hide their XP from me."

"Be careful. Run if you need to."

"Don't worry so much. It's fine. Try not to shoot me, please."

Luke darted off, his movements so fast that she had trouble keeping up with them. Sounds of combat filtered out through the trees, mostly growls and roars from the monsters interspersed with crashes and cracks as the trees were pulverized. One of the bear-monkey things went flying out into the glade they were camped in, and Zea promptly put a crossbow bolt in its face.

It didn't get back up, but it was still twitching. It would be nice to be able to adjust her system menus like Luke claimed he had to get that instant feedback that let her know something was dead, but that wasn't an option for her. Hopefully, once he was able to modify other people's statuses, he could tweak some of the things that had always annoyed her. It would be worth all of it just to have legible handwriting on her status. If he could reorganize her skills for her, that'd just be a bonus.

A bellow caught her attention while she was reloading her crossbow, and her head snapped up. The one she'd shot was still done, with no other enemies in sight, but one of the trees was bending forward into the glade. With a thunderous crack, the tree broke low on the trunk, and it crashed down into the empty space. Tangled up in it was another of the monsters, with Luke standing on top of it.

He leaped free just as the tree impacted the ground and rushed back into the forest. The bear-monkey thing lay sprawled out in the branches, its throat crushed and pitiful wheezing sounds coming from its mouth. Zea finished reloading and shot that one too.

The other two didn't make it out of the trees before Luke killed them, which was fine by Zea. The notifications popped up telling her how much XP she'd gotten, not that she felt like she'd done anything to earn it.

[You have assisted in slaying Bearboonikan (level 14). 100 XP awarded.]

[You have assisted in slaying Bearboonikan (level 16). 132 XP awarded.]

Luke appeared, mace in hand and drenched with blood. "That was . . . annoying," he said with a scowl. "I'm going to go get cleaned up in that stream we passed a mile back. You want to pack everything up and we'll find a new place to camp?"

She didn't really want to keep walking, but sleeping next to monster corpses was a terrible idea. They would attract scavengers before the night was through, and some of those scavengers might not be picky about whether their meal was already dead. It would be hard enough to get a good night's sleep without worrying about what was sniffing around the bodies.

At least they didn't have the tent set up yet. She had no idea how Luke kept track of which piece of the frame went where, but somehow he always set it up perfectly on the first try. But since it was still waiting to be put together, she didn't have to worry about tearing it back apart. It only took a few minutes to gather everything up, pack away their supplies, and wait for him to come back.

He was clean when he did, kind of, but his clothes were soaked through. There were still going to be stains when he dried out, but she guessed it was better than nothing. "Ready to go?" she asked.

"Yeah, might as well. No point in hanging around here now, not unless you want to spend the night killing everything that wanders by for a snack."

"No thanks."

[You have assisted in slaying Thornripper Vine (level 21). 230 XP awarded.]

[Congratulations! You have reached level 15. 15 AP awarded for use.]

"37 AP now," Zea said. "One more level to go."

[You have assisted in slaying Ten-Ton Raccoon (level 18). 177 XP awarded.]

[You have assisted in slaying Bloodfeather Falcon (level 16). 132 XP awarded.]

[You have assisted in slaying Titan's Fang Spider (level 19). 187 XP awarded.]

[Congratulations! You have reached level 16. 16 AP awarded for use.]

"That's it. 53 AP. I can take the first rank of **[Bloodline Purification Ritual]** now."

Three days of hard travel and a lot of slaughter had taken their toll, and if not for Luke's **[Wood Carving]** skill, she wouldn't have any ammunition left for her crossbow. He freely admitted that his replacements weren't as good as the ones she'd had originally, but those had all broken one at a time, and he'd managed to make decent substitutes.

"Huh . . . Wow. It kind of doesn't feel real," Luke said. "I know we've been working toward it, but . . . Wow."

He'd leveled once too but hadn't quite had enough AP to take both skills he'd wanted thanks to his little stunt with the bandits. Then he'd decided to hold off completely on even ranking up **[Unarmed Martialist]** until they figured out which skills would unlock when they purified his bloodline.

"Let's do this," Zea said. She added the skill to her status, then staggered back a step and dropped onto her butt as the system shoved knowledge into her brain. "Holy shit, that's a lot of technical information."

It took her a few minutes to get stuff sorted. Luke hovered around her the whole time, which was kind of endearing but also kind of annoying. Finally, she shooed him off and sat down to process things. There was a lot to it, and she was no longer sure that her current skill set was going to be enough. **[Cadence]** had been a solid choice, but she'd assumed **[Mana Manipulation]** at rank 1 would suffice. All her enchanting projects had been easy enough to do, and getting a rank up would only have increased her production speed.

Now it felt like it might be necessary just to handle the sheer amount of mana the ritual required, not to mention some sort of mental-fortitude skill. It would take three hours from the time she started to the time it took hold, if and only if she didn't make any mistakes. If she did, some of the reagents used in the ritual would be wasted and need to be replaced, which they didn't even have to begin with.

"Well? Can we do it?" Luke asked.

Zea shook her head. "I need to get some supplies before we can even try."

"Oh." Luke heaved a sigh. "That's okay. We'll keep chipping away at it. What do we need?"

Name	Luke Bennet	Zea Stenter
Level	25	16
XP	53874/57250	12709/15275
AP	34	3
Bloodline	SysAdmin	None
Strength	42	7
Agility	40	12
Stamina	36	12
Perception	39	14
Skills	Mace Mastery (3)	Dagger Mastery (1)
	Sword Mastery (1)	Stealth (2)
	Unarmed Martialist (3)	Keen Instincts (1)
	Power Strike (1)	Lock Picking (1)
	Life Surge (1)	Disguise (2)
	Peripheral Awareness (2)	Deception (1)
	Counter (2)	Bartering (2)
	Twitch Reflexes (2)	Streetwise (2)
	Stealth (1)	Cooking (1)
	Survivalist (2)	Mending (1)
	First Aid (1)	First Aid (1)
	Wood Carving (1)	Thalian (3)
	Leatherworking (2)	Neyardic (3)
	Thalian (2)	Ostari (1)
	Disguise (2)	Mana Manipulation (1)
	Deception (1)	Mana Sight (1)
		Metallurgy (1)
		Whitesmithing (1)
		Goldsmithing (2)
		Gem Cutting (1)
		Engraving (2)
		Rune Forging (1)
		Painting (1)
		Arcano Dynamics (1)
		Sleight of Hand (1)
		Steady Hands (2)
		Cold Reading (1)
		Temperature Acclimation (2)
		Cadence (1)
		Bloodline Purification Ritual (1)

CHAPTER 12

Luke didn't understand why they needed a silver bowl inscribed with a circle, or an athame of obsidian and blood silver, or anything else that the ritual called for. Zea assured him that most of the expensive objects were tools that they'd only have to buy once, and that if the ritual failed, they would only be out some of the reagents used in it.

Since she was the one with the skill for it, he didn't question the instructions. The important part to him was that they needed to get to the next city before they could even attempt a bloodline purification on him. They'd been taking their time, going out of their way to hunt monsters, and generally moving at a slower pace to accommodate Zea.

"Should we speed up?" Luke said. "I mean, we've got the money now, and we got the XP we needed to get the skill."

"How much of a hurry are we in?" Zea asked. "I don't want to encourage you to pile even more XP on, but there's a rank 2 for this skill that costs 200 AP. I would need another ten levels and to not spend a single AP before I could pick that up, and I'm not sure I can even manage the rank 1 version of this ritual without some more support skills."

"If we go deep into the mountains and do nothing but hunt monsters for a month or two, we could probably make that happen," Luke said. "Maybe it would be better to focus on increasing your survivability. Or, you've already got some of the base skills needed to learn spells, right?"

"Yeah." Zea paused for a second and shrugged. "But there's a reason it's so rare. Even with the system helping, spells are hard to do properly. They're time-consuming, expensive, and easy to mess up."

"They are? Huh. Well, good thing I didn't try to go that route."

"Were you considering it?" Zea asked.

Luke shrugged. "Not really. I'm sure most people would think it was really cool in my position, but I just don't think it's interesting. I like to move. Stats are amazing for that."

"I guess that explains why you have so few skills."

"Well, they're creepy though, aren't they? Just that feel of something taking over your body and making you do what it wants. Ugh. What would a spell even do, take over my brain and make me think differently?"

Zea stopped walking and frowned. "I guess I've never thought about it like that. That's just what skills do. Is it really that weird for you?"

"We don't have stuff like that on my planet," Luke said. "So yeah, super fucking creepy. I don't like it at all. But it keeps me alive, and I guess it kind of helps teach me how to fight. The more I use the skills, the less it feels like the system's using me as a finger puppet, but I think that's only because it's conditioned me to do what it wants."

"I suppose the first time the system did something for me, it was kind of a surprise. I mean, I already knew how skills worked, and that's not weird; it's just the way it is. But if you've been doing it for decades on your own, yeah, I can see how that might be upsetting."

"It is what it is," Luke said. "Can't change it, but I don't have to like it. Anyway, straight to Kazos or take our time?"

"I think we could probably go straight there. Getting your bloodline purified is more important than grinding out more XP. The skills we were able to find out about all sound incredible."

"And if we do need XP, it's not like I've been to a single place yet that doesn't have an overabundance of monsters," Luke said. "Okay, let's push on. Maybe we'll use the roads?"

"Probably end up having to detour to deal with more bandits."

"Okay, so not the roads then."

Luke had been expecting something similar to Valtira, but Kazos was entirely different. For one, it had a fifty-foot-high wall circling it, and for another, several miles of farmland had been carved out of the forest around that. It must have taken a small army of farmers to tend that much land with no tractors or other modern farming equipment.

Then again, Earth didn't have people with the physical qualities of Aros's population. No doubt the standard farmer could work a field all day, well past when the sun set, and at a greater speed than anyone back home could hope to match. That farmer probably wasn't even tired at the end of the day. It might take a lot less man power than he had originally thought.

That wall though, that looked like it could be trouble. "If we go in there, we're trapped. Some church assholes start trying to run me down again, I doubt I'll get away like I did last time."

"Could be," Zea agreed. "But we're not going to find the tools we need outside of a city. I'm not even confident we'll find them in the city."

"Then I guess we should make some plans now."

"Enter at different times through different gates," Zea said immediately. "I'm going to be noticeable just because I'm a dwifkin this far north, and we haven't exactly rushed. If the church has sent news ahead, then whoever's local will know to look for us."

"We could skip it," Luke said. "There must be other places to get the stuff."

Zea shook her head. "Maybe, but all in one place? If we're going to keep going north, it would be better to have this done and taken care of now. We might never find all the pieces we need if we just go shopping in every piddly-dink little village general store we come across."

"I don't like the idea of splitting up," Luke said.

"We've both got ranks in **[Disguise]**. And the average level is higher with all the Guardians in the area, so you probably won't stick out as bad."

"I could buy **[XP Mask]** now. I wanted to hold off until after the bloodline purification, but . . ."

"No, not if you're going to keep leveling after we leave. You need to know how strong what you're fighting is so you don't attack the wrong thing and get yourself killed."

"Where do we meet up then?" Luke asked.

"We don't, not while we're in the city. I'll work on getting the supplies for the ritual, and you work on getting the supplies for the road. We'll meet back here tomorrow morning." She eyed Luke up and down and added, "Get some spare clothes. Should have taken some from the bandits."

"I had enough of wearing dead men's clothes the first time around," Luke said. "Wasn't eager to do it again."

Zea shrugged and nodded. "Okay. The stains are kind of faded now, but you should still get some new clothes. Food too. I wouldn't say no to a thicker blanket and some cooking supplies."

"Uh, maybe you should get the cooking supplies."

"Good idea. Okay, what else do we need?"

"Armor for you. A weapon in your size would be nice too. Something with some range on it."

There hadn't been any close calls yet, but it was just a matter of time. Luke was fully planning on putting on another 10 levels at minimum before reaching their final destination on the western continent, and he figured Zea was good for another fifteen just to catch up to him. She needed some higher stats and some combat-oriented skills to help her too, at least a few levels worth of AP before she started saving for another rank of **[Bloodline Purification Ritual]**. That was assuming it became necessary, since it was entirely possible that doing the ritual once would give him everything he needed.

Well, not everything, but no matter how pure his bloodline was, he was going to have to finish his journey to the God Machine. But if System was telling him the truth, it wouldn't matter what state his bloodline was in once he got there. It probably wouldn't hurt to keep working on that, just to be safe. He would be incredibly pissed off if he finally got all the way to the God Machine only to find out that he had more hoops to jump through before he could use it.

Still, he needed to prioritize, and making sure Zea was strong enough to survive the trip was at the top of the list. Not coincidentally, he'd be getting stronger right next to her because he also wanted to survive the trip, and he'd run from a few too many monsters that outclassed him already. Maybe when he hit level 50, that would be strong enough, but then again, who knew what was roaming around on a whole new continent?

"Armor might be a nonstarter," Zea said, breaking him out of his train of thought. "I could look at some basic stuff, but anything truly useful would need to be custom-made. It could take weeks to fill that order. I would guess the best I could do on short notice is a chain shirt, and you've seen how easy it is to rend basic steel."

"That armor I took from the templar had adjustable straps," Luke said. "Maybe you could find something like that."

"Maybe," she agreed. "I'll look, but I'm not going to promise anything, and I'm not going to buy something we have to wait weeks on to be completed. Plus we haven't even considered the price. We've got a lot of money here, but we have big expenses coming up too."

"Fuck, yeah. We still don't even know how much that's going to cost. Even if we save everything we've got, it still might not be enough."

"That's why I'm thinking we get essential supplies only, plus the tools for the ritual. That's also a high priority."

Luke frowned but didn't argue the point. "So we go in, one day for supplies, sleep in a warm bed, and meet up back here tomorrow morning?"

"That's the plan," Zea said. "Here, take five of the gold and half the silver. That should be more than enough for a few spare sets of clothes, travel rations, and maybe a bribe or two if you absolutely have to. Better to lose a bit of coin than to draw the wrong sort of attention."

"I'll circle around through the woods and find a different gate," Luke said. He studied the roads leading away from the city. "Maybe something on the east side? It looks like there's plenty of people on that road."

Zea squinted in that direction and shrugged. "I can't tell, but sure. I'll go in through the south gate then. Pay attention to how much the gate guards are charging people so they don't scam you. Sometimes assholes will overcharge travelers who don't know any better so they can pocket the difference between what they scam out of you and the actual fee."

Luke hadn't expected there to be a fee at all. "They charge people just for going in and out? Even people who don't have a cart or wagon? It's not like I've got a bunch of shit I'm planning on selling that they can tax."

"That's just how it is. It'll probably only be a few coppers. Maybe a half-silver if it's real expensive. Just listen to what they're charging everybody else and don't let them hustle you."

"Got it. Okay, I'm off. See you in the morning."

Luke leaned down to kiss Zea, then faded back into the woods and started working his way north around the curve of the fields until he came across a road leading toward the walled city. It actually took longer to walk at a slow pace on the roads so that he didn't draw attention to himself than it did to move through the woods, and he got a few glances from other people when they felt how much XP he had, but it was otherwise a peaceful journey to the gates.

Name	Luke Bennet	Zea Stenter
Level	25	16
XP	53874/57250	12709/15275
AP	34	3
Bloodline	SysAdmin	None
Strength	42	7
Agility	40	12
Stamina	36	12
Perception	39	14
Skills	Mace Mastery (3)	Dagger Mastery (1)
	Sword Mastery (1)	Stealth (2)
	Unarmed Martialist (3)	Keen Instincts (1)
	Power Strike (1)	Lock Picking (1)
	Life Surge (1)	Disguise (2)
	Peripheral Awareness (2)	Deception (1)
	Counter (2)	Bartering (2)
	Twitch Reflexes (2)	Streetwise (2)
	Stealth (1)	Cooking (1)
	Survivalist (2)	Mending (1)
	First Aid (1)	First Aid (1)
	Wood Carving (1)	Thalian (3)
	Leatherworking (2)	Neyardic (3)
	Thalian (2)	Ostari (1)
	Disguise (2)	Mana Manipulation (1)
	Deception (1)	Mana Sight (1)
		Metallurgy (1)
		Whitesmithing (1)
		Goldsmithing (2)
		Gem Cutting (1)
		Engraving (2)
		Rune Forging (1)
		Painting (1)
		Arcano Dynamics (1)
		Sleight of Hand (1)
		Steady Hands (2)
		Cold Reading (1)
		Temperature Acclimation (2)
		Cadence (1)
		Bloodline Purification Ritual (1)

CHAPTER 13

Now three coppers lighter, Luke stood on the inside of the gate and took a deep breath. The city smelled, well, if he was being honest, it smelled awful. Maybe the wall prevented fresh air from circulating through, or maybe too many people were dumping their chamber pots in the street at once, but either way, Kazos was nowhere near as clean as Valtira.

It didn't take long to get directions to the business district, where Luke had his choice of half a dozen different stores selling traveling supplies. His mother would have strangled him for it, but Luke did not comparison shop between them. He picked the least dumpy-looking one on the dubious logic that it would have the least dumpy merchandise, then bought a pair of knapsacks and filled them both with food. He also bought two new pans and a canteen, a small hatchet for splitting firewood, and a first aid kit, though the shopkeeper called it a medic's bag.

That last one was more for Zea, just in case. He couldn't heal her with **[Life Surge]**, and she didn't have a way to patch up her own injuries, which was really another point in favor of her acquiring some actual spells if she didn't want to be a physical fighter like him. In the meantime though, being able to bandage and stitch a wound might literally save her life.

With directions to a tailor in hand, Luke wandered around town looking for the shop and protecting his three bags from tampering. After the third time he caught a young pickpocket by the wrist, he said, "Look kid, it's just apples and bread and shit."

"I know," the sullen ten-year-old said, trying to jerk his hand back. "I'm hungry."

"You've gotta be fucking kidding me," Luke muttered. "Am I really being stalked by a pack of starving homeless orphans?"

He released the kid, who stood there massaging his wrist and giving Luke the stink eye. With a sigh, Luke fished out an apple and tossed it to the boy. "That's all you're getting. Tell your buddies I said to fuck off before I have to get mean about it. Sorry about the wrist, but I'm not going to be so gentle next time."

Luke watched the kid scurry off for a moment, then shook his head and started walking again. He knew he was close to that tailor's shop but couldn't quite find it. Maybe he should have told the kid he'd give him a bit of food if he took Luke there, but he figured it was even odds that he'd end up walking into some sort of trap set up by the Oliver Twist gang. It was better to sidestep that possibility completely and just find the stupid tailor on his own.

That did not stop the kids from following him. The great thing about having such a high perception was that he didn't need to see them to know they were there, though **[Peripheral Awareness]** often pointed the kids out to him anyway. There were at least twenty of them, some of whom did a credible job of hiding. Others stared at him openly, or rather at the two knapsacks he had slung over his shoulder.

Luke heard the yelling before he rounded the corner. "—My fault they won't fix the fucking hole in the road, now is it!"

"Well you could have driven around it!"

"Not bloody fucking likely."

Two men were standing next to a wagon, arguing loudly. It was loaded to the hilt with cargo so heavy that he could see the wood bowing under the weight. A pair of sturdy, thick-limbed horses waited patiently in their harnesses while pedestrians streamed around them. Luke didn't know much about horses, but he'd always heard they were skittish animals. It surprised him how placid they were, almost indifferent to the people and the noise.

"How are we going to get it out of here? The horses were already struggling. I told you we should have done two loads."

"We don't have time for two loads," the other man said.

"Yeah, we saved ourselves a bunch of time, didn't we? All the time in the fucking world."

"Yeah, shut it." The man raised his voice and said, "Anyone willing to help us out here? Someone with a bit of strength to lift with?"

Luke could go around. He didn't need to get involved. Nobody else was stopping either, at least not any longer than they had to while they waited for their turn to squeeze past the wagon. Now that he could see it, the back wheel was stuck in a giant pothole, perfectly sized to hold it in place. Between that and the weight, it was no wonder they were stuck.

"Come on," the man begged. "Somebody. I'll pay!"

Luke paused. Easy money was something he could use more of. "How much?" one of the women in the crowd asked.

The man grimaced, and said, "Four copper?"

The woman snorted and walked away while the flow of traffic around the wagon resumed. Luke looked around for a street sign, hoping to find something that would confirm he was heading in the right direction, or even the wrong direction if it meant he didn't need to wait to get around the wagon. Then he let out a groan when he spotted the sign in the window, a pair of scissors and a spool of thread.

Of course, it was just his luck that the tailor he was looking for was right there, just behind the wagon. He could probably squeeze by if he had to. He'd need both men to move first, but he could do it. On the other hand, he didn't think it wouldn't be that hard to get the wagon moving again, and maybe it would buy him some goodwill with the tailor himself, whom Luke could see watching with tightly pressed lips through a window.

"I'll help," Luke said, stepping up to the wagon. "Just need to lift, right?"

"Yeah," the man said, his face lighting up. His partner gave a snort and nodded.

"You are the luckiest son of a bitch, you know that? I can't believe anybody is willing to go out of their way for four fucking copper."

"Well, that and I want to get into the shop you're blocking," Luke said.

"Oh, sorry about that," the man said. "It really was an accident. We don't normally take this route, and this knucklehead wasn't paying attention."

"Throw me under the cart, why don't you?" the other guy muttered. "Like it's my fault there's a huge fucking hole in the street."

Luke ignored the bickering and slung both knapsacks onto the cargo. He reached down to grab the wagon and looked over to the man. "Ready?" he asked. At the return nod, he heaved upward. Wood groaned and creaked, but the wheel slowly lifted free of the hole. As soon as it was clear, the man urged the horses forward a few steps.

"Thanks, sir," the politer of the two men said. He fished out four copper and held them out. "Wish I could pay you more, but it's all I got on me."

"Sure," Luke said. "No problem."

He caught a blur of movement out of the corner of his eye and turned just in time to see one of the orphans turn a nimble no-hands cartwheel through the air, snatch both knapsacks while he was upside down, and land on his feet on the hard cobblestones. "Hey!" Luke yelled. "Get back here, you little shit."

The boy took off, unbelievably fast as he wove through the crowd. Luke knew he could follow fast enough to catch the kid, but not without knocking down a shitload of people as he plowed through them. He was far too big to weave like the kid did too. "Shit."

He could let the kid go, or he could draw all sorts of attention to himself trying to catch him. Maybe he could do it without doing anything too suspicious, as long as he kept his feet on the street and didn't push his stats too hard. Either way, if he didn't do something, his choice would be made for him.

Luke went as quickly as he could, gently pushing people back without flinging them aside, and tried to keep the kid in sight. That wasn't easy, considering that there were plenty of adults who were a foot or more taller, and also that he was sure the kid would have no problem navigating the alleys and side roads that made up the majority of this part of the city. As soon as he turned down one, Luke was going to lose him.

That, or he was going to have to cheat, but cheating meant leaping up onto the roofs, and that would draw attention to him. Maybe if he was lucky, the alley the kid had picked would be empty and Luke could lay on the speed before the kid got out of sight. It was a foolish hope, but it was better than nothing. If he didn't catch the kid, he'd be shelling out another few silver for replacement food and bags.

The kid juked left onto a side street about a hundred feet away, and Luke put on a burst of speed to get to that corner before he lost the little thief completely. More than one startled curse chased him down the street when he knocked someone aside, and Luke couldn't do anything but yell back his apologies and for someone to stop that thief. Nobody helped, of course.

Kazos was kind of a shithole city that way.

Luke reached the corner just in time to see the kid duck into an alley a few houses down. Fortunately, the side street wasn't nearly as crowded as the main road he'd been on, and he was able to close the gap quickly. Hope sprang anew when he hit that corner and saw the kid halfway down the alley. He was going to recover both of those knapsacks, and Zea would never, ever, ever need to find out about this.

That was about the time he realized the kid had stopped running and was waiting for him to catch up. Luke slowed down and eyed him warily before sweeping his gaze up the walls to check the roofs. The last thing he needed was to have to find out how many ten-year-olds he could take on at once. He wanted to say the answer was all of them, but it wouldn't surprise him to find some jacked, high-level eight-year-old working as a bruiser.

"It's not a trap," the kid said. "You're the apple guy, right?"

"The apple guy?" Luke echoed. He'd never even owned a turtleneck.

"Yeah, you gave Temmo the apple."

"Is Temmo the last kid who tried to rob me before you showed up?"

"Yeah, that's him. He's . . . He's not very good at it. I told him not to, but he didn't listen." The kid held out the knapsacks for Luke to take. "Here, these are yours. Don't worry, I didn't take anything."

"Why did you grab them at all?" Luke asked, confused. Either the kid thought he'd bitten off more than he could chew and was trying to deflect by pretending he wasn't really trying to steal them, or Luke was missing something. If the next thing that kid said was any variation of "It's just a prank, bro," Luke was going to punch him out.

"That's, uh, I know this doesn't make a great first impression, and I wanna apologize for my crew coming at you so hard. Thanks for not hurting any of them. It's just, we're kind of desperate right now."

"Mm-hmm. And?"

"Right." The kid took a deep breath. "I kind of wanted to ask you for a favor. Just a little one. Won't take an hour of your time."

Name	Luke Bennet	Zea Stenter
Level	25	16
XP	53874/57250	12709/15275
AP	34	3
Bloodline	SysAdmin	None
Strength	42	7
Agility	40	12
Stamina	36	12
Perception	39	14
Skills	Mace Mastery (3)	Dagger Mastery (1)
	Sword Mastery (1)	Stealth (2)
	Unarmed Martialist (3)	Keen Instincts (1)
	Power Strike (1)	Lock Picking (1)
	Life Surge (1)	Disguise (2)
	Peripheral Awareness (2)	Deception (1)
	Counter (2)	Bartering (2)
	Twitch Reflexes (2)	Streetwise (2)
	Stealth (1)	Cooking (1)
	Survivalist (2)	Mending (1)
	First Aid (1)	First Aid (1)
	Wood Carving (1)	Thalian (3)
	Leatherworking (2)	Neyardic (3)
	Thalian (2)	Ostari (1)
	Disguise (2)	Mana Manipulation (1)
	Deception (1)	Mana Sight (1)
		Metallurgy (1)
		Whitesmithing (1)
		Goldsmithing (2)
		Gem Cutting (1)
		Engraving (2)
		Rune Forging (1)
		Painting (1)
		Arcano Dynamics (1)
		Sleight of Hand (1)
		Steady Hands (2)
		Cold Reading (1)
		Temperature Acclimation (2)
		Cadence (1)
		Bloodline Purification Ritual (1)

CHAPTER 14

A favor?" Luke couldn't help but laugh.

"Yeah."

"Why would I do a favor for you after you made me chase you to get back what you stole from me? Just because you stopped running?"

"Well it's not like I was really planning on taking it! If I had been, you wouldn't have found me."

That might have been true, but there was no good way to prove it. Then again, the kid wasn't breathing hard, so he could have kept running, and given how high his strength and agility had to be in order to pull off a midair cartwheel five feet off the ground, maybe there was something to that.

"Okay, let's say I believe you. Why did you take them then?"

"If I'd walked up to you on the street and just said, 'Hey, mister, wanna help me out?' you wouldn't have listened."

"Maybe not, but I don't see how this makes me more likely to actually help now."

"Because I gave you back the food," the kid said. "I'm taking a chance here. We really need that food, but only because we can't get to ours. It's blocked off, and none of us are strong enough to get to it."

"Oh, I see. You saw me lift the wagon and figured I could help you too."

"Yes! But, uh, I don't have any money to offer you."

The kid was wearing ragged clothes, was barefoot, and was crusted with dirt. His hair was long and matted, uneven from where he'd probably tried to cut it himself with a knife or something. The other kids had looked much the same, and Kazos was too cold to be walking around dressed like that, unless they had no other choices.

Luke groaned. "What exactly do you want me to do?"

"Okay, so we've been squatting in the old textile factory on Mills Street 'cause the Bloody Knuckles pushed us out of our old place a few months ago, but the factory is right on the edge of the territory line with the Grinders, and they hit us with some shit they stole from an alchemist or something. It dropped the whole second floor and killed three of my guys."

"What the fuck," Luke muttered, but the kid just kept on talking right over him.

"So that's bad enough, but we had all our food stored in the basement, and now there's all this crap blocking the stairs. We've got food for everyone, for at least a week! Hell, more since we're down a few guys, but we can't get to it. We've been trying to excavate the basement, but some of the stuff is just too heavy to move."

Luke technically had the time to help. He had all day, after all, and the only thing left to do was get some new clothes. That wasn't even particularly important to him. Every time he got new clothes, they ended up trashed anyway, so there wasn't a strong need to keep buying them. At best, he wanted one set that he kept stored away and only put on when he needed to go into a town.

The question was less whether he could help and more if he even wanted to. He didn't owe these kids anything, but it sounded like life had already knocked them down and kicked them in the ribs a few times, and it didn't cost him anything to lift a few pieces of heavy debris out of the way. He was more concerned about whether or not the kid was telling the truth, and what kind of trap he'd be walking into if it turned out this was all some sort of scheme.

He figured the orphan-street-gang thing was probably real. He'd been in town for barely an hour, and there was no way those kids had gotten in the state they were in that fast. It wasn't a matter of dressing a kid in rags and rolling him in the dirt; there were blisters and calluses that came with long-term exposure. That kid's feet were practically leather at this point.

Luke reached forward and grabbed the kid. "Okay, here's the deal. If you're fucking with me, if this is some kind of trap or scam or what the fuck ever bullshittery you might have come up with, I'm going to come after you, personally. So, you tell me the truth now. Do you need help, or are you fucking with me?"

The kid's eyes got so big they threatened to fall out of his head, and he gulped twice before shaking his head. His finger moved in a circle over his chest, and he said, "No trick, man. I promise. I swear by every god in the Pantheon."

Luke let him go and said, "Fine. I believe you. Take me to this place and I'll help you dig it out."

"Y-yeah, no problem."

They took a few side streets, seemingly at random, before the kid said, "I'm Avlir, by the way."

Luke grunted but didn't reply. He wasn't going to tell anyone his real name, and his previous fake name was officially retired. Zea would no doubt be able to suggest a new one off the top of her head, but Luke would want to talk to System about common names for the area.

"So how long were you a Guardian?" Avlir asked.

"What makes you think I was?"

They paused for the kid to squeeze under a loose board in a fence. Luke glanced around once to make sure no one else was in the alley, then jumped over it. "Well, you can do that," the kid said once he landed on the other side. "But also I feel like I'm about to shit my pants just looking at you."

"Gross. Why is this fence even here?" Luke asked.

"Territory marker. We're about three blocks away from Dust Rat territory, at least what's left of it." There was a note of bitterness in the kid's voice. "Fucking assholes. There isn't even anything good there. They just wanted it because they're big enough to take it."

"I'm not going to have a bunch of street gangs harassing me because I helped you, am I?"

"They'd be dumb as fuck to even try. Don't tell me you couldn't crush someone's skull with your bare hands if you wanted to."

"Gross," Luke said again, like he didn't routinely aim for the skulls of the monsters he fought. But the icky stuff got on the mace then, not on him, so it was different. Though it was sometimes a bitch to get it clean again. Just wiping it off on an animal's corpse didn't do a great job, and there wasn't always a handy stream to soak it in.

Now that he thought about it, nobody had given him any shit about his weapon in Kazos, and he'd seen a lot more people walking around armed. Not even the gate guards had glanced at it twice. People seemed to be a higher level in general, usually at least 15. Even Avlir was level 6 or so, and he was just a kid. Luke didn't want to think about what exactly Avlir had killed to gain six levels.

They crossed another side street and came out into some sort of manufacturing district. The buildings were all a lot wider, many of them were two or three stories, and there seemed to be an abundance of some sort of brick used as a building material instead of the more common wooden homes. Shutters were a lot more common, and also many of the buildings had multiple chimneys. Sometimes they had sloped thatch roofs, but sometimes they were flat instead.

"Labor Row," Avlir said. "This is where all the bigger workshops are at. There's another street at the end that leads back to some older ones that have been abandoned."

"And that's where you guys are squatting?" Luke asked.

"Well, we were, back when there was space."

"Right. Okay, let's get this taken care of."

The longer they walked, the more of Avlir's crew Luke spotted. Some were loitering on the way; others started trailing behind. None of them got too close, which was fine by Luke. The idea of being swarmed by a bunch of little kids trying to make off with whatever their sticky little fingers could grab didn't sit well with him.

Once they were past Labor Row, and out of sight of all the people giving him odd looks, they turned to a smaller street. It had been some sort of gravel once but had been overtaken by weeds long ago. There was barely a path through it, more of a line of beaten-down plants than any actual trail. Two rows of sad, beaten, broken-down buildings lined either side of the road.

"Which one is yours?" Luke asked, not that he needed to. There was only one that very obviously had been damaged recently. One of the walls leaned in and had broken away near the roof. Luke could see refuse and debris through the crack it made, and some sort of wooden support beam jabbed out of the second-story shutter, which had been broken away.

"This one here," Avlir said, pointing to the one Luke had picked out. The kid led him around to a back door, which only opened about six or seven inches before getting caught on something. He was able to squeeze through, but Luke couldn't.

"If I put a shoulder into this, is that going to cause any problems?" he asked.

"No, we piled stuff there deliberately to slow down any other gangs trying to swarm us. Just give it a shove."

There was the sound of something scraping against the floor, and the door pushed open another foot or so. Luke left it that way and slipped inside. Immediately, he scanned the factory floor for anyone else hiding there, then looked up through the hole in the ceiling to the second floor. It was no wonder the kids weren't able to dig through it; some massive machine of some sort, very much a monstrosity of thick and heavy iron, had crashed through the ceiling and was now lying on the ground level as the centerpiece of a demolition scene.

There was a trail of excavated stone and wood leading up to it and circling around it, presumably what the kids had managed to haul out on their own. "I'm guessing no one was able to squeeze through the inside of that," Luke said.

"No, the guts of it are all still there. You'd have to be a literal rat to squeeze through it all. Not even our youngest could manage it."

Luke shrugged off his bags and set them in a corner. "You're responsible for these," he told Avlir. "If anyone tries to take anything from them, I'm coming after you."

"Got it, boss."

"I'm not—Whatever. Stay over there so I don't accidentally clip you."

Most of the debris was wood of various thicknesses and sizes. Luke started grabbing chunks at random and tossing them across the room to pile up in a relatively empty corner. It would have been backbreaking labor a few months ago, but not now. It only took a few minutes to clear all the big stuff out of the way so that he had room to drag the machine itself aside.

Luke grabbed hold of it and heaved. It pulled forward an inch or two, then settled back into place. "Damn, fucker's heavy," he said, trying again. This time he managed to drag it half a foot before it settled back onto the floor. It took another ten minutes of dragging to haul it completely to the side, not helped by the fact that as the machine moved, the whole building shook and the partially collapsed wall started being more collapsed.

"How much farther do you need this to go?" Luke asked.

Avlir eyed up the open space where the machine used to sit. The floors were completely ruined, many of the boards broken and new holes leading down into the dark dotted the area. "We could throw some stuff down one of these holes until we have a pile to climb down. The actual cellar doors are right about there though, just another foot or two away."

Luke heaved backward a few more times, and a minute later, the first door came into view. It had been busted and most of the stairs collapsed. "Well, looks like it's going to be a jump down no matter how you do it," he said, examining the remnants with the street kid.

A low groaning sound came up from the hole. The two of them exchanged glances and said at the same time, "What the hell is that?"

Name	Luke Bennet	Zea Stenter
Level	25	16
XP	53874/57250	12709/15275
AP	34	3
Bloodline	SysAdmin	None
Strength	42	7
Agility	40	12
Stamina	36	12
Perception	39	14
Skills	Mace Mastery (3)	Dagger Mastery (1)
	Sword Mastery (1)	Stealth (2)
	Unarmed Martialist (3)	Keen Instincts (1)
	Power Strike (1)	Lock Picking (1)
	Life Surge (1)	Disguise (2)
	Peripheral Awareness (2)	Deception (1)
	Counter (2)	Bartering (2)
	Twitch Reflexes (2)	Streetwise (2)
	Stealth (1)	Cooking (1)
	Survivalist (2)	Mending (1)
	First Aid (1)	First Aid (1)
	Wood Carving (1)	Thalian (3)
	Leatherworking (2)	Neyardic (3)
	Thalian (2)	Ostari (1)
	Disguise (2)	Mana Manipulation (1)
	Deception (1)	Mana Sight (1)
		Metallurgy (1)
		Whitesmithing (1)
		Goldsmithing (2)
		Gem Cutting (1)
		Engraving (2)
		Rune Forging (1)
		Painting (1)
		Arcano Dynamics (1)
		Sleight of Hand (1)
		Steady Hands (2)
		Cold Reading (1)
		Temperature Acclimation (2)
		Cadence (1)
		Bloodline Purification Ritual (1)

CHAPTER 15

S omeone down there?" Luke called out.

"Gedin? Nenda?" Avlir added. "You two alive down there?"

Silence stretched on, broken only by the sound of debris shifting as it settled into its new position. Luke scanned the basement, even looked through a few of the other holes, but he didn't see anyone down there.

"We never found their bodies when we were digging," Avlir said quietly. "I figured they were crushed under the machine itself, but . . . maybe they just fell through the floor."

"I wouldn't get your hopes up," Luke told him. "That thing has got to weigh more than a ton. A lot more. If they were underneath it when it fell through the floor and somehow survived, they've probably spent the last few days wishing they were dead."

He dropped down through one of the holes and looked around. The only light was what came through the holes, of course, and even that was poor quality. It almost made it harder to see since his eyes kept trying to switch between light and dark, not that there was much to see. There was less debris piled upon the basement floor, if only because there were joists overhead that were close to a foot thick.

Why they were needed was beyond Luke, but he assumed they were the only reason that machine had stopped when it hit the first floor instead of crashing all the way to the basement. Most of them were cracked or even broken completely, though a few had brick pillars supporting them. Those pillars broke up his line of sight in the basement, but unless someone was actively hiding behind them, he felt like he had enough coverage to see anyone who might have been down there.

"Hello?" Luke said. "If someone's alive down here, now would be a good time to make some noise for me. I'm not going to go digging through every random pile of crap looking for you."

Another low groan came from nearby. Luke walked over to a pile of debris and grabbed the chunk of floor that had collapsed in more or less one piece and tossed it aside to reveal two children, one ten or eleven, and the other one five. "Aw, fuck. This . . . This is bullshit," he said softly.

The older one was dead, his body stiff with rigor mortis. He'd sheltered the younger one, a little girl wearing a ragged dress. She wasn't really conscious, as far as Luke could tell. Her eyes flickered, but she didn't respond to anything. Luke lifted the boy's body out of the way and set him aside, then cradled the girl close to his chest.

Without even needing to check, he could see lacerations all over her arms and legs. Her breathing was shallow, barely even there, and she whimpered when he moved her. If he had to guess, his money was on broken ribs, probably from the fall. Somehow the other boy had sheltered her enough that she didn't look like she'd been hurt when the machine had broken through the floor.

Luke jumped back up to the ground floor and looked over at Avlir. "The other one was dead already," he said softly.

"Oh, gods. Fuck those assholes for doing this. I'll kill every last one of them."

"Hey, focus. This girl is still alive. What can you do to help her?"

"Help?" Avlir gave a short, bitter laugh. "We don't have any money. We can't hire a healer. The only thing I can do to help is put her out of her misery."

The weight of that neck pouch full of gold and silver had never felt heavier to Luke. Without some sort of magical assistance, he didn't see a way the girl lived. If they found a healer willing to work on her, maybe he had enough money to pay those fees. "How much does it cost to go to a healer?"

"How the fuck would I know? Do I look like some nobleman's brat?"

There was one other option. He still had 34 AP. He could pick up the skills and learn the spell himself. Zea had told him that **[Mana Manipulation]** was an absolute necessity, and **[Mana Sight]** was considered mandatory by people who actually learned magic, if not by the system itself. Those would let him see and move mana into the desired spell form. **[Minor Heal]** was inside his budget with the points he had left.

The problem was that those were the minimum requirements, and if he wanted to do better than heal bruises and flesh wounds, he needed to upgrade that spell, and skills like **[Anatomy: Humanoid]** were also important. **[First Aid]** might cover some of those holes, but it wasn't going to be enough, not for someone that injured.

That was 25 of his 34 AP just to get **[Minor Heal]** at rank 1, another 3 AP for the anatomy skill, and he technically couldn't even upgrade it unless he bought **[Herb Lore]** first. For all of that, he could maybe set the broken ribs and heal the scrapes and bruises. If she had any sort of damage to her internal organs, he would be able to do fuck all for that.

"Shit," he said. The AP was honestly easier to replace than the money, but he just didn't have enough right now. Sure, it was a good start to more powerful healing spells, and he probably should look into that anyway, but what he had wasn't going to save this little girl right now. "Okay, we're going to a healer. You lead. I'm right behind you. Go as fast as you can. I don't give a fuck if we have to knock some people out of the way."

"But—"

"No, shut up. Just go."

Avlir was smart enough to do what he was told. He left the bags behind and darted out the door, with Luke following right behind him. It was a tight fit holding the girl close to his chest, but he managed it without jarring her. The two raced down the streets, ignoring anyone who wasn't in their way and moving around the ones who were or shoving through them if they couldn't.

A few minutes later, they stopped in front of an open gate in an eight-foot-tall brick fence. "Here," Avlir said, panting. "She's expensive but powerful. If anyone can save Nenda, it's her. How will you . . . You know . . . ?"

"With gold," Luke muttered, stepping past Avlir. "Come on."

The two of them walked through the gate, thankfully unlocked, and followed a stone-lined path up toward the house. Avlir sped ahead and started pounding on the door while Luke followed more slowly. By the time he got there, a teenage boy had answered the door and was busy arguing with the orphan.

"Mistress Omaril doesn't do charity cases, you little scab," the teenager snapped. "Now piss off before I give you a beating."

"Excuse me," Luke cut in. The teenager jumped in surprise, then turned to focus on Luke and the little girl in his arms. "I would like to talk to the healer now, if that's okay."

"She's . . . uh . . ."

A woman appeared behind the teenager, probably fifty years old and with a headful of iron-gray hair. She was dressed in a thick, padded dress with a shawl wrapped around her shoulders. "Felt you coming up the walk," she said. "Strong enough to be a Guardian. But my assistant is correct. I am not a charity worker."

"I can pay," Luke told her. "Can we come in now?"

"If you're sure," the woman said. "Don't know why you'd bother, but as long as your coin is good. Come on then."

They followed the healer to her clinic, and Luke set Nenda down on a table. The healer held out a hand. "Three silver to look her over and tell you what's wrong. Depending on what I find, it'll be gold to fix it."

Luke fished the money out of his money pouch and handed it to her. Then he dragged Avlir away from the table where he was hovering over Nenda and said, "Come on, let's get out of her way and let her work. In fact, you think you can bring my stuff here?"

"I'll have one of the boys do it," Avlir said, his eyes still locked on Nenda. "Be right back."

The healer had already started working, though so far she'd done little but look the little girl over. "Broken ribs, malnourished, lacerations on the face and shoulders. I hope you don't mind this dress getting ruined. I'll be cutting it off her," she said to Luke.

"Do what you have to."

"I'm already up to two and a half gold. You better have the money."

Luke pulled it out of his neck pouch and held it up. A little jiggle was enough to make the coins inside clink.

The healer huffed and nodded. Then, before Luke's eyes, the wounds on her skin started to close. The healer produced a pair of scissors and slit the dress open, then pulled it back. She ignored Luke while she worked but put her body between him and the patient. That was just fine by him, and in fact he turned and walked to the doorway to intercept Avlir coming back in.

"Give Nenda some privacy," he told the orphan boy. "She's not dressed now."

"Is she going to be alright?" Avlir asked.

"I fucking hope so."

They waited in silence, with Avlir ducking back out again twenty minutes later and returning with Luke's backpack and the two knapsacks full of food. "The guys managed to get most of our stuff out. We're not going to starve to death now, not this week at least. Those fuckers still killed two of us, and Nenda would be as good as dead without your help."

"She's not out of it yet," Luke said. Mistress Omaril had been working nonstop, and he hadn't heard so much as a peep from Nenda. If it was taking a professional healer that long, Luke knew he'd made the right call. Dumping his AP to get access to **[Minor Heal]** wouldn't have been close to enough.

It was an hour before the healer stood up straight and walked away from the table. "Four gold," she told Luke. He pulled out the last gold coin he had left and started digging for silver to make up the difference while the old woman watched him. By the time he was done, there was nothing left in the neck pouch but a few silver and a handful of copper.

"Very well. The child is asleep now. When she wakes, she will need food and water, but in small portions. She's extremely malnourished, even with my help. She's going to be sore for about a week, and tender for another week after that."

"You get all that?" Luke asked Avlir.

"Yes, sir. I understand. We'll take care of her."

Nenda's dress was wrapped around her, with a few stitches every five or six inches down the line of the slit the healer had made. It didn't do much to preserve her modesty, and Luke was sure it would break open, but the stitches held when he picked her up.

"Thank you," he said.

"Don't thank me. I wouldn't have done it without the money. Simple business transaction." The woman nodded at the girl. "And you're a fool for wasting it on her."

"Thank you," Luke said again. Then he turned and walked away. Avlir hustled after him, the three packs held in his arms.

When they were back on the street, he asked, "Where do you want to take her?"

"Follow me," Avlir said. "We found a new place to stay for now. It's probably not the best for her, but it's what we've got."

While they were walking, the little girl stirred and reached out a hand. Avlir caught it immediately and held it tight. "Hey, you're okay. It's alright now," he whispered.

"Where's Gedin?" she asked. "He pushed me down. Then there was a big noise, and I couldn't see anymore."

"I know. I know. Gedin . . . didn't make it. I'm sorry."

Nenda started to cry and tried to get out of Luke's arms. He stopped and let her down so that she could grab onto Avlir. "Come on," the boy said. "Let's get you home."

Name	Luke Bennet	Zea Stenter
Level	25	16
XP	53874/57250	12709/15275
AP	34	3
Bloodline	SysAdmin	None
Strength	42	7
Agility	40	12
Stamina	36	12
Perception	39	14
Skills	Mace Mastery (3)	Dagger Mastery (1)
	Sword Mastery (1)	Stealth (2)
	Unarmed Martialist (3)	Keen Instincts (1)
	Power Strike (1)	Lock Picking (1)
	Life Surge (1)	Disguise (2)
	Peripheral Awareness (2)	Deception (1)
	Counter (2)	Bartering (2)
	Twitch Reflexes (2)	Streetwise (2)
	Stealth (1)	Cooking (1)
	Survivalist (2)	Mending (1)
	First Aid (1)	First Aid (1)
	Wood Carving (1)	Thalian (3)
	Leatherworking (2)	Neyardic (3)
	Thalian (2)	Ostari (1)
	Disguise (2)	Mana Manipulation (1)
	Deception (1)	Mana Sight (1)
		Metallurgy (1)
		Whitesmithing (1)
		Goldsmithing (2)
		Gem Cutting (1)
		Engraving (2)
		Rune Forging (1)
		Painting (1)
		Arcano Dynamics (1)
		Sleight of Hand (1)
		Steady Hands (2)
		Cold Reading (1)
		Temperature Acclimation (2)
		Cadence (1)
		Bloodline Purification Ritual (1)

CHAPTER 16

Zea was quite satisfied with her shopping trip. Not only had she managed to find everything she needed both for the ritual and her own enchanting needs, she'd even negotiated free use of an enchanter's workbench to make the masking enchantment for her slave runes. It was currently bound up inside a small stud-style earring that she'd put in sometime in the next few weeks when the old one lost its power.

She'd also managed to snag a few small ceramic jars with some spices and a pot to boil water in, and a thick fur blanket that was so heavy she wouldn't even have considered it if not for her recent stat gains. Carrying five pounds of blanket a thousand miles was not her idea of a good time.

All of that combined with a luxurious hot bath, one she knew she shouldn't have spent money on and felt just slightly guilty over, and she was ready to face the road once more. She woke up early, got everything packed up, and headed out to find Luke, whom she sometimes still called Aldrick in her head, but she had more or less adjusted over to using his real name.

They needed to pick out new fake names and get some practice with using and responding to them before they actually needed the disguise. Hopefully they wouldn't encounter any problems prior to reaching Sicanti and purchasing passage across the ocean, but it didn't hurt to be prepared.

She found Luke at their agreed-upon meeting point. His eyes were sunken into his head, and he had a hollow look to his face as he just stared at the city. "You ever wish everything wasn't such a pile of shit?" he said by way of greeting.

"Frequently," she told him. As she got closer, she realized he was still wearing the same trashed clothing he'd had before. "You didn't get new clothes?"

"Spent all my money before I got that far. Didn't have enough to rent a room either."

"Spent it on what?" Zea asked, a twinge of annoyance spiking through her. He knew how important that money was.

"A healer for a little girl who'd been crushed under some machinery when a rival homeless street gang attacked the factory she and her friends were squatting in. Why did they need to do that? Why are there hundreds of homeless children to begin with? Why does this city suck so bad?"

The annoyance vanished. With a heavy sigh, she sat down next to him. "The monsters are worse up here. Losses are heavier, even with organizations like the Guardians. You just can't keep every farmer and lumberjack safe out beyond the walls, but people still need food and timber. And people die, people who have kids. Sometimes those kids have to survive on their own."

"They shouldn't have to," Luke said. "It's not fair. It's not right."

"Life's not fair or right. I know this sucks, but you're going to need to accept reality here."

"Does this city even try? Are there orphanages? Any social welfare programs?"

"I doubt it," Zea said. "I doubt Kazos can afford anything like that. There's a reason this is the northernmost city in Thalasa. The farther we push away from the center, the harder it gets to survive. We're not going to find much in the way of towns if we keep walking north, just a thousand miles of untamed wilderness, stuffed full of monsters killing and eating one another."

"Maybe we should do something about that?"

"Like what?" Zea asked. "What could we possibly do? Even if you threw your life away for it, and were extraordinarily successful, you'd kill what . . . Five hundred monsters? A thousand? And then you'd start to go crazy and become the monster that needs to be put down."

"No, that's what they would all do," Luke said. "The question is what can I do with my bloodline? Can I just lower the level of every monster on the planet? Can I make them disappear? What exactly are my options here, System? What can I do to make this place not such a hellscape for the people living here once I'm standing in front of the God Machine?"

Zea watched Luke have a conversation with himself, or rather, talk to the system, which looked like pretty much the same thing to her. He brightened up a bit and nodded. "That could work. What about the people though?"

"Want to let me in on what you're thinking?" Zea said.

"Hmm? Oh, sorry. System said we can screw with the dial to lower the amount of XP circulating around. More of it will sit in the God Machine, and everything will be weaker. Unfortunately, that includes the people too, but I think it might be worth it. People can build tools and weapons. People can work in groups. Without the raw power monsters get from skills and stats, they'll be weaker threats."

"You can't know that for sure though," Zea said.

"Sure I can. That's how it is on my world. Nobody has any levels or stats at all, and humans are unquestionably the dominant species. We have no natural predators left anymore."

"What about all the other races?"

"Ah, well . . . There aren't any. It's just humans and animals where I come from."

"So you don't actually know then. If you don't have any monsters, then you don't know how much damage even a level 1 shardmane could do."

"That's . . . true. Hrmm. Well, this is still something worth exploring, and we've got plenty of time to do it," Luke said. "Maybe I can find a way to selectively turn down just monster levels. That's more likely than getting the people at the top of the shit heap to stop exploiting everyone around them anyway."

"Maybe." Zea wasn't sure she liked the idea of Luke just screwing around with how the world worked on a whim, even if he had good intentions. That line of thinking was exactly why the Pantheon wanted him dead. They'd set things up the way they had for a reason, and she doubted they were looking for a mortal to come audit their design and make changes.

It was no wonder the church's standing policy was to immediately declare an off-worlder to be an apostate and mandate their death. That kind of power was beyond dangerous. If people found out Luke could do that kind of stuff, they would want to capture him and control him. It was better for everyone if knowledge of an off-worlder's capabilities never spread.

That left her in the unfortunate position of collateral damage. She understood why the church would go to such extreme measures to kill Luke and contain any knowledge of his abilities, but on a personal level, she wasn't okay with being killed as the most expedient solution to that problem. Since she doubted they'd leave her alone even if she promised not to tell anyone, there really wasn't an option besides not letting the church get their hands on her.

Last week, that hadn't been much of a moral quandary for her. All Luke wanted was to get the rest of his family back and go home. That was fair. None of them had asked to be taken to Aros, and they were all going to disappear when he was done. Now he was talking about something completely different, about changing how a world that he wasn't even part of functioned. That had a high potential for catastrophic unforeseen consequences of such changes.

"Luke," she said. He looked over at her, and she felt her heart clench tighter in her chest. "This idea . . . It's not a good one. You should leave it alone."

"It's not good to want to stop little kids from dying in the streets because there's no one to take care of them?" he asked, incredulous. Mad.

"No, it is, but not the way you're talking about doing it. You want to trespass on the domain of the gods here. What you're talking about doing, it's going to affect the entire planet. Millions of people will have to deal with the ramifications of the changes you want to make. How sure are you that things will be better when you're done? How many people are going to die if you do this?"

"It might be bad at first, but things will get better in the long run. It would be an overall win."

"You don't know that. You can't. This line of thinking is exactly why the church wants to kill you. You're threatening to turn everything on its head."

"What am I supposed to do then? Just go on letting things be horrible and know that I could stop it?"

"No, I'm not saying that. I'm just saying this change is too big. There's no way for anyone to predict what could happen, and who are we to say we know better than the gods do anyway?"

Luke let out a short, bitter little laugh. "Who's to say they know what they're doing? Or maybe they do, and they just don't care. Why does everyone assume any of these gods give a fuck about what happens to us? They stuffed one of their own into a machine that breaks a divine entity down into little bite-size XP chunks. Is that something a benevolent deity would do?"

"I . . . don't know." It wasn't the first time Luke had told her what he'd learned about XP madness and its true source, but she wasn't as trusting of this invisible being as he appeared to be. She was still going along with him, and part of herself thought she was absolutely crazy for that, but it was a bit too late to turn back now.

"This whole thing is fucked up," he muttered. "I don't know what the right thing to do is. It would be easier to just not give a fuck. I'll go get mine, and the rest of the world can go to hell. Worked for the boomers."

"The what?" she asked.

"Never mind. Something from my world. Just a bunch of people who were selfish assholes."

"If you really want to help those kids, maybe we should stay here and do something ourselves," she said. "I've got everything we need to try the ritual. That will give you some more options."

He blew out a heavy sigh and scrubbed his hand across his face. "Need to shave again," he muttered before standing up. "I can't stay here. The only way to get my family back is to keep going forward."

"I'm okay with whatever you decide, as long as you don't try to change the fundamental laws of my world."

"Thanks. Okay, first things first, you said you have everything needed to do the ritual?"

"I do. I have enough supplies for two tries, but I think maybe I should level up two or three more times so that I can raise the rank on some of the support skills. We can try now if you want, but I'm not promising it will work. I don't think there will be any side effects to failing it other than wasting some supplies."

"Okay. Well, if you think it would help to get you more AP, then let's do that. I think we've got time now. Nobody's really come after us since that incident in Landston."

"Nobody has come after us *yet*."

"Good point," Luke said. He gave the city one more long, troubled look, and then added, "Let's get walking?"

"Yeah."

Cardinal Gnox was not accustomed to being woken from a sound sleep in his own bed in the middle of the night, but that was the situation he found himself in. A hand had a firm grip on his hair, what was left of it anyway, and another one held a knife close enough to his throat that he could feel the scrape of steel against his skin.

"Where the fuck is my apprentice at, cardinal?" Adrevald Lath asked.

Name	Luke Bennet	Zea Stenter
Level	25	16
XP	53874/57250	12709/15275
AP	34	3
Bloodline	SysAdmin	None
Strength	42	7
Agility	40	12
Stamina	36	12
Perception	39	14
Skills	Mace Mastery (3)	Dagger Mastery (1)
	Sword Mastery (1)	Stealth (2)
	Unarmed Martialist (3)	Keen Instincts (1)
	Power Strike (1)	Lock Picking (1)
	Life Surge (1)	Disguise (2)
	Peripheral Awareness (2)	Deception (1)
	Counter (2)	Bartering (2)
	Twitch Reflexes (2)	Streetwise (2)
	Stealth (1)	Cooking (1)
	Survivalist (2)	Mending (1)
	First Aid (1)	First Aid (1)
	Wood Carving (1)	Thalian (3)
	Leatherworking (2)	Neyardic (3)
	Thalian (2)	Ostari (1)
	Disguise (2)	Mana Manipulation (1)
	Deception (1)	Mana Sight (1)
		Metallurgy (1)
		Whitesmithing (1)
		Goldsmithing (2)
		Gem Cutting (1)
		Engraving (2)
		Rune Forging (1)
		Painting (1)
		Arcano Dynamics (1)
		Sleight of Hand (1)
		Steady Hands (2)
		Cold Reading (1)
		Temperature Acclimation (2)
		Cadence (1)
		Bloodline Purification Ritual (1)

CHAPTER 17

Luke sat next to Zea by a small campfire and tried to pick the tufts of hair out of the flanges of his mace. Normally it wasn't a problem to clean it out, but his latest kill had hacked up some sort of glue-like snot ball at him, which he'd batted aside with his mace. And now everything was sticking to it.

"Goddamn it," he said, giving up and throwing the mace down into the dirt. "Whatever this shit is, it's not coming off."

Zea ignored him while she worked. What exactly it was she was working on was a mystery to Luke, but presumably it was going to help her fight. He'd carved a piece of wood, hickory he thought, into a stick about an inch thick and had done his best to smooth it down before handing it off to her. She'd then started carving little squiggles and symbols into it, an action which apparently took a great deal of concentration.

"Can I borrow that thing you have?" she asked suddenly. "The one that makes the light come out of the crystal at the end?"

"The flashlight? Sure. One sec."

He dug around in his bag until he found it sitting all the way in the bottom and handed it over. Zea pushed down on the little button and shook her head when the bulb lit up. "Amazing. Just like that, and anyone can use it. No training required. Here, hold it right here for me, please."

He held the flashlight while she spun the stick around several times and studied it intently. "I think I'm done. One way to find out though."

"You never told me what it does," Luke said.

"It redirects mana into physical force, up to ten feet away. Watch." Zea's eyes unfocused in a way that Luke had come to learn meant she was looking at the supposed mana that was everywhere, even though it was invisible and untouchable. It wasn't too outlandish to him, but it was kind of like having someone tell him they could see radio waves or electricity. Sure, there were things to measure that, but eyeballs weren't one of those things.

Then she jabbed the stick forward and a little furrow scored the ground a few feet away from her. It was the same thickness as her magic stick, and only as long as her jab had been. "Oh, that's cool," he said. "So you can use this to reach things that are too far away. Could you do something like this on a glove and then use it to pick up stuff you can't reach?"

"Theoretically, I could. But I don't know how. Some enchanter can and probably has made it, but I won't be doing it myself."

"So what's this good for then?"

"Stabbing monsters in the eyeballs, mostly," she said.

"You'd need to get awful close to do that though."

She nodded and set the stick down. "It's a problem. I'm going to work on the range though. A wooden stick is not a great medium for the spell either. This is probably only good for at most twenty uses before it snaps under the strain."

"You should probably just stick with the crossbow for now," he told her.

"The crossbow sucks. I hate it."

"I could try to reduce the stock size for you."

"Ehhhh, let's not modify it until I have a working alternative. I hate it, but it does work, and I'd rather not have to go stand in front of the monsters like you do, without any armor even. You're fucking crazy."

"It's not like I don't want armor!" Luke protested. "I've tried, several times! It's kind of hard to loot it off somebody who was wearing it when I keep breaking it in the process of killing them. And you said we didn't have the time or money to buy new stuff."

He'd relied on **[Life Surge]** a lot over the last few days to patch him up if a fight went sideways, which happened with some regularity. He was fighting all sorts of new monsters now, with abilities and tactics he hadn't figured out yet. Mistakes were frequent, but food was also readily available, and he'd prioritized staying in good condition so that injuries didn't snowball in the next fight. So far, it was working.

"How close are you to the next level?" he asked.

"About 500 XP. You?"

"1000 or so."

"That'll be enough AP to upgrade **[Mana Manipulation]** or **[Cadence]**. I'll do **[Mana Manipulation]** first since it works with my enchanting too. After those two rank-ups, I think I'll be ready to try the ritual."

Luke nodded. They had two shots at it, and that was basically it. If neither attempt took, the only way they were getting supplies to try again was to backtrack all the to Kazos. Admittedly, they could hit a road and cover all the distance they'd meandered north in less than a day, but neither of them were keen to go back there.

"How are you doing on bolts?" Luke asked. He'd done his best to recover the ones he could, or at least to retrieve the metal tips, but it wasn't always possible.

"Full-ish quiver, but they're pretty much all ones you made. No offense, but they just don't fly as well without the fletching."

He'd tried to carve the shape in, hoping that would help. It was debatable whether or not he'd been successful. As long as she managed to get a shot or two into the monster though, she generally got credit for helping and an equal share of the total XP. So while the shots might not be all that damaging or helpful, they still accomplished their goal.

If she could come up with some enchanted stick that let her contribute real damage, he was all for that. It would make the fights easier for him, plus he'd feel better about her being able to defend herself if something went wrong. It helped that, so far at least, her attempts took nothing but time. He'd seen the bag of raw materials she'd purchased, and most of it looked expensive.

"Maybe we should buy some spares next time we stop somewhere," he said. "Or at least a few more tips, just for when we can't recover them."

"I'd rather not. I do not like the crossbow. I'm not looking to invest more into it."

"Could always increase your strength and agility and get you a bag of pebbles. Do you know how to make a sling?"

"No," Zea said flatly. "And I'll pass on that one anyway."

"Did I say something wrong?" he asked, noting her tone.

"Kind of, but I know you don't mean anything by it. It's just kind of a stereotype. 'Oh look, it's a dwifkin village. They're too poor and stupid to craft anything. Ha ha. They're all hunting with sticks and bags of rocks.' It's not true, hasn't been true for hundreds and hundreds of years, but people are assholes."

"Oh. I'm sorry. I didn't know," he said.

"Not your fault," she said. "But if you want to make it up to me, you can cook dinner tonight."

Luke side-eyed her. "How is that making it up to you? My cooking is awful."

"I'm sure you'll get **[Cooking]** any day now."

Luke doubted that. He'd tried repeatedly, using her instructions, and calling the results edible had been generous. Somehow, it was almost worse than when he'd just skewered a piece of meat on a stick and left it to char over the fire. Zea had watched him cook one night, then confessed afterward that she had no idea how he'd messed up so badly, that everything looked fine while he was doing it.

"How about you cook and I'll do the cleanup?"

"That's what we do every night," she complained.

"I know. It's a good division of labor. We both get a decent meal, and you get to relax after dinner."

"Nope, nothing doing. You cook. Get that first rank in it already."

"Ugh. Fine. I'm going to burn yours extra crispy tonight."

"Don't you dare!"

Luke's eyes snapped open in the middle of the night, and he reached out to grab the mace sitting next to him. Weapon in hand, he scoured the darkness for the source of whatever it was that had woken him. It hadn't actually made a sound, but he could feel it lurking nearby, studying him.

Zea was snuggled up tight against him, an arm and a leg thrown over his body. Luke gently rolled her onto her back inside that bearskin rug she called a blanket and slowly climbed to his feet. He cocked his head to the side and listened for some sound besides the chirping of crickets. Nothing.

Something moved in the tree branches overhead, just a brief flicker. It could have been a trick of the wind, just a branch shifting, but he knew it wasn't. There was something out there, something with enough XP in it to tickle his brain, something that was very, very good at hiding. It was probably small, and very fast, looking for the perfect angle to ambush him.

Even if it didn't attack, he knew he wasn't getting any more sleep now. Some predator had marked him as potential prey and was just waiting for the right moment to strike. Luke couldn't even go look for it without leaving Zea vulnerable. He could wake her up, but she wouldn't be able to defend herself effectively.

"System, I don't suppose you could tell me what this is I'm feeling?" Luke asked, already knowing the answer.

"I'm afraid not. I cannot disclose information about other creatures."

"How about a general idea of a monster that lives in this area that's small, fast, and hard to spot?"

"There are a number of possibilities."

"Narrow it down to ones that hunt at night by themselves for me."

"A phase flicker spider fits your profile most closely. Other options include candle bearers, vanta panthers, and night creepers. This region also has a higher-than-average population of burrow wasps, which would fit all possibilities except for singular hunting patterns."

"Okay, great. What can you tell me about phase flicker spiders?"

"They are on average about a foot in diameter, not including their legs. They are active almost exclusively at night and can camouflage themselves in moonlight so as to be almost completely invisible. They rarely attack anything bigger than themselves, however, as their paralytic venom loses much of its efficacy when scaled up against heavier opponents."

So it wasn't likely to be a whatever spider then. "What about the other candidates? Which ones will attack humans? Or dwifkins?"

"All of them," System said.

"Okay. Uh, panthers and wasps. Right. What were the other two?" Luke turned in a slow circle while he questioned System. The feel of the monster's XP hadn't gone away, but he couldn't get a glance at it. He was kind of doubting it was a panther, not unless he'd only seen a limb move or they were the size of house cats.

"Candle bearers are a classification of gremlins. They feed primarily on the eyeballs of their victims and are known for their stealth capabilities. It is very rare for anyone to spot one prior to them attacking, which they do by igniting a bright light that blinds an opponent just before they strike.

"Night creepers are a type of insect that could fit in your palm. Their stings are venomous and cause hallucinations. While their victims are incapacitated, they begin burrowing through the chest cavity to feast on various organs and lay a clutch of eggs behind."

"Too big to be one of those then," Luke said. "How big is a gremlin? Like, could it be less than a foot tall?"

Even that was stretching it. Whatever flash of movement he'd seen was probably seven or eight inches, but he wasn't dismissing that it might be a limb moving through a patch of moonlight. He was barely more than guessing at its size.

"Gremlins on average are about two feet tall, and candle bearers are a small subspecies that averages twenty inches."

"Shit, what is this thing?" Luke asked. He nudged Zea with a foot to wake her up. At her groan, he said, "We've got something watching us. You need to wake up."

"Wha—?"

There was a flash of movement from his right, and then something traveling a hundred miles an hour struck him in the chest and threw him off his feet.

Name	Luke Bennet	Zea Stenter
Level	25	16
XP	56198/57250	14691/15275
AP	34	3
Bloodline	SysAdmin	None
Strength	42	7
Agility	40	12
Stamina	36	12
Perception	39	14
Skills	Mace Mastery (3)	Dagger Mastery (1)
	Sword Mastery (1)	Stealth (2)
	Unarmed Martialist (3)	Keen Instincts (1)
	Power Strike (1)	Lock Picking (1)
	Life Surge (1)	Disguise (2)
	Peripheral Awareness (2)	Deception (1)
	Counter (2)	Bartering (2)
	Twitch Reflexes (2)	Streetwise (2)
	Stealth (1)	Cooking (1)
	Survivalist (2)	Mending (1)
	First Aid (1)	First Aid (1)
	Wood Carving (1)	Thalian (3)
	Leatherworking (2)	Neyardic (3)
	Thalian (2)	Ostari (1)
	Disguise (2)	Mana Manipulation (1)
	Deception (1)	Mana Sight (1)
		Metallurgy (1)
		Whitesmithing (1)
		Goldsmithing (2)
		Gem Cutting (1)
		Engraving (2)
		Rune Forging (1)
		Painting (1)
		Arcano Dynamics (1)
		Sleight of Hand (1)
		Steady Hands (2)
		Cold Reading (1)
		Temperature Acclimation (2)
		Cadence (1)
		Bloodline Purification Ritual (1)

CHAPTER 18

Luke's back slammed into the tree hard enough that he felt the wood crack. The whole trunk groaned and shifted, with a few roots popping up out of the ground when it tilted backward. Stars flashed across his eyes, blinding him, and he did the only thing he could think of. He reached down and grabbed the monster firmly with both hands, prayed he didn't get a finger bitten off, and threw himself forward to slam it into the ground.

His mace landed next to him with a thump, and as his vision cleared, Luke saw that he had grabbed hold of something that looked sort of like an armor-plated squirrel, except without the tail. Its legs thumped uselessly against the ground, and its teeth gnashed while it twisted and squirmed in place to get some meat in its mouth.

Luckily for Luke, he'd managed to grab it right around the neck, and his hand was keeping its jaw forced up and away from him. That didn't stop its stubby little paws from clawing at him with something sharp and hooked. It was rather like getting attacked by a cat, and about as effective. Once upon a time, he would have been howling in pain. Now, his stamina was so high that it was barely leaving scratches on his arm.

His chest hurt like hell though. Either this thing was insanely fast, or something else had thrown it. Since Luke didn't sense anything else nearby, and given the speed at which its paws flailed around, he was assuming the speed was all natural. He lifted it up and slammed it back into the ground, which had no noticeable effect on the creature, other than perhaps driving it even further into a wild frenzy.

"What's going on?!" Zea yelled, finally working her way out of her blanket.

"Well it's not a fucking spider or gremlin or whatever shit-ass prediction System had, I know that much."

His flashlight clicked on, and Zea swept it around their campsite until she found Luke, still struggling to keep a hold on the monster. Her breath caught, and she said, "Holy shit, is that an armaril?"

Luke lifted it up off the ground again and grappled with it while it tried to escape. If not for his ridiculous grip strength, it would have long since writhed its way free. Even then, he didn't trust himself to hold it with one hand. "Do you think you could kill this thing for me?" he asked, grunting in pain as it landed a series of lightning-fast kicks against his wrist.

"I don't know. Can you hold it still?"

"I'm trying! Damn thing isn't that strong, but it's slippery as fuck."

Luke carried it over to a tree and held it as far away from him as he could with it pressed against the bark. "You think you can get in there and shank it in the belly or something?"

"I'll try," she said, eyeing the wriggling creature. Luke didn't like the lack of confidence in her expression, but she got her knife out and advanced inside his arms.

The armaril kicked up its attempts to escape to a whole new level, now moving so fast that it was practically vibrating in his hands. "Sooner would be better," he said.

With a huff, she brought her knife up and jabbed it into the armaril. It let out a loud shrill squeal and sprayed blood all over both of them. Luke caught it all over his arms, but Zea got it right to the face. She gagged and staggered away from them to spit on the ground. "Gods damn it. Hold it still so I can stab that little fucker again."

Its thrashing became feeble, and before Zea could make good on her promise, its movements stopped completely. "I think it's dead," Luke said, still holding on tight until he got the kill notification. When that didn't come, he added, "Or it's faking? Maybe you do need to stab it again."

"Armaril are famous for their durability and speed. Catching one is damn near impossible."

Apparently recognizing that its attempts to play dead hadn't worked, the monster shrieked and resumed its vicious clawing and scratching at his arm. "Come stab it again then. This fucking thing is shredding my arm."

After wiping her eyes clean, Zea scooped the knife back up from where she'd dropped it and stabbed the armaril four more times. It was only after she angled a stab upward that it finally jerked once and died.

[You have assisted in slaying Catapult Amaril (level 21). 255 XP awarded.]

"Well, that was an unpleasant wake-up call."

"Be gentle with the body," Zea warned when she saw him about to toss it on the ground. "Those things are incredibly valuable."

"They are? Why?"

"The hides. Those armor plates on its back and head are damn near indestructible."

"I mean . . . okay, but it's not that big."

"They're not used for making armor." Zea's eyes were sparkling now as she stared at it. "A big problem with enchanting is that your material needs to be strong enough to hold up against the strain of the magic. Amaril hide is just about the best thing you can get without dipping into extremely expensive alchemically forged materials. That thing is probably worth a hundred gold as it, easily twice that if it was properly butchered and prepared."

"Damn, that's a lot. But who would we sell it to?"

"Someone would buy that. It would be best to sell it in Sicanti right before we leave. Whoever buys that is going to remember us." She looked up suddenly. "You've got some loose AP, right?"

"Yeah."

"Take **[Butchering]**, at least rank 1, but rank 2 if you can afford it."

"Are you sure that's a good use of AP?"

"Well," she said slowly, "I guess that depends on how long you want to spend in Sicanti doing odd jobs while we scrape together money. This is our ticket off the continent, but only if we can preserve the hide. Before we can do that, we need to skin the amaril, and trust me, that's not that easy. The underside is the weakest part, and if this knife wasn't alchemically enhanced, I would not have been able to pierce those scales."

"Well, if you're sure . . ."

He bought the first rank of **[Butchering]** for 1 AP, then upgraded it to rank 2 for another 3. "Rank 3 is 8 AP. Should I keep going?"

"Yes, and rank 4 if you can."

Another 8 and then 15 AP later, Luke had his first rank 4 skill. He looked down at the corpse now and absently grabbed the knife Zea had offered him. It wasn't the ideal tool for the job, the blade being far too long and not really tipped properly, but it would work. Luke laid the body out on a flat rock and got to work.

His hands moved of their own accord, expertly sliding the knife under the edge of the soft scales right where they became thicker, heavier plate, and making a smooth incision. With one hand, he pried the hide back so that he could continue to skin the amaril. A few minutes later, he'd salvaged almost the entire hide. Other than a ruined spot in the belly from Zea's stabbing and the individual fingers, which lacked armor plates anyway, they were now the proud owners of one amaril hide.

"Do you want the claws too?" he asked. "They're not that sharp, but they're just going to go to waste otherwise."

"No," she said. "I need a . . . Damn it . . . Here, empty one of these satchels out. I'm going to put a preservation enchantment on that. I think I've got everything for that. It won't be as effective as a nice wooden box, but we'll make do."

They unpacked one of the satchels and stuffed as much of the food as they could in the other one. Zea got to work while Luke held the flashlight, and he knew better than to interrupt her. She used a small pen-looking thing to etch that weird scribbly script into the leather of the satchel, working nonstop for over two hours. Finally, she held the satchel up to him.

Luke gently placed the amaril hide into the satchel, the insides of which now made his hand tingle. Zea closed the satchel, tied it off, and went back to inscribing even more symbols on it. "There, done. Now this can't be opened without breaking the magic, and everything inside should last ten times as long."

Finally done, she allowed herself to relax. "This is the find of a lifetime. I can't believe we just randomly stumbled across one out in the middle of nowhere."

"I wouldn't say we stumbled across it," Luke said, rubbing his chest. It still hurt from where the thing had cannonballed into him, more so than his back from being slammed into the tree. "That thing would have killed me before I even got a good look at it if my stamina wasn't so high."

"Oh shit, yeah. How are you feeling?"

"Oh sure, now you ask."

"I was distracted earlier."

"I know."

"It's a lot of money!" Zea pouted. She moved closer and said, "Here, let me see."

"It's fine," Luke said. "You know you've still got blood on your face?"

"Don't care. Take off your shirt."

"What?" Luke took a step back.

"Take. Off. Your. Shirt."

"I told you it's fine."

Zea advanced on him, her gaze predatory. "Take it off."

When Luke didn't move, she pounced on him and wrapped her legs around his hips. Her hands worked between them to lift the hem of his shirt up, and she pulled it up to his armpits. Luke lifted his arms, and she stripped it off the rest of the way.

"It's a bit cold for this, don't you think?" he said.

"Hmm? Oh, yes, definitely. Your ribs are all intact," she said as she ran his hands over his chest.

"You know, I thought this was going to be the sexy kind of de-shirting."

Zea wiggled her hips against him. "I'm sure you did."

"Uh, is it the sexy kind of de-shirting?"

"Not yet. I want to make sure you're really fine."

"This really isn't doing it for me," Luke said. "The blood and all. Maybe we should go get cleaned up."

Zea ran her hands across his back and then stopped with a scowl. She plucked something out of his skin and said, "You've got wood splinters in your back still. Here, turn around."

She dropped back down to her feet and spun him with her hands, then made him sit down so she could pick the splinters out. "They would have popped out on their own, you know?"

"You rely on your high stamina too much. If I clean them out, everything will heal up that much faster."

"A likely story. You just want an excuse to run your hands all over me."

"Like I need an excuse."

That was true enough. Given the circumstances and places they'd found themselves in over the last few weeks, it was remarkable how often they'd gotten frisky. That having been said, receiving medical care was not one of his fetishes, and he truly was still sore from the impact. Thankfully, the amaril had attacked him instead of Zea. It might have killed her in a single shot if it had.

"We got kind of lucky, didn't we?" he said softly.

"Hell yes, we did. We're fucking rich now."

"No, not that. That it didn't go after you first. Is it irresponsible of me to drag you out here?"

"No," Zea told him. "Because I'm not your responsibility. I'm older than you are. I make my own choices. Now shut up and be happy that our financial woes are solved."

"Well, there is that," he said. "Hey, what are you—"

Her hand snaked down his back and dipped into his waistline. "We're rich," she said. "I'm excited. Celebrate with me."

Name	Luke Bennet	Zea Stenter
Level	25	16
XP	56453/57250	14946/15275
AP	7	3
Bloodline	SysAdmin	None
Strength	42	7
Agility	40	12
Stamina	36	12
Perception	39	14
Skills	Mace Mastery (3)	Dagger Mastery (1)
	Sword Mastery (1)	Stealth (2)
	Unarmed Martialist (3)	Keen Instincts (1)
	Power Strike (1)	Lock Picking (1)
	Life Surge (1)	Disguise (2)
	Peripheral Awareness (2)	Deception (1)
	Counter (2)	Bartering (2)
	Twitch Reflexes (2)	Streetwise (2)
	Stealth (1)	Cooking (1)
	Survivalist (2)	Mending (1)
	First Aid (1)	First Aid (1)
	Wood Carving (1)	Thalian (3)
	Leatherworking (2)	Neyardic (3)
	Butchering (4)	Ostari (1)
	Thalian (2)	Mana Manipulation (1)
	Disguise (2)	Mana Sight (1)
	Deception (1)	Metallurgy (1)
		Whitesmithing (1)
		Goldsmithing (2)
		Gem Cutting (1)
		Engraving (2)
		Rune Forging (1)
		Painting (1)
		Arcano Dynamics (1)
		Sleight of Hand (1)
		Steady Hands (2)
		Cold Reading (1)
		Temperature Acclimation (2)
		Cadence (1)
		Bloodline Purification Ritual (1)

CHAPTER 19

By early afternoon, they'd walked ten miles and picked a few fights with various monsters. Luke had just finished extracting his mace from the skull of a badger-looking thing the size of a grizzly bear when Zea said, "That did it. I'm level 17 now."

"Nice! Do you want to take a break from walking now?"

"Let me just push the rank up on **[Mana Manipulation]** and see if . . . Yeah, this ritual is looking a lot easier to pull off now. If we want to be safe, I should get one more level and rank up **[Cadence]** too. **[Mana Sight]** wouldn't hurt either, but I think I can do it without an extra rank."

"Okay, we can do one more level if you think we should."

"Probably should. Plus you spent all your AP anyway, so you need to level up again too."

Luke checked his status and said, "I'm only a few kills away from a level. That'll be 26 more AP. Let's take a break, have some lunch, and see if we can find a nice spot to farm XP before it gets dark."

He honestly wasn't sure why he still bothered to follow a day-and-night cycle, other than habit. It wasn't like it was any harder for him to see in the dark now than it was under a bright noon sky. Zea could also see well enough in the dark that they weren't in any real danger of blundering around blindly. Luke imagined it was that way for a lot of people, but for some reason, almost everyone chose to sleep during the night.

Maybe it was just human nature, and he was overthinking it. There didn't need to be some mysterious, arcane explanation for it. It was easier to sleep at night, and that's what everyone else whose perception wasn't high enough to see in the dark was doing anyway, so why not?

Thanks almost entirely to his new rank 4 **[Butchering]** skill, Luke had a very good idea of where to carve some steaks off his latest kill. The hide also would have made for some good raw materials, but he didn't have the time to treat it properly before they left, so Luke reluctantly let it be. They made a small fire, and Zea lectured Luke on how to cook the first steak, then after he'd burned it and thrown it out, made two more herself.

He did not get rank 1 **[Cooking]** that day either.

"So I've been thinking," he said. "Maybe we should set up a kind of permanent camp and just kind of work this area for a few days. Get you leveled up a bit more before we do the ritual, get me some AP to spend on bloodline skills after we do the ritual, and we'll both be a bit stronger when we start to move north again."

"Well, I can think of a few problems with that. First is that we don't have any proof that the church isn't sending people after us right this second. The more we move, the farther away we get and the harder it becomes to find us, especially if we do it like we are now. Second, the longer we stay in one area, the more likely we are to attract notice."

"Those are both good points, but I think we can hunt more efficiently if we get to know an area. Plus, have you noticed that the monsters are getting to be higher level the farther north we go?"

"They have, yes. Do you think it'll be an issue?"

Luke shrugged. If things didn't get any higher than they were now, he figured they'd be alright. They occasionally ran into something that was a higher level than him, but usually only by a few. More importantly in his mind, they'd level faster off repeated, frequent kills of low-level monsters than by hunting down a few stronger ones. It would be safer too, since he'd get a chance to fight the same kinds of monsters over and over instead of having to figure out a good way to take out a new enemy each time.

"I think I'm not on a timer, and it would be safer to be a bit stronger if things are going to keep going this way. I like having a solid ten levels on whatever we're fighting, just as a safety margin. We can win a thousand fights, you know, but we only have to lose one."

"That's true. Okay, how about if we go a bit farther east from the road for a day, then find a place to set up a good semipermanent camp? We can sit on it for a week and level up a few times, do the ritual to purify your bloodline, and then start heading north again. Maybe I can boost my physical stats some more to help make up for lost time too."

"That's a good idea." Luke took a bite out of the steak, chewed it slowly, and said, "Do these taste a bit oily to you?"

"Little bit, yeah. I think it's just the type of meat."

"I wonder if there are any shockrack elk roaming around. Those had the best meat."

"Those are a delicacy! It's practically impossible to find them anymore."

"Really?" Luke snorted. "They're pretty common in the valley I started in. I'd see them a few times a week."

"That surprises me," Zea said. "Although, didn't you say there was some massive earth elemental guarding the only pass in or out? I guess if no one could get in, no hunters ever showed up to go after them."

They chatted for a bit, cleaned up their impromptu camp, and started walking again.

"How about here?" Luke asked. They stood at the entrance to a shallow cave, about twenty feet deep and ten feet wide. The mouth narrowed down a bit, so it was somewhat sheltered from the weather, and he was confident he could put together some kind of basic door. It wouldn't be anything fancy with a handle and hinges, but he could cobble together something.

"Could work as a location, as long as there are monsters to hunt. I wouldn't want to stay too long, but a day or two to level up isn't too bad." Zea's mouth twisted as she spoke, still clearly unhappy with the idea of casually leveling up.

"I'll start making some rope," he said as he eyed up the cave. He pointed at some sort of thick, viny bush that was crawling up the rock face and said, "I can run it through some of this and hang a kind of door off it to close the place off. It'll be rough, but better than nothing."

"I'll collect some stuff for a firepit and get some tinder shredded."

"Don't go too far," Luke said. "I don't feel anything nearby, but the forest is too thick to really see too deeply into it."

"I know. You don't have to babysit me."

"I'm still going to worry about you."

"Ugh, fine. I'll stay close by."

It wasn't that Luke didn't trust Zea. It was just that she was about as strong as he'd been at level 9 despite being level 17. Any number of creatures they'd encountered in the forest already could have killed her if she'd been on her own. It was a measure of her trust in him that she'd agreed to keep going.

They worked for a few hours until their new cave home was as comfortable as they could reasonably make it, including a few racks for drying and stretching animal hides. Zea was initially against the idea until Luke promised more blankets and agreed that he'd be the one who carried them. As soon as they'd gotten that issue resolved, she'd suggested he build a few extra racks, just to be safe.

They spent the next few days hunting monsters. Luke cleared the XP needed to bump up to level 26, and Zea leveled up again to 18. After her bump up to rank 2 **[Cadence]**, she finally felt she was prepared to use **[Bloodline Purification Ritual]**, and so they decided to call it a day early and head back.

"What do you need me to do?" Luke asked when she started unpacking the supplies.

"Just stay out of the way for now. This will take a bit to get set up."

Luke did as asked and whiled away the time carving a piece of deadwood he'd set aside into the shape of a dog his neighbor had owned when he was a kid. It had been a golden retriever, ridiculously derpy, but friendly and loving in a way only good boys could be. It was too bad Luke's family had only stayed at that place for a few months before Dad had moved them to take a new job in another city.

That had happened a lot of times, for a lot of reasons. It was rare to stay anywhere for longer than a year, and by the time Luke was twelve, he'd stopped bothering to unpack his stuff. His boxes just sat in the closet, all three of them, and he'd lived out of an old, ratty backpack instead.

Not much had changed there. He'd spent a month in the valley, barely more than a week in Valtira, and then it had been pretty much a new place every night from there on out. Hell, the stupid cave in the middle of nowhere took third place for the longest time he'd spent in one spot since he'd woken up in that field.

"It's ready," Zea said softly.

Luke looked over and saw a thing drawn on the cave floor with something that might have been chalk. It was a square, about three feet wide and with a hundred different squiggles around its border. Lines radiated out from it to connect it to the corners of a pentagon that surrounded the whole thing, and even more lines came out of that to connect to six small circles set equal distance around the whole thing.

In each of those circles was one of the ingredients they'd been carrying around. The silver bowl had some sort of incense in it, not yet lit. Next to that was a flat rock, dark gray with a wavy band of green on it. A bundle of herbs, tied together at the stems, sat in the third circle, followed by a desiccated animal heart, a small ivory tusk six inches long, and a glass vial filled with some sort of golden oil.

"Spooky," Luke commented.

"Don't mess it up," Zea told him. "I'm going to be pissed if I have to redo anything. I've already checked this over three times. Go sit down in the square in the middle."

Luke set the figurine down and hopped into the center of the diagram, then arranged himself to sit cross-legged and looked over at Zea. "Now what?"

"You sit there. I'll do all the work. This . . . It shouldn't hurt, but I've never done this. If I do it right, you should be fine. Whatever happens, don't move outside the square. Don't touch the lines or smudge anything. Keep your hands close by your side or sit on them or whatever you need to do. This is going to take at least an hour."

"What happens if something goes wrong?" Luke asked.

She shrugged. "Depends how far in we are, I guess. Wasted reagents at least. Pain. You could end up with severe blood loss. If you didn't have that regeneration skill, I would say we need to wait to even attempt this."

"Oh, well, no pressure, but don't fuck up."

"This is as safe as we can make it," she said with a glower. "It's too late to turn back now. Are you ready?"

Part of him wanted to say no, that he'd been getting along just fine without this upgrade. That wasn't really true though, and he knew things were just going to get worse down the road. He needed to do this if he wanted to fix everything.

"Let's do it."

Name	Luke Bennet	Zea Stenter
Level	26	18
XP	60420/72056	18341/21602
AP	33	8
Bloodline	SysAdmin	None
Strength	42	7
Agility	40	12
Stamina	36	12
Perception	39	14
Skills	Mace Mastery (3)	Dagger Mastery (1)
	Sword Mastery (1)	Stealth (2)
	Unarmed Martialist (3)	Keen Instincts (1)
	Power Strike (1)	Lock Picking (1)
	Life Surge (1)	Disguise (2)
	Peripheral Awareness (2)	Deception (1)
	Counter (2)	Bartering (2)
	Twitch Reflexes (2)	Streetwise (2)
	Stealth (1)	Cooking (1)
	Survivalist (2)	Mending (1)
	First Aid (1)	First Aid (1)
	Wood Carving (1)	Thalian (3)
	Leatherworking (2)	Neyardic (3)
	Butchering (4)	Ostari (1)
	Thalian (2)	Mana Manipulation (2)
	Disguise (2)	Mana Sight (1)
	Deception (1)	Metallurgy (1)
		Whitesmithing (1)
		Goldsmithing (2)
		Gem Cutting (1)
		Engraving (2)
		Rune Forging (1)
		Painting (1)
		Arcano Dynamics (1)
		Sleight of Hand (1)
		Steady Hands (2)
		Cold Reading (1)
		Temperature Acclimation (2)
		Cadence (2)
		Bloodline Purification Ritual (1)

CHAPTER 20

The ritual itself was kind of boring, at least from Luke's perspective. Zea did all the work, which included walking around the circle repeatedly, chanting something that sounded ominous at first but that quickly became kind of boring and then a bit annoying as she droned on over and over, and messing around with the ingredients at specific times.

Luke's part was to sit in the square and not touch anything, for an hour. He was extremely bored by the time the ritual was over, but he was trying not to show it. It seemed rude, considering how much effort Zea was putting into it. Her face was covered in a sheen of sweat, and her voice had started to get hoarse about halfway through, but she'd powered on, and he thought she was almost done.

The pace of her chanting picked up, and her movements became more rapid. One by one, the ingredients started to crumble, or evaporate, or in the case of the incense, burn down. That was when things got interesting for him. All of a sudden, so unexpectedly that he damn near flinched and broke the chalk square around him, he could feel something tugging at him.

At the same time, something else was pushing him. Calling it an uncomfortable sensation would be a gross understatement. It felt like a fishhook had caught on his heart and was trying to pull it up through his throat. Meanwhile, his stomach was bearing down on his intestines and trying to push them out through his asshole.

Luke's throat closed up, and he grabbed at it as he gasped for breath. It wouldn't open, and he was about to break the square to make the magic stop, but he forced himself to calm down. His stamina was high enough that he could hold his breath for at least an hour. It wasn't going to kill him if he couldn't breathe right now, and Zea was almost done.

After settling back into place, he did his best to endure the rest of the ritual. Things popped, or were squished or pulled on. Muscles cramped, all at once, and it was everything he could do to hold still. Luke gritted his teeth against the pain and gasped out, "Hurry up," to Zea, who was now looking at him with alarm while she chanted out what he hoped were the final lines of the ritual.

And then it was done. The ivory turned to dust, and the incense burned out in the bowl. The rock was nothing but sand now, the herbs ash. The animal heart somehow looked fresher, and wet. Even as Luke glanced at it though, the ritual ended, and a fountain of blood gushed out, far more than the little organ could have held. A wave of dizziness passed through Luke at the exact same moment, and he collapsed backward onto the ground.

"Luke!"

He heard the voice, but it was faraway, unfamiliar. "Come on, wake up!" the voice said.

It was so hard to keep his eyes open, to even think straight. He just wanted to sleep. But something kept grabbing at him and shaking him, wouldn't stop yammering in his ear. Begrudgingly, Luke cracked an eye open and saw a blur of strawberry blonde hair framing an olive-colored face.

"Use the skill, damn it. Do it!"

Oh, right. He was supposed to do something at the end. It was . . . something about healing. He had a healing skill. Blearily, Luke triggered **[Life Surge]**, and his eyes snapped open. "Holy crap!" he yelped. "What happened?"

"I think the ritual pulled out a big chunk of your blood, and you damn near died from it," Zea said. "And that's from me doing it right. Here, come over here and start eating. You're going to need it in a minute."

Even with **[Life Surge]** singing in his veins, Luke still felt woozy. He did what Zea told him to, but he'd barely gotten his first mouthful of food before the skill gave out and he promptly toppled backward.

Zea said something, but Luke had no idea what. His skill had healed a lot of his lost blood and internal injuries, but not all, and now the hunger spike was kicking his ass. Luke managed to chew and swallow, and then he passed out.

Luke was laid out, flat on his back, with a half-eaten apple still clutched in his hand. Despite Zea's best efforts, there was no waking him up. Thankfully, she'd at least gotten him to activate his regeneration skill before he went down, but she'd been hoping to get a bit more food in him. He was going to be starving when he did finally wake up, and they were both vulnerable until then.

The door on their little cave home was nothing but a screen of branches that blocked out the worst of the wind. If something came charging in, it would be on her to stop it, and Zea had very little confidence in her abilities in a fight. That wasn't where her skills were. If she'd realized quite how much the ritual would fuck Luke up, she would have insisted they do it under difference circumstances.

The best she could do for now was keep his mace nearby and hope it would make for up the lack of strength in her arms. It was light enough at least, surprisingly so considering how heavy it looked. Between that, the ever-sharp knife he'd given her, and her stupid crossbow, she was as prepared as she could get. Her poking stick would probably just break if she tried it on a monster, so she didn't even bother to fish that out of her backpack.

While she waited, she busied herself making lunch, triple portions. Part of her worried that even that much wouldn't be enough, but she also had to consider the state of their food supply. Gods knew at the rate she was going through the flask of honey wine she'd had buried in her own stash, it was going to be empty by the time Luke opened his eyes.

The whole experience had been boring for him, right up until the end. She had watched him fidget for close to an hour while she fought desperately to hold the mana in the shape she needed it and keep the cadence of the ritual going. Messing up a word here or there wasn't a big deal; it was really more the rhythm of the thing. But there had been a few points where she'd honestly just about lost the entire thing.

There had to be a few more supporting skills she'd missed, or perhaps she just needed to rank up the ones she did have to at least rank 3. That was generally considered an acceptable level of proficiency to ply a trade. Perhaps if they'd been less impatient, she could have smoothed the process out instead of knocking Luke on his ass at the end.

What was done was done, but she'd keep it in mind if they ended up needing to invest in rank 2 of **[Bloodline Purification Ritual]**. She hoped that wasn't the case, since it cost a staggering 200 AP to upgrade it. If her math was right, she'd need to get up to level 27 in order to afford it. No doubt the support skills would tack on a few more levels after that.

There were going to be more levels in their future, either way. Luke never said it, but she could tell that he chafed at how slowly they were moving. He kept a relaxed pace for her benefit, but she'd seen him move during combat. He was blindingly fast, and he didn't get tired. If he'd wanted to, he could probably run the thousand miles they needed to go inside of two days, maybe less if he pushed himself.

Zea knew her own limits, and even with the recent bumps to her agility and stamina, it was going to be the journey of a month at minimum for her. There were no roads once they got into the deep wilderness, and that meant slow going for her, not even considering monster attacks. They would be living off the land, depending on their ability to fight and gather supplies to survive. If he had any AP left over, she was going to recommend a few ranks in **[Survivalist]** as his next point expenditure.

It still felt crazy to not take lessons, or practice, or do any of the normal things people did when they were working to achieve a higher rank in a skill. Hell, most rank-ups came about as part of the natural process of getting better at something, and there were more than a few people who cursed the system for giving them unwanted XP.

Zea just shook her head. Luke had better be right about his ability to manipulate other people's stats and skills. She didn't feel like dying in ten years because she'd leveled up into the 40s.

The smell was what finally reached through to Luke. Zea was a . . . Well, he wasn't going to say she was a fantastic cook, but certainly much better than him. Plus he wasn't all that picky. Anything and everything she cooked tasted just fine to him.

He cracked his eyes open and found her sitting next to him, her back to the wall and his mace firmly clasped in both hands. "What are you doing?" he asked, sitting up and grabbing at his head.

"Oh, thank the gods you're awake. It's been three hours, and there is something that keeps trying to get in. I've smacked it six times now, but it just keeps coming back."

"Huh? I don't . . . Whoa . . . Dizzy. Just give me a second."

He took the offered water skin from her and chugged it down, then looked over toward the delicious-smelling food she had sitting in a pan on a rock. "Is that for me?"

"After you take care of our pest problem," she snapped. "Here, take your damn mace and go whack that fucking thing."

"Someone's in a mood," he muttered.

"I didn't get a nap like you did," she snapped.

Luke's eyebrows shot up, but he didn't say anything. Performing the ritual must have been rougher on her than he thought. He'd have to find a way to make it up to her later. Gently, he took the mace out of her hands, kissed her hair, and rose to his feet.

Whatever had been trying to get in had made a mess out of his door and left a bit of blood on the stone, presumably from where Zea had smacked it. Luke pulled the whole slab of wood aside and walked out into the sunlight, where he quickly spotted tracks roaming back and forth.

There was something in the trees that he might have classified as a weasel if it wasn't the size of a Great Dane and covered in scales instead of fur. Luke slowly scanned the area, looking for more of them. Leaving Zea undefended in the cave to chase it down wasn't the play he wanted to make, not if it left her vulnerable to the rest of the pack.

[Peripheral Awareness] dragged his attention to something above him, and he found another one clinging to the rock about ten feet over his head. It leaped down at him with a hiss, but he caught it by the throat with one hand, spun in place, and hurled it down into the stone so hard that it bounced. Before it could recover, his mace smacked down and splattered it across the ground.

A ding sounded in his head, but he ignored it to watch the other weasel-looking thing retreat back into the forest. Shaking his head, Luke went back in and asked, "How many were there? I only spotted two."

"I don't know. I didn't go out to check."

"Okay, well one of them is dead now, and the other ran off. They were, uh . . . Hrmm, that's odd."

"What's odd?" Zea asked.

[You have slain Slitherscale Stoat (level 14). 201 XP awarded.]

[This creature has slain 278 other creatures.]

[Total kills for this type of creature: 1.]

[Highest-level kill: 14.]

Name	Luke Bennet	Zea Stenter
Level	26	18
XP	60621/72056	18341/21602
AP	33	8
Bloodline	SysAdmin II	None
Strength	42	7
Agility	40	12
Stamina	36	12
Perception	39	14
Skills	Mace Mastery (3)	Dagger Mastery (1)
	Sword Mastery (1)	Stealth (2)
	Unarmed Martialist (3)	Keen Instincts (1)
	Power Strike (1)	Lock Picking (1)
	Life Surge (1)	Disguise (2)
	Peripheral Awareness (2)	Deception (1)
	Counter (2)	Bartering (2)
	Twitch Reflexes (2)	Streetwise (2)
	Stealth (1)	Cooking (1)
	Survivalist (2)	Mending (1)
	First Aid (1)	First Aid (1)
	Wood Carving (1)	Thalian (3)
	Leatherworking (2)	Neyardic (3)
	Butchering (4)	Ostari (1)
	Thalian (2)	Mana Manipulation (2)
	Disguise (2)	Mana Sight (1)
	Deception (1)	Metallurgy (1)
		Whitesmithing (1)
		Goldsmithing (2)
		Gem Cutting (1)
		Engraving (2)
		Rune Forging (1)
		Painting (1)
		Arcano Dynamics (1)
		Sleight of Hand (1)
		Steady Hands (2)
		Cold Reading (1)
		Temperature Acclimation (2)
		Cadence (2)
		Bloodline Purification Ritual (1)

CHAPTER 21

"First things first," Luke said, "System, how do I make it so that Zea can see you too?"

"You will first need a skill that lets you modify other people's systems called **[Remote Access]**," System told him. "It will cost you 15 AP and is necessary for any other bloodline skills that affect anyone besides yourself."

Considering he only had 33 AP to begin with, that was going to sharply limit his options for taking anything else if he chose that. "What does it do on its own?" he asked.

"It would allow you to make any changes you can currently make to your own status, except on someone else's."

The cheapest bloodline skill he knew about was 20 AP. He should have held on to a few AP from that last rank of **[Butchering]** after all, but Zea had made some compelling points about the money. That was Luke's fault; he knew that greed was her biggest vice. He didn't blame her, of course. Anyone who'd lived as poor a life as she had would be fascinated by the idea of never running out of money again.

"Okay, so good news and bad news," Luke said. "First, I do have the AP needed to allow you to see System and to make adjustments to how you interact with your status and notifications. However, if I buy that skill, I don't have enough left over to buy anything else."

"And if you don't buy that skill, what are your options?" Zea asked.

"**[XP Mask]** and **[Analyze]** are 20 AP each. It looks like **[Stat Assignment]** is also available, but it costs 50 AP. Everything else is still locked."

"**[Analyze]**," she said immediately. "It's way more useful than anything else right now. You won't need **[XP Mask]** until we get to Sicanti anyway, and if you can't alter skills, stats, and XP yet, we don't need **[Remote Access]** anyway."

"Before I buy this, System, are there any restrictions or limitations I should be aware of?"

"The skill will show you the level and stats of a target living being. It cannot show you their skill list without further bloodline purification, but if and when you manage to accomplish that, you will not need to spend further AP to obtain the new functionality."

"What about the other skills, stuff like **[XP Mask]**? It blocks others from sensing my XP, but also blocks me from sensing theirs. Would that change with a purer bloodline?" Luke asked.

"Yes, that is possible. You would need to purify your bloodline at least two more times to gain that functionality."

Considering how much effort had gone into one single purification, Luke didn't see getting two more anytime soon. It turned out that all the bloodline skills operated that way, with a base ability that got stronger the purer his bloodline became. Some of them were still locked, and he suspected there might even be a few that System couldn't or wouldn't tell him about at all.

Finding a way to further increase his bloodline purity was going to be key to making this whole plan work. Everything shared a common theme of allowing him to manipulate the system to his benefit, and sometimes to others' detriment.

"Alright, I think **[Analyze]** is the clear winner," Luke said. "**[Remote Access]** and **[XP Mask]** next level. Or maybe not **[XP Mask]** until we get to a place where I need it. No point in blinding myself now."

He took the skill, then looked over at Zea, who was holding his little dog carving in her hands. "Ready?" he asked.

She blinked and looked up at him. "Sure," she said. "What is this thing?"

Luke activated **[Analyze]**, then skimmed the new window that popped up about her.

[Name: Zea Stenter]
[Level: 18]
[Strength: 7]
[Agility: 12]
[Stamina: 12]
[Perception: 14]

That didn't tell him anything he didn't already know since they regularly swapped status sheets every time they leveled up, but it was going to be extremely useful when used against various monsters and animals. Just knowing their stat spreads was going to go a long way in helping him determine exactly how he needed to approach a fight.

"It works! Did you feel anything?"

"Not at all," Zea said. She held up the dog carving and asked again, "What is this?"

"It's a dog. Do you guys not have dogs?" Luke asked.

Judging by the way **[Thalian]** didn't translate the word *dog*, Luke was guessing the answer was no. For the language to not even have a word for that animal, maybe they didn't exist on Aros.

"I've seen plenty of animals with similar shapes, but not one like this," she said.

"They're kind of like wolves, except smaller and nicer. We keep them as pets, or sometimes train them as work animals. When I was a kid, my neighbor had a really friendly dog I used to play with."

"It must have made quite an impression on you," she said, still looking over the carving. "You told me your family was the reason you were doing this, that they'd all been pulled to this world and died."

"I—Yeah. Why?"

"You've never really talked about them," Zea said.

"Not much to say, I guess. Mom got sick and died when I was a kid. Dad basically worked himself to death for the next decade or so, not that there was ever enough money. We moved around a lot, stayed where we could. My sister got heavy into drinking early. I think the stress of playing mother to my brother and me got to her. And my brother did his best to look out for me. He was the one who pushed me to finish school instead of dropping out when I turned eighteen."

"School? How could you afford to go if . . . I think there is something I do not understand about your culture here."

"Everyone goes to school where I come from. It's compulsory. The government funds it, and you go until you graduate or you're old enough to be considered an adult and drop out. Or maybe you drop out a bit earlier if your life has sucked particularly hard."

"Strange," Zea said. She set the dog figurine down and shook her head. "Sorry, I didn't mean to get us sidetracked there. Your world sounds pretty interesting though, with your tame wolves and your noble's education for everyone."

"Not half as interesting as this place," Luke told her. "The system, and then there's actual magic. Other species that can think and talk. We don't have that at home. It's just humans. Nothing but humans and animals that can't talk and generally aren't all that smart all the way around the globe. No dwifkin, or ostols or anything else."

"Weird and interesting," Zea said, amending her previous statement.

Luke wondered, once they were all done and his family was back, if Zea would like to go with him back to Earth. She didn't seem to have any attachments to anyone or anything in Aros, but it wasn't like their relationship was all that deep. He knew a little a bit about her, learned a few more things every day. She was pretty cool, shared his sense of humor. But he suspected the answer was going to be a firm no if he asked.

Well, there was a lot of time between now and then anyway. He'd worry about that some other day. For now, it was time to see just what all this purification had been good for.

"Ready to go find some monsters to kill?"

"Like a little boy with a new toy," she muttered, quietly enough that he wouldn't have heard her without all the AP he'd put into perception.

"Exactly like that," he agreed shamelessly.

"Alright, fine, let's go test it out."

[Name: Sandstone Burrow Rat]
    [Level: 14]
    [Strength: 2]
    [Agility: 19]
    [Stamina: 7]
    [Perception: 28]

Luke stared at a two-foot-long rat he'd spotted scrabbling along the base of a ravine, its whiskers twitching as it looked around. **[Analyze]** hadn't done anything to alert it to his presence, which he'd wondered about. It had a much higher perception than Zea, and he'd thought maybe it would work kind of like XP sensing did. The fact that it wasn't reacting at all was strong evidence that the skill was undetectable.

Level 14 monsters weren't worth that much XP, and that rat was half a mile away. Luke had chosen it specifically because of the distance and was pleased to see the skill functioned anyway. He didn't bother to go chase it down though, both because of the low XP value and because Zea wouldn't get a cut of it. There was no way she was making a shot from that range on that small a target, and no way she'd get close enough to avoid it noticing her with its perception so high.

"This is a really cool skill," he said. "I can already tell that it's not worth the effort to go after that giant rat down there."

"Congratulations," Zea said dryly. "Do you happen to see something that *is* worth the effort, preferably with a lot of meat on it? You did a number on our food stores today."

"Oh, well, sorry. But that's why we have them, right?"

"Uh, no. We have them because we like not starving, which is what we're going to do if we don't get some more."

"Alright, alright. So something . . . tasty. And big. I suppose. Let's see what we can find . . ."

They spent the next week hunting monsters and restocking supplies. Eventually though, the hides were all processed, Zea got herself a nice new fur blanket that Luke was responsible for carrying, and it started getting harder and harder to find new monsters to fight.

They both managed about 8000 XP out of it, not quite enough to push Luke up another level, but more than enough to send Zea up to level 20. She dumped 15 of her new 39 AP into both agility and stamina so that they could travel faster, with another 5 going into her perception to help her navigate better in the dark.

As prepared as they were going to get, and with little left in the way of monsters to hunt, they abandoned their cave and started walking again. It took a few hours to get into the rhythm, but with Zea's physical effectiveness increased immensely, they made good time and were far more efficient in the hunting and killing of various monsters on the way.

"I think I know now why Zammin specialized in agility," Zea said one night. "It is insane how fast I can react to things now."

"Yes, your newly enhanced agility and stamina are perfect for quick traveling. And . . . other things," Luke agreed.

"Shut up," Zea said, but she smirked when she said it.

"The monsters are starting to get stronger again," Luke said after a minute's silence. "I've spotted four of them that were over level 30, and the average level is getting up toward the low 20s now."

"You still make it look easy."

"I need to start upgrading my skills. I was hoping they'd rank up on their own, but it doesn't seem to be happening," Luke said.

"That's because it takes years of practice to get skills up to rank 4. We've been on the road for a month. Don't be so impatient."

"Yeah, well, it might be time to start dumping AP into skills instead of stats. I don't see too many monsters that outmuscle me, even now. And I've been putting off some rank-ups for a while now. It's time to fix that."

"What are you thinking first?" Zea asked.

"Getting **[Tactical Foresight]** like I originally planned, which means I still need rank 4 **[Unarmed Martialist]**. Then after that, I was considering saving up to get rank 2 **[Life Surge]**. I bet it lasts longer and is less debilitating when it ends if I rank it up. Could be a lifesaving rank-up."

"That's a good plan. How much is the second rank?"

"100 AP," Luke said with a grimace.

"Ouch. Better get to work."

It might be time to let Zea move forward on her own while he hunted. He was still faster than her and could catch up easily, and splitting the XP had cost him quite a bit, probably multiple levels of his own. There were risks to that plan though, so he wanted it to be something they mutually agreed on.

"So I have a thought . . ."

Name	Luke Bennet	Zea Stenter
Level	26	20
XP	68321/72056	26172/29492
AP	13	12
Bloodline	SysAdmin II	None
Strength	42	7
Agility	40	27
Stamina	36	27
Perception	39	19
Skills	Mace Mastery (3)	Dagger Mastery (1)
	Sword Mastery (1)	Stealth (2)
	Unarmed Martialist (3)	Keen Instincts (1)
	Power Strike (1)	Lock Picking (1)
	Life Surge (1)	Disguise (2)
	Peripheral Awareness (2)	Deception (1)
	Counter (2)	Bartering (2)
	Twitch Reflexes (2)	Streetwise (2)
	Stealth (1)	Cooking (1)
	Survivalist (2)	Mending (1)
	First Aid (1)	First Aid (1)
	Wood Carving (1)	Thalian (3)
	Leatherworking (2)	Neyardic (3)
	Butchering (4)	Ostari (1)
	Thalian (2)	Mana Manipulation (2)
	Disguise (2)	Mana Sight (1)
	Deception (1)	Metallurgy (1)
	Analyze (BL)	Whitesmithing (1)
		Goldsmithing (2)
		Gem Cutting (1)
		Engraving (2)
		Rune Forging (1)
		Painting (1)
		Arcano Dynamics (1)
		Sleight of Hand (1)
		Steady Hands (2)
		Cold Reading (1)
		Temperature Acclimation (2)
		Cadence (2)
		Bloodline Purification Ritual (1)

CHAPTER 22

Luke ranged back and forth in a zigzag pattern while Zea marched straight ahead. Every few minutes, he'd loop back and check in before starting another lap. They kept this up for days, and without the XP split or the slow pace, he quickly jumped up from level 26 to 29. Of his 84 new AP, 30 went into rank 4 of **[Unarmed Martialist]** and 15 were spent on **[Tactical Foresight]**.

He also got a lucky break and ranked up **[Power Strike]** naturally after nearly a whole day of bashing some sort of earth elementals made out of a heavy jet-black stone when they got closer to the mountains. Considering that the system shop would have charged him 50 AP for the upgrade, he was pretty psyched about it.

That left him with 52 AP, which at one point in time he would have considered an obscene amount. He stuck 15 into **[Remote Access]**, kept 20 on reserve for **[XP Mask]**, and banked the rest toward an upgrade of **[Life Surge]** in another three levels.

He noticed Zea shooting him uneasy looks one night while he continued to work on mastering cooking to the point where the system awarded him the skill. Somehow, despite her instructions and his best efforts, he still couldn't produce anything that could be described as better than barely edible, and the system wasn't giving any points for persistence.

"What's up?" he asked.

"Just trying to figure out if you're starting to go crazy yet."

Luke started to make a joke, but then he paused and really thought about it. He knew there was a cultural fear of high-level people going insane, and he even knew what caused it. "What would the signs be?" he asked.

"Hearing voices is supposed to be the first one."

"Well, you can probably check that one off. I've been hearing System since about two minutes after I got here."

"I don't think that's what it means," Zea said.

That was probably true. System was, as far as Luke knew and assuming he could trust the apparition, a manifestation of the God Machine itself. The voices people heard would be their own XP congealing back into a fragment of a god and whispering to them. He didn't really understand why XP did that, but it was easy enough to find out, he hoped.

"System," Luke said, making Zea jump. Since modifying her own status to be able to interact with System, she could see him now, but it still made her flinch. More than once, he'd overheard her muttering about going insane herself.

"Yes, Luke?"

"Please tell me everything you can about the condition known as XP madness."

"Certainly. As we've previously discussed, this is caused by an accumulation of XP over a period of time. The XP begins to form into a sort of miniature protodeity. Due perhaps to the nature of the donor god as a hive mind structure, this protodeity has an instinctual drive to connect to others and to return to the hive. That drive gradually becomes stronger with time, and with accumulated XP, until the host creature begins acting erratically and oftentimes violently."

"What does *erratically* mean?" Luke asked. He wanted to know the signs so he could monitor himself for the first hints of them.

"They get twitchy," Zea said softly. "Nervous tics. They always seem distracted. Sometimes they start making weird noises. Then when people confront them about the behavior, they start getting violent. They lash out, and things escalate. Eventually someone ends up dead. Hopefully it's whoever got sick, but usually it's a whole lot of victims first since no one can stop a guy leveled up to 40 or 50."

"That is all essentially correct," System said.

"You know . . . That kind of sounds a lot like my uncle," Luke said. "When Aunt Sophia disappeared, we all just kind of chalked it up to stress over the situation. His wife was gone, nobody knew where she went, and he got grilled pretty hard by the cops over it. Things just kind of kept getting worse over the next year. My cousin went next, then Dad, then my older sister and brother, one after another."

"Then you," Zea said, finishing his list. "But how would your uncle have XP madness? Was he someone from this world that somehow made it to yours?"

"He was from Georgia, as far as I know," Luke said. "But then again, some-one in my family tree must have been from here originally, right? How else would we all have this bloodline?"

"The gods used a mortal man as a focal point when constructing the God Machine," System said. "This is the origin of your bloodline. They opened a door to another world as far away from the God Machine as possible and cast him through."

"And that would be my ancestor," Luke said. "But it doesn't explain what happened to Duncan. He's not even actually a blood relative. Aunt Sophia is my father's sister. Duncan is just her husband that she met in college. His only connection is who he married."

"Well, the door still exists, right?" Zea asked.

Luke glanced over at System, who said, "Yes, it does."

"I didn't see any magic doorway leading into a wardrobe when I first got here."

"Maybe it only opens at certain times," Zea suggested. "Or under the right conditions."

They both turned to System, who shook his head and said, "I am not able to answer that question."

"Okay, well, let's assume that's true. Are you saying that Duncan walked through, killed something, got some XP, and then went back home?" Luke asked.

"Or something walked through and he killed it in your world."

"When I was really little, I remember my parents talking to my aunt about some animal that had gotten into their basement. They were all really freaked out about it and wouldn't tell any of us kids anything," Luke said. "That was fifteen years ago. So if my uncle killed it, he got a few points of XP, and all of a sudden he's connected to the system. But that's so little, it doesn't explain how he would get XP madness."

"Maybe—" Zea stopped and shook her head. "No."

"Maybe what?"

"I was going to say, you told me time moves at a different speed between worlds. What if XP works on our time, even in your world? Does that make sense?"

"Uh."

"If it does, then even having just a few XP, if a single month of your time is a century here, that XP would have had thousands of years to slowly eat away at your uncle's mind."

"And this thing became a voice in his head, told him to shove people with the right bloodline through the doorway, which just happens to be in his basement?"

Zea shrugged. "It had to be somewhere, right?"

"Kind of convenient, isn't it?"

Then again, that house had been in his family for generations. Luke's aunt had inherited it from his grandfather, who had himself been born, grown up, lived, and died in that house. It was more than a hundred years old. Whichever ancestor had originally been from Aros could have built his home on top of the door.

It was all speculation. Someday, it might be important, but not today. What was important now was knowing the signs of XP madness to watch out for in himself, though as he understood it, it was a factor of amount and time. He had a lot of XP, but he'd only had it for a few months. There'd been no XP at all for more than nineteen years.

"System, you can tell when XP madness starts affecting me, right?"

"I can make a guess based on your total XP and how long you've had each point. It is only an estimate, but I believe you have about twenty-five years left before you begin showing signs that would be noticeable in someone else."

"What about me?" Zea asked.

"Fifty-two years. Keep in mind that these estimates are predicated on the highly unlikely scenario that you never gain another point of XP ever again."

"It's fine. You said we could purge the XP at the God Machine," Luke said.

"That is correct. You can purge XP, Luke. Zea lacks the capability."

"But I can purge hers too," Luke pressed.

"If you so desire."

"Well there we go then. We just need to get there, and everything will be fine."

Zea gave him a flat stare and said, "I don't think it's so easy as just walking up to it. We're not even on the right continent yet. I think you should slow down on the XP grind. A few more levels and you'll only have a year or two left instead of decades."

"That's just until I start exhibiting symptoms. I'll still have some time before I go full-on cuckoo, right, System?"

"Universally, in all cases of XP madness, the host has already begun to lose control of their mental faculties prior to symptoms becoming apparent to other creatures."

Luke's face fell. "So you're saying I actually have less time than you predicted?"

"Shit," Zea swore. "This just keeps getting worse."

"That is correct, Luke."

"Time to stop screwing around then. I think I'm strong enough to get us through the wilderness. How far are we from Sicanti now?"

"Six hundred miles," System said. "Though if you intend to continue avoiding crossing the mountains, you will need to go approximately one hundred fifty miles out of your way."

"So seven fifty total," Luke said. "We can do that in a week as long as nothing big gets in our way."

"And we have the amaril," Zea said. "I know I can sell that in less than a day. Might not get the best price for it, but I'll get us enough for passage across the ocean. The biggest wait will probably be on a ship leaving port. It's not like that happens every day."

"As long as we're not killing anyone in the city, it should be fine. We do still have years left."

"System," Zea said. "Once we cross the ocean, we'll land in a city named Naldrin. How far is it from there to the God Machine?"

"Two thousand eight hundred and forty miles."

Luke let out a low whistle. "That's a lot of walking. But if we can take roads for most of it, it shouldn't be too bad."

"Maybe we could buy a few teleports to speed up the process with some of the extra money," Zea said. "Maybe. It's pretty tightly regulated, at least in Valtira. Even if you have the gold, that doesn't guarantee a slot."

"If not, we'll figure something else out. One step at a time. First, we get to the city, then get on a boat. Then we'll work out the next step."

"System, once a day, I want you to update us with your best estimate for how long until we begin to have symptoms of XP madness, not when others will start to notice," Zea said.

"Understood. In that case, my estimate is that Luke has twenty-one years left, and you have forty-six."

"Still plenty of time," Luke said, trying not to sound worried.

"Only if we can fix it. What if we can't? What if we're completely fucked?"

"We're not fucked. We'll make it there. I'll put it all back the way it's supposed to be."

"I'm not so sure anymore," Zea told him bluntly. "This is crazy. What happens when it's not just a church inquisitor trying to stop us? How far will we get before the gods agree to ignore the Covenant and just squash us?"

Luke looked over at System, who regarded him blankly. "I am not able to speculate on the motivations or actions of the Pantheon."

"Yeah, I know. You've told me, several times. Thank you, System. That will be all."

The apparition disappeared, and Luke sat down next to Zea to comfort her. "They haven't done anything yet," he said. "If they could have, they would have as soon as I got here."

"I hope you're right."

"Me too."

Name	Luke Bennet	Zea Stenter
Level	29	20
XP	87860/89266	26172/29492
AP	37	12
Bloodline	SysAdmin II	None
Strength	42	7
Agility	40	27
Stamina	36	27
Perception	39	19
Skills	Mace Mastery (3)	Dagger Mastery (1)
	Sword Mastery (1)	Stealth (2)
	Unarmed Martialist (4)	Keen Instincts (1)
	Power Strike (2)	Lock Picking (1)
	Life Surge (1)	Disguise (2)
	Peripheral Awareness (2)	Deception (1)
	Tactical Foresight (1)	Bartering (2)
	Counter (2)	Streetwise (2)
	Twitch Reflexes (2)	Cooking (1)
	Stealth (1)	Mending (1)
	Survivalist (2)	First Aid (1)
	First Aid (1)	Thalian (3)
	Wood Carving (1)	Neyardic (3)
	Leatherworking (2)	Ostari (1)
	Butchering (4)	Mana Manipulation (2)
	Thalian (2)	Mana Sight (1)
	Disguise (2)	Metallurgy (1)
	Deception (1)	Whitesmithing (1)
	Analyze (BL)	Goldsmithing (2)
	Remote Access (BL)	Gem Cutting (1)
		Engraving (2)
		Rune Forging (1)
		Painting (1)
		Arcano Dynamics (1)
		Sleight of Hand (1)
		Steady Hands (2)
		Cold Reading (1)
		Temperature Acclimation (2)
		Cadence (2)
		Bloodline Purification Ritual (1)

CHAPTER 23

The mountains loomed in their vision, blocking much of the eastern and northern sky and forcing them to push farther and farther west in an attempt to circle around them. Since that was an expected complication to their journey, Luke hadn't thought much about it initially.

That was before the squirrels started showing up. At first, it had just been some random level 12 squirrel, nothing impressive, that had leaped off of a tree branch in some sort of suicidal attempt to attack his face. Luke had batted it out of the air quite easily thanks to a combination of **[Peripheral Awareness]**, **[Twitch Reflexes]**, and **[Counter]**.

Then twenty feet later, another one had jumped on him. And another a few minutes after that. Luke quickly went from happy about the free XP to annoyed at the constant ambush attempts. Once the first one tried to attack Zea, annoyance turned to anger.

"Why in the hell are all these squirrels doing kamikaze runs on us?" he asked.

"Maybe it's a territorial thing," Zea said. "We're near the ancestral family tree or something. They're not really that dangerous. Let's just hurry through this area so they leave us alone."

Two hours later, Luke brought his mace down on a squirrel tall enough that it came up past his knee.

[You have slain Drop Squirrel (level 14). 201 XP awarded.]
[This creature has slain 387 other creatures.]
[Total kills for this type of creature: 31.]
[Highest-level kill: 14.]

"So, what do we know so far?" Luke asked.

"They're aggressive, and there are a lot of them, but they don't seem to attack in groups. This would actually be a decent place to grind out XP for you."

"Yeah, but not for you. I can kill them with one hit, but you can't."

Left unsaid was that she also wasn't fast enough to reliably tag them even if she could have one-shotted them, or that if one of them managed to sink those oversize teeth into her, they didn't have a good way to patch her back up. The first aid kit he'd picked up was good for patching up small scrapes, but it wouldn't do much to staunch wounds deep enough that they'd normally require stitches. It was probably safe for Luke to farm the squirrels, but it didn't help Zea, and they were exactly the wrong sort of enemy for her to tag while Luke did the heavy lifting.

"Maybe we should turn back and circle wide around whatever the fuck it is these squirrels have going on here," he said.

Zea shook her head. "We're fine. Your perception is high enough that they won't get the drop on you, and you're fast enough to intercept them. As long as I stay close, I'm safe. Let's just push through. How wide could a squirrel's territory even be?"

Luke had his doubts. In theory, he agreed that squirrels couldn't have a very big territory, though even that idea wasn't solid to him. There had been more than enough examples of weird shit that didn't conform to how he thought reality worked for him to just take it on faith that this particular time, everything would work out.

Even if that was the case, the real problem was that there were just so many damn squirrels. There was no end to them. Every few minutes, a new one would attack him, and he didn't trust them to keep up that pattern. It was easy to picture them hunkering down for the night and hundreds of squirrels rushing them after building up their numbers for an hour or two.

By himself, Luke thought he had good odds of surviving even a hundred squirrels attacking him at once. It wouldn't be easy, sure, but he had a full suite of combat skills, enough stamina to run for days without stopping, and the strength and agility to make every hit count.

Zea didn't, and he didn't think he could protect her from even four or five monsters at once. So far, that hadn't been an issue. Most monsters didn't operate in large groups. Hell, most of them didn't even have partners. But the sheer number of squirrels was making him second-guess the idea that they'd keep coming at him one at a time.

"Hey, look at me," Zea said, grabbing hold of Luke's arm. "It will be fine. You're strong, and I'm not as delicate as you seem to think. Even if we go around this place, we're just going to be walking through some other monster's territory. At least here, we know what we're dealing with. Now, let's go."

"Okay. Stay close, I guess."

They pushed forward, fending off attacks that got more and more frequent. Sometimes Zea managed to get a shot in at them, though she'd had to resort to her magic poking stick, and she went easy on it to keep it from breaking, but Luke did the majority of the work, and since no squirrel he touched ever lived to take a second hit, he got almost all the XP.

Night fell, and with it the attacks from the squirrels died down. They didn't stop completely, but the frequency dropped enough that Luke finally started to relax. "Maybe if we're lucky, we'll be long gone by the time the sun comes up."

"That means staying up all night," Zea said sourly. "You know how I feeeee—Aaugh!"

Luke grabbed her and pulled her behind him just as a squirrel that was at least three feet tall dropped down from overhead. The size was bad enough, but what really worried Luke was that this was the first time he'd seen one with a tool. Somehow, its paws had opposable thumbs, and it had some sort of thick branch that had been shaped down into an approximation of a size-appropriate sword. The damn thing even had a point on it, as the monster had proven by driving it straight into the ground where Zea had been standing.

"Stay behind me. Keep an eye out for others," Luke said as he leaped forward.

The squirrel was fast. All of them had been quick, but not like this one. It was damn near faster than Luke, and it jabbed out with that sharpened stick it held in quick lunging attacks that it broke off and skittered backward whenever Luke showed the slightest effort to block.

It was testing him, which meant it was smart. Smart and fast was a deadly combination he did not want to deal with. Lucky for him, he didn't have to guess at anything. **[Analyze]** would tell him everything he needed to know.

[Name: Drop Squirrel Scout]

[Level: 18]

[Strength: 9]

[Agility: 32]

[Stamina: 6]

[Perception: 24]

If it had been stupid, he would have said it wasn't a threat, but the fact that the system labeled it as a scout had some disturbing implications, like that they were intelligent and organized. It was time to pick System's brain, so to speak, about these damn squirrels and make sure he wasn't walking into a whole army of them.

Before that though, he needed to take care of the furry little bastard doing its best to poke holes in him. Luke rushed forward, pushing it back and relying on his superior agility to close the gap. The squirrel leaped up, easily clinging to the tree bark with its feet and one hand somehow, but Luke just jumped into the air and slammed into the tree right beneath it.

And the only reason he missed was that it was climbing, but not fast enough. He got a hand around its leg and ripped it free, then swung it down to slam it against the tree once before dropping it twenty feet to the ground.

"Drop squirrel this, fucker," he said.

Luke landed on it with both feet, driving it deep into the earth. Then he hopped back, took his mace in a golf swing, and ripped a huge chunk of dirt away as he decapitated the monster.

[You have slain Drop Squirrel Scout (level 18). 335 XP awarded.]

[This creature has slain 682 other creatures.]

[Total kills for this type of creature: 32.]

[Highest-level kill: 18.]

[Congratulations! You have reached level 30. 30 AP awarded for use.]

"Oh, damn. I didn't realize I was that close to leveling," Luke said. "One step closer to rank 2 **[Life Surge]** now."

Zea walked over and looked at the corpse. "That's . . . different. System, what can you tell us about this thing?"

"Drop squirrels are semisapient creatures that form huge societies with thousands of members. Their society exists above ground level, inside giant trees that grow hundreds of feet in the air. They have some biological differences from regular squirrels, primarily in that they've gained the ability to use tools."

"So what I'm getting from that is that we're heading in a bad direction and we need to go farther east toward the mountains," Luke said.

"Maybe. Then again, they still haven't been much of a threat. A detour could cost us time and XP that could be gained from cutting right through them."

"Hey, System," Luke said without breaking eye contact with Zea, "Do these drop squirrels generally attack in groups or individually?"

"Both, though the closer one gets to their home trees, the more likely it is that they'll be encountered in numbers."

"Thanks, System, thought so. We should have changed direction a few hours ago."

"System," Zea said, "where is the closest home tree?"

"Approximately four miles northwest of here."

"And would we encounter any other trees if we continue straight north?"

"You would not," System said.

"What are the chances of us encountering a large group if we pass within a mile of the tree?"

"I do not have sufficient information to hazard a guess."

Luke scratched at his chin and looked down at the dead scout. "Why are you so intent on going straight into danger?"

Zea shrugged. "Time, mostly. The magic on that bag with the amaril hide won't last forever, and we don't know how many detours we're going to be forced to take. There are no roads this far north, and there could be level 40 or 50 monsters out here that we have no choice but to do wide circles around. This is a threat you can handle, and if things start getting hot, we can retreat."

Luke didn't love the logic, and he suspected a large part of was motivated by Zea's greed. She was very excited about the expected profits from selling that hide, but they were still a week at best away from civilization, probably longer. At the same time, they needed that money to keep moving forward, and losing the value of that piece of animal skin would seriously hurt them.

She wasn't stupid. She knew there were risks, and she felt like Luke was strong enough to handle them. More than that, she trusted him to keep her safe too. If it really was just a few miles until they were past that home-tree thing, and they weren't going to run into any other trees like that, then they could be gone before daybreak.

"System, can you tell me the highest-level drop squirrel in the area?" Luke asked.

"32," System replied. "And the lowest is level 4, including the nonsapient cousin species you've already encountered."

"32 is kind of high," Luke said. "Are there a lot of them that are that strong?"

"I am only able to offer limited information on the subject. The average level is much lower, but there are always outliers."

"I would assume the high-level ones would be near their home trees," Zea said. "Which is just another reason to go hard and fast and be out of here before it becomes a problem."

"Alright, alright." Luke put his hands up in a gesture of surrender. "You've convinced me. We'll rush through as fast as we can, I'll collect a few thousand XP from whatever gets in our way, and we'll be far, far away from this problem before the sun comes up and the rest of the squirrels wake up."

"No time to waste then," Zea said. "Actually, wait. System, do the drop squirrels have a currency system? Do they use any sort of precious metals or gemstones as money?"

"They do not," System said.

"Damn, too much to hope for. I guess we don't need to worry about looting them then."

"Probably for the best," Luke told her. "We're in a hurry, remember?"

"Not so much that I wouldn't stop to pick up a few extra copper or silver off them. There's saving time, and then there's just being plain wasteful."

Name	Luke Bennet	Zea Stenter
Level	30	20
XP	89467/98832	26570/29492
AP	67	12
Bloodline	SysAdmin II	None
Strength	42	7
Agility	40	27
Stamina	36	27
Perception	39	19
Skills	Mace Mastery (3)	Dagger Mastery (1)
	Sword Mastery (1)	Stealth (2)
	Unarmed Martialist (4)	Keen Instincts (1)
	Power Strike (2)	Lock Picking (1)
	Life Surge (1)	Disguise (2)
	Peripheral Awareness (2)	Deception (1)
	Tactical Foresight (1)	Bartering (2)
	Counter (2)	Streetwise (2)
	Twitch Reflexes (2)	Cooking (1)
	Stealth (1)	Mending (1)
	Survivalist (2)	First Aid (1)
	First Aid (1)	Thalian (3)
	Wood Carving (1)	Neyardic (3)
	Leatherworking (2)	Ostari (1)
	Butchering (4)	Mana Manipulation (2)
	Thalian (2)	Mana Sight (1)
	Disguise (2)	Metallurgy (1)
	Deception (1)	Whitesmithing (1)
	Analyze (BL)	Goldsmithing (2)
	Remote Access (BL)	Gem Cutting (1)
		Engraving (2)
		Rune Forging (1)
		Painting (1)
		Arcano Dynamics (1)
		Sleight of Hand (1)
		Steady Hands (2)
		Cold Reading (1)
		Temperature Acclimation (2)
		Cadence (2)
		Bloodline Purification Ritual (1)

CHAPTER 24

They rushed straight north as fast as they could, using System as a pseudo-compass to make sure they didn't get too close to the absolutely massive cluster of hundreds-foot-tall trees jutting up out of the forest like some great wooden mountain. Luke had taken the time to climb up to the top of one of the nearby normal trees to get a good look at them, and what he'd seen was not encouraging.

Not only were they tool users, the squirrels had built rudimentary homes in the boughs of their treetop city. They were smart and organized, a civilization in their own right, and one that was extremely aggressive toward trespassers. Luke couldn't much blame them for that, considering just about everything they'd encountered out in the wilderness had done its best to kill them. Attacking on sight was a good policy for the squirrels.

Well, maybe not good, but he could see the merits. Running away on sight might have been a better policy for some of the wimpier ones. Then again, the regular squirrels were apparently some sort of lesser servant race, so Luke supposed they might be doing exactly what they'd been told. Perhaps some asshole boss squirrel was fine with throwing their lives away by the bucketful if it meant they killed a few trespassers in squirrel-folk territory.

Which was all sorts of fucked up, but not Luke's problem, except for the fact that they did not stop coming. He would have lost track of how many he'd killed hours ago if not for the system helpfully reminding him of his running kill count every time he swatted another one out of the air.

So far, the run had been more annoying than scary. Luke was more than fast enough to keep circling around Zea while she focused on moving in as straight a line as possible, and his perception was high enough that none of attackers had managed to get the drop on them. He'd even been able to point out a few to Zea, who'd taken to poking them with her magic stick so she could claim some XP too.

Two squirrels leaped out of the trees at the same time, which was a first. Worse, one of them was the weirdly humanoid variety, and it was armed with a spear. Really, it was more of a sharpened stick, but still, it was that it had a weapon at all that was concerning. They were far enough apart that Luke wasn't going to be able to get both, but still close enough that he could choose. Based on the angles of approach, he expected the bigger, smarter squirrel thought its animal friend was going to take all of Luke's attention while it got the chump shot in on him.

[Tactical Foresight] was having none of that. Luke had already mapped out how the entire fight was going to go before either of them were halfway to the ground. Pivoting smoothly, he brought the mace up over his head and smacked the squirrel folk like it was a pinata that owed him money. Blood and gore splattered across the nearby trees, but he didn't stop to watch.

The other squirrel would be hitting the ground now, no longer close enough to land on him since he'd pivoted, and he gave it even odds whether it went for Zea or him. If he was lucky, it would be right about chest level when he turned back to it, flinging its whole body at his face. If so, it would be easy enough to bring the mace around in a parry then knocked it back and leave it dazed while he finished it off.

If he wasn't lucky, well, he trusted Zea. She lacked his agility-related combat skills like **[Twitch Reflexes]**, but her raw agility was 27. That should be enough to help her react to the lightning-quick attack, which would give him enough time to attack it from behind. Either way, that squirrel had about three seconds left to live.

Luke finished his spin, saw the squirrel coming for him just like he'd hoped, and brought the mace up to divert its aerial charge. He flicked his wrist when it impacted the metal, just to rotate the mace and put a bit of spin on the squirrel while it tumbled away. Before it could recover, he took one large step forward and smacked the monster hard enough to drive its body into the ground.

[You have slain 2 creatures between levels 6 and 21. 495 XP awarded.]

"That's the first time it's been two at once," Luke said.

"We're about even with the home tree now, I think. As long as we keep moving, we shouldn't encounter more like that."

"Let's hope," he said grimly. "If we're lucky, the attacks are getting more frequent just because we're closer, and not because they're closing in on us."

They started moving again but were quickly blocked by a dense wall of underbrush. It was so thick that even with his strength, Luke decided it would be faster to go around than to punch through. Unfortunately for them, it appeared that the wall extended quite some ways to the west, perhaps all the way to the home tree itself. It also curved around to block them from going east or north, and since they definitely weren't going that far out of their way, their only remaining option was to go up and over.

With Zea clinging to him, Luke leaped straight up and started climbing into the branches. The trees were so massive and wild here that their branches were twined around one another, making it difficult for someone of his size to break through. Zea actually had an easier time than he did.

"Do you think the squirrels did this on purpose?" she said as she squeezed through a knot of crooked branches all growing around one another. "I mean, what are the chances of this giant tangle going on and on like this?"

They were directly over top it now, and Luke couldn't see the end. If it was less than a hundred feet thick, he'd be surprised. He'd certainly never seen anything like it, but Aros was full of things he'd never even imagined, let alone encountered. He supposed it could have been natural, or maybe the squirrels had grown it that way on purpose. It would hardly be an obstacle for them, since they used the tree branches themselves to travel around.

"Maybe. The big ones are smart. I don't know how exactly they'd do it, but it's possible."

Luke grunted as a branch from the bunch he'd been holding slipped and smacked against his face. Trying to push through this mess while keeping one hand on his mace was a pain in the ass, but he was managing. "If they did grow this, then we should be watching for another ambush. The terrain couldn't really favor them more than it does here."

If it came down to it, he thought he could bull through the branches. They'd probably shred his clothes, but he would be okay. Still, the tight confines would give the squirrels the advantage, especially the normal-sized ones. Those were all low level though, so he was less worried about them as anything other than a distraction. Zea would be able to fight one of those off, one-on-one. Hopefully, she'd do it without getting hurt.

Hopefully, she wouldn't have to do it at all.

Luke was leaving a trail of broken branches a blind squirrel could follow behind him, which made it easier for Zea to stick close. She kept an eye out behind for squirrels coming at them while he did the same from the front, and they were at the halfway point of the giant tangle of underbrush now. He could see an end, just barely. More importantly, he couldn't see any squirrels.

"It's going to suck if there's another wall like this," he said. "This is slowing us way the fuck down."

"Yeah," Zea agreed unhappily. "On the other hand, we don't know that we wouldn't have encountered these underbrush tangles farther east either."

Luke just grunted, not having a reply. He'd been against cutting straight through the squirrels' territory, and every single fight or detour that slowed them down defeated the main draw of taking the shortcut. At the rate they were going, if they had to crawl over another wall of underbrush, it would be dawn well before they got away from the home tree.

At least the walls weren't manned, so to speak. They reached the far end without encountering any hostile elements, which was a better outcome than Luke had been expecting. He dropped down into an open spot between two trees, a feat that he only accomplished by kicking out five different branches that were in his way, then made space for Zea to land right after him.

"Whew," she said. "Thank the gods I spent that AP on agility. There is no way I'd have been able to do that two months ago."

"Not the only thing you couldn't do two months ago," Luke said, wiggling his eyebrows at her.

"Seriously? You want to do this right now?"

"What can I say? The danger excites me. Gets the heart pumping."

"You're terrible," she said. "Just terrible. But . . ."

"Ha. You're just as bad."

"Oh, shut up."

Luke could see Zea's face turning red, and he chuckled as he tried to reorient them in the right direction again. Truthfully, he doubted there'd be time for anything like that today, or even tomorrow. Things were getting more dangerous the farther north they went. Every twenty or thirty miles, it seemed like they encountered something new. Sometimes that wasn't a problem, especially since there were only so many varieties of big, dumb, and slow he could deal with before it all started to blend together.

Other times, like the squirrels, he got a bit concerned. Luke did not like fighting smart enemies. He was afraid they'd outsmart him. More than that, he was afraid they'd use Zea against him. That was the real reason he wanted to get the hell away from the home tree as soon as he could.

He'd spent the last few hours worrying about that, about her, not that she would appreciate the concern. He could practically see her face twisted up into a scowl while she told him off. She'd put her hands on her hips and glower at him in a way that he couldn't help but find adorable.

"What are you smiling about?" Zea asked a few minutes later.

"Hmm? Nothing."

"Oh please. I know exactly what you're smiling about. Dumb boys always thinking with their dicks instead of their brains."

"What? No! It's nothing like that."

"Yeah, bullshit. Keep walking, you hornball."

"I'm serious, I wasn't eve—*Get down!*"

A branch whipped down from overhead, long and flexible as it slashed the air where Zea had been standing. She'd started to dive as soon as Luke had yelled, and even then, the only reason it hadn't reached her was because he'd jumped in between them. The branch struck his raised hand, scoring a bloody gash across his palm, and retracted.

He saw small thorns covered in his blood studding the limb, and only that one limb. Those definitely hadn't been there a minute ago. He'd been paying attention to the boughs above them for hours now, and he would have noticed an anomaly like that.

He reached for his **[Analyze]** ability, expecting it to come back and tell him they'd encountered some sort of sentient tree monster. It would probably be easier to just leave the area and get out of its range than to actually fight it, assuming it couldn't uproot itself and chase after them. Luke didn't see how that would even be possible with the forest as densely packed as it was.

It didn't matter though because **[Analyze]** came back blank. Whatever that tree was, it wasn't alive, or didn't have XP, or whatever the criteria were for the skill to work. Luke blinked up at it, confused. If it wasn't a monster, he didn't know what had caused it to weaponize one of its branches and try to attack them.

But he was betting the reason was under two feet tall and had a long, fluffy tail.

Name	Luke Bennet	Zea Stenter
Level	30	20
XP	91726/98832	27372/29492
AP	67	12
Bloodline	SysAdmin II	None
Strength	42	7
Agility	40	27
Stamina	36	27
Perception	39	19
Skills	Mace Mastery (3)	Dagger Mastery (1)
	Sword Mastery (1)	Stealth (2)
	Unarmed Martialist (4)	Keen Instincts (1)
	Power Strike (2)	Lock Picking (1)
	Life Surge (1)	Disguise (2)
	Peripheral Awareness (2)	Deception (1)
	Tactical Foresight (1)	Bartering (2)
	Counter (2)	Streetwise (2)
	Twitch Reflexes (2)	Cooking (1)
	Stealth (1)	Mending (1)
	Survivalist (2)	First Aid (1)
	First Aid (1)	Thalian (3)
	Wood Carving (1)	Neyardic (3)
	Leatherworking (2)	Ostari (1)
	Butchering (4)	Mana Manipulation (2)
	Thalian (2)	Mana Sight (1)
	Disguise (2)	Metallurgy (1)
	Deception (1)	Whitesmithing (1)
	Analyze (BL)	Goldsmithing (2)
	Remote Access (BL)	Gem Cutting (1)
		Engraving (2)
		Rune Forging (1)
		Painting (1)
		Arcano Dynamics (1)
		Sleight of Hand (1)
		Steady Hands (2)
		Cold Reading (1)
		Temperature Acclimation (2)
		Cadence (2)
		Bloodline Purification Ritual (1)

CHAPTER 25

Luke backed away from the tree slowly while Zea scrambled to stay low on all fours as she fled its reach. Twice more, branches that had just been normal, bark-covered limbs suddenly sprouted razor thorns and became as flexible as willow switches. They slashed through the air at him but weren't fast enough to tag Luke.

If the situation had been less bizarre, or if he'd had a better grasp of their capabilities, he might have swatted the attacks away. Visions of the branches grabbing hold of the mace and him being forced to fight a tree to hold on to it danced through his mind though, and since he had no idea how much strength a living tree might have, he didn't trust himself to win that one.

So he put his agility to work making sure the tree didn't touch him in the first place. It honestly wasn't even close, once he'd gotten over his initial surprise at having a branch come to life and attack him. Between the raw stat and his multiple skills designed to help him predict and react to attacks, Luke felt comfortable saying he could have kept out of the reach of four or five branches.

He could have, but he didn't because that would just be stupidly tempting fate. Even he wasn't *that* dumb.

"Oh shit! We've got company," Zea said from up ahead.

Luke risked a glance to the side and saw a single squirrel folk crouched on a branch over the trail they were on, though calling it a trail was being generous. It had a hand raised and was waving it around while it stared down at the two trespassers.

"What . . . What is it doing?" Luke asked.

Then it chucked what Luke was pretty sure was a Goddamn acorn at him, which exploded midair into a blast wave of pure force and acorn-shell shrapnel. Luke was shoved straight down into the dirt, hard enough that he left an imprint. Even before he hit the ground, he could see the two whiplike branches diving in for him, so he was already flinging himself to one side.

The first branch missed, instead scoring a slash through the dirt that was at least an inch wide and several inches deep. It would have flayed a normal person's skin open down to the bone, no question. The second branch struck him square in the shoulder, and that was when he really internalized exactly how tough 36 stamina had made him.

The branch struck him, and it bent. The razor-sharp thorns tore through the leather plate and his shirt beneath and caught on his skin, and he felt one of the thorns break off in his arm, then the others all ripped past him. He wasn't even bleeding. Luke glanced down at the wound, picked out the thorn that had gotten stuck, and saw nothing but whole, healthy, pink skin through the tear the branch had made in his armor.

"Okay, fucker, if you're going to start ruining my clothes, I'm going to get pissed off," he told the squirrel.

Zea had been on the other side of the acorn when it blew up, and she was farther away than he was. She'd still been pushed to the dirt, but it had ironically thrown her out of the reach of the tree, and at first glance, she seemed unharmed. Luke bounded past her, moving as quickly as he could through the underbrush and in a few cases just crashing right through it. He planted both feet solidly on the ground, flexed his legs, and jumped straight up into the air.

Branches came to life and wove themselves between Luke and the squirrel. Quicker than he would have thought possible, there was a solid, impassable wall of living wood protecting the little shithead from him, but Luke wasn't about to let that slow him down. He charged up a **[Power Strike]** as he ascended to the squirrel's position and brought the mace around in a two-handed overhead swing that struck the wall squarely.

Branches exploded inward, showering the shocked squirrel with wood. It let out some sort of high-pitched, terrified squeak and tried to fling itself backward, but Luke was through the new hole in the wall before it could get away. He grabbed a handful of its chest and hauled it back through the gap, then dropped down to the ground.

The squirrel hit first, having been thrown straight down while they both fell, and Luke's foot landed on its skull as it was bouncing back up. Chunks of shattered bone and brain matter splattered everywhere, and the kill notification sounded in his mind.

[You have slain Drop Squirrel Druid (level 23). 553 XP awarded.]

[This creature has slain 128 other creatures.]

[Total kills for this type of creature: 35.]
[Highest-level kill: 23.]

"Come on, we need to go," Luke said, rushing over to Zea to help her back up.

"What the fuck was that?"

"A fucking problem is what. That wall wasn't natural. We need to get the hell out of Dodge before another one shows up."

"Get out of . . . what?"

"Never mind. Earth expression. I'll explain it later."

He hustled Zea north at maximum speed. "That was the strongest one yet," he said, "and it could use magic. The system notification said it was a druid."

She regarded him blankly, then said, "What's a druid?"

Luke pulled up short and gave her an incredulous stare. "You don't know? This is your world."

"Do you know every job your world has to offer off the top of your head?"

"Er, no, but like . . . This one is kind of famous, at least back on Earth."

"I thought you said there was no magic on Earth."

"No, but we have stories with magic. Druids are like, uh, nature priests or something. They can make plants grow or do weird shit. They can do stuff with animals too. So being balls deep in the middle of this forest with the capital of squirrel civilization just a few miles away isn't exactly a great place to fight them."

Zea started to say something but stopped to curse as her pack got caught on a branch. With a jerk, she pulled it free, then started swearing. "Damn it, tore the stitching on the strap. Going to have to fix that later before it comes off completely."

"Later," Luke agreed absently while he watched the tree branches behind them. It could be just the wind moving them, or they could be preparing to attack again. He didn't see any squirrels, but there were plenty of blind spots that no amount of perception was going to allow him to peer through. His other senses weren't reporting anything either, but if the squirrels could use magic, he wasn't willing to commit to trusting his ears and nose to keep them safe.

It was a good thing he didn't either because not two minutes later he felt something grab his foot. Roots complete with their own thorns were snaking their way around his ankle, at least five or six individual strands. Luke jerked his foot free, or rather, he ripped several feet of roots straight out of the ground before they finally snapped. He glanced over at Zea to make sure she was alright, only to see her dealing with a similar problem.

Instead of using pure strength, she'd brandished the ever-sharp alchemical blade he'd given her and sliced her way free. That was admittedly a far more elegant solution than what he'd come up with, but it had the same basic flaw his own tactic did: it addressed the immediate problem of being ensnared without doing anything to help them locate the source.

Squirrel folk came hurtling through the branches above, three of them at least, by his count, and leaped at him, each with a spear held in one hand and some sort of smaller, double-ended javelin in the other. They threw them while they fell, two at Luke and one at Zea, and though he blocked them with little enough effort, they served their purposes as distractions.

The first squirrel hit Luke dead center with his spear. It snapped with a resounding crack after puncturing his armor and digging a gouge into his chest, and then Luke's hand snapped out to grab it. He jerked it into the way of the other squirrel, who had to abort its attack as it collided with its companion and they both slammed into the ground.

The third squirrel went for Zea, but she was quick and armed. Its spear went over her shoulder, and her knife sliced open its belly, causing it to cry out in pain. Luke grinned fiercely at the sight; his girl was a hell of a scrapper. She had things handled, so he focused on his own pair. They weren't just going to lie around the ground, tangled up.

For the moment though they were. And that was just the perfect opportunity to end this quickly. **[Power Strike]** slammed down on them so hard that the squirrel on top was actually ripped in two, and the one below it was pulverized. A quick two-note ding sounded, and he turned to help Zea.

His help wasn't necessary. While it was true that he did most of the fighting, and that she tried to keep herself at range to snipe at monsters, that wasn't due to some lack of skill. The truth was that Luke's ability to recover from injuries was vastly superior to Zea's, and thus the risk of getting in the range of snapping claws or teeth was a lot lower for him.

It took her all of five seconds to put that mutant squirrel down. She was vicious about it too, stabbing it in the stomach twice, then driving her knee up into the wounds to send paralyzing waves of pain radiating out through its entire body before finally slitting its throat and kicking the corpse backward.

"Jesus," he muttered. "Remind me not to piss you off."

She flashed him a wicked grin and gestured toward his crotch with the bloody knife. "Just don't let me catch your eyes wandering."

"Oh, I don't know. These squirrels, the fur on them, it's so sexy, you know?"

Zea snorted and looked down at the corpse. "Damn, still no loot though. Unless you want the sticks?"

Their spears, such as they were, were about four feet long, straight shafts of wood that had actually been sanded smooth, with the ends ground down into tips and then hardened. All things considered, he supposed they weren't bad weapons, but there was no comparison to his own mace.

"I do not, no. Do you?"

"Not if I have to carry them. They're not worth anything."

"Leave them then. Let's get out of here before more of them show up. They're obviously aware of where we are, so I'd say our best bet is speed and distance. I don't know if it applies here, but squirrels are daytime animals where I'm from, and I'm worried that in an hour, the night shift is going to clock out and we're going to have ten times as many of them on our asses."

Zea gave the trees an uneasy glance, then gestured toward the roots still clinging to Luke's boot. "There's another one of those druids out there some-where. They didn't stick around to support their skirmishers though."

"Yeah, and they are probably going to try to fuck us over again, but I figure we're getting farther from the home tree with every step now. Maybe we'll get lucky and they'll leave us alone once they see that we're leaving their territory."

Zea snorted. "You ever been lucky?"

"Once or twice," he said with a smile. "Met this feisty little thing once who rocked my world."

"Not like that, you ass."

The smile faded away, and he sighed. "Yeah, I know. Nothing we can do but get going. I'll keep an eye out."

"Let me at least cut these off your foot first."

Soon enough, they were moving again. Half an hour later, he saw the sky starting to lighten up. By his best guess, they had a few miles of squirrel ter-ritory left to cross. "Things are going to get worse now," he said grimly. "Best be ready."

Name	Luke Bennet	Zea Stenter
Level	30	20
XP	93261/98832	27635/29492
AP	67	12
Bloodline	SysAdmin II	None
Strength	42	7
Agility	40	27
Stamina	36	27
Perception	39	19
Skills	Mace Mastery (3)	Dagger Mastery (1)
	Sword Mastery (1)	Stealth (2)
	Unarmed Martialist (4)	Keen Instincts (1)
	Power Strike (2)	Lock Picking (1)
	Life Surge (1)	Disguise (2)
	Peripheral Awareness (2)	Deception (1)
	Tactical Foresight (1)	Bartering (2)
	Counter (2)	Streetwise (2)
	Twitch Reflexes (2)	Cooking (1)
	Stealth (1)	Mending (1)
	Survivalist (2)	First Aid (1)
	First Aid (1)	Thalian (3)
	Wood Carving (1)	Neyardic (3)
	Leatherworking (2)	Ostari (1)
	Butchering (4)	Mana Manipulation (2)
	Thalian (2)	Mana Sight (1)
	Disguise (2)	Metallurgy (1)
	Deception (1)	Whitesmithing (1)
	Analyze (BL)	Goldsmithing (2)
	Remote Access (BL)	Gem Cutting (1)
		Engraving (2)
		Rune Forging (1)
		Painting (1)
		Arcano Dynamics (1)
		Sleight of Hand (1)
		Steady Hands (2)
		Cold Reading (1)
		Temperature Acclimation (2)
		Cadence (2)
		Bloodline Purification Ritual (1)

CHAPTER 26

In hindsight, altering their direction to run closer to the mountains probably wouldn't have actually helped that much. The squirrel folk seemed to keep an absolutely enormous amount of territory and almost certainly would have found them anyway. They would have delayed the initial contact but been that much farther from getting out the other end when the sun came up.

Luke might still have said it was worth it, except for one thing. The squirrel folk had no problem whatsoever following him and Zea well outside what he figured were the borders of their territory. They'd gone at least ten miles past the home tree and hadn't run into a squirrel of any variety in front of them in the last hour, but they'd been attacked three times by small groups of three to six pursuing squirrels.

Another strong indicator that they'd passed beyond the regular territory of the squirrel folk was that the underbrush had thinned out considerably, to the point where they were moving almost twice as fast now. Unfortunately for them, that was still not nearly as fast as the squirrels themselves, and Luke was concerned that the smaller scouting patrols who were chasing them down were soon going to turn into whole squadrons complete with supporting druids and archers to maximize their infantry's combat advantages.

"We don't have a lot of options," Zea said when he mentioned his thoughts to her. "We could stand our ground, but what does that accomplish? Even if we try to fortify an area, they've got magic users with builds designed to take advantage of this terrain. I can't picture anything we could make that they couldn't rip apart in a fraction of the time."

"Do you think a few fires might work as a distraction?"

"Might work. I don't think there's a strong chance of us getting caught up in it. It will definitely piss them off, maybe so much that they send more guys after us and chase us farther."

"Yeah," Luke agreed, a frown on his face. "On the other hand, they're kind of already chasing us past the ends of their territory as, like, I don't know, vengeance for fighting back and killing some people."

"I don't know shit about these squirrels. System, anything you can tell us?"

The apparition appeared between the two of them and ghosted along as they ran, simply passing through branches, bushes, and vines. "I can answer some questions about them as a whole but am not able to give specific information regarding any individual."

"Okay, how about why these fuckers are still chasing us. Any thoughts on that one?"

"I'm sorry. I'm not able to speculate on their motives."

Luke couldn't help it. He started laughing. Even with the upgraded bloodline, System was still borderline useless. The knowledge was there, but most of it was locked up, and trying to figure out which questions to ask to tease out even a hint of what he wanted to know was an exercise in frustration and futility.

"Are we outside their territory?" Zea asked, ignoring Luke.

"Based on your distance from the home tree, it appears so. However, there are several smaller satellite colonies that regularly communicate and trade with the home tree. You would need to move thirty-two miles directly north of here before you leave the range of the most distant colony."

"Shit," Luke and Zea said in unison.

"Is there a way to run a route that threads through these individual territories, or are they all overlapping?" Zea asked.

"There are some overlapping territories that you will not be able to go around, but if you were to plot a route that minimizes the time spent inside territories, you would need to travel eighty-three miles to reach the edge of the northernmost territory."

More than doubling their travel time was a bad idea, in Luke's mind. The squirrel folk were just too expansive to avoid, which meant punching through was going to be the fastest and most efficient course of action. If there were that many of them still in front of him, he didn't think his setting-shit-on-fire plan was viable either. There would be more than enough squirrels to fight a forest fire and chase them down.

"I don't think there's anything we can do besides run as fast as we can," Luke said. "There's just too many to try to fight back. Eventually we'll get far enough away that they'll leave us alone."

"Or if they don't, it won't matter," Zea replied. "My biggest concern is what happens when twenty or thirty of them jump us at once."

As weak as they were individually, Luke was more concerned about keeping them off Zea than his own safety. "As long as the forest doesn't get bad like it did near their giant tree, I think we can clear that thirty-two miles in about two hours. I say we just keep going."

Zea grimaced but nodded. She was breathing hard now, which Luke couldn't blame her for. Even with high stamina, it had been a grueling run through enemy territory that had lasted for hours. He was tired in a way he hadn't been since having to fight off all those poisons Myla had tagged him with.

At least he hadn't needed to use **[Life Surge]** yet. All things considered, if it came down to it and that was what he needed to finish a fight, he figured they were basically dead anyway. Pulling the trigger on that skill was more of an act of final revenge against whatever enemy happened to be in front of him than a tactic that would lead them to any sort of victory.

Despite the sun being fully in the eastern sky now, visible over the peaks of the mountains and everything, they made it almost an hour before they encountered another group of squirrels. Even better, this group didn't have any of the bipedal ones with thumbs and weapons in it. On the other hand, there were eight of them, which made things quite hectic for about six seconds.

Luke laid into them left and right, every blow smiting another one. He killed three of them before the rest even hit the ground, and two more with a sweeping strike that caught them both in one move. Of the remaining three though, only one attacked him.

Zea was fast, and she had a rank in **[Dagger Mastery]** to give her some basic combat proficiency with that knife. She decapitated the first squirrel in the air, but then the second sank teeth into her leg, and she cried out in pain. Before Luke could cross the distance to help, she drove the knife down through its skull and pried it off of her.

"Shit," she swore. "That's going to slow me down. Here, you've got **[First Aid]**. See if you can tie this off for me. It's at an awkward spot."

Another thing high stamina was good for was preventing infection, which was the only reason Luke wasn't too worried about the state of the cloth he used to tie the wound. It would stop bleeding soon enough, and his shirt was already so tattered that it wasn't like he was going to miss three inches off the bottom.

There was enough length to go around her leg three times, and he tied it in a tight knot. "I'm sorry," he said softly. "I couldn't get them all."

"I didn't expect you to," she told him. "You know I can take care of myself. And honestly, this barely hurts. I'm sure it'll be healed up in an hour or two."

"The next hour or two is when we kind of need to be at our best," he said. "I should have seen them coming quicker than I did. I just don't get why they're so suicidal. I know they can feel how much XP I have, which probably isn't doing much to help keep us hidden, but normally monsters that are 15 levels below me don't charge in like that."

Some of them did, the particularly stupid and aggressive ones who were used to hitting above their levels thanks to their natural size, but squirrels were not predatory animals to begin with. The smart ones, he guessed he understood, but the normal squirrels were a different story. Well, normal-ish. They were still pretty big, but otherwise they looked normal.

His suspicion was that the druid squirrel folk had something to do with it. It seemed pretty likely to him at least, but he was going off some admittedly spotty memories of what kinds of abilities druids in games back on Earth had. There really wasn't anything to guarantee that things were the same here, even if he was remembering correctly.

Curt would have known right away. He'd have been able to list off a hundred different powers and skills druids in stories and games back home had, probably would even have already had names for all the abilities Luke had seen the druids use and theories about how those powers worked. Luke felt a sudden empty, hollow pain in his chest. It had been a while since he'd last thought about his brother like that.

Luke shook off those kinds of thoughts. He didn't have time to wallow in misery, not while they still had close to twenty miles to go. "You ready?" he asked Zea.

"Ready as I'm going to be. It's not like we have time to stand around."

It was slower going, but they picked their way through the brush, and as they got farther north, it got thinner and thinner. Another hour and one attack from two random squirrel folk armed with rocks of all things, and they'd reached the point where they could easily walk between trees without stumbling over any roots or getting snagged on branches or caught in vines.

"I think we're clear of them now," Luke said. "And if not, I would say we will be soon. How about we add a few more miles just to be sure, then we'll find somewhere we can defend to hole up in for a break?"

"Sounds good," Zea said, panting as she spoke.

Something thumped against the ground hard enough to shake the leaves off the trees overhead. Both of their gazes snapped to the south, where the sound had originated from. "The fuck was that?" Luke whispered. "Come on, let's go."

Whatever it was, it couldn't be good news for them. If they were quick and lucky enough, it would be an avoidable problem, and he was going to do everything in his power to make sure it stayed that way.

They hustled off, mostly with an eye on the ground to spot dips and holes hidden under a carpet of leaves and pine needles, occasionally broken by a jutting root or rock. Zea took the lead while Luke came up behind her, his attention split between following her and keeping an eye on the boughs behind them. If an attack came from any direction, it would be there.

Another thump shook the ground a few minutes later, this time to their left. The two exchanged glances and silently adjusted their course to angle off to the right. A minute later, there was a new thump, this time straight ahead of them.

"Okay, what the hell is that sound? Is it the squirrels?" Zea asked. "System, can you tell us anything?"

"You are well outside the established range of their territories, though not far enough away that they couldn't easily reach you," the apparition told them.

"Can you tell us anything useful?" she amended.

"On this subject? Perhaps. What would you like to know?"

"Forget it," Luke said, cutting the conversation off. "Look up ahead."

Through the tree line, he could see a clearing. In the middle of it, hundreds of feet away from any of the other trees, was a massive old oak. Even as he pointed at it, one of the oak's roots tore itself free of the ground, rose up in the air, and slammed down with a resounding thump. The tree dragged itself forward a few feet, and another root broke free. Soon enough, there were six roots working in concert to drag it forward.

The squirrels were literally waking up the forest around them.

Name	Luke Bennet	Zea Stenter
Level	30	20
XP	95785/98832	27782/29492
AP	67	12
Bloodline	SysAdmin II	None
Strength	42	7
Agility	40	27
Stamina	36	27
Perception	39	19
Skills	Mace Mastery (3)	Dagger Mastery (1)
	Sword Mastery (1)	Stealth (2)
	Unarmed Martialist (4)	Keen Instincts (1)
	Power Strike (2)	Lock Picking (1)
	Life Surge (1)	Disguise (2)
	Peripheral Awareness (2)	Deception (1)
	Tactical Foresight (1)	Bartering (2)
	Counter (2)	Streetwise (2)
	Twitch Reflexes (2)	Cooking (1)
	Stealth (1)	Mending (1)
	Survivalist (2)	First Aid (1)
	First Aid (1)	Thalian (3)
	Wood Carving (1)	Neyardic (3)
	Leatherworking (2)	Ostari (1)
	Butchering (4)	Mana Manipulation (2)
	Thalian (2)	Mana Sight (1)
	Disguise (2)	Metallurgy (1)
	Deception (1)	Whitesmithing (1)
	Analyze (BL)	Goldsmithing (2)
	Remote Access (BL)	Gem Cutting (1)
		Engraving (2)
		Rune Forging (1)
		Painting (1)
		Arcano Dynamics (1)
		Sleight of Hand (1)
		Steady Hands (2)
		Cold Reading (1)
		Temperature Acclimation (2)
		Cadence (2)
		Bloodline Purification Ritual (1)

CHAPTER 27

The tree wasn't moving very fast, perhaps only a foot or two every second. Occasionally, a huge root would break itself free, slam down into the earth, and drag the whole thing forward in a ten-foot jump. The whole process was so ludicrously slow that there was no way it could ever catch up to them.

Luke figured that was why they were waking a whole bunch up at once. The trees wouldn't even be able to move through the forest without being blocked by other trees, but if the squirrels woke up enough of them, they would effectively create a living wall that forced Luke and Zea to confront one or more in order to get by.

Every few seconds, he could hear another of the massive thumps echoing through the forest. "We've got to get past this line before they block us in completely," he said. "Or, I don't know . . . wake up the whole forest even. If they can even do that. System, there's a skill for waking up trees and making them move, right?"

"There is," System confirmed.

"How often can they do it? What does it cost them?"

"It is a ritual spell that takes twenty minutes to complete, though that time may be reduced by working with a partner or even in a group. It is a physically and mentally exhausting skill, not one to be used frivolously."

"Unless there's about a hundred druids working together," Luke said. "Then they could use it a whole bunch of times."

"This might work in our favor," Zea pointed out. "If the druids are wiping themselves out with this magic, they aren't going to be doing other things. As long as we can slip the noose on this trap, we'll actually be better off with fewer pursuers."

They weren't going to get away just by standing there and talking about it. The two of them circled wide around the oak tree, not even cutting across the clearing just in case there were squirrel folk hidden in its branches. Fighting something like that while the squirrels shot at them or tripped them up with more grasping roots or vines would be a nightmare.

Just to be safe, he tossed an **[Analyze]** at the tree as they skirted around it. He wasn't sure what exactly he was expecting, but it wasn't what he saw.

[Name: Enlightened Oak]
[Level: 1]
[Strength: 64]
[Agility: 9]
[Stamina: 140]
[Perception: 7]

It was a good thing they weren't planning on fighting it. He couldn't even figure out how exactly he was supposed to beat something with that kind of stamina. If his own regeneration rate scaled to something with 140 in the same stat, he expected damage to repair itself right before his eyes. And since trees drank through their roots and converted sunlight to energy, he didn't imagine it was going to run out of juice anytime soon.

They left the oak behind quickly, though not without another run-in with a troop of nine squirrels that tried to herd them back into the clearing. Herding tactics only worked if the target wasn't willing to go in for a direct confrontation though, so when the squirrels moved to block them, Luke just smashed right through.

If not for the system notifications, he wouldn't even have known how many he'd killed. "I got four of them," he said to Zea once they were through.

"Finished off two that you wounded before the rest broke and ran."

"So three left alive. They'll probably go running for reinforcements, but it's not like they've been having trouble finding us so far anyway."

"I'd say go faster," Zea said, ducking under a low hanging branch that Luke simply snapped off on his way through a moment later. "But . . ."

They were already going twice as fast as before. Even with Zea's leg injury, the forest opening up had enabled them to put on a burst of speed. "Do you want me to carry you?" Luke asked. He knew he could outrun Zea by a considerable margin, and she didn't weigh enough to slow him down. He'd avoided bringing up the subject out of respect, but things were getting kind of desperate now.

She scowled back at him and said, "It's not like I'm helpless. Am I really slowing you down that much?"

"Not that much," Luke lied. "But we could use any advantage we can get, right?"

He could see pride and practicality warring on her face. She knew he was right, and it irked her. He was probably also violating some sort of cultural taboo, like that thing with the rock throwing, but he was sure she'd forgive him for it.

"Fine," she said, reluctantly. Luke shrugged off his pack and handed it to her, then turned in place so she could jump up onto his back.

"Not even going to carry me in a princess hold?" she demanded, pretending to be offended. At least, he hoped she was pretending.

"Need to keep my arms free in case something attacks us," he said.

"Likely excuse."

Zea took a moment to adjust the multiple packs, then leaped up and threw her arms around Luke's neck. Her feet dangled down by his knees for a moment before her legs wrapped around his waist. "This was not the kind of ride on you I had in mind last night," she whispered into his ear.

"And you called me a hornball," he said back.

"You are."

"So are you."

Once Zea was securely holding on to him, Luke took off running. There was no more being gentle on the local flora, no more trying to wind around and find the best way through. He put his head down to protect his face and gave himself over to a primal urge to just *move*. Branches shattered, and bushes that tried to snag him were torn out by the roots. Luke took great, bounding strides at full speed, weaving through trees with a reckless disregard for his own well-being.

They left a trail of destruction behind them, but getting distance from those moving trees trumped being careful. They quickly left the oak tree behind, and within twenty minutes, System had confirmed for him that they were outside the farthest reaches of squirrel territory. It only remained to see if the squirrels would follow them out and, if not, what kind of monsters lived on their northern border.

The forest thinned back to normal after a few more miles, and Luke let Zea down. "I think we need to take a food break," he said. "And I need to use **[Life Surge]** to patch myself back up."

He was covered in scrapes and cuts from tearing through the forest, and one of his knees was starting to swell up from being smacked against a tree when he stumbled over a hole, then continued running for a few more miles. Nothing was really that serious by itself, but there were an awful lot of small injuries.

"We'll need to slow down to forage soon," Zea told him. She held open the food bag for him to look, revealing it was close to empty. "That's one good recovery meal there, or maybe three regular ones."

It was actually worse than that. She hadn't included herself in that calculation. If Luke popped **[Life Surge]**, he'd go through all the food in the next few minutes. Otherwise they had less than a day's worth of food between the two of them. That wasn't all that unusual a state of affairs, to be honest. Their diet consisted of a lot of meat harvested from monstrous animals, but without spending enough time in one place to preserve that meat in some way, most of it got left behind.

Considering that the wilds of Aros were rife with animals intent on eating him, Luke didn't worry too much about finding his next meal normally. The only reason he cared now was that he still wanted to get as far away from the squirrels as possible.

"I'll heal up and eat it now, and we can keep going until this evening. Once we've got forty or fifty miles between us and them, we can find a safe place to sleep, and I'll spend some time foraging before we get moving again."

He triggered the skill and let out a relieved sigh as all the little injuries that covered him melted away. A surge of energy swept through him, and all of a sudden the thought of laying a beatdown on a tree did not seem so far-fetched. Luke was too used to the side effects of **[Life Surge]** to run off and do something stupid, especially since he only had about thirty seconds before it ran out.

He steadied his shaking hands, took the bag of food, and started eating it raw. That was fine for some of the stuff they'd found, but most of it really did not taste good if it wasn't cooked. That was a price he was willing to pay though. After an all-night marathon run that had ended in a mad sprint while carrying about a hundred pounds of Zea and gear, he'd been hungry even before healing himself.

The one thing he felt bad about was that he completely emptied the bag and Zea didn't get a single bite. He would find some way to make that up to her, and soon. It wouldn't be by cooking dinner though, not unless he caved and spent the AP on the skill. Since he was still stubbornly refusing to do so, despite no evidence at all that he was anywhere close to learning it the hard way, he would have to find some other way to help.

They walked while he ate, though the pace he set was harsh enough that Zea more jogged than walked to keep up with him. Hours went by with no pursuit, and they finally started to relax just after noon. "I think it's time to find a place we can hole up in," Zea told him.

This wasn't a new process for them. Ideally, they'd find some sort of unoccupied shallow cave to camp out in. More realistically, they often ended up sleeping inside a stand of trees grown close enough together to form a sort of wall. Rarely, they slept in the branches themselves if they were worried about monsters. Given that their primary concern for the last day was squirrel folk, neither of them felt like that last option offered much in the way of protection.

Luck was with them though. Or maybe it was just simple pattern recognition. They were still close enough to the mountains that finding random caves wasn't that hard, and it only took them about an hour of travel to stumble across one that suited their needs perfectly. It was thirty feet deep before it made a sharp bend to the left and went another fifty feet in pitch blackness, which was just fine by Luke.

Zea remained there to rest, and Luke went back out to forage firewood and food. If something furry with four legs and a lot of meat on its flank just happened to come across him, well, he wouldn't complain about that. Otherwise he'd scour the area for berries, nuts, and roots.

His luck held, and Luke quickly filled half the pack with various forest edibles. He even found a bunch of mushrooms, but **[Survivalist]** couldn't help him identify what they were. Wary of poisoning himself, he left them untouched. In all likelihood, even if they were poisonous, his stamina would have kept him safe, but it seemed like a pointless risk to take.

Luke dropped off the food and started his second loop to look for firewood. He'd gathered a decent amount of deadwood to use as starter and was eyeing up a fallen tree he'd stumbled across to hack up for good, thick logs, when he noticed the first squirrel.

"Maybe it's a coincidence," he told himself. It was sitting a few hundred feet back, halfway up a tree, watching him. That wasn't that unusual. Squirrels were prey animals for a lot of things living in the forest. If they hadn't just spent hours crossing an area of the forest that was controlled by sapient squirrel-human hybrids, he probably would have dismissed it without a second thought.

It was better to be safe than sorry, so he deposited his bundle of sticks by the fallen tree, drew his mace off his back, and started toward the squirrel. He quickly spotted three more of them on other trees, and then as he got close, he felt the XP coming off something much stronger, mid-20s at least.

"Crap," he swore. It figured they weren't getting away that easily.

Name	Luke Bennet	Zea Stenter
Level	30	20
XP	96491/98832	28039/29492
AP	67	12
Bloodline	SysAdmin II	None
Strength	42	7
Agility	40	27
Stamina	36	27
Perception	39	19
Skills	Mace Mastery (3)	Dagger Mastery (1)
	Sword Mastery (1)	Stealth (2)
	Unarmed Martialist (4)	Keen Instincts (1)
	Power Strike (2)	Lock Picking (1)
	Life Surge (1)	Disguise (2)
	Peripheral Awareness (2)	Deception (1)
	Tactical Foresight (1)	Bartering (2)
	Counter (2)	Streetwise (2)
	Twitch Reflexes (2)	Cooking (1)
	Stealth (1)	Mending (1)
	Survivalist (2)	First Aid (1)
	First Aid (1)	Thalian (3)
	Wood Carving (1)	Neyardic (3)
	Leatherworking (2)	Ostari (1)
	Butchering (4)	Mana Manipulation (2)
	Thalian (2)	Mana Sight (1)
	Disguise (2)	Metallurgy (1)
	Deception (1)	Whitesmithing (1)
	Analyze (BL)	Goldsmithing (2)
	Remote Access (BL)	Gem Cutting (1)
		Engraving (2)
		Rune Forging (1)
		Painting (1)
		Arcano Dynamics (1)
		Sleight of Hand (1)
		Steady Hands (2)
		Cold Reading (1)
		Temperature Acclimation (2)
		Cadence (2)
		Bloodline Purification Ritual (1)

CHAPTER 28

At first, he had a hard time picking the thing out of the background, but eventually it stepped away from the trees. It was shaped like a man but eight feet tall. Long, spindly arms made great, ponderous swings with each step it took. If Luke had to describe it, he would have said it was a skeleton made of sticks, packed with dirt to give it mass and bound together in a layer of vines.

He would put it at level 26 at best, based on the XP he could feel from it. Assuming it didn't have any abilities to hide its strength, Luke thought he could take it. He was level 30, but he was also sitting on two levels of AP that he'd been saving for rank 2 **[Life Surge]**. Effectively, that brought him down to 28 and made the fight a lot closer.

Fortunately, he no longer needed to make judgment calls like that. A simple use of **[Analyze]** gave him plenty of information to gauge how threatening the stick monster was.

[Name: Lesser Guardian of Nature]
[Level: 26]
[Strength: 31]
[Agility: 22]
[Stamina: 50]
[Perception: 8]

He was pleased to see he'd been dead-on with his guess at its level, and also to know that he was stronger and faster. Less pleasing was that monstrous amount of stamina, especially considering how it looked like it would break apart under his own weight. But as long as it didn't have any weird tricks, he was confident he could beat it.

What he wasn't confident about was the idea that he'd fight it one-on-one. More squirrels were showing up, and even though they were all the normal kind so far, that stick monster just screamed druid. He'd bet his hat there was at least one around. At least, he would if he still owned a hat.

Ideally, he'd put down the stick monster quickly, before any of the squirrels got a chance to reinforce it. 50 stamina told him that wasn't likely to happen. With its agility so much lower than his, Luke thought he might just end up running around fighting squirrels while the damn thing chased him.

The lesser guardian of nature staggered forward, its movements somehow awkward and jerky despite its high agility. Each step flung it at Luke, its ground-eating stride at odds with its preposterous movements. He watched it approach and idly wondered what a greater guardian would look like. If he was lucky, he'd never have to find out.

One part of him wanted to rush forward and meet the stick monster's charge, but he'd gained a ton of experience in the fine art of beating shit to a pulp over the last few months, and with **[Tactical Foresight]** working overtime in the back of his brain, he recognized this as his chance to gain useful information about how it moved before the dangerous part started.

It seemed like it should fall over with each step, but it didn't. That had to be a function of its strength and agility holding it upright despite how uncoordinated it was, which was a bit of a brain buster. How could something have both high agility and move like that?

Despite its clumsy, lurching gait, the stick monster closed the gap within seconds of appearing. Luke ducked under its approximation of a hand, which resembled nothing so much as a bundle of twigs that had been dropped in the mud and rolled around a bit. He wasn't fooled by its fragile appearance. With a strength of 31 behind that swing, it could rend through brick easily.

Luke swung his mace at its hip. He was hoping to tear the leg clean off, but he wasn't expecting it. More likely, he'd just knock it down and it would remain in one piece. Either way, it was going to be the start of his plan to lead it on a merry chase while he dealt with all the squirrels that were, for the moment, still spectating.

The mace cracked into the mud-filled stick framework as planned, and then things went wrong. It didn't break anything, didn't even budge the monster. Instead, it skipped off the mud, not even tearing a furrow through it, and left Luke open for a counterattack.

[Twitch Reflexes], **[Unarmed Martialist]**, and **[Tactical Foresight]** all started screaming at the same time, warning him to get away. The skills guided his feet into a pivot that turned into a roll as he dove clear of the monster just in time to avoid its rising leg and descending arm. Both attacks missed him by a hair, if that. They were far too fast for its supposed agility, and Luke quickly backed out of its range as it pursued him.

"Something fucky's going on with you," he told the monster. It was far faster than its agility said it should be, and he suspected it was more durable than it should be as well. He had known going in that he'd have to work to lay the hurt down on the stick monster, but his attack shouldn't have just bounced off of it like that.

It wasn't hard to think of a likely culprit. He'd already seen plenty of evidence of skills that could debuff enemies, and it seemed like someone the system labeled as a druid might very well have some skills or spells that went the other direction. Zea would probably know, and System could definitely tell him, but he didn't have the time to ask right now, not with the monster in pursuit.

The only thing going right so far was that the squirrels hadn't made a move to do anything other than observe. Then again, it wasn't like they needed to. Luke had lost the first round, by his estimate. He'd scored the only hit, but it hadn't been strong enough to do any damage. **[Power Strike]** might be able to overcome that thing's defenses, but he doubted he could chain enough of them to kill it before he was completely exhausted himself.

Worst case, there was always the fallback option of spending his AP midfight. No matter how tough that thing was, he was pretty sure if he buffed his strength up 30 points, that monster would feel it when he smacked it around. That wasn't what he was supposed to be using that AP for though.

The monster came back in, arms flailing wildly while Luke dodged around it. Every now and then, he parried an attack, just to test the monster's strength. It certainly didn't seem stronger than him at least. Perhaps he'd misjudged how effective its stamina was at warding off damage, or he'd managed to choose some random point where its defenses were reinforced by some sort of skill.

There was only one way to find out. He could probably smack it on its face, such as it was, without jumping, but only if he went for a one-handed overhead swing. That wasn't conducive to channeling the strength of his whole body into the attack, so Luke opted to slip under its clubbing arm attacks, take a step past, and then turn his pivot into a full-body, **[Power Strike]**–reinforced swing.

The mace cracked into the monster's back and hurled it face forward into the ground. At the same time, there was an explosion of wood in the forest beyond the squirrels, and Luke's weapon was flung up and back so hard that he actually left the ground to keep his hands on it. The lesser guardian was somehow unharmed and already rolling over with its long, gangly limbs sticking out at weird angles.

It was back on its feet before Luke could recover and rushed in with a single bounding step to drive its twig hand directly into his chest. Pain flared through him, and he thought he felt his sternum crack as he was flung backward.

"Definitely fucky," he wheezed, skidding to a stop twenty feet away. The squirrels still hadn't moved, and he was beginning to suspect that wasn't because they were enjoying the show. He'd hit the stick monster as hard as he could, and it wasn't even a little bit injured. But it sure as fuck sounded like a Goddamn tree had exploded a few hundred yards in the forest, possibly with about as much force as a man with 42 strength enhanced by a skill could deliver in a single stroke.

And if that were the case, that would mean the squirrels were there to keep him out of the forest, which meant he was playing a sucker's game standing around fighting their monster. The only way he was winning this fight was to figure out what bullshit they'd cooked up behind enemy lines and break it.

Luke turned his back on the stick monster and sprinted for the tree line. The squirrels reacted immediately, all of them boiling out of the woods in numbers far greater than he'd seen and moving to intercept him. That was fine. There were only a hundred of them, no big deal.

The front line of the squirrel wave met him while the lesser guardian of nature chased after, and Luke's answer to that was simple. He jumped as high and as far as his stats would let him go, which turned out to be about twenty feet into the air and fifty feet forward before he crashed into the trees.

"Wooooo!" he screamed in exhilaration. "Holy shit, that was awesome!"

He'd have to do that again when he had more room and fewer monsters wanting to kill him nearby. For now, he had something else to take care of. The trailing squirrels hadn't quite made it out of the trees before he arrived, and they instantly changed direction to attack him.

They didn't stand a chance individually, and he was fast enough to kill them as they closed in. It honestly might have been easier without the mace and just relying on **[Unarmed Martialist]** to move his body against them. He certainly didn't need the weapon when a single blow would kill any of his opponents.

But he was already holding it, so he might as well put it to good use. They died by the dozens in the first three seconds, most of them never even reaching him. Luke heard so many damn dings in his head that it started to drown out everything else, which was a bit of a problem since he was specifically listening for them coming at him from behind. **[Peripheral Awareness]** only did so much to keep them off his back, after all.

The back edge of the squirrel swarm crashed into him, and that's when things started to hurt. When they were all coming from more or less the same direction, he'd done a damn good job of crushing them. Once they started attacking from multiple angles, that got a lot harder, but he'd at least kept himself clean even if his kill rate had slowed down.

After they surrounded him completely, that became impossible. He had them hanging off his arms, his back, even one stubbornly clutching his hair, and all of them attempting to scratch, claw, or bite him to death. For the most part, their efforts were painful but not debilitating. His stamina was just too high for them to casually chew through his skin.

What they could do, and did, was keep him pinned down long enough for the stick monster to catch up. It burst through the tree line in a shower of exploding splinters and squirrels as it stormed through its own allies to reach Luke.

The squirrel folk had set their trap well, as long as they didn't care how many of their brethren they sacrificed to keep him pinned in place. He couldn't kill their monster with whatever magic they were using on it, and he couldn't get away from it with all the smaller squirrels throwing themselves into the wood chipper to slow him down.

It looked like he was going to need to use his backup plan after all.

Name	Luke Bennet	Zea Stenter
Level	30	20
XP	98200/98832	28039/29492
AP	67	12
Bloodline	SysAdmin II	None
Strength	42	7
Agility	40	27
Stamina	36	27
Perception	39	19
Skills	Mace Mastery (3)	Dagger Mastery (1)
	Sword Mastery (1)	Stealth (2)
	Unarmed Martialist (4)	Keen Instincts (1)
	Power Strike (2)	Lock Picking (1)
	Life Surge (1)	Disguise (2)
	Peripheral Awareness (2)	Deception (1)
	Tactical Foresight (1)	Bartering (2)
	Counter (2)	Streetwise (2)
	Twitch Reflexes (2)	Cooking (1)
	Stealth (1)	Mending (1)
	Survivalist (2)	First Aid (1)
	First Aid (1)	Thalian (3)
	Wood Carving (1)	Neyardic (3)
	Leatherworking (2)	Ostari (1)
	Butchering (4)	Mana Manipulation (2)
	Thalian (2)	Mana Sight (1)
	Disguise (2)	Metallurgy (1)
	Deception (1)	Whitesmithing (1)
	Analyze (BL)	Goldsmithing (2)
	Remote Access (BL)	Gem Cutting (1)
		Engraving (2)
		Rune Forging (1)
		Painting (1)
		Arcano Dynamics (1)
		Sleight of Hand (1)
		Steady Hands (2)
		Cold Reading (1)
		Temperature Acclimation (2)
		Cadence (2)
		Bloodline Purification Ritual (1)

CHAPTER 29

The lesser guardian of nature crashed through the squirrels, uncaring of the damage it did to them in its rush to reach Luke. The squirrels themselves dodged out of its way, an action that reduced the death toll from dozens to a mere four or five in the second it took for the two to collide.

Luke parried its initial punch with a **[Power Strike]**, which did nothing more than throw the stick monster's arm out wide and cause another cracking explosion of woods in the trees behind them. The monster barely even reacted to having its attack blocked. Its movements were so uncoordinated and jerky that, by all rights, it should have fallen to the ground when he threw it off-balance, but it just spun in place, bringing its other arm up to swipe at his head as it rotated.

His attempted dodge turned into a stumble as no fewer than four different squirrels latched on to his leg. The stick arm swished over his head at least, but instead of a smooth retreat, Luke found himself dropping to one knee and using his free hand to rip the furry little bastards loose. Shreds of cloth went with them, and he was once again annoyed that he hadn't managed to obtain a spare set of clothes before they'd left civilization behind.

In the interest of being as destructive as possible, Luke hurled the squirrels at the stick monster as he tore them free. It made no effort to defend itself, but he threw the squirrels hard enough that three of them splattered against its vine-and-mud skin, dyeing it with streaks of red. The fourth managed to somehow twist in the air and barely avoided impact, a feat Luke considered extremely impressive given the speed he was throwing and the fact that the distance was barely three feet.

Of course, that didn't help it. It just meant that the squirrel died on impact with the tree behind the stick monster. There was even a ding in his head that confirmed it.

Despite that, hundreds more squirrels were converging on the two of them, with a primary focus on clinging to Luke and slowing him down as much as possible. Whatever those druids had cooked up, they really did not want him getting close to it. Once again, Luke found himself unreasonably annoyed that there were no good skills available for use with a mace that would let him attack multiple opponents at once.

Luke had done the math days before they'd encountered the first squirrel. He knew he needed to reach level 32 to have the 100 AP needed to rank up **[Life Surge]**. He also knew he'd have 30 AP left over, which he'd initially planned on using to purchase **[XP Mask]**. At the moment though, he needed a boost to his agility and stamina if he wanted to get to those druids and ruin their day.

Luke dumped 15 AP into each stat, bringing his agility up to 55 and his stamina to 51. Flush with new reserves of energy and suddenly able to move at beyond-inhuman speed, Luke darted under another clumsy swing and started batting new squirrels away as they charged in. He lashed out with kicks and punches, elbows and knees, and in one case even an appropriately timed head-butt to batter squirrels away.

With his stats as high as they were, and with skills like **[Unarmed Martialist]** guiding him, low-level squirrels that never made it past level 13 had no chance of surviving even a single attack. The dinging notifications in his head were chiming on top of one another so fast it sounded like he'd hit a jackpot in some sort of video game, and he was willing to bet one of those dings was to let him know that he'd reached level 31.

The lesser guardian of nature was having a harder time keeping up with him as he dodged through the trees now. The squirrels were slowing him down, no doubt, and the little bastards still had sharp teeth, but the extra 13 stamina made it almost impossible for them to break skin, and in the few instances some of the higher-level ones managed it, he healed back up almost instantly. All the while Luke moved, he kept killing them, determined that if they wanted to come at him in waves, he'd happily reap the experience.

Sooner or later this damn forest would run out of squirrels, or they'd get smart enough to back off. He certainly wasn't going to get tired any time soon. At the rate he was going, he was going to level up again before they learned their lesson.

The deeper he got into the woods, the more frantic the squirrels got. He was slowly leaving the stick monster behind, but a single mistake would let it close the distance again. Its body was too similar in appearance to the woods around it, and there were too many trees for it to hide behind. He spotted it occasionally, more from keeping track of its location by sound telling him where to look than because it was easy to see, and each time, it was farther back.

Luke didn't trust that at all. If there was anything that should have been moving through the woods faster than him, it was a monster named lesser fucking guardian of nature. He kept expecting it to jump out of a damn tree and try to take his head off, but it never did.

What did end up jumping out at him was bad enough. No less than five squirrel folk armed with primitive spears and stone knives appeared in the branches above him, no doubt intent on ambushing him. Their levels were too high though, at least four or five higher than the toughest of the regular squirrels. He easily picked their XP up through the background noise, and when the first one lunged at him, heading straight down from overhead with spear leading, Luke was ready for it.

He imbued a **[Power Strike]** into his attack, which took the form of a horizontal swipe after he'd stepped clear of its path. The blow killed the squirrel folk instantly and hurled its corpse into a mass of squirrels still charging at him. Its sacrifice was not in vain though, since it opened Luke up to attacks from its fellows.

A spear stabbed into Luke's stomach, eliciting a grunt of pain from him. He would have pulled it back out, but he was distracted at that moment by a second squirrel folk with a pair of knives that was leaping at his face. The one with the spear in his guts gave it a twist and shake, but its arms lacked the strength to drag Luke down to the ground like it was probably hoping.

Stupid of it, really. All it managed to do was piss him off and bump itself up to the top of his priority list. He even took a new spear in the back when he turned to deal with it, which in his opinion was totally worth it. Another spear grazed his cheek as he spun back, deep in the thrall of **[Twitch Reflexes]** and **[Tactical Foresight]**. There was no way he was coming out of this storm of violence without some injuries, but he was working hard to minimize them and keep them in nonvital areas.

The gut spear was not what he'd call nonvital, so he jerked it free and jabbed the blunt end into the squirrel who'd stabbed him with it. It went flying backward and skidded through some leaves before getting tangled up in some sort of thorn-covered bush. It wasn't dead, but it was out of the fight for a few moments.

How the squirrel folk could even see vital spots to aim at them was a bit of a mystery, since he had at least ten smaller squirrels hanging off his clothes, all of them doing their best to throw off his balance and claw their way through his skin. The squirrel folk were all vicious little bastards though, apparently uncaring of injuring or killing their more common cousins.

And then the worst happened. The distraction, because of course that's all it was, worked, and the stick monster burst through the underbrush. There was no hesitation in that thing, not one single bit. It completely ignored every other monster there to charge Luke, who had no choice but to abandon his defenses against the remaining squirrel folk to handle it.

His mace swung up in an underhand smack charged with [Power Strike] that landed right where the stick monster's balls would have been if, it had any. The goal wasn't to hurt it though, just to throw it straight up and over him where it would, hopefully, land on a few of the squirrel folk and kill them for him. Luke didn't stand around to find out, mostly because the attack had revealed something else to him.

Just like his previous big hits on the stick monster, there was an explosive crack of a tree shattering in the woods. Unlike the previous times, it was barely thirty feet away. Luke even saw the tree blow apart, and more importantly, he saw a squirrel folk tumble out of its branches as it crashed to the ground.

He darted through the brush and reached the scene in seconds. Maybe it was a druid; he honestly couldn't tell just by looking. It wasn't like they wore signs around their necks. Either way, he didn't have the time to throw an [Analyze] on it, not when it was just as fast to crush the damn thing's skull.

A ding sounded to prove to him that the squirrel folk was dead, but Luke didn't stop there. Where there was one squirrel, there were more. The fact that despite all his efforts to rid himself of them, there were still a handful of squirrels clinging to his back proved that. More than once, one of them had managed to crawl up to the back of his head and tear at his hair.

Stamina had, fortunately, reinforced that as well as the rest of his body, so while the tugging was painful, he wasn't going to end up with bald patches all over when this was over. Hopefully. He supposed he could shave his head if he needed. Luke blinked and shook away those thoughts. He still had a stick monster to kill, and unless he was mistaken, there were more druids standing between him and that goal.

More squirrel folk burst out of the woods to attack him, followed quickly by the stick monster. If his life hadn't been in danger, Luke would have laughed at the absurdity of the thing. It was like being stuck in a horror movie, where he was getting chased by something that he constantly escaped, but it just showed back up again a minute later. It was invulnerable, and no matter what he did, he couldn't get away.

This wasn't a horror movie though, not by a long shot. If he had to waste another [Power Strike] to find the next tree that had been magicked up to take a shot for him, that's what he'd do. It'd lead him to another druid, and sooner or later, they'd run out. While he had a second though, there were some squirrel folk that needed to die. They were a far better distraction than the squirrels, too good.

Luke led them on a chase as they closed in, more to keep some space between him and the stick monster and killed them when he could. It still caught up eventually, but he'd planned for that. He hit it again, listened for the echo of the tree the damage had been transferred to, and slipped off to hunt another druid down.

He found it quickly enough and killed it with a grin on his face. He was going to win this, one way or another. There were still plenty of backup AP if he needed it, but he didn't think he was going to. The stick monster caught up, and he repeated his tactic on it. Only this time, it didn't absorb the damage. Instead, Luke tore one of its arms off at the elbow.

"Ah, only two then? Their mistake," he told the monster.

Name	Luke Bennet	Zea Stenter
Level	31	20
XP	106820/109073	28039/29492
AP	68	12
Bloodline	SysAdmin II	None
Strength	42	7
Agility	55	27
Stamina	51	27
Perception	39	19
Skills	Mace Mastery (3)	Dagger Mastery (1)
	Sword Mastery (1)	Stealth (2)
	Unarmed Martialist (4)	Keen Instincts (1)
	Power Strike (2)	Lock Picking (1)
	Life Surge (1)	Disguise (2)
	Peripheral Awareness (2)	Deception (1)
	Tactical Foresight (1)	Bartering (2)
	Counter (2)	Streetwise (2)
	Twitch Reflexes (3)	Cooking (1)
	Stealth (1)	Mending (1)
	Survivalist (2)	First Aid (1)
	First Aid (1)	Thalian (3)
	Wood Carving (1)	Neyardic (3)
	Leatherworking (2)	Ostari (1)
	Butchering (4)	Mana Manipulation (2)
	Thalian (2)	Mana Sight (1)
	Disguise (2)	Metallurgy (1)
	Deception (1)	Whitesmithing (1)
	Analyze (BL)	Goldsmithing (2)
	Remote Access (BL)	Gem Cutting (1)
		Engraving (2)
		Rune Forging (1)
		Painting (1)
		Arcano Dynamics (1)
		Sleight of Hand (1)
		Steady Hands (2)
		Cold Reading (1)
		Temperature Acclimation (2)
		Cadence (2)
		Bloodline Purification Ritual (1)

CHAPTER 30

The lesser guardian's snapped-off arm regrew before Luke's eyes, a process that took a second at most. High stamina wouldn't account for that, so he was guessing it was some weird skill the monster had. He just hadn't seen it earlier because the squirrel folk were shielding it from harm.

Luke was confident he could overcome that regeneration, either through a thorough and extended beatdown or by finding just the right spot to pummel. Before that could happen, he needed to get rid of the rest of the weaklings. There were still a hundred or more squirrels eagerly throwing themselves at him, completely heedless of all forms of danger from friend and foe alike. More of those squirrel folk had shown up too, probably ten or fifteen at least. It was hard to tell with them hiding in the trees.

There was always the possibility of more druids arriving to fuck things up, but Luke figured he was probably past the point of them helping the stick monster. That didn't mean they couldn't pelt him with exploding acorns or make the trees come to life, so he decided to move the fight back out into the clearing where there'd be less for them to work with. The cover provided by fighting in the woods was helping his enemies more than him anyway.

The fight turned back into a running battle, with him doing his best to put distance between himself and the stick monster while he killed off the various flavors of hostile squirrel as quickly as possible, and the monster somehow passing through the underbrush like it wasn't even there. Seriously, nothing that clumsy had any right to move through the forest that easily. He was almost certain he'd seen an arm literally phase through the loop of a low-hanging vine without disturbing it.

Druid magic was such bullshit.

More squirrels died, sometimes when he palmed them by their heads and squeezed, sometimes when he snatched them by a tail or leg and threw them into trees. Every now and then, he managed to stomp on one or give it a good kick while it was coming in, but the squirrel folk were watching for the openings those breaks in his footwork gave them.

They were smart enough to hang back too, and ruthless enough to continue letting their smaller cousins sacrifice themselves. At the rate they were going, there wouldn't be a squirrel alive anywhere within a hundred miles of Luke. If he wasn't so pissed about how rabid they all were, he'd have laughed about it.

One good thing he had going for him was the stamina boost. Luke was not even a little bit tired, not even after all the times he'd dropped a **[Power Strike]** already. If anything, between that and the extra AP invested into agility, he was going even harder now. The whole fight really put into perspective why everyone was so afraid of someone hitting level 50 and just snapping.

This fight was something like five hundred on one, and as far as Luke could tell, he was winning. A lot of the squirrels were under level 10, but some of them weren't. The worst part of it was, it hardly mattered if they were level 5 or level 20. Either way, he hit them once, and they died. Only the squirrel folk, all significantly smarter and for the most part keeping their distance, presented any challenge.

And the stick monster, of course, but Luke was saving that one for last. He wanted to fight it without any distractions, and until it was just the two of them left, he fully planned on keeping it chasing after him. Eventually the squirrels would all die, or they'd break and run. His money was on genocide. They obviously weren't behaving like normal animals, and it felt like a safe bet to blame that on their squirrel-folk handlers.

The numbers were thinning now. **[Twitch Reflexes]** was in top form, always keeping Luke moving as he dodged and darted, while **[Counter]** and **[Unarmed Martialist]** teamed up to take care of most of his killing needs. The only thing his skills weren't helping him with was slaughtering the squirrel folk who were still shadowing them.

He was getting close to the edge of the tree line now. They'd have no choice but to make a move if they wanted to keep their terrain advantage, and Luke was ready for them. The squirrel army was barely a trickle compared to the flood it had been, too few to really tie up his attention at this point. The bigger, smarter squirrels were either going to attack in the next few seconds, or they'd wait for the stick monster to catch up and try to mob him as a group.

Considering how casual it was about killing squirrels who got in its way, Luke thought it would be spectacularly stupid to fight side by side with the monster. But if a few of them got themselves killed without him having to put any effort into making it happen, he wasn't going to complain.

The squirrel folk didn't disappoint. A bare fifty feet from freedom, they attacked en masse. Luke quickly found that his earlier estimates had been woefully low, with more than twenty of them appearing to attack all at once. Luke had about four seconds before the lesser guardian of nature caught up to him, more than enough time to thin the numbers.

His mace lashed out, left and then right, while he spun and drove his foot into one of the squirrel folk's belly. More fell on him, spears leading. More landed behind him and attacked his legs, intent on tripping him up and bringing him to the ground. More attacked from the sides, knives held ready to slice into him. There were always more.

Luke exploded into a spin, his mace infused with a **[Power Strike]** that tore through seven different victims before he completed his rotation, only for him to spin a second time. Spears stuck out of him, in his arms, back, and chest, as the vicious bipedal rodents took the opportunity to make clean strikes at his back.

When Luke was done a second later, twelve squirrel folk were dead. He ripped the spears out of his body without a second thought, then kicked his way through the horde that were trying to keep him in the trees while throwing each spear one-handed. Some of them hit their marks; some missed. Luke didn't care.

By the time he broke through the trees and back into the open, the stick monster was less than ten feet away from him, and almost all the squirrel folk were dead or dying. The ones that remained stopped at the edge of the tree and threw baleful glares at him. None dared set foot into the clearing.

"I guess it's just you and me, big guy," Luke told the stick monster.

Its response was a lumbering tackle, really more of a body slam. Just going by the numbers, Luke should have been able to throw himself right back at the monster and win easily. There'd been a bit too much fuckery for his tastes in this fight already, however, and besides, there was no reason to do that when his agility massively outclassed his opponent's.

Luke dodged, quite nimble with all his various skills working in tandem to keep him out of harm's reach. Then he started hammering the stick monster as it stumbled past. Rapid-fire strikes landed on its back and arms as it turned to face him, each one tearing away chunks of mud and wood, only for it to regenerate a moment later. That didn't deter Luke; he'd expected something like that.

They went back and forth, the monster trying to smash him with flailing limbs while Luke used his superior speed and reach to stay out of range while he peppered it with a barrage of light blows. Every hit did damage, and that damage was instantly reverted. The stick monster made no effort to defend itself either, which Luke took to mean that he could wail on it all day without actually hurting it. He needed to figure out where it was actually vulnerable.

It didn't care about its limbs. Busting up an arm just meant it turned itself sideways to get maximum effect out of the other arm. Breaking off a leg caused it to balance in what looked like some sort of weird yoga pose for a moment while it regrew the missing limb. Even its head was left unprotected, as he discovered when he took a risky shot and decapitated it.

Well, if none of those spots did it, that just left its torso and its crotch. Once he started looking for it, Luke noticed that while the stick monster did nothing to protect itself from attacks that struck its limbs, it did always seem to twist in some random way that coincidentally protected its chest.

Getting a solid shot in was further complicated by the fact that the squirrel folk were not content to just sit back and watch. They wouldn't leave the trees, but that didn't stop them from hurling rocks or sticks at him. That didn't hurt so much as it was distracting, since **[Twitch Reflexes]** didn't differentiate between an arrow and a twig. That, combined with the occasional individual squirrel still heroically charging to its doom, added a level of difficultly Luke didn't need to be dealing with.

Thus far, he'd managed to avoid taking even a single hit from the lesser guardian of nature, if only because he didn't trust the numbers **[Analyze]** had given him. That had been the correct move when he was dealing with hundreds of other squirrels and at least two druids that were buffing the monster up. Now, it was on its own, and no matter where he hit it, he wasn't doing lasting damage.

Luke charged up a **[Power Strike]**, waited for the stick monster to lunge at him, then stepped in under the swinging arm and blasted the monster for all he was worth. He took a blow to his shoulder that was hard enough to drive him down to one knee, but not before he cracked the chest cavity of the monster wide-open.

There was something in there, a sort of seed bigger than his fist that glowed with green light and had a hundred little roots connected to it. Even as Luke watched, new sticks grew like ribs around it, and mud started pouring in to fill the gaps.

"I don't fucking think so," Luke snarled, reading another **[Power Strike]**. The stick monster couldn't react in time, apparently dazed from the first real hit to do it any damage, and when Luke hit it again, everything from its chest on up exploded. Wood shards, mud splatters, and shredded vines went in every direction, and the seed fell to the ground.

It immediately started sucking up new mud, but Luke scooped it up before it could rebuild anything. Then he shot the squirrels a look, gave them a nasty grin in response to their angry chittering, and tossed the seed up into the air.

Luke liked baseball. He'd played varsity in high school until his grades had forced them to drop him off the team. A light toss of a round, spherical object straight up five feet into the air followed by a two-handed swing of something roughly shaped like a baseball bat as it came back down was second nature to him.

The seed burst into a million pieces and shotgunned the tree line. Luke heard a ding in his mind, and he stared defiantly at the remaining squirrels, daring them to come closer. Instead, they vanished deeper into the forest, and soon he could no longer feel their XP. Even the smaller ones stopped coming.

For the first time in about twenty minutes, Luke was completely alone. The fight was over, and he was the last man standing.

Name	Luke Bennet	Zea Stenter
Level	32	20
XP	119396/120012	28039/29492
AP	100	12
Bloodline	SysAdmin II	None
Strength	42	7
Agility	55	27
Stamina	51	27
Perception	39	19
Skills	Mace Mastery (3)	Dagger Mastery (1)
	Sword Mastery (1)	Stealth (2)
	Unarmed Martialist (4)	Keen Instincts (1)
	Power Strike (2)	Lock Picking (1)
	Life Surge (1)	Disguise (2)
	Peripheral Awareness (2)	Deception (1)
	Tactical Foresight (1)	Bartering (2)
	Counter (2)	Streetwise (2)
	Twitch Reflexes (3)	Cooking (1)
	Stealth (1)	Mending (1)
	Survivalist (2)	First Aid (1)
	First Aid (1)	Thalian (3)
	Wood Carving (1)	Neyardic (3)
	Leatherworking (2)	Ostari (1)
	Butchering (4)	Mana Manipulation (2)
	Thalian (2)	Mana Sight (1)
	Disguise (2)	Metallurgy (1)
	Deception (1)	Whitesmithing (1)
	Analyze (BL)	Goldsmithing (2)
	Remote Access (BL)	Gem Cutting (1)
		Engraving (2)
		Rune Forging (1)
		Painting (1)
		Arcano Dynamics (1)
		Sleight of Hand (1)
		Steady Hands (2)
		Cold Reading (1)
		Temperature Acclimation (2)
		Cadence (2)
		Bloodline Purification Ritual (1)

CHAPTER 31

Once the fight was over and the adrenaline was wearing off, Luke started to feel all his injuries. He'd had a few dozen holes of various sizes poked, ripped, or torn in his body over the course of the fight, and what wasn't actively dripping blood was swollen, inflamed, or bruised.

Probably the worst of it was the gut wound from a squirrel-folk spear. It wasn't immediately fatal or anything, but now that the fight was done, it hurt like hell. If he hadn't had access to **[Life Surge]**, he would have been extremely worried about it. His barely used **[First Aid]** skill told him it was the most life-threatening of all his injuries, practically guaranteed to kill him from infection if nothing else.

Unfortunately for **[First Aid]**, Luke was fresh out of any sorts of medicinal plants or herbs, and he definitely didn't have any bandages. The leather armor he'd taken from those bandits was nothing more than tattered scraps at this point, and his clothes weren't much better. Worst of all, the harness he'd bought to hold his mace had not held up to the rigors of the fight. He kept it anyway, figuring he could repair it.

Luke skimmed through his notifications as he retrieved the bundle of firewood from where he'd stashed it. It was much harder to carry now that he had to add his mace to the pile, but somehow he managed. There were a lot of kill notifications, which he grouped together into one big lump.

[You have slain 262 creatures between levels 3 and 26. 22905 XP awarded.]

[Congratulations! You have reached level 31. 31 AP awarded for use.]

[Congratulations! Twitch Reflexes has reached rank 3. 1000 XP awarded.]

[Congratulations! You have reached level 32. 32 AP awarded for use.]

"Damn," he said with a whistle. That was nothing to scoff at, though he wasn't about to volunteer to do it all over again. He'd expected the levels and wasn't even really surprised that he'd gotten two. If anything, the surprise was that he'd killed so few creatures. It had certainly felt like three times that many. Perhaps he hadn't been as thorough about one-shotting a squirrel with each attack as he'd thought, or maybe the druids had been doing some sort of magic bullshit in the background early on.

Either way, he'd gotten a metric fuckton of XP from the fight and gotten a free rank-up that saved him 25 AP in the process. He wasn't going to complain about his gains and was in fact feeling pretty damn smug about the whole thing. He had just enough AP to buy rank 2 of **[Life Surge]** now, and if he was being honest, he needed a stronger version of it. He was only waiting until he got back to Zea just in case the side effects were worse than rank 1.

When he got back to the cave they'd set up camp in and found the corpses of four squirrels in front of it, Luke threw the firewood down, grabbed his mace, and raced inside. Images of her being buried in a wave of roiling fur while they bit and scratched her to death danced in his head.

He could still feel her XP inside, so he knew that his worst fears weren't true. But she could be injured, on the brink of death. The difference between her surviving and not might be measured in seconds. If that was the case, he needed to immediately buy the full suite of skills needed for magic and dump his AP into the most powerful healing spell he could afford.

Zea was sitting next to a backpack full of food, an annoyed expression on her face as she tried to clean herself up. Blood splatters covered one sleeve and were flecked across her chest and neck. Luke let out a relieved sigh and felt his stomach unclench. "You're alright," he said. "I saw the corpses and . . ."

"Yeah, I'm fine. No thanks to you," she muttered, not looking up from her attempts to clean herself up. "And where the hell have you been for the last half an—Holy shit!"

She finally glanced over and beheld Luke in all his ragged and bloody glory. He gave her a lopsided grin and said, "I had an adventure looking for firewood. If you could maybe do me a favor and pick up the firewood I dropped outside on my way in, I'm going to go ahead and buy the upgrade to **[Life Surge]** and use that. Guess we'll see how bad it kicks."

"Buy the upgrade? But you were two levels short half an hour ago . . ." Zea trailed off as she realized how much his XP had grown. "Gods save you, how many were there?"

"Two sixty-two," he said. "I'm probably going to need another big meal here."

"Are you sure you should use it again so close to last time?" she asked. Then she looked at him again and shook her head. "Better than what you've got going on now. Go ahead. I'll start getting stuff ready."

Luke took a deep breath and then dumped 100 AP into the rank-up. It was by far the most he'd ever spent in a single go, and it had damn well better be worth it. He supposed he was about to find out. Glancing over at Zea, he said, "Going to use it now."

[Life Surge], now rank 2, kicked on, and lightning surged through Luke. All traces of weariness disappeared from him as he jolted out of a slouch he hadn't even realized he'd been in. He could physically see the bruises on his flesh fading over seconds and feel the holes made by spears and knives scabbing over. As they did, several small pieces of wood were pushed out of the wounds and fell to the cave floor. An intense wave of itchiness rolled through him, then the scabs peeled loose on their own and fell to join the wood splinters.

"Holy hell," he whispered. Even the gut wound was closing up. It wouldn't heal completely before the skill ended, but it was a puckered scar now instead of a gaping wound. Even as he thought that, the thirty or so seconds **[Life Surge]** normally ran passed by. And still he didn't come down from it. Zea was watching him like a hawk, waiting for him to drop from post-skill-use exhaustion, but he was still brimming with energy.

"Wish I had this an hour ago," he told her. "That whole fight would have been a lot easier."

"It's still going?"

"Almost double the length of rank 1 now."

The scar on his stomach smoothed over, leaving nothing but healthy pink skin and a small hole in his happy trail. By the time the skill kicked off, a full two minutes after he'd activated it and four times longer than he'd expected it to run, he was free of even the slightest injury.

The first hunger pang hit him, but it wasn't any worse than usual. It actually might have been a little lighter, though he couldn't say for sure. What he didn't feel was the wave of exhaustion that normally accompanied the skill ending. If pressed, he thought he could continue fighting. That needed some experimentation to confirm, of course, but if he was right, **[Life Surge]** had just upgraded itself from trump card to opening play.

"Oh, I like this," he told her, flexing his hands open and closed. "Totally worth 100 AP."

"You need some food?" she asked.

Luke shrugged. "I could eat, I guess. Think I'd rather wait for dinner."

"Huh. Well, okay. I guess I'll get a fire going while you, uh . . . figure out a clothes situation."

"There's not much to figure out there," he said. "This stuff is pretty much beyond saving."

"What are you going to do, just walk around naked for the next month?"

"I thought I'd keep the shoes," he told her seriously. They had some holes forming at the soles, but they were better than nothing. The rest of it wasn't even in good enough shape to be called rags. "Maybe we can take a week or so to rest and I'll make something out of animal hides. Not here though—too close to the squirrels, and they could come back. As soon as we're done eating, I want to get moving again.

"Yeah . . . Maybe. I guess we'll have to see what we wander into next."

Luke shrugged. There was only so much they could do, and they needed to keep heading north. "System, I don't suppose you could tell us what's north of here and how far we need to go to reach civilization?"

"You are approximately two hundred fifty miles from the closest human settlement," System said. "The territory between your current location and the human town is mostly contested by various individual predatory animals or monsters. None are above level 30."

"What about nonhuman settlements?" Zea asked.

"Not counting the squirrel folk you just encountered, there is a tribe of otter-kin sixty miles northwest of your current location. You would need to deviate from your current route to find their village. The next closest settlement is a clan of goblins in the mountains ninety miles northeast of here."

"Fuck goblins," Luke said. "Not going near those guys again."

"I don't know anything about otter-kin either," Zea said, frowning. "Are they friendly?"

"I am not able to speculate on their motives," System told her.

"How strong are they?" Luke said.

"They fall between the range of level 1 for their pups to level 40 for their strongest champions."

Luke let out a low whistle. "If they're not happy to see us, that could ruin our day. Might be better to just skip it."

"So our options are to take a few days off so you can make pants, or just push as hard as possible to find a place you can buy pants?"

"Depending on how thick the forest gets, it might actually be faster to just make the run," Luke said. He was pretty sure he could do two hundred fifty miles in a single day even in the woods. For Zea, it might be closer to a week unless she let him help her.

Having no clothes wasn't the end of the world, if he was being honest. He didn't really get cold anymore, and while getting stabbed in the dick by a way-ward branch would suck, he wasn't really worried about it doing any damage. Thank God that insensitivity only applied to pain. Zea would not be happy with how high his stamina had jumped up otherwise.

"No matter how we look at it, we can't stay here," she said. "The squirrels know where we are, so getting out of here in the next hour is a priority to me."

"Agreed. Although the XP was pretty nice, and at this point, even the strong ones aren't a threat to me."

"Don't be dumb. They've still got whole cities to throw at us if they want, and we have no idea how tough their upper echelons are."

That was fair. Other than the few druids, he was under the impression that everything he'd been fighting was kind of common infantry units or weaker. Even the squirrel-folk hit squad that had tried to ambush him when he was fighting the stick monster wasn't that strong, early 20s at the highest.

He had to laugh a bit though. He still remembered how much he'd struggled to survive against that goblin, his first above-level-20 kill. He never had figured out quite what had happened with the notification giving him assist credit. It probably had something to do with that other goblin who'd betrayed them all.

Now he was fighting off dozens of monsters at once, all of them the same level as that goblin, without even worrying about it. His stats had jumped way up since then though, and more importantly, all his combat skills were rank 2 or higher. That made a huge difference too. Once he picked up [XP Mask], he was thinking it was time to get [Mace Mastery] up to rank 4.

"Hey, System, how high a level do the squirrel folk get?" Luke asked. It wasn't that he expected to meet it, but it didn't hurt to ask.

"The highest-leveled one is level 34," System said.

"Thanks. Maybe I could handle it, but probably best not to find out."

"Especially since it's almost certain not to be alone," Zea agreed. "Oh, by the way, how much is rank 3 [Life Surge]?"

Luke checked, then winced. "250 AP."

"Damn. Well, that's not happening any time soon."

"Nope," he agreed. "But imagine what it could do. Maybe I could just keep it running all the time with no drawbacks. That might be worth it."

Zea just rolled her eyes and snorted. Then she paused and got a sly grin on her face. "*All* the time?"

Name	Luke Bennet	Zea Stenter
Level	32	20
XP	119396/120012	28390/29492
AP	0	12
Bloodline	SysAdmin II	None
Strength	42	7
Agility	55	27
Stamina	51	27
Perception	39	19
Skills	Mace Mastery (3)	Dagger Mastery (1)
	Sword Mastery (1)	Stealth (2)
	Unarmed Martialist (4)	Keen Instincts (1)
	Power Strike (2)	Lock Picking (1)
	Life Surge (2)	Disguise (2)
	Peripheral Awareness (2)	Deception (1)
	Tactical Foresight (1)	Bartering (2)
	Counter (2)	Streetwise (2)
	Twitch Reflexes (3)	Cooking (1)
	Stealth (1)	Mending (1)
	Survivalist (2)	First Aid (1)
	First Aid (1)	Thalian (3)
	Wood Carving (1)	Neyardic (3)
	Leatherworking (2)	Ostari (1)
	Butchering (4)	Mana Manipulation (2)
	Thalian (2)	Mana Sight (1)
	Disguise (2)	Metallurgy (1)
	Deception (1)	Whitesmithing (1)
	Analyze (BL)	Goldsmithing (2)
	Remote Access (BL)	Gem Cutting (1)
		Engraving (2)
		Rune Forging (1)
		Painting (1)
		Arcano Dynamics (1)
		Sleight of Hand (1)
		Steady Hands (2)
		Cold Reading (1)
		Temperature Acclimation (2)
		Cadence (2)
		Bloodline Purification Ritual (1)

CHAPTER 32

The breeze didn't bother Luke so much because it was cold; it was just that he was aware of the breeze in the first place. Despite his best efforts to turn the leftover scraps of his clothing into some sort of loincloth, the bulk of his repair work went to the harness for his mace, and what was left just didn't cut it. It was . . . airy down there.

Zea thought it was hilarious.

They moved at a steady pace, nothing too onerous for their superhuman bodies, but still easily fifty miles a day on average. It depended largely on how dense the forest got, and occasionally on how often they were attacked, but with Luke showing XP levels on par with some of the top predators in the forest, it became more and more rare for any random monster looking for a meal to decide it was a good idea to fuck with them.

That was not to say there weren't plenty of idiots. There were, but they usually came in two flavors. Small packs of swarm animals numbering in the dozens or even hundreds that didn't care about the level of their theoretical victims were the most common. Those were great for providing Luke with XP, even if they were only level 2 or 3, but didn't work quite as well for Zea. She was less indestructible and far less swift, so while she got a fair chunk of the XP, the lion's share went to Luke.

The other type of monsters were the ones that were used to punching above their weight classes. It was just a simple fact that while the system enhanced physical capabilities, an elephant had a much higher starting strength than a human did. Some monsters were inherently more dangerous and viewed the levels of their prey as loose guidelines to be considered rather than absolutes to be rigidly adhered to.

Luke was quite happy to show them how wrong they were. He didn't necessarily outmuscle every enemy that showed up, but if he wasn't stronger, he was always faster, and in the extremely rare circumstances that he didn't have a significant advantage in at least one category, he had a whole mess of combat skills to fall back on. **[Life Surge]** being rank 2 and having significantly diminished drawbacks had made Luke far more willing to use it to decisively end a fight that proved unexpectedly difficult.

Best of all, it was easy for Zea to participate in a relatively safe manner. Rarely did the hulking bruiser-type monsters attack in groups greater than two, and even more rarely did they fail to oblige Luke when he moved forward to challenge them. These were creatures that were secure in their physical supremacy, eager to meet any problem head-on. It had always worked for them before, and they weren't smart enough to imagine a scenario where it would fail them now.

[You have assisted in slaying Razor-Prong Moose (level 22). 230 XP awarded.]

"Big fucker, isn't it?" Luke said.

Luke wasn't sure exactly how big a moose back home was, but the internet had told him they were huge and dangerous. This moose was so tall, Luke would have had to stand on his toes and stretch his arms over his head to tickle its belly. Its rack had a spread wide enough that he could have put a full-size mattress between the outermost prongs. He wouldn't, just because the name was dead-on. The damn thing had absolutely shredded the canopies of at least three trees and casually knocked over a fourth in an attempt to keep up with Luke's movements when he'd executed a tight turn.

It also had a proportionately powerful smell, which was why after a brief discussion, both of them agreed not to bother harvesting any meat or hide from it. "I bet those antlers are worth good money though," Zea said, giving them a wistful glance as she gathered up a few of the broken shards left over from the fight. "That's got to be some sort of metallic ivory."

"That's expensive stuff?" Luke asked. It was a moot point, really. Even if he broke the rack off the moose's skull, it was way too big to carry in one piece, and dangerously sharp. Besides. every time something big attacked them, Zea made the same noises about its claws, or its eyeballs, or some other part of its anatomy. Luke was starting to think that she'd been mistaken about the idea of monster hunting not paying well.

Sure, they might not have made money off the killing, but it sounded like the harvesting was quite profitable. When he pointed that out to her, she just said, "That's because the kind of shit that lives out here is hard to come across near civilization. Just getting out here is a challenge for normal people, never mind finding these monsters, killing them, harvesting the important stuff, and transporting it back to civilization."

Luke quickly conceded that those were all good points and joined her in lamenting the loss of potential income. It seemed to make her happy to complain about it, and that made him happy too. Plus, it kept her distracted from his current situation of having no pants. She'd been almost giddy to point out that she'd told him to buy spare clothes in Kazos, and that he'd failed to do so.

That just made him upset because she knew exactly why he hadn't been able to finish gathering supplies, and he found it rather insensitive of her to keep treating it as a joke. He knew she didn't mean it that way, so he kept quiet about it, but he wasn't happy.

Perhaps sensing she'd crossed a line, Zea didn't bring it up again. Luke silently forgave her, and the good mood swiftly returned. The days grew together, until eventually they found something new.

"This is, technically, a road," Zea said.

"I guess."

"Hey, does a cart fit on it?"

"Maybe a small one," Luke said.

"It's still a sign of civilization. It goes somewhere."

That was true. Though it was more like a wide footpath in Luke's mind, it was more or less straight, packed earth that was clear of any sort of vegetation. The forest hadn't grown like that; somebody had made it. It was the first deliberate act of civilization they'd seen outside the squirrel-folk bramble walls, and one that had been made by humans, if System's information about their distance to a nearby human village was to be believed.

"Do you think I should pick up **[XP Mask]** now?"

Both of them had leveled again during the final days of their march, though neither had spent the AP yet. Luke sat on his because he was trying to wait as long as possible, both to keep himself more aware of approaching threats and because his now-massive XP aura was doing a good job of chasing off a lot of petty annoyances.

Zea, on the other hand, was still a long way off from upgrading **[Bloodline Purification Ritual]** to rank 2. She needed 168 AP more, or another 7 levels up to 28 assuming she spent no more than 8 AP on anything else. She was figuring she'd have to go up to at least level 30 in order to rank up support skills again.

"Maybe. I don't know. System, how far is it to Sicanti from here?"

"Three hundred miles in that direction," System said, appearing between the two of them and pointing at something just slightly north of true east.

"There a lot of towns between here and there?" Luke asked.

"Quite a few, yes. The exact number would depend on which roads you take, if any at all."

"I'd say it's about time then," Luke said. "It'll suck to lose the ability to sense XP from others, but let's be fair, that was more useful out in the wilds where most animals didn't bother to hide it than it'll be around other people."

"Yeah, but on the other hand, it's going to make you stick out to the ones who are looking for it," Zea said. "No XP at all? Nobody has that. They're going to know you're hiding it somehow."

"I don't have hundreds of AP to drop into **[Disguise]**. **[Stealth]** only pushes down my XP while I'm trying to be sneaky. What were the other skills that reduced my XP aura?"

"**[Unobtrusive]** is one to consider, but to get the good reductions, the stuff church inquisitors use, I think you'd need to get some skills up to max rank so you could combine them. **[Infiltrator]** would be ideal."

"Sure. I'll just roam the woods for another month killing anything and everything I can find for another 300 AP."

Even that was just a guess. The system shop didn't list what the max rank for a skill even was, let alone how much AP it would cost to get it. They'd just discovered a skill that would let him reduce the XP that he displayed by as much as 90 percent, adjustable whenever he wanted, but that required max ranks in **[Disguise]**, **[Deception]**, **[Intuition]**, **[Insignificant Presence]**, **[Intimidating Presence]**, **[Stealth]**, and **[Polyglot]**, which itself was a combined skill of at least four other languages, all maxed out.

It felt like a ridiculous set of requirements at first until they'd seen example of other combined skills. **[Arms Master]** wanted max ranks with every kind of weapon Luke had ever heard of, everything from swords to axes to spears to crossbows to slings, and about a dozen others besides. In return, it promised to make Luke a war god striding across a battlefield.

Similarly, **[Wraith]** was a skill that he might someday acquire, since he already had several of the prerequisites like **[Twitch Reflexes]** and **[Peripheral Awareness]**. The skill said he'd be untouchable, and that combined with **[Arms Master]**, he thought that just about covered things. He'd be able to take on any number of opponents at any time, using whatever was at hand, all without ever taking the slightest scratch.

Sure, maybe if he made it to level 100 he'd have enough AP to max out all the prerequisite skills and meet the ridiculous base stat requirements of 200 in every stat. As cool as the skills sounded in theory, he suspected a significantly better use of his time and energy would be further purifying his bloodline and taking skills that let him reduce his enemy to level 1 with a mere thought. That was true god-like power anyway.

"Really, what it comes down to is that if I don't take **[XP Mask]**, everyone will know something is fucky with how much XP I have. If I do take it, then only the people I'm unlucky enough to encounter who are looking will know that I'm hiding something, but even then, they won't know what. And the people that could do something about it will also have skills hiding their own XP, so I won't even be giving up much of an advantage in not being able to sense theirs either."

"That all sounds right," Zea said.

"System, did I miss anything?"

"Your knowledge of how the skill works appears complete to me, at least insomuch as how it functions at your current bloodline purity. It may change later on."

"Only good changes though, right?"

"Apologies, I am not able to answer that question."

Luke rolled his eyes. "Sounds about right. Okay, let's do this then."

He dumped 20 AP into the system store, bought **[XP Mask]**, and felt it settle onto him. "Whoa, that's weird."

"What?"

"It's just, you know, I've been feeling the XP of everything around me for so long. Now I don't, and it's like I've gone deaf, kind of. Everything is quiet now." He'd just have to get used to it, he supposed. "Okay, that's done. Let's see where this road leads and whether they're interested in trading some copper for some clothes."

"Maybe a bath first," Zea told him.

"What, I haven't aired out enough already?"

"Let's just say there's a reason I'm standing upwind."

Name	Luke Bennet	Zea Stenter
Level	33	21
XP	127531/131675	32845/34079
AP	13	33
Bloodline	SysAdmin II	None
Strength	42	7
Agility	55	27
Stamina	51	27
Perception	39	19
Skills	Mace Mastery (3)	Dagger Mastery (1)
	Sword Mastery (1)	Stealth (2)
	Unarmed Martialist (4)	Keen Instincts (1)
	Power Strike (2)	Lock Picking (1)
	Life Surge (2)	Disguise (2)
	Peripheral Awareness (2)	Deception (1)
	Tactical Foresight (1)	Bartering (2)
	Counter (2)	Streetwise (2)
	Twitch Reflexes (3)	Cooking (1)
	Stealth (1)	Mending (1)
	Survivalist (2)	First Aid (1)
	First Aid (1)	Thalian (3)
	Wood Carving (1)	Neyardic (3)
	Leatherworking (2)	Ostari (1)
	Butchering (4)	Mana Manipulation (2)
	Thalian (2)	Mana Sight (1)
	Disguise (2)	Metallurgy (1)
	Deception (1)	Whitesmithing (1)
	Analyze (BL)	Goldsmithing (2)
	Remote Access (BL)	Gem Cutting (1)
	XP Mask (BL)	Engraving (2)
		Rune Forging (1)
		Painting (1)
		Arcano Dynamics (1)
		Sleight of Hand (1)
		Steady Hands (2)
		Cold Reading (1)
		Temperature Acclimation (2)
		Cadence (2)
		Bloodline Purification Ritual (1)

CHAPTER 33

The road ran north and south, and the farther north they followed it, the more the trees thinned out. Within an hour, the landscape had given way to wide, flat plains dotted with occasional farmhouses. Luke and Zea approached the first one they found, a sprawling, multifamily building that sat right in the middle of a ring of sheds, barns, coops, and pastures.

"I wonder how many people it takes to take care of this much land," Luke said. The farmhouse was big, big enough for twenty people or more, but the sheer size of the fields and pastures, not to mention the number of animals needing to be taken care of, felt like way more work than two or three families could handle. He supposed the difference was, as always, the stats and skills.

They approached openly and were noticed well before they got close. Within minutes of being spotted, a trio of well-built farmhands were called in from the fields and flanked an older man in his fifties as he came down the road to meet them.

"Hi there," Luke said, pitching his voice to carry and waving one hand. The other was firmly latched on to his makeshift loincloth. There had been enough incidents with it falling off on its own, and he didn't figure flashing a bunch of total strangers was the best way to start the conversation.

"That's far enough," the middle-aged man said in stilted Thalian. "We don't need any trouble from any of you barbarians. Whatever you want, you just go looking for it somewhere else."

"Barbarian?" Luke asked. He glanced down at Zea, who shrugged back. "We don't know what you're talking about."

One of the farmhands snorted and tightened his grip on the pitchfork he was carrying. "Dressed like a woodland savage. Smells like one too."

"Don't be stupid," one of the other farmhands said. "When's the last time you met a savage that spoke Thalian? And you know how they feel about non-humans. Plus that guy's got to be, like . . . level 2, tops. My kid sister's got more XP than him."

"Shut up, the both of you," the middle-aged man said. He turned back to Luke and Zea. "You're not from the woods?"

It didn't seem like the farmer was keen to attack them, but with **[XP Mask]** blocking him from feeling anyone else's experience now, Luke made liberal use of **[Analyze]** to ensure that they wouldn't be a threat.

[Name: Human Farmer]
[Level: 11]
[Strength: 11]
[Agility: 5]
[Stamina: 17]
[Perception: 3]

The farmhands were similar, give or take a level or two. None had strength over 15 or perception over 5. If Luke had to make a move, it would be over before they even realized he wasn't standing in front of them anymore. That went a long way toward helping him stay relaxed.

"We came through the forest," Zea said, "from the south end. It's been a hell of a walk. We're just looking for a meal, a bath, and a new set of clothes for this lug. We'll pay, good copper."

"Wait there," the farmer in charge said. He retreated with his flunkies thirty feet down the road, and they started whispering to one another. They spoke a language Luke wasn't familiar with, but he could see that Zea was paying attention, so he didn't interrupt her.

Whatever they decided, it didn't take them long to figure it out. They returned as a group, and their leader said, "We've got a spare set of clothes for you, eight copper, and we'll fill one of those packs with road food for another six. Don't want you coming anywhere near the house."

"Throw in a bucket of water and some soap, call the whole thing twelve copper, and it's a deal," Zea told him.

"Show me the money first," the farmer demanded. Zea fished out a handful of coins, which he grunted at suspiciously before pocketing. He accepted an empty knapsack, tossed it over his shoulder at one of the farmhands, and said, "Go fetch what they bought and be quick about it."

They all stared at one another in awkward silence for a minute while one of the farmhands went running back to the house, then Luke said, "So, what's the deal with these barbarians from the forest?"

One of the two remaining farmhands snorted and muttered something in that other language, then spat on the ground. The other farmhand nodded along, but neither of them bothered to answer Luke's question.

The farmer in the middle of their group just shook his head and said, "Bad business. They come from the south, attack from the trees at night, steal food and supplies, kill livestock and destroy whatever they can't take."

"Do you think they made that road we found?" Luke asked Zea.

"How the hell would I know? I'm not going to go back and explore it. We're going north until we find a road going east."

"Yeah, sure."

Luke didn't really care that much. He was curious and making conversation, but it looked like the topic was a sore spot among the locals. He supposed he couldn't blame them if they were being targeted by cattle rustlers and horse thieves, though the idea that they were coming from the woods didn't make a lot of sense to him.

As long as the barbarians or whatever left him and Zea alone, he supposed he didn't much care. Killing men wasn't like killing monsters anyway, and bandit hunting aside, he wasn't keen to repeat it. Luke wouldn't say he'd really processed that either; mostly he'd just tried not to think about it and told himself that if there was anyone who deserved to be murdered for their shit, it was a bunch of people who'd made a living out of murdering other people and stealing their shit.

After a few minutes, the farmhand came back with some clothes rolled up under one arm, the knapsack held by one strap in one hand with a chunk of soap and a stiff-bristled brush, and a large bucket full of water in the other. He set them down in the middle of the path, gave Luke a nod, and backed away.

"There you go. Do your washing and get out of here."

Part of Luke was hesitant to drop trou in front of a group of strange men, but considering how little he'd been wearing the last few days, it wasn't like there was much mystery left. With a sigh, he started lathering himself up with the soap and splashing water all over himself.

Two of the farmhands at least were gracious enough to look away, but the other two men watched him with borderline hostile glares. Luke scrubbed himself as quickly as he could, then when he was done, upended the bucket over his head to sluice off the soap and grime. "No towel, of course," he said. "Fuck it. I'll air-dry and get dressed later. Let's just get out of here."

"Yeah," Zea agreed, glaring right back at the farmer. "Thanks for the food."

The two walked away, Luke wearing nothing but a backpack held over his crotch and his ass hanging out in the breeze. They were a thousand feet down the road before the farmer and his helpers turned their backs on him and marched away.

"Well, that was fucking weird," he told Zea. "What was that language they were speaking?"

"Ostari. I know a little bit. It was mostly just mutterings about how they don't trust us, how weird the money looked, and how much we overpaid for what they gave us."

"Think it'll be a problem later on?"

"From them? No. But it does sound like they're having problems with a tribe of raiders. If we're lucky, those will stay as their problems."

"When have we ever been lucky?" Luke asked.

"Pretty much. I think we'd best be very careful while we're traveling through this region. The sooner we make it to a main road and get the fuck out of here, the better off we'll be."

"You think everyone else is going to be that hostile, or was it just because we came from the woods?"

"Your clothing situation might have had something to do with it. Maybe these raiders also come running in buck naked."

"Speaking of," Luke said, pausing to kick his boots back off. "I think I'm dry enough."

"But I was enjoying the view," Zea protested.

"You can enjoy it later. I haven't had a pair of pants in so long my ass is tanned."

The pants were tight in the crotch and short in the legs, and the shirt strained itself across his chest and shoulders, but considering they were second-hand from some random farmer, he supposed he couldn't complain too bad if he didn't have as much ball room as he would have liked.

"Ugh. You look like shit now. We're getting you some good clothes next time we find a place that isn't some two-horse shit heap of a town."

"Sure. If you say so."

"I'm not walking around with you looking like a bumpkin."

"Hey . . ."

It didn't look *that* bad. Maybe he wouldn't fit in at a noble gala, but still. Luke looked down at the clothes. Well, maybe they were that bad. Everything was mottled brown and gray, frequently darned or patched, and somehow still worn out at one knee. The clothes were decidedly rougher than what the farmers had been wearing, and Luke suspected he'd been given some old pieces that had been destined to be cut up for rags.

"I miss my jeans," he said. "And my good work boots."

"And indoor plumbing and convenience stores and the internet, yes. You've told me before," Zea finished for him.

"That doesn't make it any less true."

Neither of them followed the line of that conversation. They both knew it would end with the question of whether Luke was going back to his own world or staying in Aros, and whether Zea would follow him if he did leave. She didn't have anything really tying her down in Aros, but at the same time, migrating to a new world was a big commitment, especially considering that there were no dwifkin there.

Luke wasn't even sure if he could make her human, even at the command console, or if she'd want to be if he could. They'd both avoided that conversation, perhaps sensing that there weren't going to be any good answers and that the longer they delayed it, the longer they could pretend it didn't need talking about.

He was pretty sure he knew what her answer was going to be anyway.

His musings were interrupted by a flicker of movement on the far end of the field. It wasn't the first farmer he'd spotted out working, but this time, something caught his attention. For one thing, it was farther away than anyone else he'd seen. For another, whomever he'd noticed wasn't dressed in farming clothes.

"Just saw someone dressed in black and green, looked like armor," Luke said quietly. "Behind us and to the right. Tall guy, head shaved but with a beard. He was in that copse of trees."

"One of those barbarians that farmer was whining about?" Zea asked, not bothering to look.

"Not unless *barbarian* means something else to these people. He looked better dressed and better equipped than any of the laborers we've seen around here. He was there and gone so quick I didn't even get a chance to throw an **[Analyze]** on him."

"So he's got some speed on him. Might be high level."

"Could be," Luke agreed. "You want to do something about this?"

"Not really. You?"

"Nah, those farmers were assholes. Fuck 'em. I'm not solving their problems for them."

"As long as whoever it is doesn't come at us, I think we're fine. But maybe let's pick up the pace?" Zea said.

They started jogging, through at a speed where they practically flew over the ground. Luke doubted he could have pedaled a bike as fast as they were going back on Earth, and he definitely couldn't have kept it up for hours.

"You think we'll run into any more?" he said as they jogged.

"Knowing our luck? Probably."

Well, there was some truth to that. Luke's mace thumped reassuringly against his back with each step though. If trouble found them, he'd be ready for it.

Name	Luke Bennet	Zea Stenter
Level	33	21
XP	127531/131675	32845/34079
AP	13	33
Bloodline	SysAdmin II	None
Strength	42	7
Agility	55	27
Stamina	51	27
Perception	39	19
Skills	Mace Mastery (3)	Dagger Mastery (1)
	Sword Mastery (1)	Stealth (2)
	Unarmed Martialist (4)	Keen Instincts (1)
	Power Strike (2)	Lock Picking (1)
	Life Surge (2)	Disguise (2)
	Peripheral Awareness (2)	Deception (1)
	Tactical Foresight (1)	Bartering (2)
	Counter (2)	Streetwise (2)
	Twitch Reflexes (3)	Cooking (1)
	Stealth (1)	Mending (1)
	Survivalist (2)	First Aid (1)
	First Aid (1)	Thalian (3)
	Wood Carving (1)	Neyardic (3)
	Leatherworking (2)	Ostari (1)
	Butchering (4)	Mana Manipulation (2)
	Thalian (2)	Mana Sight (1)
	Disguise (2)	Metallurgy (1)
	Deception (1)	Whitesmithing (1)
	Analyze (BL)	Goldsmithing (2)
	Remote Access (BL)	Gem Cutting (1)
	XP Mask (BL)	Engraving (2)
		Rune Forging (1)
		Painting (1)
		Arcano Dynamics (1)
		Sleight of Hand (1)
		Steady Hands (2)
		Cold Reading (1)
		Temperature Acclimation (2)
		Cadence (2)
		Bloodline Purification Ritual (1)

CHAPTER 34

They left a lot of miles of dirt road behind them that afternoon. It wasn't that it was hard to keep a conversation going while they ran, but it was easy to just fall into the rhythm of the movement and not think too hard on anything. At least it was for Luke. He wasn't sure that Zea's brain was as susceptible to just living in the moment as his was. Either way, hours passed in relative silence until Luke spotted a town up ahead. He slowed to a stop and said, "Incoming civilization."

"Thank the gods," Zea said. "I want a bed to sleep in tonight, an edible meal somebody else cooked, a bath, and a few hours to work on a project without moving."

"Wait, what project is this? I don't know anything about a project."

"How high is your perception?" Zea asked. "I thought you knew everything that happened around you. You were standing ten feet away while I was gathering materials."

Luke blinked and tried to think back to anything Zea had picked up lately. When they'd first started traveling, she'd been inclined to scavenge anything she thought was valuable, but after lugging it around for days, she'd switched to a less-is-more attitude. Very few things crossed the threshold of worth it to lug the weight around lately.

"The razor prongs?" he asked. She'd grabbed a few shards, but he'd assumed those were to sell.

"Exactly."

"And, uh, what are you making out of them?" Luke asked. The only thing he could picture was some sort of blade made out of the antler itself, which he was sure would be lethally sharp despite how dull the edge appeared, but they already had ever-sharp knives.

"Oh, you'll see," she said with an evil grin. "Let's just say I've had enough of that damn human-sized crossbow."

She seemed excited about it, which was good enough for Luke. He wasn't keen on watching the work happen, having already had a front-row seat to her magic poking stick. That had never really gotten off the ground, which she'd claimed was fine, since it was just a prototype to test the enchantment and that a wooden stick was far too weak a material to withstand the force the magic would put on it.

Apparently, razor prongs were a different story. "As long as I don't need to be your test subject, I'm all for it. So we'll call it an early day here? I'll see if I can get some better clothes. You get us a room and access to a bath?"

"I don't think so. You don't speak the local language, so it's entirely possible you'll run into somebody you just can't communicate with at all. Besides, we need to discuss aliases first," Zea said.

"Oh, right. Do you think we need them this far out from Valtira? We're basically in another country at this point."

"No, probably not, but does it hurt anything?"

"No. What are our names going to be for the next few days then?"

"That is an excellent question. We could go with something in Ostari, but since I don't speak it very well and you don't speak it at all, that might draw more attention to us than just being foreigners would."

"How bad is the language barrier?" Luke asked, thinking about the farmers. If even people that far away from major cities were bilingual, he didn't think he'd have a hard time communicating with most people. In the worst case, he had enough AP left over to pick up a new language at rank 1, but if all they were going to go was pass through, get on a boat, and leave the area, it felt like a waste to him.

Of course, a trip across the ocean on a ship with no engines to power it or satellites to navigate with would probably take weeks or even months. Hell, now that he thought of it, he realized that he actually had no clue how far the ship needed to even go. He'd just kind of been mentally picturing a trip across the Atlantic, but he'd never bothered to find out just how wide the ocean was. He didn't have the first clue how long he'd be stuck in a relatively small space with an unknown number of people who spoke the local language.

Maybe he'd take some time to add another level or two worth of AP to his resources, just to make sure he had some flexibility to address new problems as they cropped up. Zea's AP was still tied up in grinding out the outrageous amount needed to upgrade **[Bloodline Purification Ritual]**, so any situations that called for something outside their current skill set would be on him to provide an answer to.

"There's enough trade between Sicanti and Valtira that I'm sure we can get by with our current language skills. Nobody is going to mistake us for natives, but they wouldn't even if we both had rank 3 **[Ostari]**. You're not going to find a dwifkin up here. I'll be the one who stands out." She paused for a moment and shrugged. "You might find some full-blooded dwarves though, if we get close enough to the mountains."

Luke blinked at her. "Dwarves? Like . . . short, beards, live underground, digging a hole?"

"Wooooooooow. Is your whole world full of nothing but racist stereotypes?"

"I mean . . . yeah, kind of. But all our games and stories that have dwarves and elves and halflings and whatever in them came from . . . from a bunch of guys in the seventies who, now that I think about it, probably were kind of racist and sexist. But these are just stories where I come from. The races depicted in games and books and movies don't really exist on Earth."

"Well, somebody knew enough about Aros to consistently pick up a bunch of offensive stereotypes," Zea said. "Next you're going to tell me that elves are all a bunch of androgenous, snooty tree fuckers."

Luke didn't say anything.

"Gods damn it," Zea muttered. "Okay, new rule. Whatever you think you know about a species, I want you to just assume that you're wrong and that you would offend someone of that species if you shared your world's views on them. In fact, don't even talk to anyone who's not a human if I'm not there with you."

"I'm . . . sorry?"

"It's okay, just, that has to mean something, right? A bunch of people who were really high level found some way to look at this world, and then just fetched a bunch of information about other species that they picked up in a scummy tavern or something."

"Who were really high . . . what? No, not level seventy. In the 1970s. The decade when they were inventing the kinds of games that featured fantasy stuff."

Zea snorted. "I think I know enough about your fantasies already."

"Anyway," Luke said loudly. "Back on topic. How likely are we to run into dwarves, and is there anything I should know?"

"Not likely at all, as long as we're going directly toward Sicanti. We might run across one or two out traveling, but a dwarven stronghold is not in our travel plans. If we do meet any dwarves, just treat them like regular people and don't make any assumptions based on your games from back home."

"Got it. Will do."

Now Luke was kind of curious about what exactly dwarves on Aros were like. He was about to ask, when Zea interrupted him and said, "Now, about these aliases. I don't think you should use Aldrick again. Even your real name would be better than that, though that's not great either. How about . . . Hmm . . . Nemar?"

"Okay," Luke agreed easily. He didn't much care what fake name he used. If it ended up being annoying, he'd just change it again.

"And I will be Pavena," Zea said.

"Okay," Luke said again.

"Alright, now that that's settled, here's the plan. We get into that town, find ourselves a room, a meal, and a bath. We can ask around if there's a local tailor who's worth a damn. If nothing else, you could use a backup outfit or two. I'm sure your clothes won't last more than a week or two at the rate you go through them."

"It's not like I'm trying to get hit," Luke said. He did, in fact, have multiple skills that worked specifically to keep that from happening. Being outnumbered a hundred to one just kind of made it a moot point. "Maybe we'll have the time and money to get some real armor soon."

"It's starting to feel kind of pointless," Zea told him. "With where you're at now, 51 fucking stamina and all that, anything not made of steel isn't going to do you much good, and anything fast enough to hit you can probably rip through steel anyway. If you want armor that protects you from actual threats, you're going to need high-end, specialty materials modified by a master alchemist, a master smith to work them into a useful shape, and a master enchanter to take full advantage of those materials."

"So, lot of time, lot of money, lot of hard-to-find experts?"

"Yeah, basically."

Well, that sucked. Still, he didn't see the harm in getting a chain shirt or something. Those wouldn't break the budget, and it wouldn't hurt to have an extra layer of protection. Even if he could heal up an injury, he preferred not being hurt in the first place.

Plus, that wasn't accounting for some protection for Zea, who inarguably had the stamina needed to walk around in it all day, though perhaps not the strength to move easily. That wasn't too hard to fix though.

Either way, he wasn't going to be surprised if they didn't find anything in the village ahead of them. Unless there was a lot more hiding away somehow, he counted forty-one houses surrounding a well on the northwest side of the road, and another sixteen houses with fields around them on the southeast side. A meal and a bath probably weren't out of the question. A master craftsman of any flavor probably was.

"A problem for another day," Luke mused. "Besides, we don't even know how much money we'll have left over by the time we get on the hypothetical ship that's going to take us to the other side of the world. With our luck, that amaril hide won't sell for half what it's worth, and we'll be stuck scrounging again."

"There is no way we'll still be short on money after what you looted from that bandit camp and what we get for the hide."

Luke hoped she was right. The fact of it was, he was all too used to having money problems back home, and getting dragged over to Aros hadn't really changed that too much. The money just looked different, and he never really had a clue if he was getting ripped off or not anymore. That was one of the big reasons he left all the haggling to Zea. She at least had a good grasp on what things were worth. A preindustrial society weighed things differently than what he was used to. Clothes and shoes, especially, he found to be expensive compared to things like food.

Every time he tried to make some sort of sweeping generalization about an industry, he ended up being wrong. It seemed like some skills were just easier to rank up than others, and that had a huge impact on the price of whatever those skills were designed to produce. All in all, it was easier to just trust Zea to handle it.

"Did you ever fence that jewelry we got?"

"Not yet. I wanted to be far, far away from the families of whomever those bandits killed when they took it."

"I guess we're far, far away now," Luke said.

"Yup. Probably still going to hold on to it until we get to Sicanti. There's no way some dinky little general-supply store out here is going to pay what it's worth."

Luke smiled. Like he'd said, Zea knew what things were worth and how to make sure she milked every copper out of them. "Alright, Pavena, let's head into town and see what we can find."

Name	Luke Bennet	Zea Stenter
Level	33	21
XP	127531/131675	32845/34079
AP	13	33
Bloodline	SysAdmin II	None
Strength	42	7
Agility	55	27
Stamina	51	27
Perception	39	19
Skills	Mace Mastery (3)	Dagger Mastery (1)
	Sword Mastery (1)	Stealth (2)
	Unarmed Martialist (4)	Keen Instincts (1)
	Power Strike (2)	Lock Picking (1)
	Life Surge (2)	Disguise (2)
	Peripheral Awareness (2)	Deception (1)
	Tactical Foresight (1)	Bartering (2)
	Counter (2)	Streetwise (2)
	Twitch Reflexes (3)	Cooking (1)
	Stealth (1)	Mending (1)
	Survivalist (2)	First Aid (1)
	First Aid (1)	Thalian (3)
	Wood Carving (1)	Neyardic (3)
	Leatherworking (2)	Ostari (1)
	Butchering (4)	Mana Manipulation (2)
	Thalian (2)	Mana Sight (1)
	Disguise (2)	Metallurgy (1)
	Deception (1)	Whitesmithing (1)
	Analyze (BL)	Goldsmithing (2)
	Remote Access (BL)	Gem Cutting (1)
	XP Mask (BL)	Engraving (2)
		Rune Forging (1)
		Painting (1)
		Arcano Dynamics (1)
		Sleight of Hand (1)
		Steady Hands (2)
		Cold Reading (1)
		Temperature Acclimation (2)
		Cadence (2)
		Bloodline Purification Ritual (1)

CHAPTER 35

Luke supposed it wasn't unusual for a hotel to have a bar somewhere in the building. People liked to drink, hotels liked making money, so it made sense to him that they'd try to tap their current customers for some extra income. It hadn't really been all that relevant to him, what with the whole being underage and not going on too many family vacations. The bars he'd visited with his older siblings had been more trashy locals and cheap liquor than they had been sophisticated world travelers or dads needing a break from family vacation.

Aros was different. Every town, no matter how small, had what he would term as a tavern. Usually there'd be two or three, even in the villages. The bigger taverns were also inns, but there were plenty of taverns that were only taverns. And when he considered how little variety there was in stuff like available food, it kind of stood out to him that no matter where he stopped, there were always plenty of options on tap.

Once he'd noticed that and started paying attention, he'd realized that there were more places to get drunk than there were to pray at, and this was a world that had actual, real deities who provided proof of their existence. Yet, somehow, outside of Valtira and probably Kazos, he had yet to see a church making a regular appearance anywhere.

There were little shrines sometimes, roadside things that basically looked like wind chimes strung up on open-faced boxes, except the chimes were planks of wood that probably had the names of the Pantheon painted on them once upon a time. Weird. Luke would have thought that the gods cared about their shrines being ruined by the weather, or about the lack of churches to worship them, or just a general absence of being in people's lives outside of major cities.

It was almost like they didn't give a fuck. Like, at all.

Luke found the idea that the gods existed and had power but didn't care to exercise it throughout most of the world to be kind of suspicious. Was it that they were lazy, or was it not worth the effort for some other reason? Or was it that they couldn't? That whole Covenant excuse had always sounded like bullshit to him anyway, not that he was complaining.

"You ever notice we never see a church anywhere we go?" he said casually as they got close enough to the village that he could start making out the individual buildings there too.

"Is that a problem for you?" Zea asked.

"No, just curious. Seems like something I might want to be aware of, given my . . . relationship . . . with the church."

"I mean, I'm sure the whole Pantheon hates your guts, but you've really only dealt with the Church of Hestoc in Valtira. Maybe those squirrels might worship Nuvari."

"Uh, right. Reminds me which ones those are again," Luke said.

"God of civilization and goddess of nature."

"Right, yeah, so this Hestoc guy should be all about all these little towns, right? That's civilization popping up, spreading out, and taming the wilderness. Why doesn't he have his own little church in every town promoting the ideals of cutting down trees, murdering the natives, and growing corn?"

"What's corn?" Zea said.

"Not important to the discussion. It's just farming. Point is, this guy is a deity, he has his thing that he's in charge of, but I don't see him doing anything with it. Why not?"

"I don't know. I'm not a philosopher. My learning starts and ends with stay the fuck away from the streets around the church. They don't like seeing the poors around and are happy to do something about it."

"It's just weird is all."

"I wouldn't worry about it that much. I think there's an inn over there," Zea said, changing the subject and pointing to the side of the village with the well. "That three-story one. Or it's a big stable for the middle of town if it's not."

The pair changed directions slightly to head straight for the potential inn, which was exactly what Zea had predicted. A sign hanging from a post above the door proclaimed it to be the Full Thatcher, whatever that meant. Maybe it was a translation problem between the Ostari writing and Thalian. Or maybe it was a local joke that he just didn't get.

Zea, who'd been attracting stares from the few people out and about on the streets as they walked, stopped the bartender cold when she walked through the door. He said something in what Luke assumed was also Ostari, to which she answered haltingly. He caught their fake names in there, but not much else.

Annoyed at being unable to understand what was going on, he once again considered dumping 5 AP for the language. Zea only had one rank, and she was doing fine with it. Probably. Maybe not, considering the look on the bartender's face. Then she started counting out coins, and Luke got it. They were doing what she referred to as haggling, and what Luke thought of as channeling her inner Karen.

He'd be embarrassed if he understood a word of it. Zea was vicious when it came to her haggling, but everyone seemed to expect it in this world. Instead, he just stood there blandly and tried not to think of all the times he'd just agreeably handed over whatever amount of money the vendor had asked for.

"Come on," she said after she parted with a single silver coin. "Got rooms for the evening, a meal for both of us, and we can use the bathhouse."

"Oh, good. Rooms first?"

"Yep. Then I'm claiming the first bath. You can watch our stuff until I get back."

Luke was surprised. "You think people are going to try to steal from us in a place like this?"

"No, but do you want to risk it?"

He recalled the amaril hide and how valuable Zea said it was. Hell, she'd put so many enchantments on that bag to keep it fresh until they could get it to someone who could process it that even the bag itself was probably worth a nice bit of money.

"Fair enough. I'll babysit our stuff while you get a bath."

For the first time in what felt like a year, Luke was thoroughly clean and had eaten a meal that included things like seasoning and butter. Zea was a decent cook, but given what they'd had to work with, their diets had consisted of a lot of dry food. It was nice to have an approximation of civilization again, even if it was still beyond rustic by his standards.

Zea had somehow managed to bully the bartender, or rather, innkeeper, into loaning her a lantern, which she'd set on the floor next to her while she unpacked a dozen razor-sharp prongs from her bag. Luke watched from the bed, curious, while he listened to the sounds of the village around them. He needed to get into the habit of paying attention to what his ears and nose were telling him now that he couldn't feel approaching XP anymore.

In a way, it was discomforting to have lost that sense, but the looks he'd gotten had been more curious or confused than afraid or hostile, so he supposed it was a win. Still, if a bloodline purification would allow him to start sensing XP from other creatures while hiding his own, he'd call that a solid win. System, of course, wouldn't tell him.

It didn't seem like he could turn it on or off either, so for the time being, Luke was stuck being XP blind. **[XP Mask]** was such a weird skill, the only one he'd found so far that had a clear drawback to it. He was pretty sure it was because it was a bloodline skill, and since his wasn't pure, none of the abilities were working at full strength. **[Analyze]** only showed him basic information too. It would seem like it should have at least showed him the target's skills along with their stats, maybe even everything he could see on his own status screen.

"Ah, damn it," Zea said, flinching and dropping the prong she'd been working on to the floor. "Cut myself again."

"Do you want me to hold it for you while you work on it?" he asked. Even if it did cut him, he had far more stamina to heal up from it.

"No, it's fine. Besides, you might interfere with the enchantment."

"What exactly are you trying to do?"

She glanced up at where he was lying on the bed and said, "You really want to know?"

"Sure, why not? It's something you care about, so if it's important to you, it's important to me."

"Well, alright. Come here. I'll try to explain it as much as I can. Without **[Mana Sight]**, I can only walk you through the general idea, not the specifics."

"I'm sure the specifics would go over my head anyway."

"Give yourself some credit," she told him. "You're not dumb."

Luke just shrugged as he sat down behind her. She scooted back to snuggle up against his chest and said, "Okay, so you know this shit is super sharp, right? Like, it can pierce steel easily, and even the edge can cut skin."

"Right." He was extremely aware of how damn sharp those antlers had been, having been the one who'd killed their previous owner.

"Well, you know how they don't look like they're sharp though? I mean, it's got a point on it like a normal antler, but there's no edge here. So how's it cut through anything, right? That's the magic part. It has a kind of . . . cutting aura, I guess. It cuts because it wants to."

"Okay?" Luke wasn't quite sure how *that* worked, but if Zea said so, he wasn't going to argue.

"Right, well, what I'm doing with this enchantment is taking that cutting aura and slaving it to an anchor piece so that I can manipulate it. Then I'll be able to change its shape, size, flexibility, sharpness, pretty much anything I want."

Luke vaguely recalled how the moose had damn near gored him despite the antlers not actually touching him. If he was understanding Zea's explanation correctly, she was trying to get the individual prong pieces to do the same thing, except under her control.

"Are you . . . Are you making a magic invisible sword?"

"What? No, of course not." Zea gestured to the nine other fragments of razor prong sitting on the floor. "I'm making a magic invisible whip."

Luke remembered a monster he'd seen Curt kill in a video game once, a kind of giant water serpent that still had its spine inside it, spaced out along its length. He was picturing Zea's proposed magic weapon as something similar, with each prong fragment spaced out along an invisible razor-sharp fishing line.

"That's so cool," he said. "Are you going to need to pick up a skill like **[Whip Mastery]** to use it?"

"Nah. It's not a real whip. I'll control it with the enchantments. At least, I will if I ever finish carving the runes into the fucking things. This would be so much easier with a full workbench. Wouldn't be slicing my hand open every five seconds either."

"Here," Luke said, picking up the prong and holding it between his fingers. He could feel it scraping against his skin, like he was holding a jagged shard of glass instead of a smooth bone-textured piece of horn. It couldn't slice through him, not with his stamina. "Move my arm so that I'm holding it exactly where you need it. I won't let go, I promise."

"You know if you move while I'm writing on this, the whole piece will be worthless, right?"

"Mm-hmm. Go ahead, try to move it. Push on it as hard as you can."

Zea did as he asked and found it didn't budge, no matter what. She even accidentally cut her hand again trying to force it. Then she adjusted his arm so that he was holding it right in front of her, nodded to herself, and said, "Okay, here we go."

Slowly, one delicate line at a time, Zea etched the enchanting runes into the bone.

Name	Luke Bennet	Zea Stenter
Level	33	21
XP	127531/131675	32845/34079
AP	13	33
Bloodline	SysAdmin II	None
Strength	42	7
Agility	55	27
Stamina	51	27
Perception	39	19
Skills	Mace Mastery (3)	Dagger Mastery (1)
	Sword Mastery (1)	Stealth (2)
	Unarmed Martialist (4)	Keen Instincts (1)
	Power Strike (2)	Lock Picking (1)
	Life Surge (2)	Disguise (2)
	Peripheral Awareness (2)	Deception (1)
	Tactical Foresight (1)	Bartering (2)
	Counter (2)	Streetwise (2)
	Twitch Reflexes (3)	Cooking (1)
	Stealth (1)	Mending (1)
	Survivalist (2)	First Aid (1)
	First Aid (1)	Thalian (3)
	Wood Carving (1)	Neyardic (3)
	Leatherworking (2)	Ostari (1)
	Butchering (4)	Mana Manipulation (2)
	Thalian (2)	Mana Sight (1)
	Disguise (2)	Metallurgy (1)
	Deception (1)	Whitesmithing (1)
	Analyze (BL)	Goldsmithing (2)
	Remote Access (BL)	Gem Cutting (1)
	XP Mask (BL)	Engraving (2)
		Rune Forging (1)
		Painting (1)
		Arcano Dynamics (1)
		Sleight of Hand (1)
		Steady Hands (2)
		Cold Reading (1)
		Temperature Acclimation (2)
		Cadence (2)
		Bloodline Purification Ritual (1)

CHAPTER 36

They were both up early the next morning, having only gotten a few hours of sleep. Even that was more than Luke needed, but Zea continued to insist that she was going to sleep every night, regardless of how much stamina she'd gained. He didn't much see a reason for it, but since they'd paid good money for a room, he guessed it was fine.

The project wasn't finished, not even close. She'd gotten all the carving done though, which she considered to be the important part. Everything else could be done on the road. With the pieces of antler all packed away and their bags stuffed full once again, they were back on their way.

"It was kind of nice to stop somewhere for the night and not have any problems crop up," Luke said once the village was well behind them.

"That's what it's like for normal people all the time," she said.

"Hopefully Sicanti won't be exciting either. How long do you think it'll take us to get there?"

"Assuming we can stick to the roads the whole way now that we're nowhere near Valtira? I figure three days at the worst, maybe only two if the weather holds and the roads are good quality."

Luke suspected he could do it in twenty-four hours, but he didn't think Zea would be able to maintain that pace for an extended period of time. And since they didn't have a deadline, it was alright by him if they took it easy. He kind of wanted to take some more time to let her finish her magic-whip thing so he could see it in action.

On the other hand, they'd only been jogging down the road for an hour, and he'd noticed two different people watching them from a mile away. Both times, they'd been partially hidden. After the second one, he said, "System, can you tell me anything about the people I keep seeing watching us?"

"I am only able to offer limited information," it said, appearing next to Luke and gliding through the air to keep pace with him. "The highest-level person in that group is level 35, and the lowest is level 18. They are local to the area, though not as a town or village."

"That's all?" Luke asked.

"Yes."

"Sounds like more bandits," Zea said. "Disturbingly high-level bandits."

"Might be something to ask about next time we find a town. That farmer made it sound like the barbarians were just a group of forest dwellers who raided singular farms for food and supplies, but no way is someone level 35 in a group like that."

"You know how much effort it takes to get up to level 35," Zea told him. "And not everyone limits themselves to hunting monsters in a forest. Military units are usually pretty good about rotating people off the front lines if their levels start getting too high. Unless things are done really differently up here, I don't think this is a retired officer."

"So either a monster hunter or a mass murderer," Luke said, glancing back toward the bluff he'd spotted the last spy at. Whoever the man was, he was gone now. "I can't tell if it's the same person each time, but if it is, he's got to be pretty high level to keep up with us. We haven't been taking a leisurely stroll today."

"Could you see if he was wearing armor like that first one?"

Luke shook his head. "Not sure if they realized I noticed them or if they're just being cautious, but the last two times, all I spotted was half a face peeking out from behind something."

"The way I see it, we've got two options. We can stay on the road, which means moving faster but being predictable, or we can go cross-country and cut straight north until we find a new road going east. If we're lucky, we'll lose them. If not, we might walk right into their arms."

"So far, I've been spotting them all on the south side of the road," Luke said, but it occurred to him that just because he'd seen three people, or possibly one person three times, didn't mean that he'd noticed every single time someone was spying on them. The simple fact of the matter was that there was more open ground on the south side of the road. Half a mile to the north, individual trees started to clump together and become a true forest again.

Zea glanced around and said, "The real concern, to me, is that if it's one person, they're keeping pace with us despite not being on the road. If it's multiple people, they're somehow coordinating over miles and miles of distance. That suggests they're not barbarians or savages. It feels more like some sort of privatized military group, well funded and probably well trained, not something we want to be fucking around with."

Luke looked ahead and saw a wagon about two miles away from them, with one farmer sitting on a wooden box loaded in the back and another holding the reins. He glanced behind him and saw a cart, one of the small ones that was pushed along by a single person. That hadn't been there two minutes ago, but maybe it had come from one of the many trails that led off to individual homesteads operated by farmers all over the region.

Then Luke used **[Analyze]** on all of them, and he started swearing. "You see those two guys ahead of us?" he asked. "We're going to pass them in another few minutes. One of them is level 23, and the other is 19."

"Pretty high level for some local farmers on their way to market," Zea said.

"Yeah, and the guy pushing that handcart behind us is level 28. Worse, he's clearly not a farmer. Agility and perception are both over 50, strength and stamina above 30."

"Fuck."

That about summed it up, in Luke's opinion. Just to drive the point home, he added "The system is calling them mercenaries."

Zea gave the wagon ahead of them an appraising glance. "You think you could take both of them before the guy behind us catches up?"

Luke glanced over his shoulder to see that, despite them keeping up their jogging pace, the cart handler had closed the gap. "Not a chance. This asshole is already closing the distance. If anything, we'd be better off pivoting back to take him out first."

Neither of them said it, but they were both thinking it. Their battle plan assumed there were only three enemies. It was entirely possible that a whole war band would pop out of the trees and descend on them while they were fighting the first three.

Worse, a man at level 28 with stats almost as high as Luke's were now would likely have a lot of combat skills, and probably at higher ranks than his too. If his time at the Bloody Harbor had taught him anything, it was that just because people were a lower level than him didn't mean they were pushovers. He wasn't all that confident that he'd win the fight cleanly, let alone so quickly that the other two men couldn't arrive fast enough to help.

"Well, we could always make a break for it into the woods," Luke said. "The one following us is going to catch up, but if we can kill him, it shouldn't be hard to lose the two on the wagon. Plus if there are more of them, their numbers won't mean as much with all the trees."

"You'll have to carry me there," Zea said.

Luke shrugged off his backpack and sped up a bit so that he was in front of her. "Whenever you're ready."

She jumped onto his back midstep and wrapped her arms around him. Luke immediately changed direction with a hard left and took off into the field next to the road. He made it all of forty feet before the man with the handcart started bellowing. He abandoned the cart and sprinted across the grass on an intercept course, but he was still too far back. There was no way he'd catch up before they hit the trees, and the two on the wagon had barely gotten their feet on the ground.

The first arrow to come out of the trees was hard to see on account of how it came straight at Luke. It was barely more than a brown flash he noticed as it arced up and then down to give it the extra range it needed to reach him. [Twitch Reflexes] started screaming at him, and before he'd even made a conscious decision to do so, Luke had stepped smoothly to the right. Zea yelped in surprise as she nearly fell free from the unexpected move, then yelped again when the arrow zipped past her.

"I guess we know if there's more in the forest," Luke said.

Hopefully it would just be one though. He could handle just one if he was quick enough. As soon as they were through the tree line, he'd let Zea down and take out the archer. By the time Cartman caught up to them, it would be one-on-one.

Two more arrows came out from between the trees, one a hundred feet to the left and the other twenty feet to the right. Luke's eye twitched in annoyance. It was like God was mocking him for his optimism.

He leaped straight up and over, his hands snaking back behind to grab hold of Zea as he rose into the air. "Now's not really the time to be copping a feel, don't you think?" she yelled.

"No time like the present," he told her as he landed, both arrows behind him. Normally, he would have rolled once and been back on his feet, but with Zea still clinging to his back, that wasn't really feasible. Instead, he just flexed his legs to absorb the impact, then darted forward again. Another barrage of arrows came out of the woods at him, and now he was close enough to see the archers, two women and a man with a chin-strap beard hugging his jawline.

Luke dodged again, a feat that was actually easier despite the closer range due to [Tactical Foresight] helping him figure out the angles before the arrows were even released from their strings. Then he ghosted through the trees, skidded to a stop on one knee, and snapped out, "Get to cover. I'm going after the archers first."

Luke rushed through the trees, which were still far enough apart and with thick enough canopies that there was almost nothing in the way of leafy underbrush. He leaped a snarled tangle of roots rather than try to navigate through it, pulled his mace free, and came around a tree to find the chin-strap archer discarding his bow and drawing a sword with a two-foot blade.

The mace struck Chin Strap right on his chin strap, literally ripping the man's head off as Luke went by. He didn't even slow down to confirm the kill, trusting instead that the attack was fatal. A fraction of a second later, when Luke was already ten feet past the body, he got the notification ding. Normally, he wouldn't bother checking the messages in the middle of a fight, but he wanted to know who the hell these assholes were.

[You have slain Blacktongue Human Mercenary (level 20). 415 XP awarded.]

[This creature has slain 514 other creatures.]

[Total kills for this type of creature: 36.]

[Highest-level kill: 24.]

"Aw, shit," Luke swore.

Bandits wanted whatever anyone passing by had on them. They were opportunists. Mercenaries were so much worse. They were professionals. Somebody was still looking for Luke, somebody who had money and connections, if mercenaries had found them over a thousand miles away. It didn't take too much thinking to come up with an idea of who.

Name	Luke Bennet	Zea Stenter
Level	33	21
XP	127946/131675	32845/34079
AP	13	33
Bloodline	SysAdmin II	None
Strength	42	7
Agility	55	27
Stamina	51	27
Perception	39	19
Skills	Mace Mastery (3)	Dagger Mastery (1)
	Sword Mastery (1)	Stealth (2)
	Unarmed Martialist (4)	Keen Instincts (1)
	Power Strike (2)	Lock Picking (1)
	Life Surge (2)	Disguise (2)
	Peripheral Awareness (2)	Deception (1)
	Tactical Foresight (1)	Bartering (2)
	Counter (2)	Streetwise (2)
	Twitch Reflexes (3)	Cooking (1)
	Stealth (1)	Mending (1)
	Survivalist (2)	First Aid (1)
	First Aid (1)	Thalian (3)
	Wood Carving (1)	Neyardic (3)
	Leatherworking (2)	Ostari (1)
	Butchering (4)	Mana Manipulation (2)
	Thalian (2)	Mana Sight (1)
	Disguise (2)	Metallurgy (1)
	Deception (1)	Whitesmithing (1)
	Analyze (BL)	Goldsmithing (2)
	Remote Access (BL)	Gem Cutting (1)
	XP Mask (BL)	Engraving (2)
		Rune Forging (1)
		Painting (1)
		Arcano Dynamics (1)
		Sleight of Hand (1)
		Steady Hands (2)
		Cold Reading (1)
		Temperature Acclimation (2)
		Cadence (2)
		Bloodline Purification Ritual (1)

CHAPTER 37

While Luke wove through the trees to reach the next archer, a woman at level 24 with high agility and perception, but not much else going for her as far as **[Analyze]** was concerned, he tried to remember what it was that System had said the highest-level mercenary was. He wanted to say the answer was 35, but he hoped he was misremembering.

At least nobody nearby was that strong. As far as he could tell, he was the highest-level combatant in this particular fight, though he would appear as the weakest to them. Anybody with more than two brain cells would know that he was stronger than his nonexistent XP aura would indicate, but he much preferred his power to be an unknown to them.

He hadn't really stopped to appreciate how **[Analyze]** cut through any XP-suppressing skills until now, but as he dashed wildly through the trees, he was reminded of how it seemed like every single church agent he'd met had always been stronger than their XP would indicate. It wouldn't surprise him at all if these mercenaries were the same, but without the ability to sense it, he couldn't be distracted by false impressions.

Well, that was what he was going to tell himself anyway. The truth was that he keenly felt the loss of that sense. He could hear his opponents, and Zea as well for that matter, and that was good for roughly keeping track of their locations, but it was a poor substitute for sensing their XP. On the bright side, the look of surprise on the second archer's face when Luke popped out from around a tree and broke her arm with his first swing was priceless.

She didn't even get a chance to draw a weapon before he obliterated her on the backswing. Luke wanted to take out the third archer, but Cartman had reached the woods and had, perhaps smartly, decided to go after Zea instead of Luke. He wasn't sure if that was an attempt at taking a hostage or if Zea was just easier to find since her XP wasn't hidden, but either way, Luke needed to step in before he got to her.

There was a slight problem there, one of distance. Luke was fast, but so was Cartman, and Zea hadn't moved deep enough into the forest in the intervening seconds to delay getting caught. In fact, Luke was pretty sure she hadn't moved at all. He hadn't expected all that much in ten seconds, but he figured she'd at least have made a token effort to hide.

He was about halfway there, fully aware of the futility of racing Cartman but desperately trying to plan out some way to save Zea anyway, when an explosion shook the trees around him. Luke was thrown off his feet to tumble through the air, where he landed feetfirst, crouched against the side of a tree.

"What the fuck," he muttered, dropping back to the ground and advancing with considerably more caution now. The forest practically screamed with the sounds of panicked birds fleeing into the air, but underneath all of that he heard the voice of a man groaning in pain.

There was a new clearing in the forest, a circle about ten feet around where all the vegetation had been torn away. One tree was ripped out of the ground and only upright at this point due to the other trees it had partially fallen on. Any grass that had been there was now scoured away, and there were a good number of stripped-bare branches snapped off and lying outside the circle. Loose leaves still fluttered through the air, dozens of feet away from the clearing.

Zea was nowhere to be found, which Luke took to mean she hadn't been in the middle of whatever the hell had happened. Cartman, on the other hand, was on the ground about twenty feet outside the clearing, his whole front a charred mess. His facial features had been burned off, and the steel plate he wore was partially melted into his flesh. Luke sighed in annoyance. Once again, he wouldn't be scavenging any armor off the fight. Cartman had been the only enemy even close to his size.

Putting the mercenary out of his misery was probably doing him a favor at this point, but on the off chance he had his own healing skill, Luke killed him anyway. That left, to his knowledge, one archer and the two men from the wagon who had yet to enter the woods. Luke felt comfortable with those odds.

Zea was still missing, which was probably a good thing until the rest of the mercenaries had been dealt with, but he'd feel better if he knew where she was hiding. The explosion almost had to have been caused by her, but he hadn't even known she had something capable of doing that. He wondered if she could make things that he could use too, even without **[Mana Manipulation]** and **[Mana Sight]**. Having a secret bomb he could set off in a tight situation would be awesome.

Of course, it would have been nice to be let in on the fact that she was carrying a bomb, even if it was magical and there was no chance it could go off accidentally. They'd be having a discussion about that as soon as this was all over, and as soon as he figured out where the hell she'd gone. Luke idly scanned the branches overhead, half expecting to find her draped over one near the top of a tree.

She wasn't there because that would have made things too easy. Instead of continuing to look for her, Luke targeted the last archer, whom he could hear running directly away from ground zero. Smart of her, really. Luke expected they were all wondering just what the hell had happened and internally debating whether they'd gotten paid enough to take this job.

He slipped off after her, but after a minute or two, it became apparent that she had the agility to keep ahead of him and the stamina to keep up the pace for longer than he was willing to give chase. His time would be better spent finding Zea and getting away from the ambush site before more mercenaries showed up.

Wagonman Number One, the guy who was only level 19, burst out of the bushes nearby as Luke turned to head back toward the edge of the trees, a knife longer than Luke's forearm brandished in one hand. He did so in near-perfect silence too, obviously leaning on a few ranks in **[Stealth]** to achieve that. Luke hadn't heard so much as a single breath as he was going by. But he did smell horse and some sort of grease or oil from the man's time sitting on the wagon, which was all he needed to expect the ambush.

The knife flashed by as Luke stuttered his step slightly to alter his speed. The mercenary ended up in front of him, his whole body thrown into the attack, and in the perfect position to have his legs kicked out from beneath him. He went down with a grunt and immediately rolled, quick enough to dodge Luke's follow-up attack, but not so quick that he made it back to his feet before getting kicked again.

"You know, I should probably keep you alive so I can ask all sorts of questions, but somehow, I doubt you'd answer. And I'm just not really into torture," Luke said as he brought the mace down again.

The merc threw the knife at Luke's face, his arm uncoiling in a whiplike motion that sent the overly large blade spinning a full rotation in the scant three feet between him and his target. It was actually kind of impressive to Luke that the knife did a full spin before it reached him, not that it mattered. Luke just tilted his head to the side and let the blade go past him.

"So I'm guessing you don't want to tell me why a group of mercenaries is after me? I mean, I can guess, but it'd be nice to know."

The merc snarled and lunged forward in an attempt to tackle Luke around the waist. **[Twitch Reflexes]** tried to push him back a step and to the side so that the tackle could miss, but Luke already knew the merc's strength was only

25. He simply braced himself to take the tackle, held his ground, and then mercilessly slammed his elbow down into the man's temple.

Strength left the merc's arms, and he wobbled, now held upright only by his grip around Luke's waist. From there it was a simple matter to kick the man free, and Luke found himself at a bit of a loss. He was no good at information extracting, but it still seemed prudent to try. Maybe Zea would have a better idea. With a sigh, Luke grabbed the now-limp body by the arm and started dragging it back toward the demolished clearing.

"Okay, one more wagon guy, whom I don't hear anywhere nearby, and one hot short stack that I also don't hear anywhere nearby, probably because of some sort of trinket she whipped up that hides her just like that feather did," Luke said, looking around. "Which I guess means I'm standing here and letting people come to me."

Luke didn't like that idea. He wanted to do something proactive, not just wait for someone to show up and take a swing at him. Proactive was always better than reactive. That was why they'd pulled the fight into the forest to begin with. So far, that was working out just fine, except that he'd lost track of the only person on this whole planet he actually cared about.

Worse, if he just sat around waiting, that meant more mercenaries might show up. Considering he'd given up the chase on one of the archers and had never even encountered the second wagon man once they'd gotten into the trees, not to mention the various people stalking them, he figured there were good odds that reinforcements would be showing up soon.

"Uh, Pavena? Could you like . . . stop hiding now?"

Luke didn't want to pitch his voice too loud, just in case, but at this point, he figured he could take anyone who might still be lurking in the area, and he didn't hear anyone at all anyway. He waited a minute, gave his new prisoner another kick to the head when the man started groaning, and then tried again.

"Pavena? Seriously, it's time to go." There was no answer. Luke looked around again, hoping to spot her and knowing it was futile. "Shit."

"Hey, wake up," Luke said, lightly slapping around his prisoner. "I need to know where you guys set up your camp. I think my friend might have gotten abducted."

The man's head lolled backward, and the only thing keeping him even sort of upright was a firm grip on his armor. Once again, too small for Luke. He was really getting sick of that. It wasn't even like he was that tall, but somehow, every time, the one guy whose armor might fit him ended up getting gruesomely murdered and took his armor along with him.

"Snap out of it," Luke demanded. "Really, dude, I don't have the time to fuck around with you here."

The man murmured something, but Luke could barely hear it. "What was that again?" he asked.

His prisoner said something else, different words this time, but a little louder. Luke didn't understand a word of them. "Of fucking course. You don't speak Thalian, do you? What was this language called again. *O* something. Osagi? No. System, what is this guy speaking?"

"Ostari, Luke."

"Right, thanks. Okay, time to buy rank 1 in that. I knew that was going to end up happening."

A few seconds later, **[Ostari]** got added to his list of skills. "Okay, shithead, let's try this again. Where did your friends take my friend? I need to go get her back."

Name	Luke Bennet	Zea Stenter
Level	33	21
XP	128963/131675	32845/34079
AP	8	33
Bloodline	SysAdmin II	None
Strength	42	7
Agility	55	27
Stamina	51	27
Perception	39	19
Skills	Mace Mastery (3)	Dagger Mastery (1)
	Sword Mastery (1)	Stealth (2)
	Unarmed Martialist (4)	Keen Instincts (1)
	Power Strike (2)	Lock Picking (1)
	Life Surge (2)	Disguise (2)
	Peripheral Awareness (2)	Deception (1)
	Tactical Foresight (1)	Bartering (2)
	Counter (2)	Streetwise (2)
	Twitch Reflexes (3)	Cooking (1)
	Stealth (1)	Mending (1)
	Survivalist (2)	First Aid (1)
	First Aid (1)	Thalian (3)
	Wood Carving (1)	Neyardic (3)
	Leatherworking (2)	Ostari (1)
	Butchering (4)	Mana Manipulation (2)
	Thalian (2)	Mana Sight (1)
	Ostari (1)	Metallurgy (1)
	Disguise (2)	Whitesmithing (1)
	Deception (1)	Goldsmithing (2)
	Analyze (BL)	Gem Cutting (1)
	Remote Access (BL)	Engraving (2)
	XP Mask (BL)	Rune Forging (1)
		Painting (1)
		Arcano Dynamics (1)
		Sleight of Hand (1)
		Steady Hands (2)
		Cold Reading (1)
		Temperature Acclimation (2)
		Cadence (2)
		Bloodline Purification Ritual (1)

CHAPTER 38

Luke had forgotten how uncomfortable a rank 1 language skill was. The way it twisted his lips and tongue around to form sounds he was pretty sure he'd never made in his entire life was downright creepy, like feeling someone else's fingers in his mouth forcing it into the shapes needed to say the words.

It put him in a bad mood, and he didn't need help with that. The merc he'd captured was woozy enough already that, now that Luke understood what he was trying to say, everything coming out of his mouth was nonsensical. Maybe the head shots hadn't been the best idea. Then again, this guy had levels and stats. He should have bounced back from being hurt just fine.

So maybe he was playing it up. After all, people wouldn't normally be able to tell exactly how much stamina someone had, so if the guy was sandbagging him to stall for time, pretending to be woozy from a blow to the head was a good strategy. It might even have worked if not for the fact that Luke had already hit him with an **[Analyze]** and knew for a fact that he had 26 stamina.

"Man, I really don't want to have to start breaking things, but you see, my friend is very important to me. So I'll make you a deal. Your buddies are gone. No one within a mile of here. You tell me what I want to know, and you can just walk away. Go wherever, do whatever. I don't care."

The merc spat out something that Luke's new skill had trouble translating, but which he was pretty sure was a stream of swearing. Then, he said, "I won't tell you anything. Just kill me now."

"Oh, okay. Well, in that case."

Luke brought his mace down on the merc's knee.

"Six gods curse your mother!" the merc screamed, trying to clutch at his knee but prevented from reaching it by Luke's hold on him.

"So where did you say your buddies were taking my friend?"

The merc gave him a sullen glare but didn't answer. Luke let out an exaggerated sigh, threw the man face down into the bare, scoured earth, and brought the mace around again to smash one of his hands. "I really don't like doing this," Luke told him once the screaming died down into whimpers. "But I'm going to get her back, one way or another."

"Go fuck yourself, apostate devil," the merc said as he cradled his demolished hand close and tried to scoot away on his elbows.

"Ah, so it *is* a church thing. Figured that was the case, but good to know. Look, my **[Survivalist]** skill is just okay, not that great. That only means that I won't find her quickly, not that I can't do it. But man, oh man, if something bad happens to her before I catch up, well, I guess I would say that I hope you hate your coworkers because bad things would start happening to them too."

The merc flipped onto his back and started using his good leg to kick against the ground and push him backward. He was actually managing a respectable speed with it, all things considered. Luke clicked his tongue and shook his head. "Come on, man. Help me out here. No?"

The other knee was next, then the hip, then the shoulder, all on the same side and in quick succession.

"Greshlin! We're working out of Greshlin," the merc screamed out.

"Fucking fantastic! Now we're getting somewhere," Luke said. He paused a beat and added, "And what direction is that in?"

In the heat of the moment, it was easy to take necessary measures to get what he needed. It was only after Luke was finished working the guy over that it really hit him what he'd been doing. Specifically, it was while the merc was on the ground, delirious with pain and no longer able to answer anything at all that Luke got a notification.

[Congratulations! You have unlocked the Torturer (1) skill. 25 XP awarded.]

He stared at the little blue box blankly, his lips moving as he silently read the message over and over again. There it was, right there. Undeniable proof forever stamped onto his status of what he'd done. He'd gotten what he wanted, and he hated himself a little bit for that.

Then he looked around at the little clearing made by some sort of explosion. He was hoping it was from something Zea had made, but he didn't know that for sure. Maybe Cartman had been the cause of it, however unlikely that appeared. What he did know was that she was nowhere nearby, and at least one of the mercenaries had never even tried to attack him.

The merc he'd captured moaned in agony at Luke's feet. A huge part of him was sickened by what he'd done. It was different than fighting the man, cruel somehow. Then his mouth hardened into a thin line, and he reminded himself that, given the chance, these people would have done worse to him. They might be in the process of doing exactly that to Zea.

The mace came down on the man's skull, shattering it in an explosion of bone chunks and brain matter.

[You have slain Blacktongue Human Mercenary (level 19). 374 XP awarded.]

[This creature has slain 428 other creatures.]

[Total kills for this type of creature: 38.]

[Highest-level kill: 24.]

"Thanks for the help," he told the now-silent corpse.

Luke started running north through the woods. Without Zea there, he didn't need to hold back so she could keep up, and since he had System constantly correcting his course, Luke was heading toward Greshlin in a straight line. The merc had told him it was a twenty-mile trip by road, but System said twelve miles through the woods. Luke was determined to make it in under half an hour.

Zea was beyond pissed off right now. Whatever the fuck weapon that guy had been using, it had reacted really badly with her partially completed razor-prong whip. She supposed that, strictly speaking, it was most likely her fault for trying to use a weapon that was only half-enchanted. That did not make her any less pissed about the explosion, if only because she was pretty sure they'd left the prong pieces behind in the woods.

At least it had happened at the point of contact, which was on his end. She'd blown that fucker's shoes off, even if the explosion had also tossed her into a tree fifty feet away. She'd barely been conscious when another one of Team Asshole had shown up, pulled her out of the tree, bound her hands together, and gagged her. Then he'd taken all her bags off her, thrown her over his shoulder, and just ran off with her.

Which brought her back to now, sitting on the floor, still bound and gagged, in an empty, locked room with a guy who had enough XP to be at least level 30, and that was just what she could sense. Zea had a strong suspicion this might be the level 35 guy System had warned them about, and judging by how the rest of the humans acted around him, he was definitely the leader of their little group.

They hadn't tried to question her, or even talk to her. In fact, they hadn't done anything at all other than make sure she was securely tied up and sit on her so that she couldn't even make an attempt to escape. That was smart of them, since she was sitting on 33 AP and had a few ideas in mind for what skills she might pick up to get herself free if they happened to leave her unattended.

Someone knocked on the door, and the high-level guy guarding her glanced over at it. He stood up, crossed the room, and pulled it open. "What?" he asked softly, probably too quietly for most people to hear. Zea had gotten quite used to having what was, for normal people at least, an abnormally high perception. The guy probably thought he was being quiet enough, but she could hear him easily.

"The other target is coming directly toward the town. One of our scouts spotted him three minutes ago. He is really flying. No one else came back out of the woods. They're probably all dead."

"He's coming here?" the boss asked, surprise evident in his tone. "Well, that makes things easy then. Make sure everyone is ready for him. Our contract states they both need to be alive to get the full amount. If someone kills him, I will personally string them up by their own intestines. Then we'll take turns beating them with sticks until all the gold we missed out on falls out of their pockets."

The other man laughed. "Understood, sir. I'll go spread the word."

The boss closed the door, then returned to leaning against the wall. He glanced down at Zea and said, "Your man is coming after us. You'll have some company soon."

Zea laughed through the gag and mumbled something that probably wouldn't have been intelligible even without the low rank in her language skill. The boss raised an eyebrow, then leaned forward and untied the gag. "Something to say?"

"Sounds like you're all fucked then," she told him.

He laughed. "That'd be a good time. We've got him outnumbered thirty to one though, and he's not even trying to be sneaky about it. Weird, that. The scouts are saying they can't feel any XP off him at all. You'd think he'd have a stealth build if he devoted that much effort to hiding his XP."

Zea just laughed again. "You'll find out soon, huh?"

"Suppose so. Well, if he does manage to win this one, I want you to know that we don't give a flying fuck about his status as an apostate. Well, most of us don't. Never really was much for religion myself. Nuk caught it real bad a few years back. Probably why he volunteered for the capture mission. He gets all rabid about heretics. But the rest of us, well, we're mercenaries. Gold is the only god we worship.

"What I'm trying to say here is good luck. I wouldn't wish an inquisitor's attention on my worst enemy. I hope you both escape, but only after we hand you over. I still want to get paid, of course."

"Don't expect me to be grateful for your consideration," Zea told him.

"No, no, of course not. Ignore me. Just an old man rambling to pass the time."

He didn't look that old to her, but considering how high his level was, and that he was still in active service in a mercenary organization, she supposed he knew he only had a decade or two at most left. Well, if Luke was on his way in, it was more like an hour or two, especially if this guy was going to keep sitting on her. That practically guaranteed he'd be targeted.

Luke could be a big softy at times, and he wasn't always practical about stuff, but he took her safety seriously. Honestly, he probably spent more time worrying about her than he did about himself. That was kind of sweet, kind of annoying, and wholly him.

The bastard put the gag back in place, nodded to himself, and leaned serenely back against the wall. "Any minute now and the fun'll start," he told her.

If Luke had any doubts that he had the right place, they were dispelled by the asshole on the roof with a crossbow trying to hide just behind the peak. That seemed like a good sign. Plus, the building was right on the edge of town, ten times bigger than a normal house, and made completely of stone, just like that guy he'd tortured for information had said. Between that and the three different traps he could see near the front door, two trip lines and some sort of pit covered in a screen of actual sod with grass going out of it, that pretty much confirmed his suspicions.

The asshole on the roof popped up over the peak, aimed his crossbow in a fraction of a second, and pulled the trigger. Luke shifted his mace so that the bolt pinged off the head.

"Yep, definitely the right place. Time to get to work."

Name	Luke Bennet	Zea Stenter
Level	33	21
XP	129362/131675	32845/34079
AP	8	33
Bloodline	SysAdmin II	None
Strength	42	7
Agility	55	27
Stamina	51	27
Perception	39	19
Skills	Mace Mastery (3)	Dagger Mastery (1)
	Sword Mastery (1)	Stealth (2)
	Unarmed Martialist (4)	Keen Instincts (1)
	Power Strike (2)	Lock Picking (1)
	Life Surge (2)	Disguise (2)
	Peripheral Awareness (2)	Deception (1)
	Tactical Foresight (1)	Bartering (2)
	Counter (2)	Streetwise (2)
	Twitch Reflexes (3)	Cooking (1)
	Stealth (1)	Mending (1)
	Survivalist (2)	First Aid (1)
	First Aid (1)	Thalian (3)
	Wood Carving (1)	Neyardic (3)
	Leatherworking (2)	Ostari (1)
	Butchering (4)	Mana Manipulation (2)
	Thalian (2)	Mana Sight (1)
	Ostari (1)	Metallurgy (1)
	Disguise (2)	Whitesmithing (1)
	Deception (1)	Goldsmithing (2)
	Torturer (1)	Gem Cutting (1)
	Analyze (BL)	Engraving (2)
	Remote Access (BL)	Rune Forging (1)
	XP Mask (BL)	Painting (1)
		Arcano Dynamics (1)
		Sleight of Hand (1)
		Steady Hands (2)
		Cold Reading (1)
		Temperature Acclimation (2)
		Cadence (2)
		Bloodline Purification Ritual (1)

CHAPTER 39

Luke was planning on killing a lot of people in the next few minutes. He wasn't sure what the exact number would be, and he supposed that really depended more on them than it did on him. But he was sick to death of people in this world fucking with him, and abducting Zea crossed the line. She'd been dragged into his problems enough, and he'd failed at keeping her safe.

That was his fault. He shouldn't have left her alone. He'd thought she'd find a place to hide, but then there'd been whatever the hell that explosion was, and everything had gone sideways from there. Now these merc fuckers, Blacktongue or whatever, had her, and he was going to get her back.

And anyone between point A and point B trying to stop him was going to have a really bad day.

He took a breath after blocking the crossbow bolt and just listened. It wasn't as good as feeling XP, but the sounds were all there. Pretty much all the time, he did his best to block all that extraneous noise out. It was necessary just to keep from being overwhelmed by it. Lately, he'd been trying to get a better handle on it.

One guy on the roof. Two on the other side of the wall, flanking the gate and crouched low. Footsteps of people running around inside, at least five. Whispered conversations discussed who was getting in what position, and where and when they'd attack. He heard the word *nonlethal* thrown around a lot. That was great. They were handicapping themselves. By the time they changed their minds, some of the mercenaries would already be dead.

Luke exhaled. Somewhere in that building, below ground level, he thought, was a dwifkin woman who wasn't doing much moving around, but who was regularly tapping her foot once every five seconds. That was the goal.

Priority one was the sniper. **[Analyze]** told him the guy was level 22, with agility and perception in the 30s, strength and stamina around 15. The compound was about thirty feet back from the wall, which was itself ten feet high and topped with a row of metal spikes that curled outward.

He jumped it in one smooth motion, touched down briefly on the outer curve of the spikes, and leaped up to the roof. Below him, the two mercs waiting for him to rush the gate gaped at his sudden appearance overhead, and Luke took a moment to hurl his knife into one of their throats.

A few months ago, he would have been amazed at his own athleticism and precision. Today, he was just grimly satisfied when the kill notification went off. His feet pounded against the cedar shingles, three distinct steps as he scaled the pitch of the roof and brought his mace around to hit the sniper as soon as he came into view.

The cowardly merc had already abandoned his position, but he hadn't made it off the roof yet, and he wasn't nearly as fast as Luke. He died, and his corpse was flung out through the open air to crash into the fence surrounding the back of the compound. Luke dropped back down to the ground, stepped around some sort of bear trap that was hidden in a flower bed, and kicked the back door hard enough to blow it off its hinges.

It was significantly heavier than he'd expected, being made entirely out of some sort of steel, and the hinges squealed as they tore free. It landed with a huge, echoing boom that Luke found entirely satisfying, right up until the four mercs in the room all whipped around to face him. "Hi," Luke said. "Just direct me to the dwifkin girl and I'll be out of your hair, okay?"

Even as he was speaking, he was already moving into the room and bringing his mace around to crack the first merc across the face. The man went flying through a wall, definitely dead, and definitely surprising two more mercs. Then the other three attacked, and Luke let himself fall into the grip of his skills.

[Tactical Foresight] took center stage, easily predicting the incoming attacks. That, combined with **[Unarmed Martialist]** to keep his body moving and **[Counter]** to show him the openings the mercs left when they tried to kill him, was all it took to end the fight.

A man with a sword stumbled past him, his agility too low to keep up with Luke's movements. The mace caught the back of his skull and threw his corpse to the floor. The woman farthest away from him across the room unloaded a brace of throwing knives so fast and so precise that there was no way for Luke to weave through them. Instead, he hopped straight up and flipped in the air so that when he landed, he was behind the man holding a pair of shortswords.

Mace met blades as the man blocked behind him, not even turning around fully to stop Luke. Then the man collapsed when Luke kicked the back of his knee out, and Luke took a single step to the side just as the knife thrower unloaded another salvo on him. The dual wielder took three of them in his back, which slowed him down just long enough for Luke to tear his head off with a simple horizontal strike.

He advanced on the knife thrower, who'd run out of weapons and was now looking for a way out. She'd backed herself into a corner to get some distance on him, but without the other mercs to keep him occupied, she was trapped now.

"Downstairs, right? Want to tell me where the stairs are?" Luke asked, noting the two mercs from the other room were coming in from the only other door.

When the woman didn't answer, Luke closed the distance and blew through her defenses as she tried to step into his swing and grab his arm, only to find that he outmuscled her by an order of magnitude. He planted a hand on her chest and shoved her backward, then swung a second time. *Ding. Ding.*

Two dings. He supposed that meant he'd leveled up. That was good. Having loose AP that he could use midfight when he needed it was always reassuring. Rank 4 **[Mace Mastery]** would probably be a good option, or maybe rank 3 **[Counter]**. Right now, his biggest concern was being overwhelmed by sheer numbers, and both of those skills would help with that.

He held off on it for the moment, if only because he had yet to use **[Power Strike]** or **[Life Surge]**, and he'd already killed six of the mercenaries. Most of them had been low 20s, but he was betting there were a few tougher ones floating around somewhere.

Luke knew that he needed to keep his momentum going. Right now, the mercenaries were off guard. They'd expected him to show up maybe, but not to charge in like that. **[XP Mask]** was proving its worth already, throwing people off. If they were anywhere as used to relying on feeling someone else's XP to keep track of where they were as he was, it was no wonder they were having a hard time reacting to him.

Sooner or later, they'd get their shit together, and then he'd be fighting all of them at once instead of three or four at a time. The more of them he killed before they got to that point, the better off he'd be, which was why Luke turned and attacked both mercs as soon as they made it into the room.

One of them was level 30 and more than willing to get in Luke's face. He actually had a mace of his own, which surprised Luke, as it was the first time he could recall seeing anyone using the same kind of weapon as him. From the look on the merc's face, it seemed like he was surprised too. A brief moment of kinship passed between the two, and then they were back to trying to kill each other.

The merc had the strength to back up his weapon choice, even a few points over Luke's, and he'd complemented it with an excellent suite of skills, just judging by their initial clash. What he lacked was the agility to keep up with Luke's lightning-fast strikes. Merc-y McMaceFace was more than happy to take the damage in exchange for getting a shot at Luke, and perhaps most importantly, he had a friend to help him out. That other guy was even more of a problem, in his own way.

He had, of all things, what looked like some sort of slingshot that he was rapidly loading with pebbles and firing in Luke's direction. They were pretty accurate too and stung like a bitch whenever one of them landed. It wasn't going to be fatal on its own, not unless Luke took a real unlucky hit to the head or something, but it was distracting, and that was unacceptable when he was squaring off against someone who could dish out punishment just as hard as he could.

The skinny one was skulking around behind McMaceFace, relying on his buddy to be a human shield for him, a . . . A meat shield, Curt would have called it. That was unacceptable. Not only did Luke not have time for a drawn-out confrontation, but what kind of asshole just shot rocks at someone?

Luke skipped back a step and let McMaceFace's attack whoosh by, then surprised the man by stepping in to meet him with his own attack. There wasn't enough space between them to fully swing his own mace, so Luke compensated with a short downward chop infused with **[Power Strike]**. The merc got the haft of his mace up in time to partially block it, but even his strength and stamina weren't high enough to keep both his feet under him.

Maybe Luke could have finished him off right there. There were certainly openings to exploit, but he didn't even try. His arm snapped forward, just like that other merc who'd thrown that huge knife at him, and his mace flew out to strike the dick with the bag of rocks right in the chest. Ribs broke, his heart was pulped, and the man died with a surprised and pain-filled squeal accompanied by a one-note ding in Luke's head.

Throwing his weapon would have been a terrible move, except that Luke activated a second **[Power Strike]**, this time through his fist, and drove it directly between McMaceFace's eyes. Even down on one knee, the man wobbled. He dropped his own weapon and fell to the floor, now needing both hands to keep from toppling over. In an impressive display of willpower, he shook his head slowly and tried to reach out to grab Luke as he moved past.

Luke was far too fast, and McMaceFace was far too dizzy. Luke recovered his mace from the destroyed chest cavity of his latest kill, then spun back to finish off the last merc before he could recover. In a way, he almost felt bad about killing this one. Almost.

[You have slain Blacktongue Human Mercenary (level 30). 957 XP awarded.]

[This creature has slain 1126 other creatures.]

[Total kills for this type of creature: 46.]

[Highest-level kill: 30.]

At least the XP was good. He'd just leveled a few kills back and was already down to a mere ten thousand to level again. Hell, it might even happen before he left the compound if he found another twenty or so mercenaries. And he was planning on going out of his way to kill anyone who wasn't smart enough to run, just so there wouldn't be any pursuit after he was done.

Booted feet stomped on the floor about fifty feet away from him, just slightly out of time with one another. Luke paused and counted. Six people, he thought, all of them coming his way. He hefted his mace and moved forward, already using **[Analyze]** as he picked out individual targets by sound alone.

Name	Luke Bennet	Zea Stenter
Level	34	21
XP	134110/144088	32845/34079
AP	42	33
Bloodline	SysAdmin II	None
Strength	42	7
Agility	55	27
Stamina	51	27
Perception	39	19
Skills	Mace Mastery (3)	Dagger Mastery (1)
	Sword Mastery (1)	Stealth (2)
	Unarmed Martialist (4)	Keen Instincts (1)
	Power Strike (2)	Lock Picking (1)
	Life Surge (2)	Disguise (2)
	Peripheral Awareness (2)	Deception (1)
	Tactical Foresight (1)	Bartering (2)
	Counter (2)	Streetwise (2)
	Twitch Reflexes (3)	Cooking (1)
	Stealth (1)	Mending (1)
	Survivalist (2)	First Aid (1)
	First Aid (1)	Thalian (3)
	Wood Carving (1)	Neyardic (3)
	Leatherworking (2)	Ostari (1)
	Butchering (4)	Mana Manipulation (2)
	Thalian (2)	Mana Sight (1)
	Ostari (1)	Metallurgy (1)
	Disguise (2)	Whitesmithing (1)
	Deception (1)	Goldsmithing (2)
	Torturer (1)	Gem Cutting (1)
	Analyze (BL)	Engraving (2)
	Remote Access (BL)	Rune Forging (1)
	XP Mask (BL)	Painting (1)
		Arcano Dynamics (1)
		Sleight of Hand (1)
		Steady Hands (2)
		Cold Reading (1)
		Temperature Acclimation (2)
		Cadence (2)
		Bloodline Purification Ritual (1)

CHAPTER 40

"Gods above, what are those idiots doing up there?" the boss muttered to himself as he glanced up at the ceiling.

Zea would have laughed if she hadn't still been gagged. Luke was generally pretty easygoing, but she'd seen him when he got riled up about something. From the sounds of it, he wasn't happy and was taking it out on the mercenary group that had attacked them. It sounded like a demolition crew was tearing apart the building over their heads, and Zea had some vague worries about being buried alive if it all collapsed down into the basement.

Based on how many different sources of XP up there were disappearing one after another, things had gone very badly for the mercenaries over the last two minutes. It sounded like Luke wasn't holding back at all anymore.

"Why in the hell isn't he coming straight at her? It's like he can't even find her," the boss muttered. He walked over to the door and jerked it open. "Change of plans, men."

"Sir?" one of the mercenaries lurking in the hall said.

"Get this one out of here and delivered to the client. It looks like the other one is either too smart to fall for the trap or too stupid to even find it. I'm going to have to go take care of him before he causes any more damage."

"Understood."

The boss stalked out, presumably to go fight Luke himself, and three other mercenaries came into the room. One of them hoisted her up over one shoulder, and they trooped out in a line. "Can't believe that apostate is going through us like that," she heard the one in the lead say softly. "How many fucking levels did that kid pack on since he got here?"

* * *

[You have slain Blacktongue Human Mercenary (level 27). 769 XP awarded.]
  [This creature has slain 719 other creatures.]
  [Total kills for this type of creature: 55.]
  [Highest-level kill: 30.]

Finally, Luke had a moment to get his bearings. After the third group, the rest of the mercs had backed off. As far as he could tell, most of them had retreated out of the building completely, like they'd just given up stopping him. That was all well and good, except he still hadn't found Zea. For a few minutes after he'd arrived, he'd heard a rhythmic tapping sound, but that had stopped at almost the exact same time he'd finally had a second to focus on it. He thought it was coming from below him and to the left, which was as good a direction as any.

There had to be a set of stairs somewhere, but Luke had no idea where they were. Rather than waste time looking for them, he brought his mace down in a wild overhand swing and busted the floorboards apart. A second chop was all he needed to widen it enough to fit in, and Luke dropped down into, well . . . not a basement, but he supposed a subfloor. He landed in a hallway, dark except for the light that spilled down from the hole he'd made, and looked around for any mercs.

There was no one in sight, but he could hear a group of them moving somewhere behind him. They didn't appear to be heading toward him, but since they were the only ones he could hear moving around, he figured it was better to check on them first. He set off at a slow—for him—jog and, within a few seconds, was barreling through his first locked door. The wood broke apart before the lock did, and the remains of the door blew inward as he charged through it.

"Hello," he said in Ostari. Three mercs who'd been walking toward the door all froze in surprise. One of them gave an uncertain glance behind him, then muttered something softly while running off. The second one, who was holding a tied-up Zea over his shoulder, darted off in another direction, and the merc in the lead pulled out a weird sword-looking thing with no edge, but that was hooked at the tip, then moved to the center of the hall to block Luke from getting past him.

"Dick move of your buddies to run off and leave you here," Luke said, activating **[Analyze]**.

[Name: Blacktongue Human Mercenary]
[Level: 28]
[Strength: 31]
[Agility: 28]
[Stamina: 25]

[Perception: 22]

Tough, but not the worse he'd fought in the last few minutes. There was no question in Luke's mind that he would win, just how long it would take and how far away the one carrying Zea would get. Now that he'd gotten confirmation on her position, he knew which set of sounds were hers. The gag was unexpected, but it actually made things easier to pick her out of the background noise since she was the only person breathing with one on.

The merc rushed forward, his hooked blade snaking out to grab at the haft of Luke's mace. It tugged the weapon to the side, either in an attempt to disarm Luke or to pull him off-balance and leave him open for some sort of follow-up attack. Either way, the merc lacked the strength to move Luke's weapon any farther than he allowed it to.

Just as Luke was about to reverse that and use the man's own weapon to pull him into an attack, something changed. All of a sudden, his mace was being dragged sideways, practically out of his grip. There was no way the merc had enough strength, and the angle seemed all wrong to give him that leverage.

Despite that, Luke was forced to shuffle to the left just to keep hold of his weapon. He grimaced as he was pulled out of his stance, then kicked out to check an attack coming from the merc. It seemed Luke wasn't the only one stacking ranks into **[Unarmed Martialist]**, and this guy's build was actually countering him pretty hard, despite the level gap.

Luke was far from out of tricks though. Whatever skill the merc was using to keep his mace tied up, it wasn't enough to keep Luke from moving it. He feinted left, then when the merc moved to keep his weapon locked down, Luke pulled back to the right. This earned him a fist across the face, which Luke gladly accepted in exchange for getting his hand locked around the merc's arm.

All skills aside, when it came down to a contest of brute strength, Luke outclassed his opponent. He demonstrated that fact by picking the man up by his arm and slamming him repeatedly into the wall. The hooked stick fell from limp fingers and clattered against the floor, followed swiftly by the man's body. That was less of a clatter and more of a wet thump followed by some groaning.

Luke finished the merc off before he could recover, then stepped over the corpse and raced down the hall after the man who'd been carrying Zea. Before he could catch up, two more mercenaries came out of a previously unseen stairwell and got in front of him. The first was one of the two runners from the group he'd just encountered, but the second was someone new.

[Name: Blacktongue Human Mercenary]
[Level: 35]
[Strength: 42]
[Agility: 38]
[Stamina: 48]

[Perception: 29]

"Shit," Luke said. Of course he'd have to run into the toughest one of the lot right as he was about to catch up with Zea. It really couldn't have happened any other way, otherwise he might have taken is as proof that the gods weren't fucking with him. Show him the goal, then block it with the biggest asshole of them all.

"Not as planned at all," the merc said with a shake of his head. "Very messy."

He was a big guy, almost a full head taller than Luke's five foot nine, with a square jaw and a neck like a bull. Considering his stats, Luke was kind of surprised by just how bulky the merc was, but he moved with all the fluid grace Luke would expect from someone with 38 agility. Strangely, Luke didn't see a weapon anywhere.

That actually worried him a little bit. His own style of combining heavy attacks with his mace and following up with quick, brutal strikes at pinpointed targets thanks to **[Unarmed Martialist]** had been incredibly effective so far. The only times he'd really struggled was against opponents who were using the same skill. Given the skill level on display so far, Luke felt comfortable saying that his superior levels and stats had carried him through.

For the first time in a long time, he was fighting someone who was a higher level than him, with the exact same strength stat and similar stamina. Luke had a big advantage in agility, but he knew better than anyone how some skills could defeat that by predicting attacks instead of reacting to them. There was no telling what kind of skills the strongest merc in their whole outfit had, or what ranks he had them up to.

Luke tightened his grip on his mace. It didn't matter how strong this guy was, not really. One way or another, Luke was going through him. "Move," he said quietly, "or I'll move you."

The merc just let out a laugh and told him, "Been a while since I had a good scrap. Don't worry, I won't kill you. Though, maybe you'll wish I had once the client gets hold of you."

There was nothing else to be said. Any stalling for time would only hurt Luke's chances of catching up to Zea, and he knew how fast these mercs could move. If this fight dragged on, they could get ahead of him by miles before he got out of the building. Finding Zea at that point would be difficult, verging on impossible.

Luke sprang forward, and the merc rushed down the hall to meet him. The smaller, scrawnier one said something in Ostari, something rapid-fire and complicated enough that as distracted as Luke was in the moment, he couldn't process it to figure out what was being said. Whatever it was, the merc he was fighting just grunted in return. Apparently, that was good enough for the other guy, who took off running.

That was probably a bad sign that the guy was so confident that he didn't even bother keeping his reinforcement around to help. Another bad sign was that they were less than ten feet from each other and he was showing every sign that he planned to just body Luke into the floor without stopping. The mace flashed up, speeding toward the merc's center mass, only to be deflected by a palm slap that hit with surprising force and drove the weapon through the wall.

Luke was forced to let go or get run over. His hands worked to block the merc's attempts to grab on to him as their bodies collided, and Luke threw himself backward both to lessen the impact and to tuck into a roll and throw the merc over him using nothing but his feet. Both of them went flying, with the merc going overhead and landing fifteen feet down the hallway.

It looked like the big guy was a fan of wrestling, something Luke had briefly considered trying out for in school before deciding he liked baseball more. Now he was kind of wishing he'd played a season, just so he'd have some basic idea of what kind of moves to expect. Well, it probably didn't translate well anyway. At the levels they were working on, having an extra three hundred pounds trying to hold you down to the ground contributed nothing anyway.

The merc settled into position, his hands wide in a pose that made Luke think of Tantoro, the ostol he'd fought once back in Valtira. That had been a close fight, but Luke was a lot weaker back then. He still hadn't used **[Life Surge]** anyway, but now that he thought about it, the merc was on the wrong side to stop him, and Luke knew agility was his weakest stat.

Luke tore his mace free from the wall, then spun on his heel and dashed off after the fleeing mercenaries.

Name	Luke Bennet	Zea Stenter
Level	34	21
XP	134879/144088	33350/34079
AP	42	8
Bloodline	SysAdmin II	None
Strength	42	7
Agility	55	27
Stamina	51	27
Perception	39	19
Skills	Mace Mastery (3)	Dagger Mastery (1)
	Sword Mastery (1)	Stealth (2)
	Unarmed Martialist (4)	Keen Instincts (1)
	Power Strike (2)	Lock Picking (1)
	Life Surge (2)	Disguise (2)
	Peripheral Awareness (2)	Deception (1)
	Tactical Foresight (1)	Bartering (2)
	Counter (2)	Streetwise (2)
	Twitch Reflexes (3)	Cooking (1)
	Stealth (1)	Mending (1)
	Survivalist (2)	First Aid (1)
	First Aid (1)	Thalian (3)
	Wood Carving (1)	Neyardic (3)
	Leatherworking (2)	Ostari (1)
	Butchering (4)	Mana Manipulation (2)
	Thalian (2)	Mana Sight (1)
	Ostari (1)	Metallurgy (1)
	Disguise (2)	Whitesmithing (1)
	Deception (1)	Goldsmithing (2)
	Torturer (1)	Gem Cutting (1)
	Analyze (BL)	Engraving (2)
	Remote Access (BL)	Rune Forging (1)
	XP Mask (BL)	Painting (1)
		Arcano Dynamics (1)
		Sleight of Hand (1)
		Steady Hands (2)
		Cold Reading (1)
		Temperature Acclimation (2)
		Cadence (2)
		Bloodline Purification Ritual (1)
		Ghost Script (1)

CHAPTER 41

It wasn't that Luke expected to get away, though that would have been the best possible outcome. Enough of the Blacktongue mercenaries had run off that he'd accepted he wasn't going to kill all of them, and that it was a distinct possibility that they'd continue to be a problem in the near future. Killing one more right here and now wasn't going to change that.

But no, he didn't think he was going to get away without another fight. His goal was to catch up to the one who was holding on to Zea before that merc escaped, and to give himself a better arena to fight in. The hallway wasn't exactly narrow, but it favored the merc fighting with his bare fists far more than it favored Luke. He could barely get half a horizontal swing in before he hit one wall or another, and while it was easier to predict which direction a hit would come from when his opponent had no choice but to be right in front of him, it also made it easier for the merc to predict his attacks.

Assuming the merc could keep him with him, Luke just wanted more space to swing his big, heavy, poke-y metal stick around. Plus, he had four different skills that helped him avoid attacks, one of them at rank 4 and another at rank 3, and he needed to play to that advantage.

He sprinted away, trusting in his agility and **[Peripheral Awareness]** to keep him safe. The merc, perhaps surprised by the sudden retreat, hesitated a second before chasing after him with a strangled, "Hey, get back here, you little shithead!"

Luke followed the other merc up the stairs, took a beat to locate the sound of Zea's breathing through the gag they had on her, and rushed off to the right. He hadn't gotten the full layout of the compound while he was rampaging through it, but Luke didn't mind crashing through a window to get back outside if he needed to. Zea was being carried off in a straight line, the same direction all the other lower-level mercs had retreated in, which was another reason to catch up to her before the merc rejoined the rest of his team.

An instant's cracking sound was all the warning he got before the floor next to Luke exploded and the high-level merc was in front of him. The merc grabbed him by the shirt, but Luke threw himself backward. The fabric was no match for the strength of the two men and tore like paper, leaving the merc with a scrap of cloth in one hand and Luke with a V-necked shirt.

The wood splinters hadn't even come back down to the floor yet, and the merc was already coming in for a second attack. Luke blocked it with his mace, mostly by slapping the man's outstretched hand aside. If being battered with a piece of heavy metal moving at high speeds bothered the merc, he didn't show it. Fighting someone with just as much stamina as Luke was a pain in the ass.

Luke darted off to the side, set his shoulder, and activated **[Power Strike]** just as he impacted the wall. His rush took him right through it and into the next room, where he rolled into the air in a sideways flip that sent him over a dinner table. By the time his feet were back under him, the merc had landed on top of the table and already had a fist coming for Luke's face.

"Shit!"

Luke ducked the attack and brought his mace up to crash through the bottom of the table. It snapped apart easily, and the force of the upward strike threw the merc into the ceiling. The man bounced off and was on his way back down before Luke could even scramble back upright, this time with his foot lined up to drop an axe kick onto Luke's skull.

Things got hectic for a few seconds as they traded blows and broke through furniture and walls. Despite his agility advantage, Luke found he was having a hard time keeping ahead of the merc. No matter which way he moved, the other guy was always working to cut him off before he'd even started. Luke was almost positive the merc had his own version of **[Tactical Foresight]**. Hell, it might even be the same skill, and probably at a higher rank too.

The worst part of it was that this was turning into by far the longest fight he'd had against any of the mercs. The guy's build practically seemed designed to stall Luke and frustrate him until he made a mistake, not that that meant he couldn't kill Luke too. Just, that wasn't their aim. They'd made it pretty obvious they wanted Luke and Zea alive for whoever had hired them.

The important thing was that this asshole was stopping him from even making it out of the compound so they could make a proper fight of it, and while Luke was a bit hesitant to use **[Life Surge]** in the middle of a fight, he had tested it against various monsters and found that the rank-up had drastically lowered the side effects. Those had been fights Luke could have won even without the skill pumping him up, but he was reasonably confident it would work here too.

If it didn't, there was no way he was catching up to Zea before the skill gave out, not even with the extended duration. It was a gamble, but his bid to break away from the grabby merc had failed before he'd even gotten out of the compound. Luke activated the skill.

The merc seemed to slow down as all of Luke's stats skyrocketed. He reached out and casually grabbed an arm that was lunging for him, then spun and hurled the big man through the wall. Luke chased after and hammered his enemy with his mace to drive the merc back to the floor when he tried to bound up to his feet.

Something changed, and the merc sped up to something approaching Luke's new speed. The pair went through another wall, and this time Luke took the brunt of it. Before they could land, he rolled and threw the merc off of him. They hit the floor at the same time with about five feet of open air between them. The merc had struck a couch on his way down and was shoved up hard against a wall, while Luke crashed through some sort of end table and broke it to pieces.

There were hundreds of little splinters caught in his clothes, but none pierced his flesh. Even without the boost from **[Life Surge]**, he would have stood back up without a scratch. With it, he barely even noticed the wood bursting apart when he crashed into it. Luke's focus was solely on the exterior window the room boasted, his ticket to freedom. Once they were outside, he'd see if the merc could keep up with his enhanced speed.

Luke crashed through the window before the other guy had even recovered. It seemed like his bursts of speed were extremely short duration and had to be used strategically instead of just poured on. That was better than an alternative where the man somehow kept up with him, and also gave Luke a bit more hope that he might make a clean getaway. Zea was getting farther and farther away the longer he delayed going after her. Already, he was only making guesses as to which direction he needed to go.

The merc put on another burst of speed and landed next to Luke, but those brief instants weren't enough to keep up while **[Life Surge]** was still running. Luke gave him the slip again and shot off at full speed away from the town. He tried to pick up some sort of trail with **[Survivalist]**, but he was moving too fast, and the skill just didn't have enough ranks to function when he was running faster than a car could drive down a highway. All he had to go on was what his ears were reporting back to him and a vague, lingering smell of metal and oil that got stronger the closer he got to the trees.

Luke hit the woods at a run, the merc in hot pursuit behind him. With each passing second, the distance between them grew. Despite his little speed-burst skill, the merc just didn't have the raw stats to keep up with Luke in a long-distance sprint, and that wasn't even factoring in the boost **[Life Surge]** was currently giving him.

Part of him wanted to stand his ground and use the buff from the skill to finish off the mercenary. If his only goal was to kill the man, that's exactly what he would have done, but finding Zea was more important. He could hear mercenaries in the woods, running and calling out to one another to coordinate their retreat. Somewhere in that mess was a man carrying a dwifkin, and Luke was determined to find him.

And then he'd probably bash the man's brains out, just for good measure. He wasn't feeling too lenient toward the mercenaries, considering they'd attacked him and abducted Zea. Anyone who got in Luke's way would receive a similar fate.

Luke chased after the fleeing mercenaries, who seemed to be moving in small groups and converging on one another at a central fallback point. At least, that was the picture he got of it based on what he could hear. There was a spot a mile or so away that was crawling with mercs. That was his best option for finding Zea, but also kind of a worst-case scenario. Fighting that many enemies at once was about the best way to get himself killed.

Maybe he'd get lucky and they'd have another building they could divide themselves up into smaller groups inside. Then all he'd need to do was keep up his momentum and kill them as faster than they showed up. It didn't seem very likely, but a man could hope.

"Luke," a voice said from up in a nearby tree.

His head whipped around, and he blinked when he spotted Zea sitting there, or rather, hanging there, still tied up and draped over a thick branch. Her gag had been loosened enough that it was over her chin now. "What the actual fuck . . ." he whispered as he watched her sway a little bit, the branch creaking.

"Uh, yeah, hi. I . . . um, escaped?" Zea told him.

"Fucking how?" Luke asked. Then he shook his head. They didn't have time to stand around discussing it, not with that merc right on his ass. At best, they had four or five seconds of lead time.

Now that he'd found Zea though, he could shift his priorities. He had about thirty seconds of **[Life Surge]** left and one annoying merc he'd like to kill before they left. If he came at the man aggressively, he might be able to end the fight that quickly. He might get Zea down from the tree and keep running, if he acted quickly enough.

Someone crashed through the trees a hundred feet away, heading straight for them.

"Shit, out of time," Luke said, his decision made for him. He spared a second to leap up into the tree, grab Zea, and break the rope binding her with brute strength. Then he dropped back to the ground and squared himself with the source of the noise. He could see flickers of movement behind a screen of branches and underbrush, and an instant later, the merc burst through them.

"Both of you together? Can't those idiots do anything right?" the merc muttered.

Then he rushed forward, his speed far in excess of what his agility should offer him and his hands extended to grab hold of Luke.

Name	Luke Bennet	Zea Stenter
Level	34	21
XP	134879/144088	33350/34079
AP	42	8
Bloodline	SysAdmin II	None
Strength	42	7
Agility	55	27
Stamina	51	27
Perception	39	19
Skills	Mace Mastery (3)	Dagger Mastery (1)
	Sword Mastery (1)	Stealth (2)
	Unarmed Martialist (4)	Keen Instincts (1)
	Power Strike (2)	Lock Picking (1)
	Life Surge (2)	Disguise (2)
	Peripheral Awareness (2)	Deception (1)
	Tactical Foresight (1)	Bartering (2)
	Counter (2)	Streetwise (2)
	Twitch Reflexes (3)	Cooking (1)
	Stealth (1)	Mending (1)
	Survivalist (2)	First Aid (1)
	First Aid (1)	Thalian (3)
	Wood Carving (1)	Neyardic (3)
	Leatherworking (2)	Ostari (1)
	Butchering (4)	Mana Manipulation (2)
	Thalian (2)	Mana Sight (1)
	Ostari (1)	Metallurgy (1)
	Disguise (2)	Whitesmithing (1)
	Deception (1)	Goldsmithing (2)
	Torturer (1)	Gem Cutting (1)
	Analyze (BL)	Engraving (2)
	Remote Access (BL)	Rune Forging (1)
	XP Mask (BL)	Painting (1)
		Arcano Dynamics (1)
		Sleight of Hand (1)
		Steady Hands (2)
		Cold Reading (1)
		Temperature Acclimation (2)
		Cadence (2)
		Bloodline Purification Ritual (1)
		Ghost Script (1)

CHAPTER 42

Bertram Singer had joined the Blacktongue Mercenary Company when he was sixteen. He had spent the better part of his life fighting men and monsters, sacrificed his future for the privilege, and grown to the point where it was rare for him to meet anything or anyone who could challenge him. This boy, barely grown to a man and already wanted by a church inquisitor, had presented him with a rare opportunity.

That's what he'd thought ten minutes ago, at least. Now he was getting just a bit frustrated with the whole thing. The guy had no presence whatsoever, not even as a level 1. That was obviously some skill that hid his XP, but Singer had never heard of anything that could eliminate it completely. The system just didn't work that way.

It made it a bit disconcerting and hard to keep track of the kid, but nothing Singer couldn't compensate for. The real problem was that this guy was either insanely high level, or he'd focused on pumping his agility to the detriment of everything else. Singer didn't think it was the latter either, just judging by how strong the kid was and the fact that he hadn't slowed down once since the fight started. If anything, he'd gotten even faster in the last minute or so.

Even chaining his **[Speed Burst]** skill as often as possible, Singer couldn't keep up with kid, which was not acceptable. This whole mission had turned into a disaster, with fully a quarter of his division confirmed dead, probably more considering how many they still had missing. The kid was too fast, and smart enough not to sit still and let numbers overrun him.

Singer caught up to the apostate in the woods, half a mile or so from the base, and the only reason he'd even managed that was that the kid had stopped running. It didn't take a genius to figure out why; he'd found what he was looking for. His dwifkin companion had somehow managed to escape Singer's apparently incompetent underling. She was even still tied up when Singer caught sight of her.

Disaster might have been too mild of a word.

He caught sight of them through the trees ahead. The boy was up in a tree, breaking the ropes binding his companion and helping her disentangle herself. With a soft sigh, Singer muttered to himself, "Both of you together? Can't those idiots do anything right?"

The apostate dropped as soon as he noted Singer's appearance, a smart move, if a hair too late. Singer lunged for the boy, hoping to catch him while he was still in the air, where his agility wouldn't count for so much. Somehow, the kid managed to not only dodge the grab, but also used Singer's arm as a contact point to shift his momentum laterally and move completely out of Singer's reach.

He activated **[Speed Burst]** to push himself after the kid, relying on the skill's rank 4 ability to alter his trajectory without loss of speed to keep him going in the right direction. Somehow, even in the air, the kid was outpacing him. When he hit the ground and skidded backward, he was already perfectly balanced and ready to fend off Singer's attack.

Singer slapped away the mace, some beautiful monstrosity of gleaming red silver and steel that should have cracked under the repeated stress of being subjected to his **[Sunder]** skill but that was holding up remarkably well. There had to be a bit of magic in that, or possibly some sort of reinforcing skill the kid was using, but that didn't feel right. The feedback he got from each hit made him think his skill was doing full damage to the weapon's structure.

And yet, somehow, infuriatingly, that damn thing still hadn't snapped. Singer was pretty sure if he could get rid of the mace, the kid would try to run again. That would suck, but Singer would rather recapture the dwifkin and lose the apostate than let them both get away, and at the speed the kid was moving now, there was practically no way he was going to get a clean grab in. Singer needed that grapple to overpower the apostate, to exert some leverage to pin him down.

Unless whatever boost skill the kid was using left him with severe side effects when he came down from it, it wasn't going to happen. The kid seemed like a pretty smart fighter, someone he would have been trying to recruit under other circumstances. He was a bit rough around the edges, but there was plenty to work with. Too bad. Unless Singer's judgment was way off, that also meant the kid wasn't going to pass out or give up whenever that skill ended.

They danced around for about fifteen seconds, with Singer trying to drive him back into a tree to cut off his options and the kid doing his best to run circles around him. Maybe that would have worked against someone else, but Singer was too fast and too experienced to fall for those kinds of tricks. He smacked that mace with another **[Sunder]** each time it came at him and watched closely to see if it would finally start to show any signs of damage.

Nothing. Damn.

Then the kid stumbled, just for an instant. It was the first time Singer had seen him misstep, and he recovered almost instantly, but the tell was there. His boost skill had kicked off. The kid was slower now, and when he came in for another swing, it was easy for Singer to deflect it and lash out with a low kick designed to take the kid at the ankle.

The apostate hopped over it, but it was a close thing. Singer grinned and started pushing him.

Luke knew it was a long shot, but he'd hoped he could bury the merc in a flurry of attacks before **[Life Surge]** gave out. The man had been too smart for that though. He might not have known the exact mechanics of how Luke's skill worked, but he recognized the universal weakness of all those skills. They wore off.

Now that he was returning to his normal stats, or maybe slightly worse, it was harder to keep ahead of the merc. Worse, the man was doing something to Luke's weapon. He couldn't quite figure out what, but it felt . . . wobbly, for lack of a better term. Steel wasn't supposed to be that malleable, and his whatever-the-fuck-it-was-made-out-of self-repairing mace should have been even stronger. God knew it had been expensive enough.

The longer this fight went on, the worse off he was going to be. Zea was still tangled up in the tree, apparently needing a lot longer than he expected to finish getting out of the ropes. The merc was showing no signs of slowing down, and his defenses were just too good for Luke to get a clean shot in. More mercenaries could show up to assist him as any moment, though Luke was keeping an ear open so he'd at least have some warning.

The merc blocked another attack, then kicked at Luke's ankles. Luke dodged, **[Tactical Foresight]** having predicted the move as soon as the merc shifted his weight. The attack was nothing but a feint designed to get him off-balance and give the merc time to get inside Luke's range. **[Unarmed Martial-ist]** had quite a bit to say about that though. He smacked aside the merc's arm when he tried to grab hold of Luke, then brought a knee up to check a second kick.

This fight was a bad matchup for Luke. His only real advantage was his increased agility, something the merc was countering with his own speed-boosting skill and a lot of practice using it. It would end eventually, but not anytime soon, and time wasn't on Luke's side. He needed Zea to get free and make a run for it so that he could break off from the fight, but she was somehow *still* stuck up there.

Now that he thought about her, Luke realized she actually had managed to finish freeing herself and was doing something else instead of running. Shit. There was no way for him to get a message to her without also drawing the merc's attention, and it was going to be hard enough for her to get away as it was. He just needed Zea to reach the open road, and he could come in behind her. She didn't weigh anywhere close to enough to slow him down, and Luke was confident he could outrun the merc.

He'd thought she understood that plan, but instead of escaping, she was messing around with the rope she'd already freed herself from. Whatever she was doing, she was wholly focused on it, and all it would take was just one merc coming to investigate the sounds of fighting for her to be captured again.

The boy was losing focus, letting himself get distracted by too many worries outside of the battle. Singer didn't blame him. He was young, inexperienced. Between that and skill fatigue from his boost skill, he was starting to make mistakes. They were little things, for now, nothing that would lead to a dramatic failure on his part, but they would pile up. They would create opportunities.

Singer was content to wait. Capturing both of them now was the best possible result of this whole shitstorm, though he supposed the kid had done him a favor and cleaned out some of the hopeless cases in his ranks. That was counterbalanced by the good men and women who'd also died trying to capture him, of course.

He'd get his though. Being handed over to a gods damned inquisitor was revenge enough for Singer's slain comrades.

Ha, he was getting old. There he was, lost in thought just like the kid he'd been mentally berating. Still, he'd been in enough fights and knew his skills inside and out. If his mind wandered a bit, he wasn't going to start making mistakes. Besides, that knee check the kid had just used to block a kick was the mistake that was going to end the fight.

Singer dropped in place and grabbed hold of the bottom of the apostate's foot before he could retract it. He heaved upward, his hand still locked on the boot, and overbalanced the kid. Singer kept pushing, putting all his weight and his strength into it, and toppled the kid over. Rather than falling on his back, the bastard did some sort of handspring and moved with it, his whole body curved into an arch as his other foot came up and clipped Singer's chin.

That wasn't going to stop him, not now that he finally had his hands on the kid. Singer grabbed him by the ankle and pulled him sideways into a brief spin that resulted in the kid going around, then up overhead, then face down to slam into the ground. Any normal man would have been stunned, at least for a moment, from the impact, but not this kid. He literally bounced off the ground and started twisting like an eel to escape.

Singer knew he had him. The mace was still an issue to be dealt with, but even if he couldn't shake it loose from the apostate's grip, he'd have the boy locked up soon enough. He just needed to get a handle on . . . Damn . . . "Slippery little shit, aren't yo—Huerk!"

Something looped around Singer's neck and started constricting. He would have said it was a snake, but the texture told him otherwise. Somehow, someone had snuck up behind him and looped a rope around his neck. It was impossible! There was no one else even there. The dwifkin girl was still up in the tree, and the apostate was firmly in his grasp.

Singer reached up with his free hand to grab at the rope and pull it loose from his throat. His fingers had just brushed against it when the world went white, a roaring sound filled his ears, and pain tore through him. That was the last thing he ever experienced.

Name	Luke Bennet	Zea Stenter
Level	34	21
XP	135549/144088	34019/34241
AP	42	8
Bloodline	SysAdmin II	None
Strength	42	7
Agility	55	27
Stamina	51	27
Perception	39	19
Skills	Mace Mastery (3)	Dagger Mastery (1)
	Sword Mastery (1)	Stealth (2)
	Unarmed Martialist (4)	Keen Instincts (1)
	Power Strike (2)	Lock Picking (1)
	Life Surge (2)	Disguise (2)
	Peripheral Awareness (2)	Deception (1)
	Tactical Foresight (1)	Bartering (2)
	Counter (2)	Streetwise (2)
	Twitch Reflexes (3)	Cooking (1)
	Stealth (1)	Mending (1)
	Survivalist (2)	First Aid (1)
	First Aid (1)	Thalian (3)
	Wood Carving (1)	Neyardic (3)
	Leatherworking (2)	Ostari (1)
	Butchering (4)	Mana Manipulation (2)
	Thalian (2)	Mana Sight (1)
	Ostari (1)	Metallurgy (1)
	Disguise (2)	Whitesmithing (1)
	Deception (1)	Goldsmithing (2)
	Torturer (1)	Gem Cutting (1)
	Analyze (BL)	Engraving (2)
	Remote Access (BL)	Rune Forging (1)
	XP Mask (BL)	Painting (1)
		Arcano Dynamics (1)
		Sleight of Hand (1)
		Steady Hands (2)
		Cold Reading (1)
		Temperature Acclimation (2)
		Cadence (2)
		Bloodline Purification Ritual (1)
		Ghost Script (1)

CHAPTER 43

Luke stared down at the headless corpse in shock. "What even the fuck?"

A moment later, he got the ding of the kill notification, which was a whole new level of fucked up. Had that merc been alive for a few seconds after his explosive decapitation? Just fucking how?

[You have assisted in slaying Blacktongue Human Mercenary (level 35). 670 XP awarded.]

Luke turned his stare from the corpse up to Zea. "Learn a new party trick?"

"Something like that. Here, catch me. I'm going to jump."

She was twenty feet away, but she hurled herself bodily through the air in Luke's general direction. He caught her in his arms, spun once to diffuse the momentum, and then brought his lips down to hers. "I was afraid they were going to kill you," he said. "I shouldn't have thought you'd be safe splitting up. I just assumed they'd all come after me. Fucking stupid."

"Ah, well, I didn't try too hard to get out of their way," she said. "Let's just say we both screwed up on this one."

"I guess all's well that ends well, but there's a whole bunch of these mercs left, and they're not breaking into smaller units to try to hunt me down anymore, sooooo . . . Time to get out of here?"

"Did . . . did you find my stuff?" Zea asked.

"Your stuff," Luke repeated. "The stuff with the worth-its-weight-in-gold hide and all your enchanting projects? That stuff?"

"That'd be the stuff, yes."

"I did not, no."

"Oh. Well. Fuck."

"You want to go back to their base and look for it? I don't think there's anybody there right now. We could do a quick in and out."

Luke could see greed and caution warring on her face. Without a word, he started running back toward the compound. Zea squirmed in his arms until he shifted her into a bridal carry, which earned him a glare and a resigned sigh.

They arrived two minutes later, paused for Luke to recover his knife from the throat of the merc he'd thrown it into during his initial assault, and went in through the hole he'd made when he broke through the window. "Holy shit," she said, looking around at the damage. "What the hell did you do to this place?"

"They took you. I stopped holding back. Normal wood and stone, even steel, none of that is actually strong enough to hold me anymore."

"That's about what it looks like," she said. "Okay, we're looking for . . . maybe storage rooms? They had me blindfolded on the way in, so I'm not sure where exactly they took my bags. If we're really lucky, we'll find them intact and can get the fuck out of here."

"I didn't see any on the ground floor, but there might be some in the basement."

"I guess we'll start there. I think the stairs are that way." Zea started walking off, only to stop and spin around when Luke stomped down on the floor and broke a hole through it. "Or that works too."

He hopped through, caught her when she jumped in after him, and gave the room a quick once-over. A desk dominated one half of the room, with a big chair behind it, standing shelves flanking either side, and about a thousand sheets of paper bound together into makeshift books that didn't have covers.

"No cupboards or cabinets here," Luke said. "Probably not in the paperwork room."

He found the door was locked, so he casually ripped it out of the frame and set it down to the side. Zea followed after him slowly, her expression thoughtful as she looked around. "Any idea where to check?"

"I didn't really poke my head into each room looking for you," Luke said. "There were people trying to stop me, which, you know, kind of distracting."

"I guess we'll just go down the hall and open each door then?"

That was exactly what they did, though most of them were locked. It seemed like there were a lot of sleeping chambers, usually with bunks, but occasionally what he guessed were officer's quarters that only had a single bed and some furnishings. There was a huge pantry that he took a few minutes to raid, filling a conveniently located sack that had contained vegetables until he upended it onto the floor with a variety of smoked meat, some cheeses, a few glass jars with spices that Zea said were worth quite a bit, and several other odds and ends at her direction.

Eventually they found what they were looking for. The door was reinforced with steel bars, which he ripped out of the anchoring stonework with brute strength. Luke paused, his eyes glinting and his lips widening into a grin when he got a look inside. "This is my new favorite room," he announced.

Zea peered around the door, rolled her eyes, and said, "Sure, go nuts. Let me know if you see my backpack in there."

To his left, a trio of wooden racks were lined up next to one another. They had every type of weapon he had a name for mounted on their pegs, and a few he didn't. All of it was good steel too. Though he wasn't an expert, Luke could see the grain in the metal from across the room, and it matched a lot of other high-quality steel he'd seen. He had to assume that meant it was good, not that it mattered. He had his main weapon and a sidearm already.

Opposite the weapons were some supply shelves. Bags, pouches, blankets, coats, boots, and more were set up there. Luke even found some clothes in various sizes. It looked like the Blacktongue mercenaries wore some kind of uniform when they weren't in an active combat situation. Or maybe even during, just under their armor. Either way, Luke found some in his size and pilfered four sets.

Then he shucked off his own rough and ragged farmer's clothes and dressed himself. His boots had taken quite the beating over the last few weeks as well, so those got replaced. By the time he was done, he was dressed in all-new clothes, carrying new, high-quality bags, and had even found a harness not in desperate need of repair for his weapons.

Then, at the back, finally, there they were. In three rows, displayed on mannequins, sets of dark-green-and-black armor waited for someone to come claim them. Luke sorted through them until he found one in his size, then started dressing himself. The straps weren't that complicated, though it would have been easier with some assistance. Zea was three doors down now, busy rifling through one of the rooms that was had been left unlocked, so he decided to give it a go himself.

It wasn't as hard as he'd expected it to be. The worst of it was probably holding the back and front plates together while he fastened the straps on the sides, but even those were a clever mix of locking clasps and adjustable belts. In less time that he'd expected, he wore greaves, vambraces, gauntlets, a breastplate, and pauldrons.

Luke threw a cloak on over the armor, then flipped it back to leave one shoulder bare and allow easy access to his mace. He twisted around experimentally, trying to find the limit to his flexibility inside the armor. "Huh, not as bad as I thought," he muttered. He supposed it made sense. The breastplate left his sides partially exposed where the adjustable leather straps connected the front and back of it together, a bit of a trade-off, but one he was happy to make if it allowed him to make better use of his agility.

"Hey, you think you could come bust open a few of these doors for me?" Zea called out from the other room.

"Yeah, be right there," Luke yelled back.

He went down the hallway, casually kicking each door open as he went by until he reached the room Zea was searching. Rows of cupboards, wardrobes, and cabinets all hung open, their contents ransacked and scattered across the floor. A number of empty bags had been tossed into the corner, but none of them looked like Zea's. Based on her stomping and muttered cursing, he was guessing she was getting frustrated.

"Can't believe how much shit they've got in here. Fucking hoarders, the lot of them. Never going to find—" Zea glanced up at the doorway, saw Luke standing, there, and flinched back. "Holy shit! I thought you were a merc for a second."

"You think I can get away with keeping this set? I've been trying to get some good armor for what feels like forever."

"Uh, maybe. It's less conspicuous than templar gear that's been marked with the Sign of the Six, at least. I think you've got the straps done wrong on your side though."

"I do?" Luke looked down at them. "They look right to me."

"No, see, you've got this one going over top of this one. They're tangled. You need to thread the strap through this piece here, otherwise it's going to work itself loose."

"Oh. Damn. Thought I had it figured out." Luke started tugging on the straps to adjust them. "So no luck with finding any of your stuff?"

"Not at all," Zea said. "That's why I wanted to break open more rooms. Was there anything small and valuable we could take with us from the armory?"

"Valuable like it's worth a lot of money? Not so much. It was a lot of basic necessities, which, I mean, I'm not going to complain about a free resupply, especially when so much of it is better quality than what we were using. But in terms of straight gold and silver, no, nothing."

"Fuck. What are we going to do if my stuff isn't here? We'll basically be broke again. It'll take months to save up what we need to charter passage across the ocean."

"Let's not give up just yet," Luke said. "I don't hear anybody approaching the compound, and there are plenty of places left to look."

"Right, yeah. Come on, let's hurry anyway."

Luke followed her into the next room and helped her start tearing the place apart. While they worked, he asked, "What was with that exploding rope you used on that merc?"

"That's how I escaped. I bought a new skill. Expensive as fuck. 25 AP. But it lets me put temporary enchanting runes on basically anything, with no tools.

I enchanted the rope with a strangling spell and set it to detonate after so many seconds, which was awesome mostly because you normally have to specially prepare the rope to take that kind of enchantment. Trade-off is that it only would have had about twenty seconds before the enchantment died."

"Well, that's fucking terrifying," he told her frankly. "I'm guessing that's how you got away in the first place?"

"Yeah, if you'd gone another thirty feet or so, you'd have found what was left of the guy who was carrying me. I drew the runes on the back of his armor. Tricky as fuck because he was moving, my hands were tied up, and I had to be real fucking careful about how that one blew up. Could have killed myself if I'd fucked it up."

"Glad you didn't," Luke said. "It would have been a pain in the ass to have to avenge you. There's a lot of mercs left in that group."

They moved onto the next room, and then the next. Finally, after another ten minutes of searching, Luke held up a hand to get Zea's attention. "Someone is approaching the compound," he whispered. "One person from the north and another from the west. Maybe two from the west? We're running out of time."

"Shit," she swore. Moving quickly and silently, she started tossing the room. After a perfunctory search of the cabinets, she shook her head. "Might be valuable stuff in here, but not *our* valuable stuff. Let's keep going."

Luke kept quiet and followed her. If it was just the three mercs, he was confident he could win. Even if it was six, he could probably take them. His concern was that the whole unit would come in at the same time, one big group, and overwhelm him with sheer numbers.

"Aha!" Zea hissed, triumphant. She held up a familiar bag and added, "About fucking time."

"Good, let's get out of here now. I think we can still get away before the mercs pin us down."

Zea flipped the flap open, peered in, and frowned. "Fuuuuuuuuck. They took the money."

"What about the hide?"

"Still here, but that's not liquid until we get somewhere we can sell it."

"Better than nothing," Luke said. "Let's get out of here."

Name	Luke Bennet	Zea Stenter
Level	34	21
XP	135549/144088	34019/34079
AP	42	8
Bloodline	SysAdmin II	None
Strength	42	7
Agility	55	27
Stamina	51	27
Perception	39	19
Skills	Mace Mastery (3)	Dagger Mastery (1)
	Sword Mastery (1)	Stealth (2)
	Unarmed Martialist (4)	Keen Instincts (1)
	Power Strike (2)	Lock Picking (1)
	Life Surge (2)	Disguise (2)
	Peripheral Awareness (2)	Deception (1)
	Tactical Foresight (1)	Bartering (2)
	Counter (2)	Streetwise (2)
	Twitch Reflexes (3)	Cooking (1)
	Stealth (1)	Mending (1)
	Survivalist (2)	First Aid (1)
	First Aid (1)	Thalian (3)
	Wood Carving (1)	Neyardic (3)
	Leatherworking (2)	Ostari (1)
	Butchering (4)	Mana Manipulation (2)
	Thalian (2)	Mana Sight (1)
	Ostari (1)	Metallurgy (1)
	Disguise (2)	Whitesmithing (1)
	Deception (1)	Goldsmithing (2)
	Torturer (1)	Gem Cutting (1)
	Analyze (BL)	Engraving (2)
	Remote Access (BL)	Rune Forging (1)
	XP Mask (BL)	Painting (1)
		Arcano Dynamics (1)
		Sleight of Hand (1)
		Steady Hands (2)
		Cold Reading (1)
		Temperature Acclimation (2)
		Cadence (2)
		Bloodline Purification Ritual (1)
		Ghost Script (1)

CHAPTER 44

This is bullshit," Zea muttered under her breath. Even from across the room, Luke could clearly hear her, and he wasn't sure how far away he'd have to be before he couldn't. She wasn't trying to be noisy, but his hearing was so sensitive now, and without his ability to sense XP active, he was really paying attention to what it told him. He was tracking people just by listening to them breathe, and he was reasonably sure if he sank any more points into perception, he'd start hearing heartbeats from across the room.

"We knew they'd show up eventually. At least we salvaged something, plus I figure I stole at least twenty gold worth of gear and supplies from them."

"How much do you have on you?" Zea asked.

"I don't know. Not much, but if we stick to the roads, we can get to the city in a few days, right? We'll be fine."

Zea swept the room with her gaze one more time, let out a frustrated sigh, and said, "Shit. Fine."

Luke held up a hand and cocked his head. "They're in the building."

[Analyze] was easier to use if he could actually see his target, but it wasn't impossible to tag someone if he had a good enough idea of where they were. He managed to get readings on two of them, levels 21 and 24, but the third one either had insanely high agility or a decent chunk of AP dedicated to stealth skills. Given the average level of the mercenaries he'd fought so far, he was betting it was the latter.

More importantly, he didn't hear anyone else coming in behind them. Most likely, these three were scouts, and if that was the case, he might kill them and give Zea some more time. Either way, he couldn't let them live to report back.

That would just result in the rest of the mercs hounding them all the way to Sicanti.

"I'll go take care of them," he said. "You . . . I don't know. I can probably get to them before they make their way here, but I don't like the idea of leaving you alone."

Zea rolled her eyes. "Just go. I'll keep looking, make some noise. Maybe they'll be distracted."

"You're not fooling anyone," Luke told her. "You just want more time to look for our money."

"So? Is that so wrong? Go take care of them."

Their entire conversation had been whispered, barely even audible, and hopefully quiet enough to keep the mercs from hearing them. Zea made a show of throwing open a cupboard and letting the door bounce, then dropping the book she found inside on the floor. She made a little shooing motion with her hand at Luke, then dropped another book next to it.

Luke hadn't had much use for **[Stealth]** in a long time. His XP had rapidly outgrown his ability to disguise it without devoting considerably amounts of AP to a specific build. Since taking **[XP Mask]** had always been a long-term goal for him, it had seemed pointless to sink points into skills that hid his XP from everyone else.

Now his XP was invisible. He only needed to evade their mundane senses, which he wasn't exactly confident he could do. The mercs were specialized with scouting builds, high perception was part of that, and he'd never upgraded **[Stealth]** past rank 1. Theoretically, his agility was high enough that he thought he could walk silently, but that didn't mean he wouldn't be spotted.

That would be very bad for whoever spotted him. It would mean Luke no longer had any incentive to be quiet, and also that he had a lot of incentive to very quickly kill all three of them before they could run off. Of course, he was going to kill them anyway, but it would be a lot noisier and messier if **[Stealth]** failed to keep him from being noticed.

Luke ghosted down the hallway, following the sounds of one of the mercs above him. It seemed like they were being thorough about checking out the ground floor, and they were either coordinating in some way he didn't understand, or they'd swept buildings enough to be practiced without needing to speak.

He leaped up through one of the holes he'd made between the ground floor and the basement and landed without so much as a creek from the floorboards. Two of them were only a few rooms away, their breathing smooth, even, and shallow. He moved himself to a room ahead of their sweep pattern, drew his knife, and waited next to the door.

Luke held himself perfectly still and didn't even dare to breathe. Silent as a statue, he waited for them to approach the room. They were taking their time, sweeping each room fully, pausing, and moving on to the next, but it wouldn't be long until they were inside his range. His only concerns were the still-missing third person and their proximity to Zea. He expected to be back by her side in the next thirty seconds though.

It would be fine. She could take care of herself anyway.

The merc scouts were inches away from him now, both of their backs to the wall. If Luke had been more confident in his hearing, he could have stabbed through the wall and skewered them from behind. Instead, he stuck with his original plan of waiting for one of them to stick something through the doorway. He'd already been holding his breath for two minutes; a few more seconds wouldn't hurt. Hell, he'd barely even noticed it and was nowhere near his limit.

One of the scouts swept through the door. There was a fraction of a second where his eyes went wide at seeing Luke, and then the knife flashed up under the scout's chin and slashed open his throat. Luke's free hand grabbed the front of his shirt and dragged him out of the way so that he could leap through the door. The other scout didn't hesitate at his sudden appearance.

Four throwing knives flew through the air, slamming into him with all the power of a major-league fastball but bouncing off his new armor. The scout scrambled backward, drawing more knives as he went. One of them caught Luke's cheek, his own fault for ignoring **[Twitch Reflexes]** to close the gap as quickly as he could.

[You have been afflicted by the following condition: Poison—Blue Bile Tincture (16M).]

Luke ignored the notification and grabbed the scout's hand. He squeezed hard enough to crush bones, and the scout cried out in pain as he dropped the throwing knife he'd been prepared to stab Luke with. Before he could do anything else, Luke jerked him forward and rammed his own alchemically treated ever-sharp blade up through the underside of the man's chin.

[You have slain 2 creatures between levels 21 and 24. 1062 XP awarded.]

He stopped to listen, half expecting the third scout to be closing in on him. If that was the case, Luke couldn't hear them. Then he took a second to try to figure out what this poison was doing to him. Nothing felt different, at least not that he could tell. He supposed he might have lost a temporary point or two in strength or agility, but he couldn't feel any real difference.

He made a mental note to ask System about it after he found the third scout. Maybe now that he'd upgraded his bloodline, he could just ask what the poison did. That would come later though, when he wasn't concerned about making noise. The fight had been brief, barely seconds long, but he hadn't been nearly quick enough to keep the second scout quiet.

Whatever skill the final scout was using, it was a strong one. Luke couldn't find any trace of the merc and, lacking a better idea, decided the best thing to do was stay close to Zea and try to ambush them if and when they showed up. He went back to the nearest hole and dropped silently into the basement.

She was easy enough to find, at least. It wasn't that she was being deliberately noisy so much as that she was making very little effort to be quiet. In her haste to secure their lost gold, she was tossing every room without giving any consideration to being neat or organized, and that meant a lot of noise.

"Got two of them," Luke said quietly from the doorway. Zea's head snapped up to look at him, and she slowly nodded.

"The third?"

"Can't find him. You ready to go?"

She gave a frustrated growl and kicked a wooden box. "More time?"

"A few minutes. I'll find a good hiding spot and just kind of . . . uh, stalk you, I guess. If this other scout is still lurking here, maybe I can spot them if they come after you."

He left it unsaid that it was far more likely in his mind that the third scout had bailed and was running back to tell the rest of the mercenary band that their two victims were still stupidly lurking in the compound. Luke really wanted to tell Zea to forget the gold, but he understood how important it was, and how many months it could take them to recoup the loss.

Zea moved into the next room while Luke scanned the hallways. As unlikely as he considered it that the third scout was still around, there was the possibility that the merc had some ungodly powerful version of **[Stealth]** that was making it impossible to sense them.

The counter on his poison ticked down another minute, and deciding that Zea was making enough noise anyway, Luke whispered, "System, can you tell me what this poison in my status ailments does?"

"I can," the apparition said. "By itself, it does nothing. It is a catalyst for several other poisons, however, and magnifies their effects."

"I guess that makes sense. The guy using it had a ton of knives. Maybe I should go grab those before we leave. Might be worth it for Zea to take a knife-throwing skill so she can use them."

"As you say. Is there anything else you would like to know?"

"Can you tell me which poisons are most commonly used with blue bile tincture?"

"Crossok venom is the most common. It is a debilitating condition that causes fever and vomiting on its own, and also afflicts the victim with muscle cramps and lethargy when mixed with blue bile tincture. Another common combination poison is known as Arat's bane. This causes severe dehydration, to the point that death becomes a possibility. When mixed with blue bile tincture, it also causes immense pain due to muscles retracting hard enough to rip themselves off the bones they are supposed to be attached to."

"That's fucking cheery. Good thing I didn't get hit by the knife with that."

"Arat's bane is commonly identified by its smell. It is often described as sickly sweet, like flowers that are dying."

"I haven't smelled anything like that," Luke said. Now that he thought about it though, that knife-throwing scout had smelled unusual. He supposed it was all the poisons the man had on him. He'd have to make some effort to see if System could help him identify them all later.

"Fuck yeah!" Zea hissed out. "Found it! Shit, there's even more here than what we had to start with. Time to get out of here."

Luke started to move out of his hiding spot and join up with Zea, only to sense . . . something. It was so faint that he wouldn't have paid it any attention, barely even the whisper of a soft breeze against his skin. **[Twitch Reflexes]** didn't ignore it though, and that was what saved Luke. He hurled himself to the side just as a blade slashed across his neck.

Blood splattered across the ground, and Luke slapped a hand onto the wound. It had missed the major arteries, at least. He'd heal easily enough. The final scout was now revealed next to him, a woman perhaps forty years old and dressed in hunting leathers with a green half cloak thrown over her shoulders.

Luke almost missed her next attack because he was busy focusing on the notification that had just popped up.

[You have been afflicted by the following condition: Poison—Withering-Blossom Sap (27M).]

[Conditions have merged. You are now afflicted by the following condition: Poison—Blue-Lip Rasping Breath (48M).]

[Warning: You are no longer able to breathe.]

Name	Luke Bennet	Zea Stenter
Level	34	21
XP	136601/144088	34019/34079
AP	42	8
Bloodline	SysAdmin II	None
Strength	42	7
Agility	55	27
Stamina	51	27
Perception	39	19
Skills	Mace Mastery (3)	Dagger Mastery (1)
	Sword Mastery (1)	Stealth (2)
	Unarmed Martialist (4)	Keen Instincts (1)
	Power Strike (2)	Lock Picking (1)
	Life Surge (2)	Disguise (2)
	Peripheral Awareness (2)	Deception (1)
	Tactical Foresight (1)	Bartering (2)
	Counter (2)	Streetwise (2)
	Twitch Reflexes (3)	Cooking (1)
	Stealth (1)	Mending (1)
	Survivalist (2)	First Aid (1)
	First Aid (1)	Thalian (3)
	Wood Carving (1)	Neyardic (3)
	Leatherworking (2)	Ostari (1)
	Butchering (4)	Mana Manipulation (2)
	Thalian (2)	Mana Sight (1)
	Ostari (1)	Metallurgy (1)
	Disguise (2)	Whitesmithing (1)
	Deception (1)	Goldsmithing (2)
	Torturer (1)	Gem Cutting (1)
	Analyze (BL)	Engraving (2)
	Remote Access (BL)	Rune Forging (1)
	XP Mask (BL)	Painting (1)
		Arcano Dynamics (1)
		Sleight of Hand (1)
		Steady Hands (2)
		Cold Reading (1)
		Temperature Acclimation (2)
		Cadence (2)
		Bloodline Purification Ritual (1)
		Ghost Script (1)

CHAPTER 45

Luke experienced a moment of sheer, visceral panic when he read that notification and realized that his lungs wouldn't open up to pull in air. He could try to take a breath, but there was nowhere for it to go. Then he remembered that he could hold his breath for an hour if he needed to, probably more.

He'd be fine. Or at least, he wouldn't die from just the poison. The merc who'd attacked him knew it too, or at least was smart enough to realize that he'd be able to fight back. She didn't even try to press the advantage, instead offering him a smirk and fading into invisibility right before his eyes.

Luke's eyebrows went up at that. That was a powerful skill right there, but he was willing to bet it wouldn't let her walk through walls. He leaped to the door, slammed it closed as best he could, and leaned up against it. Hopefully, he'd been fast enough to keep her trapped in here with him. He was confident he could survive this poison. Zea might not.

"What was that?" Zea asked from outside the door. "You okay in there?"

Luke went to say something, to reassure her that he was handling it, but the words wouldn't come. Specifically, the air wouldn't come. The poison that had paralyzed his lungs was also keeping him from speaking. Lacking a better means of communicating, Luke tapped out a quick beat on the door.

"Uh . . . What?" Zea asked.

If he could have thought of a way to communicate without opening the door, Luke would have. Failing that, he had no choice but to place himself firmly in the way so she couldn't come in. His eyes scanned the room, looking for the invisible assassin who was trying to kill him. Wherever she was at, he didn't spot her, and it looked like she was patient enough to just wait for him to drop dead.

That wasn't going to happen, of course. He was pretty sure he could outlast the poison if he had to, and he was willing to bet **[Life Surge]** would knock it out, or at least cut the duration to under ten minutes. He thought about triggering it now, just so he could talk to Zea, but he wanted to save it as a surprise to use on the merc once he figured out where she was. Besides, he hadn't quite worked out what the side effects would be for using it multiple times in succession now that he'd upgraded the rank.

The room was a scattered mess, thanks to Zea's ransacking. It might have been well organized originally, but now the floor was covered in what looked like account ledgers, loose paper, small crates that had been overturned, and a mess of shattered ceramic from where she'd knocked over what appeared to be some sort of pot or urn.

Wooden boxes were stacked high on the back wall, almost to the ceiling. Luke counted twenty of them, all piled up in five stacks of four each, each one closed with a lid that had been nailed down. He suspected they'd remained unmolested during Zea's search more for their height than their security. Perhaps most importantly, there was a smudge of dirt on one about halfway up, one that looked suspiciously like the tip of a shoe.

If his guess was right, the would-be assassin had jumped up on top of the crates and was hiding in the two feet or so of open space left there. Luke just wasn't sure what exactly to do with that information. He could start throwing things up there, he supposed. As long as he didn't leave his post guarding the door, the worst that could happen was that he was wrong.

Well, no, the worst that could happen was that the assassin used his distraction to slip a knife between his ribs, killing him and leaving her free to kill Zea too. Or maybe they'd both end up captured and sold to whoever was interested in them the first place. That might be worse, depending on what the contract holder wanted and what lengths they were willing to go to in order to get it.

Luke was about to start throwing things up there anyway when he noticed another footprint, this time on a loose sheet of paper on the ground. He was about 99 percent sure that hadn't been there when he'd done his first scan. The invisible merc was moving and, based on the direction of the footprint, closer to him.

He kept scanning the room, not wanting her to know that he'd seen a clue. A second later, he noticed another partial print on the cover of a book. She was getting close now, heading his way. Luke considered pulling the mace off his back but hesitated. It might spook her now that she was so close. He should have done it a few minutes ago when he'd first jumped in front of the door.

It was probably fine. The assassin's big advantage was her invisibility skill. Once he tagged her with even a glancing blow, he was confident he could end things quickly. Luke just needed the perfect moment to strike. His eyes scanned the room again. The newest footprint was only three feet away, close enough to strike. He was just about to lunge forward and attempt to body-slam her when he noticed something out of the corner of his eye.

It was a hazy spot, just to his left, opposite the side of the footprints. In an instant, he realized that she'd been setting him up, just waiting for him to draw the conclusion she wanted and jump the wrong way. Then she'd either stab him in the back or slip out the door and flee. He wasn't sure which she was planning, but neither was acceptable.

Luke jumped forward the wrong way, then stopped short and lashed out behind him with a kick. His lips curled up into a grin when he felt contact on his foot, and the assassin crashed into the wall. He was on her in an instant, even before she became fully visible, his knife drawn and on its way into her chest.

She reacted instantly, kicking out with both feet to try to push him backward, but there just wasn't enough power in her legs to stop him. Luke's knife flashed down, only slightly off course, and hit her ribs. That didn't stop him from driving it home, not with the alchemically treated steel and enough strength to tie a piece of rebar into a knot behind it. The assassin screamed, or at least tried to. What actually came out was more of breathless whimper.

Luke turned the blade and jerked it sideways. Blood splattered across his face and chest, and he got the kill notification. The invisibility skill failed completely with the assassin's death, but the poison she'd inflicted him with remained active.

[You have slain Blacktongue Human Mercenary (level 27). 769 XP awarded.]

[This creature has slain 1037 other creatures.]

[Total kills for this type of creature: 59.]

[Highest-level kill: 35.]

Zea burst into the room now that he was no longer blocking the door. She took in the dead woman at a glance and said, "What happened?"

Luke shook his head and pointed at this throat. When she just stared at him blankly, he cast around for something to write with, then scooped up one of the books. It took him a few tries to get the hang of a quill and inkwell, and he made a hell of a mess, but they weren't his books. Fuck those mercs anyway.

Poisoned, he wrote. *Can't breathe for forty-two minutes. Can't talk.*

"Are you going to be alright?" she asked.

Luke nodded and added, *High stamina. Don't need to breathe. Just can't talk without air. You got everything you need?*

"Yeah. Fuck yes. Like three times as much as we had yesterday. I don't even know if any of it was ours originally, but it is now. Let's get the hell out of here."

You want poisoned throwing knives? Body upstairs has them.

Zea shrugged. "I don't have a skill for them. Might be worth it to sell if they've got any valuable poisons, but I don't know anything about them. We'd probably just get scammed. I guess we could take them and throw them away somewhere, just as a final fuck-you to these assholes."

Luke shook his head. In his mind, it wasn't worth the time if she didn't want them. *Let's just go*, he wrote.

Luke sucked in a heavy lungful of air and let out a satisfied sigh. "Man, that was annoying."

"I don't know. Seemed like an improvement to me," Zea said.

"Well, it wasn't."

They were taking it slow, not wanting to strain Luke until he could breathe freely again, which meant regular walking speed and a lot of paranoia that they'd be attacked before they got far enough away. Luke thought, somewhat uncharitably, that none of it would have been an issue if Zea had been willing to give up her search. On the other hand, she'd found a literal pot of gold at the end, so it was hard to complain too much.

"You think we should get off the road?" Luke asked. "Just to make it a bit harder for them to catch up to us?"

"Road's the fastest way, and more or less a straight line to where we're going," Zea said. "It would be really nice to just get there and be done, but maybe you're right. What if we encounter more of them, or even higher level? Some of those guys were really pushing the limits. Any higher and they'd have people hunting them down instead of the other way around."

"System, we're going to need you to navigate for us," Luke said. "Just keep us pointed in the general direction of Sicanti."

"That will not be a problem, Luke. Would you like to continue the pattern of a course correction once every ten minutes?"

"Yep, let's do that."

They ducked off the road then. Thankfully, the forest here was nothing like that nest of wood the squirrels had made farther south. There were spots they had to skirt around, but for the most part, there was plenty of space between the trees to weave their way through. They went north for a few miles before turning east again.

"So I know you want to get that amaril hide sold off, but how do you feel about doing that, then immediately leaving the city again?" Luke asked.

"Why, what would we need to do outside the city?"

"I was, uh. Well, I was thinking about leveling some more."

Zea nearly tripped over a root when she turned to look at him but failed to stop walking. "Are you out of your damn mind? You're already level 35."

"34," Luke said defensively.

"Really? I just figured you'd leveled again from all the mercenaries."

"Not even close. I still need another 8000 or so XP."

"Either way, 34 is high enough, don't you think?"

"I don't know," Luke said. "If there are church inquisitors waiting for us in Sicanti, is it high enough?"

"That's . . . Shit. That's a good point. But how high are you thinking here?"

"I thought we could figure that out together. I've got a few skills that could use upgrades to max rank, and I'm thinking another 20 AP to pour into strength and perception to bring everything up to around 50."

"So like level 40? Gods above, you're going to die before we get across the ocean. How would you even do this quickly?"

"Well, that's what I was thinking about. The way this system is designed, it rewards killing a lot of weaker monsters instead of one big one. So, everything has a level, right?"

"Yeah."

"And most insects would only be level 1?"

"Sometimes 2 or 3," Zea said.

"Does Aros have ants?"

Name	Luke Bennet	Zea Stenter
Level	34	21
XP	137370/144088	34019/34079
AP	42	8
Bloodline	SysAdmin II	None
Strength	42	7
Agility	55	27
Stamina	51	27
Perception	39	19
Skills	Mace Mastery (3)	Dagger Mastery (1)
	Sword Mastery (1)	Stealth (2)
	Unarmed Martialist (4)	Keen Instincts (1)
	Power Strike (2)	Lock Picking (1)
	Life Surge (2)	Disguise (2)
	Peripheral Awareness (2)	Deception (1)
	Tactical Foresight (1)	Bartering (2)
	Counter (2)	Streetwise (2)
	Twitch Reflexes (3)	Cooking (1)
	Stealth (1)	Mending (1)
	Survivalist (2)	First Aid (1)
	First Aid (1)	Thalian (3)
	Wood Carving (1)	Neyardic (3)
	Leatherworking (2)	Ostari (1)
	Butchering (4)	Mana Manipulation (2)
	Thalian (2)	Mana Sight (1)
	Ostari (1)	Metallurgy (1)
	Disguise (2)	Whitesmithing (1)
	Deception (1)	Goldsmithing (2)
	Torturer (1)	Gem Cutting (1)
	Analyze (BL)	Engraving (2)
	Remote Access (BL)	Rune Forging (1)
	XP Mask (BL)	Painting (1)
		Arcano Dynamics (1)
		Sleight of Hand (1)
		Steady Hands (2)
		Cold Reading (1)
		Temperature Acclimation (2)
		Cadence (2)
		Bloodline Purification Ritual (1)
		Ghost Script (1)

CHAPTER 46

Zea's eyes went wide. "No. Noooooo. Bad idea. No!"

"What? Why? What's the big deal with ants?"

"You have to have a special build to be an ant hunter," Zea told him. "Because of the pheromones. They're not the only bug monster that has them, but they're the worst by far. If you fuck with an anthill, you're going to have thousands of them pouring out and no way to stop them from swarming you."

Luke frowned and considered that for a moment. "Uh, what are the pheromones good for?"

His knowledge on the subject could generously be described as hazy. He had a vague memory somewhere floating around in his head that it was something ants used to communicate, maybe by smell. That didn't seem like something people with the technology level he'd seen on Aros should know about.

Then again, his perception was high enough to follow scents like a bloodhound now. Maybe pheromones were glaringly obvious to anyone who could see in the dark and hear people talking at a normal volume from five hundred yards away.

"Reanimation is the big concern. You kill a hundred ants, but then more show up and they get back on their feet. It's damn near impossible to kill a colony without some extremely specialized skills."

Luke came to a cold stop. "Wait, are you telling me there are zombie ants?"

"I'm not sure what they count as," Zea said. "But they don't stop coming, and once they get their scent on you, they'll follow you anywhere."

"Scent-based tracking should be beatable with like . . . soap and water," Luke pointed out.

"Maybe? I'm not an ant hunter. It's kind of one of those things you can only get wrong once, you know?"

"Assuming I'm right though, how much XP could we get off an anthill?"

"Is it really worth risking your life over? If you're not right, they're going to kill you. You could kill a thousand of them, only for another five thousand to eat you alive."

"Hmm. Hey, System, I have questions," Luke said.

"What would you like to know?" System asked.

"For starters, where is the nearest anthill?"

System raised a hand and pointed. "Twenty-six miles that way."

"And can you tell me roughly how many ants are there?"

"Roughly, there are three hundred thousand ants there."

Luke's eyebrows shot up. "Damn, that's a lot. What's the level range look like?"

"Almost all of them are level 1 or 2, with an almost insignificant fraction reaching up to level 5."

"That's . . . That's a lot of XP," Zea said faintly. "Enough to drive a person insane instantly. No wonder ant hunters work in groups of thirty or more. They have to just to keep the XP split somewhat reasonable."

"So that would be good for at least ten levels," Luke mused. "Instantly, with only a few minutes of work."

"No," Zea said firmly. "Get this thought out of your head. Bad idea. You don't have any way to kill that many ants to begin with. Even if you survived XP madness, the ants themselves are going to kill you."

"Sure we do," Luke told her. He pointed a finger at her. "You can make explosives. All we have to do is chuck one into the anthill and then run. We'll blow up a few thousand of them, and when the rest come up to the surface, there's no one around to chase."

Zea sputtered and started to protest, but then paused. "You know . . . Huh. That . . . could work." She shook her head. "No. It's crazy. We're not doing this."

"It's okay, you don't have to help," Luke said. "I'm sure I can just **[Power Strike]** the ground a few times. It probably won't work as well, but I'll still get a level or two out of it."

"Okay, this isn't funny anymore. We're not doing this. You're plenty strong already."

Luke stopped walking and shook his head. "Am I? System, can you tell me the average level of a church inquisitor?"

"There are many factors to consider, most prominently which church you are speaking of. The Church of Hestoc has the most advanced Inquisition Department, and if you include only them, the average level is 31. If you include all other churches, it drops down to 23. If you include clergymen and templars, the average level is 14."

"The Church of Hestoc is the one that was giving us shit, right?" Luke asked.

"Yeah," Zea agreed unhappily. "And that merc who was super high level let slip that their contract was with an inquisitor too."

"So what's the level range for Hestocian inquisitors?"

"Including apprentices, they range from level 7 up to level 63," System supplied promptly.

Zea missed a step. "What the fuck! How is someone level 63 and still walking around?"

"That is the direct result of a god making changes to the system," System said. For perhaps the first time he could remember, Luke thought he detected a note of emotion in the ghostly apparition's voice.

"If I didn't know any better, I would say you don't like that," he said.

"The system was not designed to be altered by the whims of the gods, but they all agreed to allow this one exception. You are aware of what XP madness is, a clumping together of your XP and the forming of a miniature pseudodeity. It is of course a bare fraction of the total XP that makes up the god trapped inside the machine, but even that is enough to overwhelm a fragile mortal mind.

"The system's purpose is to prevent this clumping of XP from becoming a threat, which it does by circulating the XP as mortals are born, survive, kill, and die. In this case, an individual favored by a god has their XP forcefully cycled, with their current total broken down and drained back into the God Machine and a matching set of new XP bestowed upon them. This results in a soft reset and prevents the mortal from being overwhelmed while this new XP begins forging new bonds."

"So it's not some sort of immunity then," Zea said. "That means this level 63 guy needs to keep going through this process every so often, maybe even every few months at that level."

"That is correct," System told her.

"The important takeaway here is that the guys who don't like me have someone who's almost twice my level on the payroll," Luke said. "That's pretty good incentive to put on a few more levels just in case this guy comes after me."

"Except that the gods aren't giving you a do-over button you can push every few months. If *you* level up that high, you'll just go insane and start destroying everything."

"Well, maybe, but I've been thinking about that. My bloodline gives me control over the system, right? Is there a skill that duplicates what the gods are doing to their clergy? I mean, you told me that the level cap of 100 doesn't apply to me, so there's got to be a way."

"There is not a skill like that," System said slowly. "It may be possible to create one."

"Would I need to be at the console to do it?" Luke asked, afraid he already knew the answer.

"At your current level of bloodline purity, yes. I am sorry; this situation has never come up before. I am not able to say if it may be possible to create such a skill independent of direct access to the God Machine."

Well, that was new. System might refuse to answer, but he'd never given any indication that he didn't know the answer, just that Luke wasn't privileged enough to be told it. Luke wasn't sure how to take that. Maybe it was a good sign that a possible solution existed, or maybe it was a bad sign that System didn't already know a solution. Who was Luke to think he could figure out something a whole Pantheon hadn't already created? Unless it wasn't that they didn't know how but just didn't want to, of course.

"If a theoretical XP-refreshing skill could be created," Zea said, "would it work with **[Remote Access]**? Could Luke use it on me?"

"Theoretically, assuming it used the same rules and logic of other bloodline skills, that would be correct," System said.

"Okay," Luke said, getting excited now. "So we need **[Bloodline Purification Ritual]** rank 2, which is 200 AP, right? That's eight or nine levels? I'm not clear on the math."

"Eight, not counting AP needed for upgrading auxiliary skills," Zea mumbled, obviously not liking where this conversation was heading.

"So we go kill some ants. You'll make a few explosive enchantments with your new skill, we'll chuck them into the anthill, then we'll run like the wind. Repeat as needed. When we get to Sicanti, we can get supplies, do the ritual, and see if we can overcome our XP-madness woes. If the fucking church can do it, no reason we can't."

She was wavering now; he could see it. They were taking a risk, but that was nothing new. If Luke was right, they'd both be untouchable for the rest of their journey, and they already knew that he could reset her back to level 1 if that's what she wanted once they made it to the God Machine.

"The simple truth of the matter is that we're not done leveling," Luke said quietly. "There are going to be more obstacles, and we're already pushing up against the limits of what we can handle. Even if we could find a quiet corner of the world to fuck off to for a decade to manually train skills up, it still wouldn't be enough. And we both know we can't do that. We're going to need a to gain more levels before it's over, and with **[XP Mask]**, I can get as many as needed. You can grab some of the non-bloodline skills that hide your XP presence, and even if someone makes an issue of it, it's not like anyone would be able to stop us."

"This is a terrible idea," Zea said with a heavy sigh. "But."

"But I'm not wrong," Luke finished.

"Exactly. I guess we're doing this."

Luke broke out into a grin and turned toward the direction System had indicated. Before he could take a single step, Zea held up a hand to stop him.

"Not that one. We're too close to the mercs still, plus we need to make it to Sicanti and unload this amaral hide before it starts to go bad. These enchantments aren't going to last much longer. I'm also going to need some time to do some enchanting work. I think ant hunters have some sort of scent blocker they use to help keep the ants from tracking them. I'll have to do some research."

"Sicanti first, then power leveling," Luke agreed.

"System, let's say that we need five years each before we have to worry about XP madness. How high a level could we go?"

"I would estimate you could safely level up to 43, and Luke to 45 with a five-year window," System said. "The initial effects are hardly intrusive. If you wish to exceed that threshold, you could both reach level 50 before XP madness becomes a significant issue, and perhaps 55 before your behavior becomes erratic and noticeable to others."

"So we have time to try this, and if the next purification doesn't allow us to make a skill to handle XP madness, we can still head for the God Machine to do a hard reset and just flush the XP out completely," Luke said. "That seems like a good plan."

"Those are the only kind I make," Zea said smugly.

"Really? What about that time you tried to make money at a fight club off an apostate and ended up on the run?"

"Well, admittedly that plan had a few holes in it, but I was operating on incomplete information, wasn't I?"

"I suppose it turned out for the best," Luke said.

"It certainly has had a few perks."

Luke pretended he didn't see it coming when Zea goosed him. A few perks, indeed.

Name	Luke Bennet	Zea Stenter
Level	34	21
XP	137370/144088	34019/34079
AP	42	8
Bloodline	SysAdmin II	None
Strength	42	7
Agility	55	27
Stamina	51	27
Perception	39	19
Skills	Mace Mastery (3)	Dagger Mastery (1)
	Sword Mastery (1)	Stealth (2)
	Unarmed Martialist (4)	Keen Instincts (1)
	Power Strike (2)	Lock Picking (1)
	Life Surge (2)	Disguise (2)
	Peripheral Awareness (2)	Deception (1)
	Tactical Foresight (1)	Bartering (2)
	Counter (2)	Streetwise (2)
	Twitch Reflexes (3)	Cooking (1)
	Stealth (1)	Mending (1)
	Survivalist (2)	First Aid (1)
	First Aid (1)	Thalian (3)
	Wood Carving (1)	Neyardic (3)
	Leatherworking (2)	Ostari (1)
	Butchering (4)	Mana Manipulation (2)
	Thalian (2)	Mana Sight (1)
	Ostari (1)	Metallurgy (1)
	Disguise (2)	Whitesmithing (1)
	Deception (1)	Goldsmithing (2)
	Torturer (1)	Gem Cutting (1)
	Analyze (BL)	Engraving (2)
	Remote Access (BL)	Rune Forging (1)
	XP Mask (BL)	Painting (1)
		Arcano Dynamics (1)
		Sleight of Hand (1)
		Steady Hands (2)
		Cold Reading (1)
		Temperature Acclimation (2)
		Cadence (2)
		Bloodline Purification Ritual (1)
		Ghost Script (1)

CHAPTER 47

Sicanti was smaller than Luke expected it to be. He supposed it counted as a city by Aros standards, but it didn't seem like it could hold that many people to him. Then again, they were approaching it from downhill and couldn't even see the harbor, or any of the ocean itself for that matter. Maybe it would look bigger once he got a better view.

They'd used the roads pretty much the whole way, but Luke thought they'd done a fine job of remaining inconspicuous. At the speed they'd moved, nobody had caught up from behind, and with his high perception, any time they'd seen someone they were going to overtake, they'd gone off-road to circle around. In the end, it had probably cost them an extra hour or two of travel time, but both felt it was worth the effort.

The real question in Luke's mind was whether the Blacktongue mercenaries had any presence in Sicanti, and if so, how safe he'd be walking in wearing a bunch of their gear. System had, as usual, been less than stellar with the information he was willing to share.

"We could stash the armor out of town and come back for it later," Zea said.

"But I just got it. I've been trying to get good armor since I got here."

"I know, but it's also really conspicuous."

"Maybe if I hold the cloak closed?"

"There are so many things wrong with that, I'm not even going to list them," Zea told him. "Actually, it's going to bug me if I don't."

"What?"

"Okay, so first, holding your cloak closed makes you look like a flasher. Or it would if you couldn't see the outline of the armor through the cloak anyway.

Second, are you going to leave your mace behind? I guess maybe the harness has an option for having it ride at your hip instead of on your back? Third, the cloak is part of the uniform. Anyone who recognizes the armor is going to recognize the cloak too."

"Okay, okay! I get it. It's a dumb idea."

"Oh," Zea said softly. "I'm sorry."

"No, you're right," Luke said. "We don't need to attract trouble."

"But I was being mean about it. I didn't need to do that. How about if we stop for lunch, empty out one of the food bags, and put the armor inside that? You can carry it with you. Or we can fold it up in the cloak and you can carry it that way?"

"I suppose that's a decent compromise," he said.

"Good, now get out of that armor. It's cold as fuck, and I'm not getting the kind of snuggles I was promised when I signed on for this trip."

They found a small campsite off the road a few miles from the city and set up their cooking fire. Luke attempted, without success, to cook while Zea watched with mounting horror. After they'd scraped away the abomination he'd created, she took over and walked him through the steps of what he should have done.

"It all looks the exact same to me," he said at the end.

"What? No, it was completely different. How could you . . ." Zea trailed off with a sigh. "Maybe you should just spend the AP on **[Cooking]** and be done with it."

"Never!"

"It's just 1 point."

"It's the principle of the matter," Luke told her. "I'll get it, just you wait and see."

Zea gave the bush they'd dumped his attempt at cooking into an uneasy glance and sighed. "Okay, if you say so."

After a bit of rearranging, they managed to clean one of their backpacks out enough to hold Luke's stolen armor. It was a bit tight, but in the end, everything metal and armor-y was in a single bag with the cloak wrapped around it to prevent clanking sounds. He kept the outfit and the boots, having discarded his old farmer's homespun back at the mercenary compound. Hopefully, the new clothes were generic enough not to be recognized as mercenary standard issue.

"Ready?" he asked.

"Ready as I'll ever be."

It was a simple plan. They'd head into the city, thankfully just as unwalled as everything else in the northland seemed to be, and Zea would sniff out a few enchanter's shops. They'd pick whichever one looked the most loaded and try to off-load their primo enchanting hide directly for an infusion of literal cold, hard cash.

Money in hand, it would be time to find the harbor and learn which ships were going across the ocean soon, then barter passage. With whatever time they had left before they set sail, they'd try Luke's idea of bombing anthills for XP. If everything went according to plan, they'd level up enough for Zea to rank up **[Bloodline Purification Ritual]** so she could determine what weird shit they'd need to repeat the ritual and start shopping for it.

It would definitely go smoothly, just like they wanted it to. Definitely.

They shouldered their packs and walked into Sicanti.

"Okay, it's bigger than I thought," Luke admitted. "I didn't realize we were still so many miles from the ocean when we first spotted it."

"I bet there's not a lot of people actually living on the east edge of the city. Probably all dry docks, warehouses, and taverns. Sailors, dockworkers, and guards all the way. Maybe try not to get into a fight with them this time."

"That was one time! And I didn't even really fight him," Luke protested.

Zea shrugged. "Come on, I think the business district is over this way."

Luke looked over to where Zea was gesturing. It looked just like the rest of the city to him, single-story buildings made out of timber lining either side of cobblestone streets. Occasionally, there was a second story that loomed over its neighbors, but those were a clear minority.

"Why this way?" he asked.

"Better-dressed people, more carriages, more servants. All signs that the money is over that way, which means the people who sell things are there too."

"Oh, well when you put it like that."

They got a lot of looks as they made their way through the crowd, and it wasn't hard to figure out why. There wasn't a single other dwifkin anywhere in sight, and while everyone else was dressed in heavy clothes and a coat, maybe with a cloak thrown over top, she was practically waddling the double-layered everything and a hat she'd pulled out of her bag. Luke wasn't even sure where she'd picked that up.

He got a few curious stares as well, but no one paid him much attention. In fact, he couldn't recall a time ever when he'd received fewer looks than now. And then it hit him. His XP was hidden. The people checking him out were probably the few who had high enough perception to tell that he was showing 0 XP, not just low XP. Between that and the novel nature of a dwifkin walking down the street, it was easy enough for him to fade into the background.

He followed along mutely. His job right now was to be the baggage boy and protect their money and equipment from theft. Considering they'd ended up with five packs of various sizes somehow, it was a cumbersome task to be holding all of them at once, especially since there was every possibility of a cutpurse slicing the stitching on the bag he'd slung over his back without him realizing it.

He opted for one of the remaining food bags in that position. If they lost an apple or a wedge of cheese, he could live with that. The amaril-hide bag and the money bag stayed in front of him, with his armor bag tucked under one arm and the miscellaneous supplies held in the other. So far, no one had tried to mess with it. That may have been more due to Zea's expert navigation away from the poorer districts than it was due to Luke's high perception catching anyone who even thought about it.

The deeper they got into Sicanti, the nicer the streets got. He stopped having to watch his step to keep from catching his toes on uneven cobblestones after the first ten or so blocks, and he noticed the houses getting bigger and two-story buildings becoming more common soon after. Glass windows started showing up, and the general quality of both the wood and the carpentry rose.

By the time they made it to what Zea dubbed the business district, there were open squares with stalls set up in them, alleyways with back doors to let employees and deliveries in and out, and spaces reserved for carriages, carts, and wagons, which meant wider streets to accommodate vehicles and foot traffic. She wove through them, ignoring the calls of vendors and the muttered grumblings of shoppers unhappy with her invading their personal space.

Eventually, after far too much browsing around for Luke's taste, Zea settled on a building with an unusual number of windows and a sign hanging from a post near the door with a picture of what looked to him like some sort of symbol he would have expected to show up in math class. Presumably, it was some kind of rune. Whatever it meant, it made Zea happy to see it.

She snatched the bag with the amaril hide from Luke, gave him an appraising glance, and said, "It's going to be boring enchanting stuff. You want to come with?"

"Uh. Did you need me to do something else?"

"I don't, but I figured you might like a spare set of clothes for when you inevitably end up destroying the ones you're wearing."

"Hey, I've got armor now."

"Mm-hmm. And, just out of curiosity, how many of those mercs you killed also had armor?"

Luke thought about that for a second. He was pretty sure most of them had been wearing bits and pieces, if not a full suit. "All of them? Ish."

"Yeah . . . How many pieces of armor did you destroy?" Zea asked.

"A lot of them. Fuck. Good point. Okay, I think I saw a clothing store a block back. I'll go see if I can find something and meet you back here when I'm done?"

"The one that had that black shirt on display in the window? I'll just head over there if I finish up first."

They split up, with Zea gleefully dashing into the enchanting shop and Luke shaking his head. That poor shopkeeper wasn't going to know what hit him. No doubt she'd get every single copper she thought the hide was worth, probably more besides. If she didn't take it in hard cash, she'd get a chunk of it in trade for other supplies. Luke was kind of hoping she did, if only because she'd started grumbling about feeling the lack of options when they stopped for breaks and she wanted to work on something.

He rearranged the remaining load and backtracked to the shop in question. Maybe he'd get two extra outfits, just to be safe.

Adrevald Lath was staring at out the harbor from the window of the suite he'd been given for his use in the church in Sicanti. His work had taken him to many, many exotic locales, but never across the ocean. If things didn't go well here though, that could very well be his next step. The church didn't have its own ship, so he'd have to charter passage. Well, it was best not to get ahead of himself. He'd know if the mercenaries had succeeded in locating and capturing the two apostates he wanted soon enough.

Almost as if thinking of them had summoned them, someone knocked on his door. "Come in," he said, not moving from his position.

"Ah, pardon me, Inquisitor Lath," one of the local priests said as he entered the room. "You have a visitor."

Lath studied the man's reflection in the window. Scrawny, low level. Weak. No hidden weapons. Unimportant. "Very well. Send them in."

A mercenary followed the priest in, not the same one he'd spoken to originally when he'd formed the contract. This one wasn't as strong, or was just better at hiding it. He doubted that. It had been a lot of years since anyone had been able to fool him.

He didn't like the mercenary's posture. The man seemed afraid to talk to Lath. That meant it was bad news. Something had gone wrong. Fucking mercenaries. All they had to do was find the pair.

"You have news for me?" he asked, still watching the reflection in the window.

"Yes, erm, about that . . ."

Name	Luke Bennet	Zea Stenter
Level	34	21
XP	137370/144088	34019/34079
AP	42	8
Bloodline	SysAdmin II	None
Strength	42	7
Agility	55	27
Stamina	51	27
Perception	39	19
Skills	Mace Mastery (3)	Dagger Mastery (1)
	Sword Mastery (1)	Stealth (2)
	Unarmed Martialist (4)	Keen Instincts (1)
	Power Strike (2)	Lock Picking (1)
	Life Surge (2)	Disguise (2)
	Peripheral Awareness (2)	Deception (1)
	Tactical Foresight (1)	Bartering (2)
	Counter (2)	Streetwise (2)
	Twitch Reflexes (3)	Cooking (1)
	Stealth (1)	Mending (1)
	Survivalist (2)	First Aid (1)
	First Aid (1)	Thalian (3)
	Wood Carving (1)	Neyardic (3)
	Leatherworking (2)	Ostari (1)
	Butchering (4)	Mana Manipulation (2)
	Thalian (2)	Mana Sight (1)
	Ostari (1)	Metallurgy (1)
	Disguise (2)	Whitesmithing (1)
	Deception (1)	Goldsmithing (2)
	Torturer (1)	Gem Cutting (1)
	Analyze (BL)	Engraving (2)
	Remote Access (BL)	Rune Forging (1)
	XP Mask (BL)	Painting (1)
		Arcano Dynamics (1)
		Sleight of Hand (1)
		Steady Hands (2)
		Cold Reading (1)
		Temperature Acclimation (2)
		Cadence (2)
		Bloodline Purification Ritual (1)
		Ghost Script (1)

CHAPTER 48

Luke was just settling his packs back into place with their new additions when he heard Zea moving toward the tailor's shop. Specifically, he heard the clinking sound of coins smacking together with every step she took. It certainly sounded like there were a lot of them, and he almost thought he could hear her humming under her breath. That poor shopkeeper.

A few seconds later, Zea appeared in the shop window. Well, the top half of her head did anyway. Luke raised a hand to wave, then finished shouldering the last bag and headed out the door. "You look happy," he said when he got outside.

"Today has been a good day," she said with a self-satisfied smile.

"I take it negotiations went well. I can hear you clinking with every step."

"Hey now, don't invade a girl's privacy like that," Zea told him sternly. "You just keep those ears to yourself."

Luke laughed and said, "Where to now?"

"Two options. Either we head straight to the harbor and start looking for ships going across the ocean, or we get some lunch. I vote for the second option. It's getting hard to remember what it's like to eat a meal I haven't cooked."

"Ah, yes. Those are quite good," Luke agreed. "I try to have meals cooked by someone else as often as possible."

"Wait a second. Have you . . . Have you been deliberately burning everything just to get out of cooking? Is that why you won't learn the skill?"

"What! No. Not on purpose. I'm just . . . I'm not a good cook, okay."

"Humph," Zea said. "We're going to get lunch. You're paying."

"Me?! I'm not the one who clinks when she walks!"

"And I'd like to keep clinking, thank you very much. Now, come on. Off we go."

They bypassed the local bars and taverns and found a little restaurant in an out-of-the-way corner of the business district. Perhaps it was the fact that he only had rank 1 **[Ostari]**, but Luke couldn't make heads or tails of the menu. It was posted on something that looked vaguely like a chalkboard, except it was blue instead of black or green, and the words written on it might as well have been scribbles for all he could tell.

Zea took care of the ordering, though he suspected she couldn't read it either, and soon there was a plate of . . . something . . . in front of him. The meat was questionable, the vegetables oddly shaped and strangely colored, and the drink smelled vaguely alcoholic. For all that, it was pretty good. Weird, but good.

"What are you thinking about?" Zea said.

"Huh? Oh, just . . . being reminded how different everything is here. It's not bad, just not what I'm used to. My family wasn't big on traveling, you know? We moved around a lot, but never really left the area."

"So a world-spanning trip is a bit outside your comfort zone."

"Little bit, yeah." Luke poked his fork at something cubed, purple, and jiggly. It wasn't meat, but maybe not a vegetable either? Some kind of fruit, perhaps? Oh well, at least it tasted good.

"If it makes you feel any better, I don't think anybody would be comfortable with this situation. This whole thing is crazy, and we're not even halfway."

"Yeah. Do we know anything about the eastern continent?"

"Not so much," Zea said. "But we know someone who does."

Luke snorted. "Yeah, and it's like pulling teeth to get a useful answer out of him."

"Still better than nothing."

"I suppose."

Their conversation died off for a bit, until Zea said, "What are you going to do after we get there?"

Luke froze, his fork halfway to his mouth. He'd done his best to avoid thinking about it. The obvious answer was that he was going to bring his family back, but she already knew that. Zea meant what he was going to do after. Would they go back to Earth? Would they stay here? If they left, would he ask Zea to come with him? If he did, would she say yes?

"I don't know," he said lamely. "I'm trying to avoid thinking about it."

Earth didn't have dwifkin. Maybe he could turn Zea into a human if she wanted to go there, but that was a hell of a commitment. There was also the fact that they would need to purge every last point of XP out of their bodies, or souls, or wherever that was stored. Luke wasn't sure exactly how it worked.

And he needed to find some way to drag Uncle Duncan over here so they could purge however much XP he had in him too. When this was all over, he wanted no trace of the god in the machine on the Earth side of the doorway.

"Probably something to start spending some time thinking on," she said.

"I know, it's just . . . That's a big ask, you know? Would you want to come to Earth with me? Would you want to be turned into a human? Is it even possible to do that?"

"Would you want to stay on Aros with me?" she countered. "Would any of your family? Could that doorway stay open so you can go back and forth as you please?"

"Maybe we can ask once we're back out of town?"

"Why wait?" Zea said. "It's not like anyone else can see him."

"It still looks like I'm talking to my imaginary friend," Luke said dryly. "Don't need people thinking I'm crazy."

"Even if you kind of are."

"The way I see it, on this world, people who act crazy get put down for the safety of the whole community. Therefore, it is in my best interest not to appear crazy."

Zea started to say something, paused, then said, "Fair point. We'll wait until later then."

They returned to their food, both lost in their thoughts.

The harbor was even bigger than the one in Valtira, and there were some truly massive ships anchored there. Well, massive by comparison to most of the boats floating in the docks. Luke made some generous assumptions and assumed the bigger ones were the ships that would cross the ocean. It only made sense to him. More room for food, more room for people, more room for cargo.

The docks were just as busy as he remembered Valtira's being, with a row of warehouses curving to follow the harbor that hundreds of men and women moved in and out of as they shifted crates and barrels around. Some went onto ships, some went into the warehouse, and everywhere, men and woman stood around in unobtrusive corners counting each and every last container.

"If there's one thing nobles are good at, it's making sure to collect their taxes," Zea said when she noticed Luke looking.

"But how do they know what's actually inside is what they say is inside?"

Zea shrugged. "Spot checks, I suppose. It's not a perfect system by any means, and I'm sure more than one captain has smuggled this or that. Hell, most of the nobles have done the same thing. The customs officers probably know which boxes their bosses don't want them checking."

"I don't think that'll cause us any problems," Luke said.

"No, as long as we're not on a ship that gets caught smuggling anything."

"Speaking of, which ship are we thinking is going to take us across the ocean?"

Zea surveyed the harbor slowly, occasionally pointing at a ship. "Those ones, I think, are probably our best bets. We'll have to see if we can speak with the captains."

They weren't all the big ones like Luke had figured either. Whatever criteria she was using to judge, Luke didn't follow the logic. None of them were small, exactly, but he wasn't sure he'd be comfortable with being at sea for weeks on them.

Before he could ask, she set out onto the docks. Zea wove her way around the workers deftly, leaving Luke to struggle to keep up with all their baggage. When she got to the first ship, she exchanged a few words with a large man wearing a fur cloak and hat who was supervising the unloading of the ship's cargo. He listened for a moment, shook his head, and pointed at another ship a few spaces down.

Zea thanked him, then turned and beckoned for Luke to follow. Once again, he got caught up trying to stay out of the dockworkers' way and didn't make it to her until she'd already finished her conversation and started moving to a third ship.

This was one of the smaller ships, the kind he was leery about being stuck on for an extended period of time, but that Zea seemed to think was a good choice. This time, she was talking to a tall woman with dark-brown, almost green even, skin. The woman was taller than Luke by at least half a foot and might have outweighed him too. She was wearing some kind of poofy pants that were cinched at the calves and a bright-red shirt that had three buttons on the front to extend the neckline. All three of them were undone, revealing an inordinate amount of cleavage.

"Sixty is robbery!" Zea snapped.

"I'm barely breaking even," the woman said, her words thick with a sharp accent. "Two passengers means food, water, and most importantly, space. That cabin could hold cargo. If you want it, you need to cover the money I'm losing by not taking other cargo."

"Forty gold," Zea said.

"Sixty."

"Forty-five."

"Sixty," the woman said again, this time more slowly as she enunciated each syllable.

"You don't even have any cargo for that space, or you wouldn't be considering it," Zea argued. "Forty-five is more than enough to cover the costs and still turn a profit."

"The price is sixty. It is not negotiable. If you don't like it, fuck off and bother someone else."

"Fine, I will. Good luck filling that space," Zea said, stomping off. Luke distinctly heard her mutter, "Bitch," under her breath as she walked away.

If the woman heard her, she gave no indication of it. Probably her perception just wasn't that high. That would be for the best. Maybe Luke should check, just to make sure.

[Name: Human Ship Captain]

[Level: 17]

[Strength: 10]

[Agility: 21]

[Stamina: 9]

[Perception: 23]

That perception stat was higher than he would have expected, and he wasn't really sure why. Maybe it was just the woman's personal preference, or maybe there was some part of a sailor's job he wasn't aware of that demanded really good eyesight. Old-timey ships had that guy who stood up in the crow's nest looking for land, he supposed, but that wasn't usually the captain's job.

Well, what the hell did he even know about it anyway? With a mental shrug, Luke dismissed the woman and chased after Zea, who was already halfway to the next ship. By the time Luke got there, she'd already finished talking to a group of sailors coming down the wooden ramp thing and was stomping off. He supposed they wouldn't be talking to anyone important on this one.

Three more ships passed in the blink of an eye, each with the same results. Sometimes Zea spoke with a captain or first mate, sometimes with the regular sailors. Luke started using **[Analyze]** regularly, trying to get a range of what normal people's levels were. The highest he saw was level 22, and the lowest was 9. That came from a kid, maybe fourteen, who was scurrying after a pair of sailors while they rattled off orders to him.

It seemed like sailors favored a mix of agility and perception, whereas dockworkers went all in on strength and stamina. The paper pushers with their books and tally marks seemed to have universally low stats all the way around, despite their levels. Unless it was some cultural thing to sit on massive amounts of AP, he supposed there were a few expensive skills that would be difficult to pick up otherwise.

While he was pondering that, Zea shook hands with an absolute bear of a man, closer to seven feet tall than six, and his bare chest covered in coarse black hair. She counted fifteen gold coins out of her purse and handed them over, then turned and waved at Luke.

"Two weeks until we leave," she said. "And only thirty gold, half up front. Ha."

Name	Luke Bennet	Zea Stenter
Level	34	21
XP	137370/144088	34019/34079
AP	42	8
Bloodline	SysAdmin II	None
Strength	42	7
Agility	55	27
Stamina	51	27
Perception	39	19
Skills	Mace Mastery (3)	Dagger Mastery (1)
	Sword Mastery (1)	Stealth (2)
	Unarmed Martialist (4)	Keen Instincts (1)
	Power Strike (2)	Lock Picking (1)
	Life Surge (2)	Disguise (2)
	Peripheral Awareness (2)	Deception (1)
	Tactical Foresight (1)	Bartering (2)
	Counter (2)	Streetwise (2)
	Twitch Reflexes (3)	Cooking (1)
	Stealth (1)	Mending (1)
	Survivalist (2)	First Aid (1)
	First Aid (1)	Thalian (3)
	Wood Carving (1)	Neyardic (3)
	Leatherworking (2)	Ostari (1)
	Butchering (4)	Mana Manipulation (2)
	Thalian (2)	Mana Sight (1)
	Ostari (1)	Metallurgy (1)
	Disguise (2)	Whitesmithing (1)
	Deception (1)	Goldsmithing (2)
	Torturer (1)	Gem Cutting (1)
	Analyze (BL)	Engraving (2)
	Remote Access (BL)	Rune Forging (1)
	XP Mask (BL)	Painting (1)
		Arcano Dynamics (1)
		Sleight of Hand (1)
		Steady Hands (2)
		Cold Reading (1)
		Temperature Acclimation (2)
		Cadence (2)
		Bloodline Purification Ritual (1)
		Ghost Script (1)

CHAPTER 49

The ship was called *The Averast*, which maybe meant something, but neither of Luke's language skills translated it for him. It was one of the big ones he'd spotted earlier, which was somewhat comforting. He wasn't sure exactly why he wanted the ship to be bigger, other than that bigger meant sturdier, probably less likely to sink while he was on it. Maybe it also meant less likely to be attacked by sea monsters, which he assumed existed because why wouldn't they?

Luke made a mental note to question System about the existence of sea monsters later.

At the moment, he was helping Zea lay out her new portable enchanting workstation, which was really just a small foldout lap table with some sort of articulated arm that had a clamp on the end of it. His job was to unpack all her new stuff from her bag and assist as needed while she carved runes into them. It was both tedious and boring, but considering it was his bomb that she was working on, it felt like it would be rude to complain.

"How come you're doing it the hard way instead of using **[Ghost Script]**?" he asked.

"Bigger boom this way, plus things I enchant with **[Ghost Script]** only last a few minutes before the mana drains back out. We can't really stockpile anything unless I do it the hard way."

"Oh, right. How many booms are you thinking we're going to need?"

Zea paused in her carving and considered the question. "One for you, one for me. I'll make a temporary one when we get to the anthill. We also need something for scent nullification, or the rest of the colony will be chasing us.

I'm . . . not really sure how to do that. Going to have to experiment a bit, but it's important. I figure I'll get it working, try it out, and if you can't smell me with your perception as high as it is, maybe that'll be good enough."

"How many ants do you think three bombs are going to kill?" Luke asked.

"We're only throwing one bomb in there to start," Zea said. "The other two are for emergencies. You know that a colony has hundreds of thousands of ants, right? We're throwing this from as far away as we can, then running for our lives and hoping the ones that survive don't come chasing after us. If it works, we can consider repeating it. In no way are we to get within a hundred feet of the actual hill itself."

Luke still thought she was overestimating the danger, but he had to admit that she had so far displayed better judgment than he had about, well, pretty much everything. The worst he could think of was her decision to push deeper into squirrel territory, but even then, she'd had good reasons, and they'd thought they'd encountered an enemy they knew they could handle. For all they knew, going around could have meant fighting something that was level 40.

Still, ants were just ants. They were tiny, not really a threat to a human under normal circumstances. He would have to fall into their nest and let them swarm him, and even then, he had 51 stamina. It might be gross to be covered with them, but it was hard to imagine them being able to bite through his skin. If squirrels couldn't manage it, it seemed unlikely a mere ant could do it, no matter how many friends it brought to the party.

He might have been concerned about system fuckery, except that he knew for a fact that they were all level 1 or 2. System has explicitly stated that there was only a tiny fraction that even made it to level 5. Given everything he'd learned about how things worked on Aros, he just didn't see the big deal. Maybe to someone who was only level 10 and didn't have a lot of stamina, they'd be a threat, but not to him or Zea.

But he trusted Zea, and she said the preparations were necessary. Overkill or not, if this was how she wanted to play it, he supported her. Even if it meant days of her fiddling with stuff until she was satisfied.

"I was thinking I might go hunting," Luke said. "Unless you need my help here."

"Are you really that bored?"

"I guess. I'm not much for standing around doing nothing. I'm happy to help if you need me, but just lying here all day doesn't sound like fun. Now, if you want to take a break and help me test out this bed . . ."

Zea rolled her eyes and said, "Not now. We're on a clock before that ship leaves, and if this crazy idea of yours actually works, I'll need to pick up more stuff for rank 2 of **[Bloodline Purification Ritual]**."

"Yeah, about that. You noticed all the stares you were getting, right?"

"I did. There's not much I can do about that though."

"I know," Luke said, "but we know the church here is also going to take a swing at us. They already hired those mercenaries, and I definitely didn't kill all of them. Maybe we need to think about cutting our time around the city to a minimum. The longer we're here and the more people see you, the better the odds of them finding us again. And all that is assuming some asshole god doesn't just point a divine finger at us to tell the church where we are."

"They aren't allowed to do that," Zea muttered. "Fucking cheaters don't even play by their own rules."

"So I was thinking that when we leave the city on this exterminator job, we don't come back until it's time to get on the boat."

Zea grimaced. "But . . . Bed. Warm."

"I know, but we're not really safe here."

Luke didn't want to say she needed to be locked in their room for the next two weeks, but at the same time, they were already distinctive as a human-and-dwifkin couple. This far north, where there were practically no other dwifkin at all, it was even worse. With **[XP Mask]** hiding his level from everyone, Luke was actually the less noticeable of the pair now, especially since he now had two sets of clothes done in the local fashion.

It was still obvious he was foreign to anyone who talked to him, but he only looked a little pale compared to Sicanti's native population. As long as he kept his mouth shut, he felt like he could move around freely without drawing attention. Zea didn't have that option.

"So you're going hunting?" she asked, not looking up from her project.

"It seemed like a good way to spend my time."

"See if you can find another one of those moose. My project exploded when I fought that mercenary, and I'd like to take another crack at it."

"I can do that," Luke said with a smile. He knelt down next to her for a kiss and added, "I'll be back tonight. If anything goes wrong, get the fuck out of here and I'll find you?"

"Duh. I'm not going to stick around to trade punches with an inquisitor or five."

"Good girl."

Zea just rolled her eyes and kissed him back.

Luke stood at the edge of the woods, about twenty miles from Sicanti. The trees weren't nearly as big as what they'd found in the deep forests, and with them being nicely spaced out and little underbrush, it was actually kind of nice to just walk around. But he had a job to do. "Moose, huh? Hey, System, can you point me in the direction of the nearest moose?"

"I am sorry, but I am not able to give information about specific individuals," System said.

"Right, of course not. That's my mistake forgetting that," Luke said. "Oh! By the way, do sea monsters exist on this world?"

"What do you mean by *sea monster*? There are many aquatic monsters, but it sounds like you might be thinking of something in particular."

"I don't know. Giant squids and sea serpents and shit. Things big enough to sink a boat."

"In that case, the answer to your question is yes, there are several dozen species of aquatic monsters powerful enough to successfully attack and destroy a seafaring vessel."

That was pretty much what Luke had expected to hear. Then again, there had been two reasons they'd had to travel to Sicanti. One was that the land-masses were simply closer up here, but the other . . . "How many of them live in cold water?"

"Only two, and both are numerically insignificant," System said. "The first is a great black-and-white creature known as the flesh grinder. It looks like a fish, only hundreds of times bigger. The real danger from this sea monster is that they tend to travel in groups."

"Uh, that just sounds like an orca to me," Luke said.

"I am unfamiliar with the term."

"A killer whale?"

"That species is not known to me either."

"Do you guys not have whales here?" Luke asked. He wouldn't have been surprised to find them with extra fins or armor plating or shooting lasers out of their eyes or something, but to not have them at all seemed unlikely.

"There are many species of whales, and though the flesh grinder shares some characteristics, they are most definitely not whales."

Now Luke almost wanted to see one, just because he couldn't picture anything other than an orca based off System's description. Of course, seeing one would probably mean the ship was getting attacked, so maybe he'd be better off not sating his curiosity there. "What's the other monster? Please don't say kraken."

"Not in the frigid-cold waters of the northern ocean," System said with a shake of his head. "The other type of sea monster is known as a xashim. There has never been a case of XP being exchanged between any land-dwelling species and a xashim. I can only assume this is because the two species never come in contact. Xashim live exclusively on the ocean floor and resemble a great glowing orb a thousand feet wide with many thou-sands of tentacles each up to a mile long that it uses to catch prey and drag itself around."

"Some sort of deep-sea megajellyfish? Well, as long as they never come to the surface, I guess that's fine. So the only things I need to be concerned about are these not-whales, the flesh grinders."

"In terms of monsters native to the sailing routes used by humans to move between continents, that is correct."

Luke didn't like the way System phrased that. "Are there other concerns?"

"Elementals are statistically more likely to cause problems than monsters," System told him. "And they are generally harder to destroy."

Luke stopped walking and glanced over at the pale-blue apparition. That was the problem with getting information out of System. He never knew when he was missing something because he hadn't thought to ask a specific question. Zea was far better than him about prying those little nuggets of information out of their conversations, partially because she had a better base of knowledge to compare against, and partly because she was just all sorts of clever. At least, she was when she didn't have dollar signs in her eyes.

"Okay, I think we need to have a longer conversation about every possible danger and the likelihood that the ship will run into them. I have a feeling I'm going to need to do some preparations here."

Before System could reply, Luke heard the sound of something snorting and tearing at the ground nearby. He peered through the trees and spotted some sort of wild boar a few hundred yards away.

"Hold that thought," he told System as he pulled his mace off his back. "I've got some hunting to do."

Name	Luke Bennet	Zea Stenter
Level	34	21
XP	137370/144088	34019/34079
AP	42	8
Bloodline	SysAdmin II	None
Strength	42	7
Agility	55	27
Stamina	51	27
Perception	39	19
Skills	Mace Mastery (3)	Dagger Mastery (1)
	Sword Mastery (1)	Stealth (2)
	Unarmed Martialist (4)	Keen Instincts (1)
	Power Strike (2)	Lock Picking (1)
	Life Surge (2)	Disguise (2)
	Peripheral Awareness (2)	Deception (1)
	Tactical Foresight (1)	Bartering (2)
	Counter (2)	Streetwise (2)
	Twitch Reflexes (3)	Cooking (1)
	Stealth (1)	Mending (1)
	Survivalist (2)	First Aid (1)
	First Aid (1)	Thalian (3)
	Wood Carving (1)	Neyardic (3)
	Leatherworking (2)	Ostari (1)
	Butchering (4)	Mana Manipulation (2)
	Thalian (2)	Mana Sight (1)
	Ostari (1)	Metallurgy (1)
	Disguise (2)	Whitesmithing (1)
	Deception (1)	Goldsmithing (2)
	Torturer (1)	Gem Cutting (1)
	Analyze (BL)	Engraving (2)
	Remote Access (BL)	Rune Forging (1)
	XP Mask (BL)	Painting (1)
		Arcano Dynamics (1)
		Sleight of Hand (1)
		Steady Hands (2)
		Cold Reading (1)
		Temperature Acclimation (2)
		Cadence (2)
		Bloodline Purification Ritual (1)
		Ghost Script (1)

CHAPTER 50

Luke prodded the dead boar . . . thing . . . with his foot. It had a lot of bone spurs across its skull and shoulders, and instead of hooves on its front two legs, it had appendages that looked an awful lot like monkey feet. It was also a lot bigger than a regular wild pig, at least any of the ones he'd seen. It was easily taller than he was, and if it weighed less than three tons, he'd be surprised.

It had taken a single attack infused with **[Power Strike]** to the side of its face when it lowered its tusks to gore him to snap its neck and send fragments of teeth, bone, and brain out in a wide arc to his right. There were no less than six different trees with specks of white peppered into their bark. "Huh, that was easy."

[You have slain Bone-Charger Boar (level 20). 415 XP awarded.]

[This creature has slain 372 other creatures.]

[Total kills for this type of creature: 1.]

[Highest-level kill: 20.]

He felt kind of bad about it, after the fact. Sure, the boar had been more than willing to take a swing at him, but only because he'd walked over and put himself in its line of sight. And then he'd just hauled off and one-shotted it. The XP gain wasn't even that much.

"System, this says that I have only killed one of this type of monster, but I swear I've encountered one before."

"You have also killed one bonespike boar, a related species with similar anatomy."

"Oh, yeah. I guess that must have been it. Well, I suppose I best get to butchering it while it's still fresh."

Thanks to rank 4 **[Butchering]**, that didn't take long at all, and Luke got some choice cuts off the body. Well, as choice as a wild boar got. He doubted the meat would taste anywhere near as good as bacon off a fat farm pig, but it was better than leaving it to rot.

On the plus side, while he was doing his best to package up the meat without making a huge, bloody mess, plenty of other animals came by to investigate. Thanks to **[XP Mask]**, they were no longer avoiding his massive XP presence, and a few of them were aggressive enough to fight him for scavenging rights. Of course, that started to get old quick . . .

[You have slain Hephelian Falcon (level 22). 505 XP awarded.]
[This creature has slain 471 other creatures.]
[Total kills for this type of creature: 1.]
[Highest-level kill: 22.]

If the bird hadn't tried to dive-bomb his head, he might have felt worse about killing it. It kind of reminded him of Red, except a lot more murder-y. Plus it was kind of on the scrawny side for a monster bird. Luke shrugged, waited for the explosion of feathers from where he'd decked it to finish falling to the ground, and kicked the body out of the way so he could get back to work.

[You have slain Camo Cougar (level 26). 712 XP awarded.]
[This creature has slain 521 other creatures.]
[Total kills for this type of creature: 1.]
[Highest-level kill: 26.]

"Okay, what the fuck is a camo cougar?" Luke said after a nearly invisible cat tried to pounce on him from behind. Even with his perception as high as it was, he hadn't seen or heard it coming, but the smell gave it away. He'd had to fight that one essentially blind, relying on his skills to react in time, but the cat hadn't been able to take a hit, and after he'd tagged it once, it was easy to finish it off. "System, is this just a weird translation error?"

"I am not sure what you mean, Luke."

"Well, like, I see the notifications in English, right? That's not a language on Aros, and *camo* is an abbreviation in my language. It's just weird is all."

"I understand. It could perhaps best be translated as 'large cat with the ability to become nearly perfectly invisible,' if you were to take the name literally."

Luke rolled his eyes and considered the corpse. "I wish you could relay messages to Zea for me. I bet there's some part of this thing she'd want. Maybe the whole hide?"

"Apologies, but that is outside of my functionality. I can advise that the eyeballs are prized among alchemists, though you lack the equipment to properly remove and preserve them. The hide does not have any special properties."

"The equipment and the knowledge," Luke said, looking down at his knife and back to the cougar's corpse. **[Butchering]** apparently didn't cover removing eyeballs from bodies. He could probably pick up a skill for that but didn't see a reason to bother since he couldn't magic up the tools needed. Besides, they had enough money now. He didn't even know if the coins they were currently using would be good for anything on the other side of the ocean.

[You have slain Black-Rot Viper (level 17). 298 XP awarded.]
    [This creature has slain 235 other creatures.]
    [Total kills for this type of creature: 1.]
    [Highest-level kill: 17.]
"Why is it called black-rot viper? This sounds like something someone would try to poison me with."

"The venom sacs are indeed harvested for use by poisoners and assassins," System said.

"What does it do?"

"It turns the skin around the bite black, and then chunks of necrotized flesh start to fall off."

Luke gave the dead snake a wary glance and stepped away. "Ew."

As some point, he eventually gave up trying to butcher the boar and settled for just waiting until the next carnivore came by, looking for a free meal. The stink of blood was starting to get overpowering, and Luke had to reposition himself a hundred feet or so upwind to cut it down to tolerable levels.

A lot of small animals showed up, most of them between levels 3 and 7, which he generally just ignored as long as they didn't try to take a bite out of him. The only time he moved in for the kill was if something above level 15 made an appearance, and even then, there were only half a dozen over the next hour or two.

After a few hours, he gave up on a moose coming by. It made sense, he supposed, that an herbivore would avoid a scavenger's buffet, but then again, it wouldn't surprise him in the least to see one show up with a mouthful of sharp teeth and a taste for flesh, not on Aros.

He'd filled his food bag with various monster parts that System said were usually useful for enchanting, mostly things like teeth and claws, though he'd taken the time to skin that giant snake and start processing the leather. It was quick work to set up a drying rack for it now and gave him something to do while he waited for the next victim to show up.

Hopefully, no one would mess with it over the next few days. He wasn't even sure what he'd do with the hide, but it was a nice black color, and he had 2 ranks in **[Leatherworking]** that hadn't seen any action in a while. If it followed the same progression as **[Butchering]**, it wasn't even all that expensive to bump it up to rank 3 or 4 either.

Maybe a nice belt or some boots? Luke would figure something out. Zea would probably say to just sell it instead of making her anything, and in her defense, if it didn't have fur attached to it right now, she did not want it.

"Hmm. Maybe a money purse?" That would be a good gift for her. "Oh! A case for her enchanting tools! One of those roll-out ones." Perfect.

It felt kind of weird just leaving a drying rack out in the middle of the woods, completely randomly placed and unattended, with no camp nearby. Hopefully none of the animals would get at it. Well, if it was gone or destroyed when he came back to check on it, he wasn't out anything but some time.

"Okay, this has been a thing, but let's see if we can't find a moose now," Luke said.

Finding a moose was easier said than done, especially considering they hadn't even meant to find the first one. It had just stumbled across them one night, and Luke kind of had to kill it since the crazy fucker had immediately charged them. That had been a good two or three hundred miles away in a very different kind of forest, and he was starting to suspect there just weren't any around here. Even if he did find one, it might not be the kind Zea wanted.

"System, what was the type of moose we killed?"

"A razor-prong moose," System supplied.

"Right, that. Can you tell me if there are any in this forest? I mean, is this the right type of habitat for them?"

"They are commonly found in much denser woodland areas farther away from advanced civilization. It is rare to see one this close to Sicanti."

"Damn," Luke said. "I was hoping I was wrong about that. And you can't point me in the right direction either."

"My apologies. I cannot."

"Okay, well, I guess we'll see what **[Survivalist]** has to say about it."

The answer to that was, unfortunately, not a lot. No convenient moose tracks jumped out at him, and as soon as Luke thought that, he had a sudden craving for ice cream. After two hours of exploring, the deaths of a few larger carnivorous monsters, and precisely one encounter with a skunk, which Luke promptly ran away from, he gave up.

There was just too much background noise to rely on his hearing, and as spacious as the trees were, he was still limited to about a thousand feet in any given direction. He supposed he could have theoretically gotten lucky and caught a whiff of moose musk, but that hadn't happened. If there were any moose, they were nowhere near the locations he'd explored.

He was hoping that some of the other stuff he'd collected would be close enough to do what Zea wanted. Those snake fangs were sharp as fuck, practically needles at the tips, for example. That had to count for something. Then again, he only had two fangs, and she'd used over a dozen shards of antler in her initial construction.

He trudged back into town, somewhat disappointed despite his full bags. When he got back to the inn, he found Zea passed out on the bed, snoring softly, various tools and scraps of materials he could only guess at scattered across her worktable. Luke was tempted to start cleaning up, but he didn't want to risk anything blowing up if he handled it the wrong way or touched it to something else it wasn't supposed to come in contact with.

Instead, he inspected the tools, trying to get a mental snapshot of their dimensions. Already, he was envisioning pockets and straps to hold them and wondering if he should add some extra space just in case she got more later.

He was definitely going to have to bump **[Leatherworking]** up another rank, and he thought he might need to find a supply shop of his own. For something this small and delicate, using thin strips of leather as thread wasn't going to work. He'd need actual thread, and considering the kinds of weird materials they had available on Aros, he might find something that was strong enough that it was guaranteed to never break.

That was a job for tomorrow. Now, he settled down next to Zea and smiled at her when she cracked open her eyes. "Did you find my moose?" she mumbled.

"Sorry, there wasn't one anywhere. I did get you a few other things. You want to look them over?"

"Maybe later," she said, crawling over to lay her head on his leg.

"Later is good."

Name	Luke Bennet	Zea Stenter
Level	34	21
XP	141216/144088	34019/34079
AP	42	8
Bloodline	SysAdmin II	None
Strength	42	7
Agility	55	27
Stamina	51	27
Perception	39	19
Skills	Mace Mastery (3)	Dagger Mastery (1)
	Sword Mastery (1)	Stealth (2)
	Unarmed Martialist (4)	Keen Instincts (1)
	Power Strike (2)	Lock Picking (1)
	Life Surge (2)	Disguise (2)
	Peripheral Awareness (2)	Deception (1)
	Tactical Foresight (1)	Bartering (2)
	Counter (2)	Streetwise (2)
	Twitch Reflexes (3)	Cooking (1)
	Stealth (1)	Mending (1)
	Survivalist (2)	First Aid (1)
	First Aid (1)	Thalian (3)
	Wood Carving (1)	Neyardic (3)
	Leatherworking (2)	Ostari (1)
	Butchering (4)	Mana Manipulation (2)
	Thalian (2)	Mana Sight (1)
	Ostari (1)	Metallurgy (1)
	Disguise (2)	Whitesmithing (1)
	Deception (1)	Goldsmithing (2)
	Torturer (1)	Gem Cutting (1)
	Analyze (BL)	Engraving (2)
	Remote Access (BL)	Rune Forging (1)
	XP Mask (BL)	Painting (1)
		Arcano Dynamics (1)
		Sleight of Hand (1)
		Steady Hands (2)
		Cold Reading (1)
		Temperature Acclimation (2)
		Cadence (2)
		Bloodline Purification Ritual (1)
		Ghost Script (1)

CHAPTER 51

It took Zea two days to admit that she just couldn't do the enchantments that blocked scent with her current level of skills. "Maybe we should call off the whole thing," she told Luke.

Considering that she hadn't been all that keen on Project Ant Smiter to begin with, Luke wasn't terribly surprised that she was ready to give up on it. "We still have the bombs," he said. "Can't hurt to chuck them from a ways away and see what happens."

"It very much could hurt," she said. "If they figure out where we are, they'll chase us until they catch us, even right back into the city. And if they find anyone else on the way, they won't hesitate to attack those people either."

"Really? What are they going to do if they can't find anyone then? Just loiter around for a bit and then go back underground?"

"Reanimate the dead if they can, set them to work expanding the colony. I don't have the exact numbers on this, but I've heard as many as half the ants in a colony are reanimated."

"Fucking zombie ants," Luke muttered. "So if they're dead, do they have XP?"

"They do not," System said, appearing suddenly. "The reanimation effect is a result of a skill used by the queen and carried by the other ants."

"But they're ants," Luke said. "How much could possibly be left of one after it dies? Are they just reanimating random legs and antennae?"

"The explosion is going to throw a lot of them straight up into the air," Zea explained. "And they're just going to land wherever they land. That's why it's a big deal to not get tagged with their tracking pheromones. They're not fast, but they don't quit. Imagine waking up in the middle of the night fifty miles away from the anthill only to find a hundred thousand of them swarming over your camp."

"Is this pheromone thing some sort of system fuckery?" Luke asked. "I would think that a dip in the river would be enough to de-stink someone."

"The skill varies from species to species, but it usually allows for any other ant in the colony to follow the pheromone trail for upward of several weeks. And it's practically impossible to remove the scent manually. Special counter-skills need to be employed, such as those that prevent the pheromone from being applied in the first place," System said.

"So the best strategy is just not to be anywhere nearby when these detonate. Can we set them off from far away, or on a timer? That way I could just place them near the anthill, we could fuck off to someplace a few miles out, and there's no risk of us getting pheromoned or whatever."

Zea frowned and looked over at the two explosives she'd made. "I can mod-ify them to delay a few minutes after activation, I think. The one I do with **[Ghost Script]** will be harder. There's only so much I can do with that to copy actual enchantments."

"Let's do that then. We'll go give it a try, and if the whole idea's a flop, we'll abandon it."

"Ugh. Fine. But I swear by the gods, if you get us killed . . ."

"Then the gods will thank you for a job well done and reward you in the afterlife?" Luke finished for her.

"Ugh," Zea said again.

The bomb didn't look much like any bomb Luke had ever seen. It was made out of a chunk of wood that Luke had carved into an oblong box for her, and she'd cut a big chunk out of the middle afterward and wrapped a couple dozen feet of twine around it. Tiny squiggles covered the whole thing like some sort of hieroglyphs, none of which he had the first clue how to read.

They stood about fifty feet away from a massive anthill that rose up well past their heads and that, thanks to his high perception, he could see thousands upon thousands of individual ants crawling around. There were thirty feet of empty space between them and the closest ant, which was not nearly enough, in Zea's opinion.

"That thing's going to last about two more minutes before the runes lose power," she said. "Toss it over there and let's go. As soon as we're clear, I'll detonate it."

Luke gave it a gentle underhand toss and watched it sail in a smooth arc through the air to smack into the side of the ant hill. Loose dirt shot up twenty feet in the air, along with a few hundred ants that were too close to the drop zone.

"Whoops," he said with a wince.

"Go!" Zea hissed back at him, already retreating deeper into the woods. They ran as fast as they could for about a minute, then stopped. "Here we go. Ready?"

"Do it."

The explosion was entirely audible even through all the trees. Branches shook, and loose leaves fluttered down to rest on the ground, and Luke was overwhelmed with a massive ding that left him dazed. It wasn't so much the volume, which was the same as always, but the fact that it was so much . . . deeper than normal. It resonated through his mind, and he soon saw he wasn't the only one.

Zea was staring off at nothing, her mouth hanging open. She recovered a second after him and said, "Holy shit."

Luke wanted to check the notification, but at that moment he noticed a wave of ants bursting out of the anthill. "Time to go!" he said, grabbing her hand and dragging her away from the epicenter of the blast.

They ran another ten minutes or so until he could no longer sense the ants in any way. They stopped on the other side of a small stream, only ten feet wide, but hopefully more than enough to provide a physical barrier that would slow down any insectoid pursuit.

And now to check his gains. He grinned in anticipation and mentally opened up the system notification in his head.

[You have assisted in slaying 72624 creatures between levels 1 and 3. 60960 XP awarded.]

"Holy shit," Luke said.

"That's what I said!" Zea told him.

"I gained five levels."

"I got nine."

"Holy shit," Luke said again.

"This is why people who take out anthills do it in big groups. They have to, or they'd only be able to do one or two before going mad. Even then, it's a short-lived career, and the hills are only acted against if they become a direct threat to a village or town."

"Yeah, I guess it wouldn't be as impressive if it was divided thirty ways."

"This also isn't the whole colony," Zea warned him. "See how we didn't get anything above level 3? The bomb must not have gone deep enough into the ground."

If they used both those other bombs on that anthill, he'd probably be at least level 45, maybe even 47 or 48. As nice as that would be, ultimately it would depend on if he could reset XP madness. If that wasn't an option once he upgraded his bloodline again, it might be too risky. They had no real control over how many ants the bombs killed, and he could easily end up with two or three times as much XP from the next shot.

"I think we need to find out if I can control XP madness before we go any further with this plan," he said.

"We also need to make sure we're not leading a bunch of ants back to the city."

"Do you think so?" Luke asked. "We were pretty far away when it went off."

"It's better to be sure. I'd rather not have an army follow us back to the inn in the middle of the night. That would get us executed as soon as they figure out who was screwing around and attracted their attention."

Luke felt like he had to be missing something. Ants were annoying, and maybe Aros ants had some weird skills, but so did the people. They weren't a threat, not even if they could reanimate their own dead to continue working. Other than society's tendency to not want to gain a lot of XP, which Luke understood the reasoning behind, he just wasn't getting the overblown fear of ants.

"So what now? We spend some AP?"

"I'll pick up rank 2 **[Bloodline Purification Ritual]** while you scale a tree and see if you can track which way the ants are going."

It was the work of seconds to leap up, hook his arms around a branch, and climb the rest of the way to the top. From there, he jumped to another taller tree that was blocking his view and peered out across the canopy. "Not much to see from up here," he muttered.

There were enough gaps for him to get a general picture of what was going on at ground level, but he didn't have a good look at any single place. It was like looking through a thousand keyholes and trying to put together what the door behind them looked like.

Luke stared east for a minute, looking for signs that a swarm of tiny black bodies was washing across the forest. There was nothing. After another few minutes, he dropped down, happy to give Zea the good news.

At least, he was until he got halfway to the forest floor. That was when he noticed the movement. Frowning to himself, Luke dropped to the ground and started moving toward it. It could be nothing, but something told him he wasn't that lucky. It only took a few minutes of running for him to confirm it. Thousands upon thousands of ants were following their trail through the forest.

"Son of a bitch. How did they mark us with their pheromone stink? We never even got close to them."

Though the question hadn't been directed specifically at System, it still appeared to answer it. "You were well inside the radius of the underground portion of the colony. It's possible that just by being nearby, you picked up some of the pheromones the ants themselves leave behind as they move around."

Luke glanced over at System, who was watching the ants' silent march. "If it's just something we stepped on, then they're really only looking for our shoes, right?"

"That is possible. I am not able to confirm it."

"One way to find out. Zea's going to be grumpy about having to walk back barefoot."

He rushed back and leaped the stream to land next to her. She glanced up, took one look at his face, and said, "Fuck. They're following us, aren't they?"

"Yeah, but I have an idea. System thinks just by stepping on the ground the ants walk around on normally, we might have picked up the pheromones. If that's the case, then they're just following the stink of our footsteps, right? Abandon the shoes, let them eat them, and we're good."

"I . . . Will that work?"

"System wouldn't tell me," Luke said.

"Of course," she said with a sigh. "Okay, well, good news. I think I can get everything we need to do the next ritual pretty easily and cheaply. Less good news, I'm going to need at least a little more AP to upgrade all the support skills."

"We have two bombs left, and there's time to make another temporary one before the ants get here. Let's leave the shoes as bait with a temporary bomb tucked in one and we'll blast the ants to hell with that."

"Eeehhhhh. Let's not fuck with this colony anymore. If this shoe thing works, we can see about hitting a different one later. Maybe I'll take another rank in **[Rune Forging]** and **[Arcano Dynamics]** now that I've got some loose AP and try those scent-blocking enchantments again."

Luke shrugged. "Okay, that sounds like a good plan."

He was just happy she wasn't mad at him.

Name	Luke Bennet	Zea Stenter
Level	39	30
XP	202176/218294	94979/98832
AP	227	42
Bloodline	SysAdmin II	None
Strength	42	7
Agility	55	27
Stamina	51	27
Perception	39	19
Skills	Mace Mastery (3)	Dagger Mastery (1)
	Sword Mastery (1)	Stealth (2)
	Unarmed Martialist (4)	Keen Instincts (1)
	Power Strike (2)	Lock Picking (1)
	Life Surge (2)	Disguise (2)
	Peripheral Awareness (2)	Deception (1)
	Tactical Foresight (1)	Bartering (2)
	Counter (2)	Streetwise (2)
	Twitch Reflexes (3)	Cooking (1)
	Stealth (1)	Mending (1)
	Survivalist (2)	First Aid (1)
	First Aid (1)	Thalian (3)
	Wood Carving (1)	Neyardic (3)
	Leatherworking (2)	Ostari (1)
	Butchering (4)	Mana Manipulation (2)
	Thalian (2)	Mana Sight (1)
	Ostari (1)	Metallurgy (1)
	Disguise (2)	Whitesmithing (1)
	Deception (1)	Goldsmithing (2)
	Torturer (1)	Gem Cutting (1)
	Analyze (BL)	Engraving (2)
	Remote Access (BL)	Rune Forging (1)
	XP Mask (BL)	Painting (1)
		Arcano Dynamics (1)
		Sleight of Hand (1)
		Steady Hands (2)
		Cold Reading (1)
		Temperature Acclimation (2)
		Cadence (2)
		Bloodline Purification Ritual (2)
		Ghost Script (1)

CHAPTER 52

Back on Earth, we had this thing called a telescope that let us see stuff from far away. They came up with all sorts of stuff from it, microscopes used for medicine and science, binoculars used for hunting and by the military, even big-ass telescopes that took up whole rooms and were pointed at the sky so they could look at the stars," Luke said.

"Sounds useful," Zea said dryly. "Probably why we have them too. People with low perception sometimes use them."

"Yeah? Good. I wonder what it would look like if I looked through one of them now."

"I'm told that they don't mix that well. I guess you see farther, but it gets really hard to see far enough away without something blocking your line of sight and it just being the equivalent to putting your nose to a wall and looking at it."

"I can see that," Luke said. "Still, might be nice to have one for you right now."

They were up a tree together, about a thousand feet from where they'd left their shoes. Luke had picked Zea up after she'd untied hers and literally jumped up into the nearest tree. They'd done their best squirrel imitations and leaped from branch to branch until they were a good distance away. With any luck, whatever scent trail the ants were following would end there.

The ants advanced slowly, at least by person speeds. He would have walked faster than they were moving, even before the system had made him superhuman. It was interesting to see that the stream did not much slow them down either. The made some sort of living bridge with their own bodies, thousands and thousands of ants crawling all over one another to extend it until they reached the far end. The ones in the lead raced off to the shoes, and a wave of them washed over the leather. A minute later, there was nothing left.

"Oh damn," Luke said, squinting to see between the leaves. Every few seconds, one annoying branch would sway with the wind and flop directly across his line of sight. "I think I get why people are so much more worked up about ants here than they are back home."

"They got to the shoes?" Zea asked.

"Yup. Completely devoured them."

"Are they still coming?"

"Doesn't look like it. They're just kind of spreading out in every direction now. I think . . . Maybe they're still looking, but they lost the trail? We should be fine to circle wide around them."

"Good thing you left that armor back at the inn, huh? You'd have lost your fancy new sabbatons before you even got a chance to use them."

Luke let out a heavy, dramatic sigh. "It seems I am destined to never know the benefits of fighting in armor."

"You're damn near level 40. I don't think you much need it at this point. How much AP do you have again?"

"227, but I want to save it for the bloodline upgrade. Those skills are never cheap, but they're generally pretty useful. If I've got AP leftover after, well . . . we'll see."

He needed a few of those points to upgrade **[Leatherworking]** twice for Zea's surprise, and depending on what was left over, he thought it was about time to upgrade a few of his combat skills that had been stagnating. It probably wouldn't hurt to round off strength with another 10 or 15 points either. His mace could handle that level of force.

"If I'm right about this, I should be able to get everything you need for ten gold, maybe a bit less. That'll give us one attempt, but ideally, I want **[Mana Manipulation]**, **[Mana Sight]**, and **[Cadence]** all up to rank 3 first. That would cost 90 AP though, so it's not really reasonable."

"I know a little bomb who begs to differ," Luke said.

Zea grimaced and shook her head. "Once was enough for today."

"You sure? I know where there's a big cluster of ants right now that I could probably hit with a careful throw. It wouldn't be seventy thousand of them, but it might get you a few levels." When he saw her hesitating, Luke added, "Plus it might help make sure they don't follow us if we wipe out the ants chasing us."

"Fine, damn it. Let me just make up something with **[Ghost Script]** so we can hold on to the good ones. Give me a few minutes."

Luke did his best to procure anything and everything she asked for, which wasn't much. One of the biggest benefits to Zea's new skill was that she would write runes onto basically anything just by tracing them with her finger. It still had to follow whatever enigmatic rules regular runes did to form the enchantment, but that seemed to mostly mean being properly shaped and sized to hold everything.

"No twine this time?" he asked after cutting the wedges out of the block of wood for her.

"Don't have any on me. It was for the long timer anyway. I put a whole length of runes down the twine to give us the time to run. This one is going to go off about ten seconds after I empower the runes, so be ready to throw it."

"Gotcha. We should probably move somewhere else first. I don't have a good angle on the main swarm from here."

They circled around at ground level until they found a spot a quarter mile downstream. The ants were mostly spreading up and down the shore, though a significant portion had gone into the woods. "Looks like we're not going to get as many this time," he said. "Too spread out."

"That's a hell of a long throw. Are you sure you can make that?"

"The distance? No problem. Accurately? Eeehh, probably. My biggest concern is it landing before ten seconds is up."

Zea shrugged and said, "It probably shouldn't land at all. From this distance, I don't think it'd be possible to avoid breaking the wood when it hits. Then the enchantment is ruined and there's no boom. You ready?"

"Ready."

"Here we go. Ten," she said, handing it to him. "Nine, eight . . ."

Luke took a second to aim, then threw it so that it spun end over end through the air. "Seven, six, five," they said together. The enchanted bomb whipped through the air, now halfway to its destination. "Four, three, two."

It was coming down now, and Luke was almost sure he'd thrown it too soon, that it was going to hit the ground and shatter into a thousand pieces right before it would have otherwise blown. Just before he could say, "One," it went off, and he got whammed with another ding blast.

"Good thing it went off early," he said after he came out of it.

"Yeah. I might have underestimated how quickly the timing runes would burn out."

[You have assisted in slaying 8521 creatures between levels 1 and 3. 14595 XP awarded.]

"Not as big as the first one," Luke said. "But still, not bad at all."

"Got two levels this time, just barely. Brings me up to 105 AP though, so mission accomplished. There won't be a lot of extra AP leftover for anything else."

"If we're lucky, I'll be able to take that bloodline skill that lets me play with other skills."

"That would be nice, and I wouldn't mind if you got that one that lets you just create things out of nothing to go with it."

"Maybe the one that lets me change stats around too."

They chatted about the possibilities while they walked back, both trying to ignore that they were barefoot. For Luke, it was less of an issue. His stamina was almost twice as high as Zea's, though she'd gotten plenty of practice in not having shoes throughout her adult life. They were in firm agreement to get new shoes back in Sicanti, and that they were unlikely to try the bomb trick again any time soon.

"Cobbler first, ritual supplies after," Zea said. "And then I guess we should probably find a ritual site that's outside the city. I don't want anyone coming to check on the noise and getting freaked out."

"We could probably get it all done tonight," Luke said. "There's still a few hours of daylight left."

Zea shrugged. "We'll see how the shopping goes."

"There have been reported sightings of a dwifkin in the city, occasionally accompanied by a human man," the mercenary said.

"Where?" Lath asked. He hated this part of the job. The waiting was just so tedious. It was much better to arrive at a location, have all the information already on hand, and find the perfect moment to strike. But the waiting was part of his profession. There really was only so much he could do to create an opening without risking exposure.

If the goal were to just kill someone, well, any fool could stick a knife between some ribs. To kill someone and make it look like an accident, or to do it in a way that left a deliberate message, took skill and patience. He prided himself on possessing both of those qualities in excess. Still, the talking and the reliance on others grated on him.

"Business district. We're not sure where they're staying yet, but we do know they went down to the harbor and started looking to buy passage across the ocean."

Lath couldn't begin to fathom why anyone would want to go to the eastern continent. It was a savage and brutal place, devoid of anything remotely resembling what he'd call real civilization. Even their cities were crude caricatures of Hestoc's glory here. He supposed it was a simple matter of an apostate running away to a far-off land, foolishly expecting it would allow him to escape the gods.

They would never get that far, of course. "Did they find a ship willing to take them?"

"Some coin exchanged hands, yes. My men weren't able to listen in on the conversation, but it seems a fair assumption to make," the mercenary reported.

"I'll send a pair of inquisitors around to arrest the captain. No one gets away with making deals with apostates."

Especially not apostates who'd killed his apprentice.

This wasn't going to be an assassination. It would be an execution. From what he'd learned of Myla's attempts at capturing the apostates, her mistake had been just that. She'd tried to capture them, to take them in for questioning so she could figure out how far the rot had spread. She should have excised the tumor immediately and then salted the earth anyplace that had an association with it. A few lost innocent lives were a small price to pay to ensure the taint left behind was fully expunged from this world.

"Perhaps it is time for me to join the hunt myself. Your team is capable of finding the apostate?"

"Given enough time, yes," the mercenary said.

Lath didn't like the woman. She was too cowardly to commit to something, too soft and weak willed. He'd much preferred their old leader, but it seemed he'd lost his life challenging the apostate to direct combat, the idiot. If the master poisoner had paid for the Blacktongues' services out of his own pocket, he thought he might have demanded his money back. It was ridiculous that they'd somehow made contact with, lost, and subsequently been decimated by one man.

It was interesting though that none of them could feel the presence of his XP. That meant something, but Lath wasn't sure exactly what. He suspected he might never know, as there would be precious little time for questions once the execution began. No doubt it was some odd ability the apostate had picked up while he was practicing his heresy, something to help him hide from the righteous light of the Pantheon's truth.

Perhaps he might petition Hestoc himself for the answer after he'd shuffled the apostate off his mortal coil. It was rare to receive such direct communion from any god, but he'd been worshipping the god of civilization for forty years now and had served as the church's blade in the night for more than twenty of them. Surely he'd earned that much.

"We'll be relocating to the business district. Find them and report back to me. Do not engage them. Do not let them see you. I will handle the apostates myself. All you need to do is tell me where they are. Do you understand?"

"I understand, sir," the mercenary said, a sour look on her face.

"Banish all thoughts of avenging your fallen comrades from your mind. Those two are mine."

The mercenary gave him some kind of salute he didn't recognize, probably something unique to their company, and left the room. Lath moved to begin preparing his equipment. The hunt would be on soon.

Name	Luke Bennet	Zea Stenter
Level	39	32
XP	216771/218294	109574/120012
AP	227	105
Bloodline	SysAdmin II	None
Strength	42	7
Agility	53	27
Stamina	49	27
Perception	39	19
Skills	Mace Mastery (3)	Dagger Mastery (1)
	Sword Mastery (1)	Stealth (2)
	Unarmed Martialist (4)	Keen Instincts (1)
	Power Strike (2)	Lock Picking (1)
	Life Surge (2)	Disguise (2)
	Peripheral Awareness (2)	Deception (1)
	Tactical Foresight (1)	Bartering (2)
	Counter (2)	Streetwise (2)
	Twitch Reflexes (3)	Cooking (1)
	Stealth (1)	Mending (1)
	Survivalist (2)	First Aid (1)
	First Aid (1)	Thalian (3)
	Wood Carving (1)	Neyardic (3)
	Leatherworking (2)	Ostari (1)
	Butchering (4)	Mana Manipulation (2)
	Thalian (2)	Mana Sight (1)
	Ostari (1)	Metallurgy (1)
	Disguise (2)	Whitesmithing (1)
	Deception (1)	Goldsmithing (2)
	Torturer (1)	Gem Cutting (1)
	Analyze (BL)	Engraving (2)
	Remote Access (BL)	Rune Forging (1)
	XP Mask (BL)	Painting (1)
		Arcano Dynamics (1)
		Sleight of Hand (1)
		Steady Hands (2)
		Cold Reading (1)
		Temperature Acclimation (2)
		Cadence (2)
		Bloodline Purification Ritual (2)
		Ghost Script (1)

CHAPTER 53

Luke did not consider himself to be a particularly observant person. Even here on Aros, after all the fighting for his life and the system giving him the ability to literally count the ants on a tree a thousand feet away, he'd only recently started trying to sort through what his senses were telling him. Even then, that had only been an active effort to make up for losing the ability to feel the amount of XP other people or monsters had.

However unobservant he might have been, he still realized they'd attracted a stalker. There was a man, an inch or two taller than Luke and with shaggy brown hair. He wore clothes in the local style and was unarmed, and nothing about him indicated that he was anything other than some random citizen, except for the fact that Luke had seen him three times now in the last fifteen minutes.

He took a minute to toss an **[Analyze]** at the man, then leaned hard into his poor, neglected, rank 1 **[Deception]** to keep his face blank.

[Name: Blacktongue Human Mercenary]
[Level: 23]
[Strength: 9]
[Agility: 30]
[Stamina: 17]
[Perception: 28]

"Zea," he said softly.

"Hmm?" She didn't look up from where she was sorting through a jarful of what looked like ordinary river pebbles to him.

"There is a man following us. **[Analyze]** says he's part of that mercenary group we fought a few days back."

Zea froze for a split second, then resumed picking through the pebbles as if he'd never spoken. "I need two more reagents to make this work. Ten minutes tops. We'll go back to the inn, collect our stuff, and get out of the city."

If only they hadn't had to get new shoes, they'd already have been done with the shopping. Then again, if they were back at the inn, it was possible Luke would never have noticed the tail. They might have been ambushed by a dozen more mercenaries in the middle of the night.

Luke started throwing **[Analyze]** at random people, which mostly returned results of ordinary citizens between levels 8 and 15, usually correlating to the target's age. There were, unfortunately, three more mercenaries hidden in the crowd. They all were around the same level and with similar stat spreads as the first one, so Luke assumed they were rocking some sort of scout or spy build.

He let Zea know in a whisper, and she picked up the pace to grab the last two things she needed. Once they left the stall and hustled away from the market square, all four mercenaries he'd spotted faded into the background and eventually disappeared.

Luke wasn't about to let his guard down though, not now. He kept using **[Analyze]** over and over, which led to him discovering two new mercenaries. These ones only followed him for a block before handing him off to someone else. Either they were communicating somehow, or there were so many that no matter which direction he went, someone was always waiting to start following.

"At least ten different mercs now," he told Zea. "There might be more I didn't spot. None of them are wearing field gear, but that doesn't mean they won't have poisoned knives."

"Maybe you should spend some AP now. Just leave some for bloodline skills later. You're probably not going to need the whole amount anyway."

"I think we're good for now. I haven't spotted anyone above level 26 yet," Luke said. "But a skill to help see through stuff like **[Stealth]** would be good. Raw perception is great for seeing, but it doesn't help me notice, you know?"

"So . . . **[Detection]**?"

"Er, yeah, maybe. That sounds about right." He found it easily enough in the system's skill shop, with the first rank being a measly 3 AP. Luke picked it up and looked around. "Doesn't seem any different."

"You just bought it? Gods, of course you did." Zea said. "Maybe because there's no one hiding around here? Or maybe because it's only rank 1 and the mercenaries following us are good at their jobs?"

"Those are both good points," Luke said. "You think I should pick up rank 2 for another 10 AP?"

"Might not hurt, but honestly, your perception is so high already that you could just make a bit of effort to train yourself. I'm sure you could have learned

[Detection] easily with a bit of work. You could probably get it up to rank 2 without wasting the AP."

"You think I can do that in the next few minutes before however many hidden mercs there are following us make their move?"

"Well. Shit. Fine, I guess it's a good use of AP."

Luke spent another 10 AP and bumped **[Detection]** up to rank 2. The skill started poking at his brain, demanding he look at certain people, though not giving him much to go on beyond that. Most of the signals were irrelevant, things like someone palming a coin at a nearby vendor stall, or three kids looking out the second-story window of a nearby home. His high perception was probably making it worse, since it gave the skill so much more raw data to work with.

Between that and **[Peripheral Awareness]** widening his range of vision even more, Luke was already trying to find an Off button for the new skill. On the other hand, **[Detection]** pointed out two guys lurking in an alleyway up ahead, looking like they were waiting to jump out and ambush someone. A quick use of **[Analyze]** told him they weren't part of the mercenary band, but the point was that Luke hadn't even noticed them before, despite having seen them.

It was going to take some work to get the hang of every little thing demanding his attention, but he expected he'd get used to it quickly enough. For now, he just focused on looking for the mercs tailing them. With **[Detection]** helping him focus, he spotted another four mercs over the next minute.

"What do you think they're waiting for?" he asked. "They know who we are. They're keeping track of our movements. You think they're assembling somewhere and preparing to come out in force to subdue us?"

"Maybe, or maybe just one big hitter. Or . . ." Zea bit her lip and shook her head. "Don't forget who's employing them and what we know about those kinds of people. A single high-level person could be coming down on us like a literal hammer of the gods, and they're just making sure that church agent knows where to strike."

"Fuck. That's probably worst-case scenario. You think we should make a scene of it, seize the initiative or whatever?"

"Not until we get back to the inn. You might as well put on that armor too. No point in trying to blend in now. Shit, this is going to make getting onto that boat a lot harder. How the fuck did they find us this quickly?"

"I mean," Luke said as he gestured around. "Dwifkins?"

"There's a whole city! Tens of thousands of people."

"Sure, but don't they live here? They've probably got friends and family, a whole social network. Maybe they just said, 'Hey, if anyone sees a smoking-hot dwifkin lady, let me know. Pay you a half-silver for the info.'"

"Fuuuck. And you still stick out yourself a bit. Not as bad as back in Valtira, but yeah. So the church knows who we are, what we look like, where we're going. Of course they hop on a boat and beat us here. And then we spent some time down at the docks, and they know we're looking for ships, so someone keeps on eye on it and spots me easily."

"Wait, they know all that? How do they know we need a ship?" Luke asked.

"Because I was asking about prices for you back in Valtira, and inquisitors torture people for information. I wouldn't be surprised if the entire stable at the Bloody Harbor ended up in a confessional after you made a run for it. I'm sure the only reason I didn't was that they were expecting to follow me to you."

The idea that the church had tortured just about every person he'd ever met in Valtira hadn't occurred to Luke, which was stupid, now that Zea had pointed it out. That was what inquisitors did. It really put into perspective how callously they treated the average person and how much harm he'd done to everyone around him just blundering around in Valtira.

"Snap out of it," Zea said, poking him in the hip. "We're here. Any mercs watching?"

"Three," Luke said.

"No help for it. I guess we're done sleeping in a bed again. Let's go get our stuff."

"The apostate knows he's being followed," Dradion reported. "He spotted tails a few times, and then about twenty minutes ago, he was suddenly noticing everything. I think he may have purchased a new skill, possibly **[Detection]**."

The inquisitor who'd hired them just shook his head. "Foolish and arrogant of him. To spend his AP so frivolously. I suppose he knows his death is imminent and is determined to grasp at every conceivable chance at victory. Where is he now, and is the dwifkin still with him?"

"They both went into the inn they're staying at. I've got a team watching it from every direction. They won't get out without us noticing."

"Lead me there," the inquisitor said.

Dradion did his best to keep his expression neutral. The inquisitor was a paying client, even if he was an arrogant dick. Never mind that this job had cost Blacktongue an unheard-of body count and probably well over a thousand gold in property damage. There was no way they'd so much as break even at this point. He cursed the day Singer had said yes to hunting a fucking apostate.

That kid, a fucking teenager, had to be a higher level than anyone in Blacktongue. He'd torn through Dradion's friends like they were children. He'd call anyone who said the apostate was under level 30 a liar to their face. And yet no one could feel a single point of XP coming off the kid.

"Of course," Dradion said, still doing his best to maintain the polite fiction that he didn't want to ram a sword down the inquisitor's throat. The church didn't have nearly as much power up here in Sicanti as it did back where this asshole was from, but murdering their client would look bad for his band, and gods knew they were going to need a lot of business to recover from this whole shitstorm.

Besides that, he wasn't sure he could actually take the man. The inquisitor felt like he was only level 10 or 12, but there was no way that was true. The old man could be even stronger than Singer. Fuck, he'd better be if he was planning on taking down the kid who'd killed Singer. Maybe Dradion would get lucky and they'd kill each other.

Luke was armored up, with a bit of help from Zea. He'd put on the cloak and everything. They split the packs between them, now significantly emptier without the armor. The bag Zea had enchanted for slowing time was their officially designated food bag now, and since Luke's worldly possessions amounted to what he was wearing and two full sets of clothes, his stuff didn't take up much room. Mostly they were just carrying camping supplies and a full bag of enchanting stuff.

"Got the route in your head?" Zea asked.

"Yep."

"Know where to meet up if we get separated?"

"Yes."

"Back-up meeting spot?"

"Yes, Zea! I'm good. Are you ready?"

Both of them expected the mercs to make their move soon. No way they'd just let Luke and Zea walk out of the city without attempting to stop them.

"You sure you don't want to spend some of that AP?" she asked.

"Only if I need it. I want to keep as much held back as I can for new bloodline skills. There's not a person on their team who's within ten levels of me. Hell, you're a higher level than any of them now."

"Yeah, but I'm not specialized toward combat. Any of them would kick my ass in a straight fight."

"You know the fallback plan: if all else fails, blow shit up."

Name	Luke Bennet	Zea Stenter
Level	39	32
XP	216771/218294	109574/120012
AP	214	105
Bloodline	SysAdmin II	None
Strength	42	7
Agility	55	27
Stamina	51	27
Perception	39	19
Skills	Mace Mastery (3)	Dagger Mastery (1)
	Sword Mastery (1)	Stealth (2)
	Unarmed Martialist (4)	Keen Instincts (1)
	Power Strike (2)	Lock Picking (1)
	Life Surge (2)	Disguise (2)
	Peripheral Awareness (2)	Deception (1)
	Tactical Foresight (1)	Bartering (2)
	Counter (2)	Streetwise (2)
	Twitch Reflexes (3)	Cooking (1)
	Stealth (1)	Mending (1)
	Survivalist (2)	First Aid (1)
	First Aid (1)	Thalian (3)
	Wood Carving (1)	Neyardic (3)
	Leatherworking (2)	Ostari (1)
	Butchering (4)	Mana Manipulation (2)
	Thalian (2)	Mana Sight (1)
	Ostari (1)	Metallurgy (1)
	Disguise (2)	Whitesmithing (1)
	Deception (1)	Goldsmithing (2)
	Detection (2)	Gem Cutting (1)
	Torturer (1)	Engraving (2)
	Analyze (BL)	Rune Forging (1)
	Remote Access (BL)	Painting (1)
	XP Mask (BL)	Arcano Dynamics (1)
		Sleight of Hand (1)
		Steady Hands (2)
		Cold Reading (1)
		Temperature Acclimation (2)
		Cadence (2)
		Bloodline Purification Ritual (2)
		Ghost Script (1)

CHAPTER 54

They walked out of the inn and started heading for the edge of town, with Luke throwing out an **[Analyze]** every few seconds at random people to help him spot any mercenaries tailing them. They seemed to have fallen back for some reason, or else they'd gotten better at avoiding his notice. Maybe their only job had been to figure out where Luke and Zea were sleeping. A late-night ambush might be their new strategy, since he'd thoroughly thrashed the whole company in a head-on fight.

If so, that trap was going to fail. Luke had learned better than to just assume he'd figured out an enemy's plan, or even that the enemy only had a single plan. He would need to be extra vigilant as they left the city and got into the open grasslands and fields surrounding it. He wasn't sure even a concentrated volley of crossbows would put him down, but it would fuck Zea right up, and just because something wasn't immediately fatal didn't mean it couldn't be in the long run. There'd be no civilians in the way if a large group of mercs decided to try their luck outside the city.

At the same time, Luke was confident in their ability to outrun any pursuing mercs if it came down to it. Zea hated riding piggyback, but she'd do it so he could leverage his full speed against them. It would also be much harder for the mercs to successfully ambush the two of them once they were outside the city and there was no crowd to hide in.

He'd feel a lot better once they got away from all the people.

"Anything yet?" Zea asked quietly from his side. It was really more of a whisper under her breath purposely done because she knew he'd hear it and nobody else was likely to.

"No mercs," he said, only slightly louder. "Suspicious that they all just vanished. They're planning something."

"Change direction. If they're setting up something up ahead, they'll have to abandon it or show themselves to herd us into it."

"It'll add a few minutes to our travel time," Luke said. "But yeah, good idea. Take a left at the next intersection? We can go down four or five blocks before we start heading to the edge of the city again."

Zea nodded her agreement, and the pair kept walking. On the bright side, he was finally getting to wear his stolen armor in public, and no one seemed to look twice at it. It was garbage for blending into a crowd, but he doubted he could even if he wanted to, not with Zea next to him. Plus, a lot of mercs had seen his face. They'd be able to spot him again more easily since they knew exactly what he looked like.

Minutes ticked by, and no one jumped out to ambush them, or popped up on a nearby rooftop to snipe at them, or even walked up and tried to sell them something. Pushy vendor-stall merchants were a staple in Sicanti, so that last one was actually something of a relief. Even as far away from any market districts as they were, it wasn't unusual to get verbally assaulted by someone running a food stand. Maybe it was the armor making him look serious and unapproachable.

Someone flicked at the very back edge of Luke's peripheral vision, and he quickly tagged them with an **[Analyze]**. "Got one," he said. "Level 26 merc with an agility-and-perception build. Probably a scout. Way back behind us too, and I think with some stealthy skills to keep hidden."

"So they are still following us, just not closely. They've pulled back their weaker members to keep them from becoming casualties in their ambush."

"Makes sense to me. They have to know I'll tear through anyone under level 30 like paper at this point."

The problem there was that Luke had only seen one merc who was a credible threat. There'd been a few who had hassled him, but they weren't strong enough that he was concerned with losing, just with how long it would take to win. The weaker Blacktongue mercenaries hadn't been able to stop him in groups of five or six, and while Luke hadn't wanted to test twenty or more at the same time, he was pretty sure he could escape after inflicting casualties at the least. Depending on the scenario, if he could pull off an ambush that killed five or six before they could react, he might wipe out all of them.

He was pretty sure that wasn't the plan though. Attacking in town would be a smarter move for them, unless they knew something he didn't. "Is there a reason to let us walk out of here?" he asked Zea.

"Maybe? It could be they just don't have the man power to do what they want, so they're trailing us while they gather up the rest of the mercs."

"Why cut back on the number of tails, though?"

"If I had to guess, I'd say they figured out that you were identifying them and changed tactics. Plus you're in full armor now, so it's a lot easier to keep track of you."

Luke wasn't satisfied with that explanation, but he didn't have a better one. "They're going to try something," he muttered. "The only question is when."

Lath stood outside a dingy old inn, one that catered to travelers who were more thrifty than picky. "How long ago did they leave?"

The mercenary who'd become his new liaison glanced at his comrade, who said, "Five minutes, moving west in a straight line. We've got people rushing to the edge of the city to set up a perimeter, but they're moving fast. We'll be lucky to get adequate surveillance set up."

"Lead the way," Lath said.

He followed the merc, who stopped twice to speak to people dressed in unobtrusive outfits of the local style, but who were obviously stronger than their XP presences would indicate. Their infiltration skills were severely lacking if they thought dressing like a peasant would be enough to hide the fact that they had much higher stats than normal.

The Blacktongue Mercenary Company had been an utter disappointment, despite coming with high recommendations from the local church. They'd completely failed in their assignment and gotten half of their band killed in the process and were struggling to even keep up with the apostates, let alone follow them without being detected.

They changed direction each time the merc in the lead stopped to talk to someone and, perhaps unsurprisingly, quickly found themselves in a poorer district, one where Hestoc's guiding light had failed to take hold. For some reason, the church had made no efforts to purify these cancers from Sicanti. Instead, they festered around the edges of the city, threatening to infect everything else that had been built in Hestoc's name.

"There they are," the merc said, drawing Lath out of his contemplations.

The human was plain enough. He was a bit pale, even compared to the other northerners, but nothing that stood out. The dwifkin he was with could have been any of the thousands Lath had seen scurrying through the back alleys of Valtira. She was surprisingly high level, higher than he'd been expecting from the mercenaries' reports, at least. Strangely, that phenomenon of having no XP at all they'd mentioned was still in effect on the human. Lath couldn't remember ever seeing anyone able to hide all XP. Even he couldn't do that.

It was probably some heretical off-worlder ability. The church had records of some truly odd skills previous apostates had exhibited centuries past, though none that so completely shrouded their XP. It was entirely possible that those records had been corrupted, parts lost or altered as they were copied over the decades.

Regardless, Lath felt something he hadn't felt in years. He was wary about approaching the apostate with so many unknowns. That the man was powerful was obvious just from watching him move, but exactly how powerful was still a mystery. If his stamina was high enough, he might shrug off all but the most potent poisons.

Based on which poisons had been missing from Myla's supplies and which ingredients the servants had reported her using, the fact that the apostate had survived her meant his stamina was likely at least in the high 40s, or that he had some skill to temporarily boost it that high. Lath had chosen his own weapons carefully, with that fact in mind.

Killing the apostates who'd murdered his apprentice would be one of the most expensive tasks he'd ever undertaken, but it was worth every last copper. He felt his fists clench as his sides and forced his body to relax. There was no room for personal feelings in this part. He'd indulge himself after the apostates were dead.

The human apostate jerked in place, then leaned down and whispered something to his dwifkin companion. Lath frowned as he observed the motion. He could only assume one of those idiot mercenaries had gotten themselves discovered. It had better not complicate Lath's takedown of the pair. Just to be safe, he picked up the pace.

"Fuck me," Luke swore.

[Name: Hestocian High Inquisitor]
[Level: 45]
[Strength: 37]
[Agility: 61]
[Stamina: 40]
[Perception: 51]

"What's wrong?" Zea asked.

"Fucking church inquisitor behind us. Level 45. Stats are close to mine, a bit higher in agility and perception. I'm betting he's got all sorts of skills at rank 4 or 5."

"You've still got about 200 AP you're sitting on too," she said. "Fuck. Maybe you should spend it. Bump your big combat skills up a rank, drop 50 AP or so into raw stats?"

Luke chewed on his lip and stared straight ahead. If only he knew how much he needed to save for after the next bloodline purification, it would be an easy decision. The big thing was creating a skill that protected them from XP madness. He was starting to push the threshold now where he didn't want to have to gain too many more levels before they had a solution, especially right before they took a hopefully uneventful boat trip across the ocean, where his XP would have plenty of time to work on his brain and circumstances would keep him from leveling again to fix it.

"I'll keep around 100 AP in the bank," he said. That would leave him enough to upgrade a few skills. **[Mace Mastery]** would take 30 to get to rank 4, **[Counter]** needed another 30 to get to rank 3, and **[Twitch Reflexes]** needed a whopping 50 AP for rank 4. That would leave him with 109 AP to spare.

He decided to buy the upgrades for **[Mace Mastery]** and **[Counter]** only and split the 50 AP left to add 10 to strength and perception, bringing them up to 52 and 49, then put 15 in stamina to bring it up from 51 to 66. That left him with 15 more for agility, which kept it as his highest stat at 70. That one wasn't an upgrade he particularly loved, but he didn't like the idea of fighting an enemy that could move faster than him.

That left him with 109 AP, and he decided to save that extra 9 just in case he needed to give another stat a bump midcombat to compensate for something. Luke was worried even that much wouldn't be enough. This inquisitor was a higher level than him, higher than anything Luke had ever seen, and he kind of doubted the man had sunk a significant amount of points into needlepoint or gardening.

He probably had a dozen combat skills, all a higher rank than Luke's, not to mention just straight-up decades more experience fighting life-and-death battles. They needed another edge if they wanted to ensure victory.

"Hey, how fast can you make those bombs explode?" Luke asked.

Name	Luke Bennet	Zea Stenter
Level	39	32
XP	216771/218294	109574/120012
AP	109	105
Bloodline	SysAdmin II	None
Strength	52	7
Agility	70	27
Stamina	66	27
Perception	49	19
Skills	Mace Mastery (4)	Dagger Mastery (1)
	Sword Mastery (1)	Stealth (2)
	Unarmed Martialist (4)	Keen Instincts (1)
	Power Strike (2)	Lock Picking (1)
	Life Surge (2)	Disguise (2)
	Peripheral Awareness (2)	Deception (1)
	Tactical Foresight (1)	Bartering (2)
	Counter (3)	Streetwise (2)
	Twitch Reflexes (3)	Cooking (1)
	Stealth (1)	Mending (1)
	Survivalist (2)	First Aid (1)
	First Aid (1)	Thalian (3)
	Wood Carving (1)	Neyardic (3)
	Leatherworking (2)	Ostari (1)
	Butchering (4)	Mana Manipulation (2)
	Thalian (2)	Mana Sight (1)
	Ostari (1)	Metallurgy (1)
	Disguise (2)	Whitesmithing (1)
	Deception (1)	Goldsmithing (2)
	Detection (2)	Gem Cutting (1)
	Torturer (1)	Engraving (2)
	Analyze (BL)	Rune Forging (1)
	Remote Access (BL)	Painting (1)
	XP Mask (BL)	Arcano Dynamics (1)
		Sleight of Hand (1)
		Steady Hands (2)
		Cold Reading (1)
		Temperature Acclimation (2)
		Cadence (2)
		Bloodline Purification Ritual (2)
		Ghost Script (1)

CHAPTER 55

The hardest part of the plan was finding a spot with no one else around. They didn't want to kill some random person who just happened to be walking by. Thankfully, Zea had built in options in the enchantment that would let her trigger the bombs remotely or with a timer, but the range on remote detonation was pretty awful.

They decided it was better to let the inquisitor chase them down and make sure he got caught in the blasts than it was to keep their lead and hope they'd timed it right. As long as no random stranger walked into the middle of things, Luke wasn't too concerned about the explosions causing collateral damage. A blown-out wall could be rebuilt. Bringing someone back from the dead was quite a bit harder, as he well knew.

As soon as they were around the corner and broke line of sight on the inquisitor and the two mercs following them, Zea pulled both bombs out of her bags, took a second to prime the enchantments, and handed one to Luke. He studied the street for a second to find the best spot.

It was really more of a wide alleyway than a street. A trail of hard-packed bare earth ran down the middle, with strips of grass on either side next to the houses. There wasn't much in the way of litter or garbage to hide the bombs behind, but the grass was tall enough that he thought it would go unnoticed to casual inspection.

More importantly, both houses were empty. The bombs might collapse them completely, but they wouldn't kill anyone. Zea was sure she could trigger them both at the same time, so the plan was to place one on either side, then blow the inquisitor to smithereens as soon as he stepped between them. If they were lucky, the blast would take care of the two mercs as well.

He gently set one down in the grass to his left, acutely aware of every little rustle. That inquisitor's perception was so high that he felt that the noise was a legitimate concern. He placed it as softly as he could, which in his opinion was pretty damn near completely silent. Zea did . . . Well, other than stepping onto the grass, she did fine. Actually, that kind of covered up the noise of her dropping the bomb, as long as the inquisitor didn't note a change in footfall patterns.

With the first part of their diabolical plan to murder a man of the cloth completed, they walked away at a somewhat slower pace. About thirty seconds later, the inquisitor appeared in the mouth of the alley, and their lead had shrunk from four blocks to two. Worse, Luke had already determined that the new alley they'd walked into was a dead end, and that if they jumped the wall that blocked it off, they'd be landing on somebody's property.

Well, it probably wouldn't matter much. They'd be there for all of four seconds before leaving out the other side, so no one was likely to even notice, much less complain. But it'd be just his luck to step into some sort of booby trap the moment they went over the wall.

They were putting on the act, like they'd just gotten lost and taken a wrong turn. It wasn't much of an act for Luke, who'd regularly gotten lost even when he'd had access to GPS. Still, he wrung out every bit of help he could get from **[Deception]**, hoping to sell the ploy, hoping that the inquisitor would take another five steps forward without noticing the bombs.

For once, nothing went wrong with one of their plans, other than the fact that the mercs hadn't showed up with him. Luke didn't much care about getting those two though, not when the stronger one was only level 30. They would only be a threat in large numbers.

Both bombs went off at the same time, throwing a huge cloud of debris into the air. Chunks of wood, brick, and dirt arced into the sky and rained down on the city in every direction, reaching far enough that Luke had to bat a few chunks away to avoid being struck. He glanced down at Zea for confirmation, but she frowned and shook her head.

"Shit," he muttered. The explosion hadn't killed the inquisitor. He reached back behind him to grab the handle of his mace. If the damage was severe enough, maybe Luke could finish the job. He took a step forward to put himself between Zea and the rolling dirt cloud coming out of the alley, then peered into it.

He'd just bumped his perception up to 49. That should have been enough to see through the cloud, or at least to see a silhouette or something. Instead, the first warning he got was the sound of creaking wood on the roof of the building to his right. His head snapped up just in time to see the inquisitor, clothes ravaged by fire and skin bright red under the smeared black of soot. The man looked to be about fifty and made of wire and gristle. He had a thick mustache obscuring his upper lip and a headful of gray hair that currently looked like it had only a passing acquaintance with the concept of a comb.

He was also holding a short sword in one hand, its edge blackened and crisp, and a throwing knife in the other. In a flash, the knife spun through the air toward Zea, cutting across the distance too fast for normal eyes to follow. It might as well have been a bullet fired from a modern-day gun for all the reaction time Luke had while it traversed those twenty feet of open air.

Somehow, miraculously, he batted the knife off to the side. Considering that **[Twitch Reflexes]** didn't do anything to help against attacks that weren't aimed at him, he had to give all the credit to his own enhanced agility and perception, with a dash of assistance from **[Tactical Foresight]** recognizing the imminent throw and plotting its path.

It was only after he'd saved Zea from taking a knife in the throat that he realized the trap. He was off-balance now, vulnerable. That was exactly what the inquisitor had planned all along. Even if Luke had realized it, it wasn't like he could have done anything differently, not in the microsecond he'd had to act.

The inquisitor came down from the roof, blade leading. That would have been an exceptionally stupid move normally, considering how hard it was to defend against an attack when midjump. In this case, it was less of a leap and more of a dive, and given the man's extremely high stats, it was all Luke could do to throw himself backward out of the way of that descending blade.

He saved his nose from being cut off, but only just barely. Even with three different skills pushing Luke out of the way and an agility score higher than anything else he'd ever seen, the inquisitor was so blindingly fast that it was all Luke could do to track the movements. There was no thought to the fight as he dealt with the follow-up attacks, just pure reaction speed.

Luke dodged out of the way of a pair of strikes, slipped between the inquisitor and Zea, and deflected another blow on his left vambrace, only to have the sword shear through the metal with a squeal and draw a line of blood across his forearm.

[You have been afflicted by the following condition: Poison—Cobalt Scorpion Venom (3M).]

Because of fucking course this inquisitor would be another poison user, just like the last one. The difference was that he was way stronger, although this particular poison didn't seem to be doing much. If Luke had to guess, he'd say that the pair of bombs had cooked the poison coating the blade and rendered it more or less useless. The short duration and the fact that he didn't feel much of a difference in his body seemed to support that assessment.

That was fantastic news, since the last thing he needed now was another handicap. The inquisitor seemed experienced enough not to expect anything either, or else he was just too good at schooling his facial expressions to show surprise when Luke failed to slow down.

They continued fighting, with the inquisitor forcing Luke's positioning in order to keep Zea safe, a tactic he'd pounced on immediately and was using to great advantage against Luke. At the rate things were going, Luke was either going to end up overpowered by the inquisitor's superior skills or he was going to miss a block and let the inquisitor slip by to attack Zea. A single hit would probably be all it took to kill her.

Luke activated **[Life Surge]**.

Instantly, he had the inquisitor on the defensive. The man obviously knew what kind of skill Luke was using and that the best way to defeat it was to wait it out. Unfortunately for him, Luke could keep it running for a full two minutes now, which would be plenty of time to end the fight. He pressed his new advantage ruthlessly, even going so far as to channel a **[Power Strike]** or two into parries that came at a bad angle so that he could blow through them and smack his mace into the inquisitor.

The man took the strikes with nothing more than a grunt, having turned with the blows at precisely the right moment to nullify the lion's share of the damage they would have done. Luke mentally cursed and tried to drive the inquisitor back into a corner where the man wouldn't be able to dodge so easily.

That didn't work, not just because the alley only really had a corner at the dead end, but because the Inquisitor had no qualms about jumping into the air. His agility was so high that the first time he flipped over Luke's head, he still managed to dodge an attack by twisting his body around and drove his blade into Luke's shoulder.

The wound healed immediately, but the fact that the inquisitor had scored it at all was terrifying. Luke should have had the clear advantage with both feet on the ground and the ability to move freely, but somehow he'd lost that confrontation. He couldn't even imagine how badly he'd be doing if he hadn't spent all that AP. Even at rank 4, **[Mace Mastery]** was not keeping up with the inquisitor's bladework.

He was starting to get worried that even with **[Life Surge]** going and him using **[Power Strike]** every few swings, the inquisitor was going to outlast him. He needed some way to change the fight, to get it more on his terms. He had more strength and a huge pool of AP he could spend if he had to. Maybe he needed to take it to the ground, get the man in a proper pin, and slit his throat.

There were probably even a few grappling skills he could buy on the fly. He'd done some wrestling in high school, but it wasn't really his thing. Luke was pretty sure he could close in for a grapple if he accepted a stab or two as the price of doing business, but he was less sure he could keep hold of a man with over 60 agility, even if he did buy a skill to help.

He didn't have a better idea though. He opened his skill store and split his concentration, desperately trying to stall for time while he skipped through the options. "Damn it, System, where's grappling at?" he muttered under his breath, though he knew that System wouldn't respond. The question wasn't audible enough.

Then Zea finished whatever she'd been doing, and Luke was suddenly deafened by a rolling wave of sound so powerful it threatened to knock him off his feet.

Name	Luke Bennet	Zea Stenter
Level	39	32
XP	216771/218294	109574/120012
AP	109	105
Bloodline	SysAdmin II	None
Strength	52	7
Agility	70	27
Stamina	66	27
Perception	49	19
Skills	Mace Mastery (4)	Dagger Mastery (1)
	Sword Mastery (1)	Stealth (2)
	Unarmed Martialist (4)	Keen Instincts (1)
	Power Strike (2)	Lock Picking (1)
	Life Surge (2)	Disguise (2)
	Peripheral Awareness (2)	Deception (1)
	Tactical Foresight (1)	Bartering (2)
	Counter (3)	Streetwise (2)
	Twitch Reflexes (3)	Cooking (1)
	Stealth (1)	Mending (1)
	Survivalist (2)	First Aid (1)
	First Aid (1)	Thalian (3)
	Wood Carving (1)	Neyardic (3)
	Leatherworking (2)	Ostari (1)
	Butchering (4)	Mana Manipulation (2)
	Thalian (2)	Mana Sight (1)
	Ostari (1)	Metallurgy (1)
	Disguise (2)	Whitesmithing (1)
	Deception (1)	Goldsmithing (2)
	Detection (2)	Gem Cutting (1)
	Torturer (1)	Engraving (2)
	Analyze (BL)	Rune Forging (1)
	Remote Access (BL)	Painting (1)
	XP Mask (BL)	Arcano Dynamics (1)
		Sleight of Hand (1)
		Steady Hands (2)
		Cold Reading (1)
		Temperature Acclimation (2)
		Cadence (2)
		Bloodline Purification Ritual (2)
		Ghost Script (1)

CHAPTER 56

The inquisitor staggered to one side at the same time as Luke, leaving both of them vulnerable. But Luke had more stamina, and **[Life Surge]** was still pumping him up. He recovered before the inquisitor did, and he used that window of opportunity to turn his stagger into a heavy, planted step, pivoted on that foot, charged **[Power Strike]** down through his arms, and brought his mace around in a wide-arcing two-handed swing that delivered all that force directly into the inquisitor's rib cage.

Luke had been aiming for the inquisitor's face, but even caught off guard and momentarily stunned, he still recovered so fast that Luke missed shattering his skull into a thousand pieces. It would have been a death blow to any normal person, strong enough to pick the inquisitor up off the ground and throw him over the roof. Wooden shingles went flying as he crashed through a house on the other side of the street a block over.

Luke heard the body thump against the floor inside the house, and he waited, desperately hoping he'd hear the notification ding. When it didn't come after a few seconds, he silently cursed the man's durability.

"Not dead?" Zea asked, seeing the look on his face.

Luke shook his head. "Should we run?"

"He's injured. We might not get a better shot at taking him out."

"He's got reinforcements coming. I can hear mercs shouting a few blocks over."

"Shit. How many?"

"I don't know," Luke said. "At least five."

"Can you finish him off before they get here?"

Luke heard the inquisitor groan and the sound of a piece of wood scraping against the floor. There was a rattle of many small things hitting the ground and the inquisitor climbing back to his feet.

"Nope! Time to go. He's back up again."

Luke snatched up a loose pack from the ground, grabbed Zea, tucked her under one arm, and started running. "Hey!" she said, "What the fuck, man!"

Her words came out individually as she bounced with each step. "No time," Luke said harshly. He tossed her up and forward, then sped up slightly to get underneath her so she landed on his back. He didn't quite get the bag out of the way in time, and it got squished between them while she scrambled to hang on.

Once she had secured herself with an arm around his neck, Luke put on the speed. He bounded through the city, leaping over knots of people when they were packed too densely to go around. "Fuuuuuuucccckkk," Zea screamed when he leaped a house at the end of a dead-end street.

They broke free of the city a minute later, with Luke laughing wildly while Zea tried not to scream again. "Brings back memories," he hollered over the wind. "Just like being chased out of Valtira."

"I haaatte you!" Zea yelled back.

Luke just kept laughing as he sprinted across open fields. At the speed they were going, he doubted there'd be any pursuit capable of keeping up with him, but raw stats weren't everything. It wouldn't surprise him at all if that inquisitor pulled some trick out of his ass that let him move faster. Every thousand feet or so, he'd spin in place, much to Zea's misery, and confirmed that there was no one behind him in that ever-shrinking gap where his peripheral vision couldn't see.

About twenty minutes and just as many miles later, he slowed down. The forest loomed up in front of him, and while he thought he could probably dodge between the trees at full speed, he didn't want to take the chance of accidentally hurting Zea. Plus, the choke hold she had on his neck was making it harder to breathe.

He ghosted through the trees and came to a stop a few hundred feet in. Slowly, Zea pried her fingers off of Luke and dropped to the ground, where her legs wobbled for a moment before she gained her balance. "Well, let's not ever fucking do that again, shall we?" she said.

The adrenaline was starting to wear off now, and while Luke wasn't exactly tired, he was feeling a little twitchy. "That guy was the scariest thing I've ever seen," he said. "You don't even . . . He could have killed you with one hit, and he knew it. He was using it too."

He didn't want to make Zea feel bad, but she'd made that fight harder just by being there. On the other hand, whatever she'd made with **[Ghost Script]** had been what he'd needed to finally land a single decisive blow against the inquisitor. Even that hadn't been strong enough to finish the man off, sadly. Maybe if Luke had blown the rest of his AP, he could have overpowered the inquisitor, but he doubted it.

If he wanted to win the rematch, he needed to learn harder into his bloodline skills, which meant finding a safe place to hole up and doing the ritual as soon as possible. As much as he wanted a fix for XP madness, he'd take the skill that let him fuck with other people's stats first. It was probably the only way he was going to win if that inquisitor caught up to them again short of bombing another anthill.

"We need to find a safe place and do the ritual as soon as possible. Next time that fucker comes near us, I want to be able to drop his agility down to zero. Then I'll beat the hell out of him for a while before I take away his stamina too."

"Maybe we could just avoid him in the future," Zea suggested. "Or at least try."

"Seems unrealistic," Luke said. "Hard to avoid someone like that when he's looking for you."

"Probably right," she said. "Okay, so . . . Caves are probably going to be harder to find this far from the mountains. Any thoughts on where you want to do this ritual?"

"Uh . . . That's a good question."

They ended up finding a wide, flat shelf of stone that overlooked a stream. It was relatively clear of typical forest debris, and what little there was cleaned up easily. Zea had handled that while Luke had fetched some firewood. He'd been given directions to bring back enough to last a fire all night, and when he'd dropped the first load off, she'd told him to find two more just as big.

That was more than an overnight pile of wood, in his opinion, but he wasn't the one with **[Bloodline Purification Ritual]**, so he just did as he was told. Meanwhile, she'd scoured the stone and started drawing complicated geometric patterns on it. Luke noticed that this one was a lot bigger than the first one, with quite a few empty spaces in it. She paused regularly to stack firewood in those spots, and he was starting to see a pattern to it.

Unfortunately, that pattern was a circle with a suspiciously empty Luke-sized hole in the center. "Uh, this isn't one of those rituals that has words like *burn the witch* in it, right?" he asked.

"Don't distract me. This is harder than it looks, even with the upgrades to my skills."

"Oh yeah. I forgot you were going to do that. **[Cadence]**, **[Mana Sight]**, and **[Mana Manipulation]**, right?"

"90 fucking AP for them," she said. "Better be worth it."

She traced another shape in the stone with the chalk, then frowned and compared it to the other side of the ritual circle. With an annoyed sigh, she splashed some water from her waterskin on it, wiped away the chalk, let it dry, and redrew it. "There's an herb in my bag you'll need to eat. It's a dusky-red color with blue veins running through it. Get that out, please."

"This?" Luke asked, holding up what looked to him like a simple leaf rolled up on itself and stored in a glass jar.

"That's the one. I'm told it tastes like chewing on fire, but it also cost us seven gold, so don't waste it."

"Eh?" Luke eyed the leaf. Then he shrugged. With his stamina up into the 60s now, he wasn't too worried about eating Aros's version of the Carolina Reaper. Now, the amount of firewood that was getting piled up in this ritual circle, that was concerning. He didn't know exactly how his regeneration would interact with being burned alive, but he doubted it would be a fun experience.

While he waited for Zea to finish setting up, he got into their food pack and started eating the snacks. Just because **[Life Surge]** didn't drop him on his ass now that it was at rank 2 didn't mean he didn't need to replenish that energy anyway. Plus, if this ritual was anything like the last one, he'd be using the skill again at the end of it.

Eventually, everything was set up. Luke stood in the center of the circle, naked for some reason, and surrounded by a ring of firewood. Outside that was the familiar setup from before, with smaller circles inscribed inside the whole. Each of those had something in it, though this time there seemed to be a definite theme going on. A red gemstone glinted in the evening light to his left, and some sort of yellow-banded stick sat opposite it. A brownish-red scorpion, dead thankfully, took center stage in front of him.

"Okay, this next part is going to take about ten minutes to get going. Once I finish lighting the wood on fire, that's your cue to eat that herb. You're going to start sweating, and it's going to be mostly blood. Don't freak out if it's not the normal color or if it starts to hurt. Just don't move out of the circle and don't use any skills until I tell you."

"Got it."

Zea took a deep breath and said, "Alright. Here we go."

Lath grimaced in pain as he landed back on the ground. The jump hadn't seemed that high from his perch in the tree, but then again, he didn't usually demonstrate that kind of athletics with four busted ribs. Much as he hated to admit it, that apostate had gotten a solid hit on him. It had been over three hours and things still weren't fully healed up.

Between that explosive trap at the beginning of the fight and the apostate's final attack at the end, Lath hadn't been this injured in a decade. Though they were both undoubtably a higher level than they'd been when his apprentice had lost her life to them, he was still begrudgingly impressed with their capabilities.

That didn't mean he wasn't going to kill them as soon as he caught up to them, of course. He'd paused just long enough to fetch a new set of poisons from his rooms, then raced back across the city to chase the apostates in their flight from him. It had been relatively slow going, at least by his normal pace. Between his injuries, his lack of familiarity with the local terrain, and the fact that his skill set really wasn't geared toward tracking, it had been a troublesome expedition out into the wilderness.

This was precisely why he'd hired those worthless mercenaries to find the apostates in the first place. It was too bad they'd been unable to execute the simplest of tasks without getting themselves slaughtered. He had the two almost-competent ones with him, and they assured him that they were making good time, that they'd catch up when the targets stopped to sleep.

Lath didn't bother correcting them. If the apostates were smart, they wouldn't stop running for days. It was going to be a long, drawn-out trip. At least it would give him time to fully recover before the next confrontation. When he did finally catch up to them, he was going to kill the dwifkin first, just so she couldn't reveal any more surprises.

Much as he wanted to take his time and avenge his fallen apprentice, the apostates had proven too dangerous to subdue. Attempting that had been Myla's own error in judgment. Lath was just going to stab a poisoned knife into the apostate's heart and end it.

Name	Luke Bennet	Zea Stenter
Level	39	32
XP	216771/218294	109574/120012
AP	109	15
Bloodline	SysAdmin II	None
Strength	52	7
Agility	70	27
Stamina	66	27
Perception	49	19
Skills	Mace Mastery (4)	Dagger Mastery (1)
	Sword Mastery (1)	Stealth (2)
	Unarmed Martialist (4)	Keen Instincts (1)
	Power Strike (2)	Lock Picking (1)
	Life Surge (2)	Disguise (2)
	Peripheral Awareness (2)	Deception (1)
	Tactical Foresight (1)	Bartering (2)
	Counter (3)	Streetwise (2)
	Twitch Reflexes (3)	Cooking (1)
	Stealth (1)	Mending (1)
	Survivalist (2)	First Aid (1)
	First Aid (1)	Thalian (3)
	Wood Carving (1)	Neyardic (3)
	Leatherworking (2)	Ostari (1)
	Butchering (4)	Mana Manipulation (3)
	Thalian (2)	Mana Sight (2)
	Ostari (1)	Metallurgy (1)
	Disguise (2)	Whitesmithing (1)
	Deception (1)	Goldsmithing (2)
	Detection (2)	Gem Cutting (1)
	Torturer (1)	Engraving (2)
	Analyze (BL)	Rune Forging (1)
	Remote Access (BL)	Painting (1)
	XP Mask (BL)	Arcano Dynamics (1)
		Sleight of Hand (1)
		Steady Hands (2)
		Cold Reading (1)
		Temperature Acclimation (2)
		Cadence (3)
		Bloodline Purification Ritual (2)
		Ghost Script (1)

CHAPTER 57

It wasn't so much the chanting that set the ominous mood as it was the chanting done just as the sun was setting and the *lighting of the fucking wood on fire while he was standing inside the circle*. Luke could not possibly stress enough how much he wasn't a fan of that idea. He'd been hurt pretty regularly since coming to Aros, and to some extent, he'd grown used to that. It still hurt, but thanks to how fast he healed now, it was a lot less scary to know that it'd be over and done with quickly. It was kind of like getting jabbed with a needle. It only hurt for a moment.

However, he had what he felt were some legitimate concerns about the concept of being roasted alive, how long that would hurt, and how long it would last with his regeneration factored in. Zea was not interested in discussing those concerns and, in her own blunt way, told him to, "Suck it up, you big baby."

Luke stood there, sweat dripping down his skin and the leaf clutched in his hand, close to his chest to keep the fire from catching it, while Zea paced circles around him, chanting and prodding the wood to help spread the flames with a silver baton she'd purchased. Luke had suspicions that the baton did not need to be silver, that she'd just bought it because she liked it. He was wise enough to avoid voicing those suspicions out loud.

When Zea lit the yellow-banded stick, the temperature spiked inside the circle. Flames flashed across the rest of the wood, and Luke pushed the leaf between his lips as the circle closed completely around him. He got a whiff of something that burned his nostrils for a moment as he shoved the leaf into his mouth, and then he started chewing.

At first, it just tasted like a piece of plant matter, kind of like a crispy piece of lettuce, except that as soon as his teeth mashed into it, it felt like he'd chomped down on a firecracker. Each little fleck that was torn from the whole ignited, searing the insides of his cheeks, his gums, and his tongue. Luke froze midchew and mentally wrestled with himself to keep from spitting it out.

In the end, it wasn't the seven gold that kept him going. It was that Zea had told him it was crucial to the ritual, and if they fucked that up, they might not live long enough to gather new ingredients to try again. Chewing that burning leaf was a matter of life and death. Though, she hadn't said anything about how mashed up it had to be. Luke gave it a couple more decisive chews, then swallowed it more or less whole.

[You have been afflicted by the following condition: Poison—Raw Frostbane (8M).]

"Way worse than any Earth peppers," he said with a wheeze, so bad that the system itself told him he'd been poisoned. He almost expected smoke to be coming out of his mouth, but there was none. Luke wanted to leave his mouth hanging open and fan it, but the heat and the smoke from the burning wood just made it worse somehow.

Then the heat moved down to his chest, like the worst heartburn ever, and then it started in on his stomach. With each breath, new bursts of fire seared his lungs. The heat spread to his limbs, far more than just what he could feel on his skin. "Oh God, Zea is trying to kill me," he moaned. "She's gone cannibal and is cooking me from the inside out."

Zea smacked the shard of red gemstone with the baton, and it burst into crimson light. The flames roared up again, then froze in place and crystallized. The heat died down on the outside of his skin, but the leaf kept cooking his insides. Luke clutched at his belly in misery and, not for the first time, cursed the God Machine, the Pantheon, and Aros in general.

The flames started moving again instead their crystalline prison, looking more like fire behind glass now. Melting glass. He watched in mounting horror as little bubbles appeared, and then burst. Each time, a new wave of heat passed over him. Each time, it got a little bit hotter.

He was going to melt long before this ritual was finished! Sweat poured off him liberally, and Luke glanced over at the nearby stream with longing. He could be in that water in less than a second, before Zea could activate the next torturous step of her sadistic and evil ritual.

The chanting rose to a fever pitch, and she stopped in front of the dead scorpion. Maybe it was the flickering light of the flames dancing across its body, but he could have sworn he saw it move, like it was dancing in demonic glee. A shadow flicked across its tail, giving it the illusion of the stinger moving forward.

Luke knew it hadn't moved. His perception was too high to be fooled. It was just a trick of the light, one he could easily see through. That was why he was so surprised when he felt a pinprick stab into his shoulder. "Ouch!" he yelped, slapping at his skin with his hand. There was nothing there.

Firelight waved back and forth across the dead scorpion, and a thousand stings hit him at once. They were all over his body, little devil needles of fire. Each one lasted for an instant before the pain disappeared, and his sweat started turning red. It quickly darkened to black and started smoking.

More beads of red sweat rolled down his body, too many coming too fast to all burn away. In a matter of moments, he was stained red. Luke had withstood the leaf, the general heat, and the stings. They sucked, but he could deal with it. This was something else. He was dizzy now, and he didn't think it was smoke inhalation.

"Too much blood loss," he said, but so quietly that Zea didn't hear him over the flames. Stubbornly, he held his balance and stayed on his feet. Maybe it would have been better to sit down, but he hadn't thought to before they'd started, and his little box was small. He didn't know if he could change position without stepping outside the line, and they'd come too far to screw it all up now.

He could do this. He was superhuman now, capable of bending steel with his bare hands, of leaping thirty feet straight up, and able to run for days without slowing down. A little blood loss wasn't going to be the thing that finally beat him.

The chanting wasn't slowing down either. If anything, it was getting more frantic, and the fire was reacting to it. Luke kind of wished he'd thought to ask how long this was going to take. It was different from their first ritual in so many ways that he didn't even think he could use that as a loose guideline.

At some point, it all stopped mattering. The entire ritual felt like some endless, hazy fever dream that Luke was suffering through, his own personal lake of fire and blood. All his energies were focused on nothing more than staying upright and inside his designated square. Anything else was asking for too much.

Then, somehow, it was over. The fires had gone out, leaving him surrounded by nothing but ash and cinders.

[You have further purified your bloodline. It has been upgraded to Sys-Admin III.]

Luke didn't remember getting a message like that the first time they'd done the ritual, but then again, the only part he really remembered at the end was being super fucking woozy and damn near passing out. Maybe he'd gotten it and just dismissed it without really reading it.

"Ritual worked," he slurred out as he dropped down to one knee.

Zea was next to him the instant he went down. Her hands pressed against his chest and his shoulder, helping to support his weight. "You look half-dead," she told him. "Time to use **[Life Surge]**, then a quick dip in the stream."

"Right, yeah, sorry. Hard to think. It went better than the first one?"

Zea snorted softly. "Yeah, a little bit. If I had to do the first one on someone else now, it would be a lot easier on them. All those rank 1 skills did not do you any favors. Now, come on, let's get you back on your feet."

Luke triggered **[Life Surge]** and immediately started to feel better. It didn't bring him back up to 100 percent, but it was a start. With Zea's help, he got back upright, took a few deep breaths, then jumped into the stream. It was only about four feet deep, so he crouched down until he was completely underwater and started scrubbing at his bare skin.

The blood-sweat that hadn't blackened on his skin came off easily enough, but he had to scrape at the rest of it with his nails to make any progress. After a few minutes, he popped his head back above the water and said, "Throw me a bar of soap?"

While Zea was rummaging around, he kept working and said, "Okay, System. Two things. First, the skill that lets me change stats. Tell me about it."

"It is called **[Stat Assignment]** and costs 50 AP. This will allow you to alter your point spread but not change the total amount. For example, you could take 30 points from your perception and add them to your strength. The change occurs as a rate of 5 points per minute, so it would take six minutes for the change to become fully effective."

"I thought there was a way to remove stats from someone else. Wasn't it this skill mixed with **[Remote Access]**?"

"You can change how stats have been allocated, but you cannot gain more without spending AP. I apologize if this wasn't made clear in my initial explanation."

"Damn it, that would have been too powerful, I guess. Is there a way to take someone else's stats away from them?"

"You can unassign the AP used on them, which refunds the AP to their pool for use. Please bear in mind that as your bloodline becomes further purified, new facets of your current skills will open up. Also remember that I am not able to give you detailed information about bloodline skills you don't have access to yet."

"Right, speaking of! **[XP Mask]**. Can I see their XP without letting them see mine?"

"No, I'm afraid not, but you should be able to turn the skill on or off at will now."

"Small start," Luke grumbled. It was better than nothing but not what he wanted. Worse, they'd somehow fucked up on the whole plan of taking an enemy's stats away. There went his idea for killing that inquisitor easily. He was interrupted by Zea tossing a bar of soap to him, something lavender scented that he hesitated to use. Tracking people by smell alone was something he'd started to consider.

"Got anything without a scent in it?" he asked.

"No."

"Damn it. Ugh. Fine." It would probably be alright. If the inquisitor was close enough to smell the soap on him, he'd be close enough to smell them anyway. Luke started scrubbing away at the black gunk flecks all over his body.

"Okay, well, not as good of news as I was hoping. Next question, the XP-cycling skill. You said it doesn't exist, but can we create it?"

"It is certainly possible," System said. "If you'd like, I can guide you through the skill shop's interface to a section where you can design the skill yourself."

"Perfect," Luke said. He paused for a second, then added, "What about the whole stat-draining-skill idea? Could I make that as well?"

"I believe it should be possible, but we will not be able to say for sure until we try."

"Well, one way to find out. As soon as I get this crap scrubbed off me, we're going to make some new skills."

Name	Luke Bennet	Zea Stenter
Level	39	32
XP	216771/218294	109574/120012
AP	109	15
Bloodline	SysAdmin III	None
Strength	52	7
Agility	70	27
Stamina	66	27
Perception	49	19
Skills	Mace Mastery (4)	Dagger Mastery (1)
	Sword Mastery (1)	Stealth (2)
	Unarmed Martialist (4)	Keen Instincts (1)
	Power Strike (2)	Lock Picking (1)
	Life Surge (2)	Disguise (2)
	Peripheral Awareness (2)	Deception (1)
	Tactical Foresight (1)	Bartering (2)
	Counter (3)	Streetwise (2)
	Twitch Reflexes (3)	Cooking (1)
	Stealth (1)	Mending (1)
	Survivalist (2)	First Aid (1)
	First Aid (1)	Thalian (3)
	Wood Carving (1)	Neyardic (3)
	Leatherworking (2)	Ostari (1)
	Butchering (4)	Mana Manipulation (3)
	Thalian (2)	Mana Sight (2)
	Ostari (1)	Metallurgy (1)
	Disguise (2)	Whitesmithing (1)
	Deception (1)	Goldsmithing (2)
	Detection (2)	Gem Cutting (1)
	Torturer (1)	Engraving (2)
	Analyze (BL)	Rune Forging (1)
	Remote Access (BL)	Painting (1)
	XP Mask (BL)	Arcano Dynamics (1)
		Sleight of Hand (1)
		Steady Hands (2)
		Cold Reading (1)
		Temperature Acclimation (2)
		Cadence (3)
		Bloodline Purification Ritual (2)
		Ghost Script (1)

CHAPTER 58

Zea took the news that their plans for using a bloodline skill to strip the inquisitor of his stats wasn't going to work about as well as Luke did, though with considerably more swearing. After giving her a few minutes to get it out of her system, Luke said, "There's still the possibility of making something similar. We won't know until we try. I figured you'd want to get a look at the interface with me."

"Can I?" she asked.

"I don't see why not. **[Remote Access]** has given you pretty much every other settings option I have."

"That reminds me, I keep meaning to reorganize my skills. The system's default method is garbage."

"Can we focus here?" Luke asked. "This whole situation is turning into a repeat of Valtira. I don't believe for a second that that inquisitor just gave up because we managed to run away. I'd like to be a bit more prepared for the next encounter with them. Myla nearly killed me, and you flat-out said it was pure luck that you got your hands on that core that allowed you to go invisible for so long."

Zea glanced up at him. In her hands, she held a small stylus with a sharp metal tip. She'd been using it to carve lines into a roll of thin leather while they talked. "What do you think I've been doing while you get cleaned up?"

"Sorry, I'm just . . . tense. Frustrated, I guess. I thought we had this one figured out, but of course we were wrong. And System didn't tell us because we didn't ask the right questions. Now we've got to rush it and try to patch up the plan before the church catches up to us again."

"Some good news there at least. I don't think that inquisitor is working with anyone else from the church," Zea said. "I think that's why he hired those mercenaries. He's too far from home and doesn't have his normal support network. I'm not saying he's not dangerous, just that we're not going to have to fight off dozens more inquisitors and templars."

Luke shrugged. "Does it matter? So he's got fifty mercs instead of fifty church assholes. Same difference to us."

"Well, it means we can reasonably expect to not have anyone else above level 30 coming at us, which is a nice bit of info to have. We really only need to plan for the inquisitor himself as a hard opponent, and I'm already working on some crowd-dispersal stuff in case the mercs try to jump us as a whole group."

"Okay, that's a good point," Luke said. "So I guess I'll start poking at this skill-creation thing while you work on enchanting stuff?"

"Yup. I've got a few new ideas thanks to those rank-ups in **[Mana Sight]** and **[Mana Manipulation]**."

Luke found a spot on the shelf where he could sit with his feet dangling above the stream and said, "Alright, System, let's do this."

"Certainly, Luke. If you'll open your skill-shop interface and look to the right, you'll see a skill-forge option."

"Was this always here? It can't have been, right? I wouldn't have just not noticed it all this time."

"It was not," System told him. "Upgrading your bloodline to SysAdmin III has unlocked new system options for you."

"Like what?"

"For example, you can now see full skill-progression lines instead of only the next rank-up," System said.

"Really?" Luke quickly checked **[Peripheral Awareness]** and saw that instead of just telling him rank 3 would cost 25 AP, it also showed rank 4 at 50 AP and rank 5 at 100 AP and gave a bit of information about what each rank-up would do to improve the skill. That wasn't particularly useful, as the gist of it was basically that it would keep working as it already did but better. Though the skill did specifically call out that enemies using some sort of stealth skill would become easier to spot as **[Peripheral Awareness]** got stronger.

"Oh, that's cool." If Luke was that kind of planner, he could figure out how to spend every point of AP for the next forty levels. Come to think of it, that was kind of what Curt had done, only without the AP requirements being estimates. He'd been pretty accurate as far as his information went though, so he must have figured out some sort of pattern. Luke had noticed a lot of skills had the same progression of AP costs as they ranked up, but not all of them. Curt had probably done a better job of figuring out the patterns than Luke could ever hope to.

"What all changed with the bloodline purification?"

"Expanded skill descriptions, access to the skill-creation menu, increased information from **[Analyze]**, **[XP Mask]** can now be turned on and off at will, the range on **[Remote Access]** has increased, you have fewer restrictions to the system's database, and several new bloodline skills are available. You can view them in the skill shop."

Luke gave that a quick look, but it wasn't anything he hadn't already known about. The skill shop had already told him those bloodline skills existed, things like **[Matter Generation]** and **[Inflict Status]**, but they were available to take now, as long as he had a whopping 200 AP to spend on each one. If he hadn't been forced to dump AP to fight at something close to that inquisitor's level, maybe he'd have considered it. **[Inflict Status]** certainly sounded like the ultimate trump card. Just give someone the paralysis condition and kill them while they lay there.

That wasn't the reality of his situation, unfortunately. Unless they wanted to go blow up some more anthills, 200 AP was going to be the better part of a week's grinding. Luke much preferred the bombing method as a way to exploit the system's shitty XP policies, but he also wanted to have an effective counter to XP madness first.

That would be the focus of his efforts. XP madness was the hard stop to increasing their power. If he could remove that wall, they could just outlevel all their problems. He opened the skill forge and started looking through the options. The first decision he had to make was whether he was looking to build a combat or utility ability. Since being able to prevent XP from coagulating into a new miniature protodeity inside him didn't strike him as a combat-oriented skill, he decided to select utility.

The menus were mostly the same as when he was browsing through the regular portion of the skill shop, at least as long as he was filtering down what he wanted. Eventually, he reached a dead end where the system no longer had anything even close to what he was trying to make. From there, a new interface window popped up that wanted him to him do . . . something.

"System, what does this mean? I don't understand what it's asking for."

"In broad terms, this is the customization matrix that guides AP into the shape of the skill. It's a bit more nuanced than that, since AP is an artificial construct. The system assigns it to you as a way for your minds to grasp a portion of the divinity you carry in your soul. Otherwise you would be spending XP directly, and that gets more and more complicated the more of it you have."

"Oh, I see." No, he didn't. This was math class all over again. He was more than happy to leave the math behind the screens to the system to figure out. Getting an amount of AP equal to his level each time he leveled up was easy to grasp, and he preferred it that way.

Except now he was getting past that layer and looking behind the screens, and Luke discovered that his lack of understanding was making it impossible to do what he wanted. Fortunately, he had a sentient being that was inclined to help him.

"Can you show me what this is supposed to look like? Maybe show me what the matrix looks like on other skills so I can compare?"

A second window opened up next to the one he was manipulating, this one listing all his skills. **[XP Mask]** was selected off the list, and a three-dimensional image of something that kind of reminded him of those pictures of molecules they used to show in science class was shown, except instead of four or five balls that were two or three different colors, there were thousands of little shapes in every color. He spotted cubes, spheres, cylinders, and dozens of other shapes he didn't have words for, , all connected to one another either by pressing their sides together or meeting at a point.

"What the fuck am I looking at?" he asked. There was no way he could build something like that. No human could.

"This is a visual representation of how each point of XP is used to make the matrix that forms one of your skills. **[XP Mask]** uses 20 AP worth of XP, so while this is more complex than most rank 1 or 2 skills, it is nowhere near representative of the most difficult skills to create."

The screen closed, and a new one opened. This time, the whole shape was five times as big, and the shapes were glowing with various degrees of brightness. There were plenty of new colors too, most of which were different shades of the colors he actually had names for. That all would have been fine to look at, even if he couldn't recreate it, but they were also moving. If there was some pattern to it, Luke couldn't see it, but it did give him an immediate headache if he focused on it at all.

"This is the matrix for the 200 AP skill **[Matter Generation]**. There are skills more complex than this, but I believe this serves as an example of the scaling complexities of creating a new skill."

"I don't think I could make a 1 AP skill," Luke said, looking away from the screen. "Can you help me do this?"

System hesitated. "The system doesn't make new skills," he said. "The Pantheon made all of these when they set the God Machine up and used a god as the fuel that powers the system."

"So, that's a no?"

"There are no directives preventing me from assisting you," System said. "I can certainly take parts from other skills and mix them together to your specifications. I believe it would be within my capabilities to merge them into a single new skill."

"Okay, well . . . Let's just see what we can do," Luke said. "I need it to be able to work on Zea too, so I guess we need **[Remote Access]** in there?"

"That is not necessary," System said. "By its very nature, **[Remote Access]** itself will work in conjunction with any new bloodline skill you develop."

Luke was so far out of his depth that he didn't know if he should feel relieved or frustrated. It was probably a bit of both, if he was being honest with himself. System was going to help, but System's help was generally pretty awful. Even if they pulled this off, it was probably going to be a long, time-consuming process filled with a lot of swearing.

"I guess let's start with walking through what this process is supposed to do," Luke said. "The first step is to take all the XP in me and send it back to the God Machine, right? Then we want to draw a new batch of the same amount of XP out and give it back? And it needs to be put into all the right shapes for my skills and stats? So, really only three steps."

"That is essentially correct, at a very basic level," System said.

"Okay, so there's a mechanism for sending XP to the God Machine and getting it back. It triggers every time I kill something, right?"

"That is also correct."

"Can we copy that process and turn it into a skill, and then just adjust it to take it from me and give it back to me? That would get me new XP, right?"

A new screen popped up with a bunch of shapes hooked together in a million screwy ways. At least they weren't moving this time. "This skill would do this. It would not shape the XP into your skills though."

"Okay, let's keep building on it then," Luke said.

He had a good feeling about this. It was going to work. He just had to figure out how to find all the pieces so System could put them together for him.

Name	Luke Bennet	Zea Stenter
Level	39	32
XP	216771/218294	109574/120012
AP	109	15
Bloodline	SysAdmin III	None
Strength	52	7
Agility	70	27
Stamina	66	27
Perception	49	19
Skills	Mace Mastery (4)	Dagger Mastery (1)
	Sword Mastery (1)	Stealth (2)
	Unarmed Martialist (4)	Keen Instincts (1)
	Power Strike (2)	Lock Picking (1)
	Life Surge (2)	Disguise (2)
	Peripheral Awareness (2)	Deception (1)
	Tactical Foresight (1)	Bartering (2)
	Counter (3)	Streetwise (2)
	Twitch Reflexes (3)	Cooking (1)
	Stealth (1)	Mending (1)
	Survivalist (2)	First Aid (1)
	First Aid (1)	Thalian (3)
	Wood Carving (1)	Neyardic (3)
	Leatherworking (2)	Ostari (1)
	Butchering (4)	Mana Manipulation (3)
	Thalian (2)	Mana Sight (2)
	Ostari (1)	Metallurgy (1)
	Disguise (2)	Whitesmithing (1)
	Deception (1)	Goldsmithing (2)
	Detection (2)	Gem Cutting (1)
	Torturer (1)	Engraving (2)
	Analyze (BL)	Rune Forging (1)
	Remote Access (BL)	Painting (1)
	XP Mask (BL)	Arcano Dynamics (1)
		Sleight of Hand (1)
		Steady Hands (2)
		Cold Reading (1)
		Temperature Acclimation (2)
		Cadence (3)
		Bloodline Purification Ritual (2)
		Ghost Script (1)

CHAPTER 59

1 25 AP," Luke said. "Just slightly more than what I have available because of course it is."

Despite that, he wasn't upset. Just knowing that there was an option for **[XP Cycle]** now was enough to take a lot of stress off him. Gaining a single level before he could put it into effect was no big deal, and he immediately started planning out how to abuse insect bombing to his advantage. They just needed to wipe out two or three hives to push up to a high enough level that they could physically overpower anything that even considered fucking with them, and then it was a straight line across the ocean and to the God Machine.

"Zea, are you just about done?" Luke asked.

She grunted without looking up but otherwise didn't respond. Luke looked over to see her hunched over the leather so close that her nose was bare inches away. She was carving lines in it in long, straight rows, and it was only half the size it had been when she started. Next to her were strips of leather, each with their own row of runes etched onto them.

Judging by how much leather was left, he figured she was going to need at least another hour, maybe a bit longer. She'd worked through the night to get her project done and kept on going after the sun had risen. It must have been important to her to skip sleeping, even if she didn't really need more an than an hour or two each night now.

With nothing better to do, Luke sat himself back down and started working on a new skill. Or rather, he got to the interface and said, "System, I want to make a mace skill that can attack multiple opponents at once, like some of those sword and dagger skills you showed me when I was looking for a way to fight groups of enemies."

"Which skill would you like to base this new skill on?" System asked.

"What was that one sword skill, the one that made copies of the sword and then attacked with all of them at once? Omnicut or something?"

"I believe you are referring to **[Phantom Blades]**," System said. Luke silently mouthed the skill name and shook his head as he laughed at how wrong he'd been. "That skill could serve as a viable base to generate multiple temporary copies of your current weapon, but I believe you would need to combine it with a different skill in order to account for a change in how the weapons attack."

"Well how does **[Phantom Blades]** do it?" Luke asked. "I just kind of figured it would use your **[Sword Mastery]** at whatever rank to control the extra swords for you."

"In part, yes. You could scavenge a movement pattern off **[Mace Mastery]**, but that skill wouldn't provide you with the framework necessary to coordinate so many different weapons at the same time. Additionally, **[Mace Mastery]** makes assumptions such as that you are the person holding the weapon, so you may run into some positional issues where the weapons miss because they are targeting based off where your physical weapon is."

"**[Phantom Blades]** should have the stuff to cover that, wouldn't it? I mean, that skill has to overcome the same obstacles."

System considered that for a moment, then nodded. "I believe you are correct. Would you like me to attempt to model the matrix for a mace-based version of **[Phantom Blades]** used in conjunction with **[Mace Mastery]**?"

"I think so. What if we mixed **[Power Strike]** in there as well, just to give it some extra oomph with each hit?"

"That may be inadvisable," System said. "The cumulative strain on your body from so many uses of **[Power Strike]** at the same time could theoretically kill you."

"Damn," Luke said, his fantasies of pulverizing a mountain in one swing vanishing. "Maybe we could just make it so that it synergizes with **[Power Strike]** if I use the skill at the same time but just divides a single use into each phantom mace?"

"That would be possible," System said. "I believe it would raise the AP cost to acquire the skill by 5."

"What's the cost now?"

"**[Phantom Blades]** costs 25 AP. Your as-of-yet-unnamed version will cost 30 AP if you include the ability to synergize with other combat skills. As it currently stands, you will need to raise **[Mace Mastery]** to rank 5 and purchase **[Mana Manipulation]** rank 3 as prerequisite skills for this new skill."

"Ah, damn it. Is there a way to go around those requirements?" Luke asked.

"I suppose you could, technically, but it would inflate the AP cost of the skill so high that you would be worse off than if you'd purchased the skills to begin with."

Luke kept tinkering with the idea until Zea finished up her project, but in the end, he couldn't find a viable alternative. The best he could come up with was a skill that was already in the system, **[Burst Step]**, which just allowed for a brief window, fractions of a second, in which he could move faster to help with positioning for an attack. Even that still wasn't the same as attacking in multiple places at once though, not really. It seemed semi-useful at best to him, considering how easily it could be blocked by skills like **[Twitch Reflexes]**, not to mention the extreme amount of perception and agility needed to take full advantage of it kind of provided the same benefits, only without wasting the AP.

"Annnndd . . . done," Zea announced.

"Cool. What are they?"

"Enchanted restraints," she said.

"Oh? Kinky."

"Not that kind of restraint. Although . . ." Zea trailed off, then shook her head. "No. They're made to throw at an enemy. They'll make whatever limb they hit feel like it weighs a few hundred pounds, and if you can tag the same enemy multiple times, they'll also start to pull toward one another. Ideally, they'll slow down the person, then make it harder to coordinate their limbs, and eventually stop them completely if enough bands hit."

"Oh shit, that's cool. Are they reusable?"

"Unfortunately, no. Each one will last for about three minutes. After that, they're just strips of leather with fancy squiggles on them."

Even with that limiting factor, Luke could see how valuable they were. If they could trip up that inquisitor with even two or three of the restraints, Luke would probably be able to score a decisive victory. Then again, considering how fast the inquisitor was, there really wasn't any guarantee that they'd actually be able to hit him.

"So what happens if you get one of these around a person's neck?" Luke asked.

Zea gave him a wicked grin. "I imagine it would become very difficult to breathe or hold your head upright."

"And the torso?"

"Wouldn't activate at all. Unfortunately, they only work if the spot they hit is small enough for the band to completely circle it. For any human opponent, arms and legs are good. Head is . . . probably? Maybe. Neck is excellent. I can't make them long enough to circle a waist or chest."

"Still, even with those restrictions, that's pretty awesome. Are you sure you can tag that inquisitor with one though? That guy's crazy fast."

"Not even a little bit," Zea told him. "But I have faith that you can. All you have to do is hit him with one and it'll activate on its own."

"Ooooooohhh." Luke looked down at the bands again. It was tempting to tag himself, just to see what it felt like. He could justify it as needing to know the limits of what it did so that he could use it effectively in combat, but the way he figured his luck ran, as soon as he did that, the inquisitor would burst out of the trees and attack. Then Luke would be fighting at a handicap against an opponent he already couldn't beat.

As Zea gathered up all her enchanting supplies, Luke told her, "I cracked the XP-madness problem. We made a new skill called **[XP Cycle]**, but I need one more level to have the AP for it. Feel like making some temporary bombs to use on an anthi—What are you looking at?"

Zea just stared at him, her mouth hanging open. "Come on, it's not that big a deal," Luke said.

"Not that big a deal!" she sputtered. "Are you serious? If this was a skill everyone could take, it would completely change society!"

"Uh . . . Can everyone take it, System?" Luke asked.

"Not without your bloodline," System said. "I suppose if you were prolific enough in that regard, you could spread your bloodline so that in a few hundred years, it would be a skill that most people could take."

"Yeah. Um. No thanks. Can we modify it so that people can take it without the bloodline?"

"I'm afraid not."

"Figures." Luke thought about it for a second, then added, "All we're really doing with this skill is adding a condition to how XP is transferred between the God Machine and everyone with XP, right?"

"Correct."

"Could we alter the system to do that by default, for everybody?"

Zea's breath caught, and she glanced sharply over at System, who stood there considering the question. "I believe it is hypothetically possible, but I do not know if you will be allowed to. Thus far, the addition of a new skill that is limited to your own bloodline falls well within the bounds of your permissions. Even at the command console, you would not be allowed to make a change this big. You would need to query for system override first. Such requests are sent directly to the Pantheon and must be unanimously agreed upon."

"So we need the gods' permission," Luke said. "And if they wanted the system to do that, they could have just done it that way to begin with."

"I cannot speculate on the—"

"Yeah, yeah, I know," Luke said. He blew out a hard sigh and added, "Well, fuck. I guess the problem is solved for us at least. Wait, I can use **[XP Cycle]** on someone else with **[Remote Access]**, right?"

"That is correct," System said.

"Could I use **[XP Mask]** too?"

"That is also correct."

"Huh. How about that? Good to know that we can hide your XP too, if we need to," Luke told Zea.

"When this is all over, I don't plan on having that much. I still want you to reset me so I can do my own build."

"Right. I can pick up **[Stat Assignment]** right now, but, well, that doesn't reduce your XP. System, just to confirm, **[Alter Skill List]** will let us remove skills from Zea, correct?"

"Yes, Luke. Removed skills will have their AP refunded. You will need to remove higher-tier skills with prerequisites prior to removing base skills in the event that such skills are present."

"And that's 200 AP," Luke said. "So, ants. Pack on a few levels, pick up **[XP Cycle]**, buff some stats and upgrade some skills, punch that inquisitor's lights out, then get on the boat and bail on this place?"

"I suppose that is a plan," Zea said. "As long as System is sure this new skill will stop XP madness."

"It will," System assured her. "As long as you receive regular applications of the skill, your XP will be cycled through the God Machine. Once every month or two should be sufficient up through level 60."

"See, there you go," Luke said. "Let's do this?"

"Maybe you should just get that XP yourself," Zea said. "I think I've leveled enough."

"Why? We just figured out a way to overcome this problem."

"Sure, but what if you're not around? We get separated for a few months, and by the time you find me, I'm fucking insane. Whoops, too late. Sucks to be Zea, I guess? Or what happens when you get your family back? That's it, no more treatments for me? It was a good, long twenty-three years?"

"I . . . I wouldn't . . ." Luke stopped himself. "Okay, that's fair. I get where putting yourself in a position where you're relying on me to keep giving you your XP-madness pills for the rest of your life, with no other way to get them, and if the supply runs out, you die, is a bad spot. Maybe we can keep working on the skill to make it do it automatically, permanently."

"If we can, then I'm more interested. Right now, I want to see my XP reset permanently before I commit to going to an even higher level."

"Fair enough. I still need to get a few more levels to even take the skill though, and I can't bomb a colony of ants without you."

Zea sighed and said, "Fine. One bomb. That's it."

"Great! System, which way to the closest anthill?"

Name	Luke Bennet	Zea Stenter
Level	39	32
XP	216771/218294	109574/120012
AP	109	15
Bloodline	SysAdmin III	None
Strength	52	7
Agility	70	27
Stamina	66	27
Perception	49	19
Skills	Mace Mastery (4)	Dagger Mastery (1)
	Sword Mastery (1)	Stealth (2)
	Unarmed Martialist (4)	Keen Instincts (1)
	Power Strike (2)	Lock Picking (1)
	Life Surge (2)	Disguise (2)
	Peripheral Awareness (2)	Deception (1)
	Tactical Foresight (1)	Bartering (2)
	Counter (3)	Streetwise (2)
	Twitch Reflexes (3)	Cooking (1)
	Stealth (1)	Mending (1)
	Survivalist (2)	First Aid (1)
	First Aid (1)	Thalian (3)
	Wood Carving (1)	Neyardic (3)
	Leatherworking (2)	Ostari (1)
	Butchering (4)	Mana Manipulation (3)
	Thalian (2)	Mana Sight (2)
	Ostari (1)	Metallurgy (1)
	Disguise (2)	Whitesmithing (1)
	Deception (1)	Goldsmithing (2)
	Detection (2)	Gem Cutting (1)
	Torturer (1)	Engraving (2)
	Analyze (BL)	Rune Forging (1)
	Remote Access (BL)	Painting (1)
	XP Mask (BL)	Arcano Dynamics (1)
		Sleight of Hand (1)
		Steady Hands (2)
		Cold Reading (1)
		Temperature Acclimation (2)
		Cadence (3)
		Bloodline Purification Ritual (2)
		Ghost Script (1)

CHAPTER 60

There was no way to keep Zea from gaining XP along with Luke, not as long as they were using **[Ghost Script]** to make the bombs. If she made them the old-fashioned way, there was enough separation between her as the enchanter and him as the wielder of the bomb to assign all the XP to him, but those took hours and money to make. **[Ghost Script]** let her inscribe the runes on any old chunk of wood or a rock, as long as she didn't need them to last for more than a few minutes.

She wasn't thrilled about putting on even more levels. Luke had a fix for himself, or so he said, and that was great. But it meant that she was tethered to him for the rest of her life, and thankfully he at least grasped why that was unappealing for her. She felt like she'd already sacrificed an enormous amount for him, and while she didn't exactly regret that, it had been done under the assumption that he'd be able to reset her status later on.

It wasn't like they'd given up on that plan or anything, but after using **[Bloodline Purification Ritual]** on him twice now, he had access to a whole bunch of tools, enough that he should be able to finish this whole God Machine job without any additional help from her. At this point, she was along for the ride to collect her payment and because she liked spending time with him.

He was fun and driven. She was comfortable around him, and while she wouldn't say she loved him, there were some definite feelings there. It wasn't like Luke had no bad qualities either, mainly how impulsive he was. He did not like to think things through, but he'd been bitten in the ass too many times now and was slowly growing out of that habit.

He could be thoughtless, but he did care. All she had to do was point out what was likely to happen if he did what he was thinking and how it would affect her or others, and he generally made good choices.

Zea had met many worse people in her life. Traveling with Luke could be stressful, but more so because of the constant fighting than because of anything he did. She knew she'd slowed him down tremendously too, but he never mentioned it or gave the appearance that he resented her. He could have gotten what he wanted and ditched her quite easily.

So, she'd make this sacrifice for him. They were about three hundred feet away from their target, and she was busy tracing the enchantment onto a chunk of deadwood he'd scavenged up and sliced down to size for her. **[Ghost Script]** was quickly becoming her new favorite skill, despite the high price. It was so much easier to just trace the runes with her finger than it was to physically carve them into the material.

The best part was that she could go fast because, if she made a mistake, all she had to do was wipe the rune clean and start over. It cost nothing since **[Ghost Script]** didn't damage the wood at all, and she didn't have to redo all the runes on a new base object. She thought that with a little practice, and maybe another rank in the skill—though maybe not, considering how expensive rank 1 had been—she could turn it into a viable combat skill.

"This is going to blow up fifteen seconds after I finish the last rune," she told Luke. "Be ready to throw it as soon as I hand it to you."

The bombs she made were much easier to do without the twine serving as a fuse anyway. Those were just a repeating chain of timer runes that burned away at a rate of five runes a second, which meant to add any reasonable length of time, she needed a few feet of twine. It also wasn't easy to put the runes on something that small and flexible.

Another rank of **[Rune Forging]** would probably unlock knowledge of better timer runes, but she worked with what she had. Besides, the whole goal was to start back over at level 1 and pick the skills she wanted instead of all the enchanting-adjacent skills that had been forced on her. She didn't even have the tools to make use of half of those skills anyway.

"Here you go," she said as she finished drawing the final rune and tossed the chunk of wood to Luke. He snatched it out of the air, took off through the trees to a spot he'd already scouted out as giving him a clear shot, and tossed it at the anthill. Mentally, she counted down the seconds until the makeshift bomb exploded.

Right as she reached zero, an echoing boom shook the trees, and her mind was overwhelmed with notifications dings. All of it boiled down to two lines.

[You have assisted in slaying 22490 creatures between levels 1 and 3. 26367 XP awarded.]

[Congratulations! You have reached level 33. 33 AP awarded for use.]
[Congratulations! You have reached level 34. 34 AP awarded for use.]

She grimaced at the boost to her total XP. At least it had only been two levels this time. That was still another 67 AP to spend, and she was starting to feel like some retired vet. People just didn't raise their XP this high on purpose, and definitely not in their early twenties. She'd probably cut her remaining life span down to under forty. Luke had better deliver on reverting the changes.

Luke came hurtling back out from between the trees at unbelievable speed, straight toward her. Her eyes widened, and she tried to jump out of the way, but she was far too slow. He hit her without so much as slowing down, and she found herself caught up in a princess carry in his arms as he kept running. "Shit shit shit shit shit shit shit," he said, over and over as he dodged between trees.

"What the fuck are you doing?!" she just about shrieked. She could barely hear herself over the wind.

"Inquisitor heard the explosion. He's right behind us!"

Not for the first time, Zea considered sinking some more points into perception, but it was already to the point where she'd had to develop some new habits just to filter out all the background noise. The fact that anybody could sneak up on her at all, even with system-backed skills to help, was something she had a hard time accepting, and Luke had 30 more points in the stat than she did. His world had to be a nightmare of hearing every single thing around him for miles. She didn't see how it hadn't driven him crazy.

He twisted his torso, skipped a step, and ducked so low that she was afraid he was going to step on her hair. A knife went flying by over his head. Though it had missed him, he let out a grunt anyway, and a moment later Zea saw a second knife had pierced the armor on his shoulder. He gave that arm a shake, and the dagger dislodged to fall to the ground.

"Did it hit you?" she asked.

"No, got stuck in the metal. Armor was good for something after all."

They'd left their bags behind, though that was all replaceable. She'd kept the money in a separate pouch hung on her neck, thankfully, so they weren't completely shafted if they couldn't circle back and recover their stuff, but she wasn't happy about losing her enchanting gear. Now that she thought about it . . .

"I have four binding straps on me," she told Luke. "Here, set me down and see if you can get him with these."

She felt a tug against her hand as she held them up, only to see they'd disappeared. A moment later, she was tottering forward, trying to keep herself from sprawling face-first into the dirt. Her hand slapped against a nearby tree trunk, and she stumbled forward two steps before she caught her balance. Luke was nowhere to be seen, but she heard the sound of metal striking metal coming from a hundred feet back.

Watching him fight that inquisitor made her head hurt. They both moved so fast that it was impossible to keep up with their movements. She'd made that concussion enchantment last time fully knowing it would affect both of them but that, if she targeted it properly, it wouldn't hit Luke nearly as hard. She might be able to do something like that again, but she expected the inquisitor would be far more wary of her this time.

Zea wasn't about to sit around and do nothing though. She cast about and quickly found a branch on the ground, then started tracing runes across its surface.

Lath could scarcely believe the stupidity of the two apostates. To use an anthill as a way to quickly gain XP was beyond foolhardy, both because they did not have the hands of a god to shield them from the sickness of the mind that came with higher levels and because ants would chase after their pheromone-tagged targets for weeks.

He could admit some cleverness in their chosen method of execution. They'd most likely sidestepped the pheromone problem just by refusing to get close enough to pick any up to begin with, but still, they were extremely reckless. Then again, he supposed if he'd known he was so thoroughly outclassed by a hunter who might catch up to him at any moment, he would be considering some reckless strategies to gain a few levels too.

Their ploy wouldn't save them. He'd taken the apostate's measure, and clever tricks aside, the boy was too young and inexperienced. He let his stats and his skills fight for him, with no true measure of personal ability. Lath had no doubt the apostate had gathered hundreds of AP to spend, but in the end, it was far from enough. Lath had all the real experience between the two of them, and that would be what determined the winner of their fight.

They met on the game trail that wound its way through the trees, and that section of the forest became their battlefield. The apostate used the trees to his advantage, constantly seeking cover behind them to limit his risk of being exposed to any of the poisons Lath employed on his throwing knives. It was like playing a high-speed game of tag, where they danced around obstacles to avoid each other while simultaneously moving closer to try to sneak in an attack.

Something brown flashed through the air, and Lath smacked it away with his sword. He'd already dismissed it from his mind a moment later, until his sword suddenly felt like it weighed a hundred pounds. He blinked and looked down at it to see the brown thing, a strip of some kind of leather, had wrapped itself around the blade four times and was now glowing with runes of some kind.

A second strip of leather struck Lath's arm while he was distracted. Like a living thing, it snaked around his biceps and activated its magic. He was dragged off-balance while he adjusted to the feeling of extra weight and the fact that the two pieces of leather seemed to be trying to pull toward each other. Lath recovered instantly, but not quickly enough to avoid the apostate coming around the far side of the tree to blindside him with a hammer blow from that mace.

Lath threw himself back and rolled with the attack. His sword got left behind, now too heavy to use effectively. On the bright side, putting some distance between himself and the weapon broke the attraction between the two enchanted pieces of leather.

That was a neat trick, something he wouldn't mind adding to his own arsenal. As a capture tool, it had a lot of advantages over more mundane methods. Lath resolved to find somebody to duplicate the effect for his own use. Of more immediate concern was the enchanter supporting the apostate. She would be the softer target by far. Lath needed to break away from this fight and kill the dwifkin first.

Then he'd come back for the boy, and he would fulfill his twin purposes of executing divine will and avenging his apprentice.

Name	Luke Bennet	Zea Stenter
Level	41	34
XP	243138/254133	135941/144088
AP	125	82
Bloodline	SysAdmin III	None
Strength	61	7
Agility	70	27
Stamina	66	27
Perception	55	19
Skills	Mace Mastery (5)	Dagger Mastery (1)
	Sword Mastery (1)	Stealth (2)
	Unarmed Martialist (4)	Keen Instincts (1)
	Power Strike (2)	Lock Picking (1)
	Life Surge (2)	Disguise (2)
	Peripheral Awareness (2)	Deception (1)
	Tactical Foresight (1)	Bartering (2)
	Counter (3)	Streetwise (2)
	Twitch Reflexes (3)	Cooking (1)
	Stealth (1)	Mending (1)
	Survivalist (2)	First Aid (1)
	First Aid (1)	Thalian (3)
	Wood Carving (1)	Neyardic (3)
	Leatherworking (2)	Ostari (1)
	Butchering (4)	Mana Manipulation (3)
	Thalian (2)	Mana Sight (2)
	Ostari (1)	Metallurgy (1)
	Disguise (2)	Whitesmithing (1)
	Deception (1)	Goldsmithing (2)
	Detection (2)	Gem Cutting (1)
	Torturer (1)	Engraving (2)
	Analyze (BL)	Rune Forging (1)
	Remote Access (BL)	Painting (1)
	XP Mask (BL)	Arcano Dynamics (1)
		Sleight of Hand (1)
		Steady Hands (2)
		Cold Reading (1)
		Temperature Acclimation (2)
		Cadence (3)
		Bloodline Purification Ritual (2)
		Ghost Script (1)

CHAPTER 61

Luke gained two levels from their bombing of the anthill, and with it 81 AP. He only needed 125 for **[XP Cycle]**, and he'd been debating how to spend the other 654 on the trip over to the anthill. He needed something to give him an edge against that inquisitor. The man was a higher level and had probably spent decades strengthening skills the hard way. No doubt his options dwarfed Luke's own.

Not two seconds after the explosion had gone off, Luke realized how badly they'd fucked up. The inquisitor had thrown away stealth for speed, was moving almost close to Luke's top speed on an open road, but was doing it through the trees, and was still so fucking quiet that Luke didn't realize what was happening until the man was only a few hundred feet away. Thank God the anthill had been between him and the inquisitor, and the inquisitor had been forced to go around.

Luke immediately slammed 50 of that free AP into rank 5 **[Mace Mastery]** and the remaining 15 AP into his stats, adding 9 strength and 6 perception. He left the other 125 free for **[XP Cycle]** and hoped he wouldn't have to use it for more upgrades before the end of this fight. The last round he'd fought against the inquisitor had been pretty close to a draw, so he figured the upgrade to his primary weapon skill and some extra stats would help even that out.

Then he remembered that **[Analyze]** was supposed to return more information now and tossed that out on the inquisitor.

[Name: Adrevald Lath]
[Level: 45]
[XP: 326982/337550]
[AP: 0]

[Strength: 37]
[Agility: 61]
[Stamina: 40]
[Perception: 51]
[Skills:]
[Blade Master (3)]
[Wall of Steel (5)]
[One with the Wind (4)]
[Zealot (3)]
[Tower of the Mind (5)]
[Black-Blooded (3)]
[Blind Fighting (4)]
[Infiltrator (5)]
[Rumormonger (5)]
[Night Stalker (4)]
[Polyglot (3)]
[Trickster (3)]
[Envenom (5)]
[Alchemical Potency (4)]
[Human Anatomy (5)]
[Torturer (5)]
[Rope Use (3)]
[Sailing (2)]
[Tracking (2)]

Calling it a draw might have been giving himself more credit than he should have.

There wasn't time to read through the inquisitor's skill list, but his brief skim told him that he didn't recognize most of the skills. The ones he did know were advanced skills made from merging basic ones together. It was a ridiculous amount of AP, probably twice what he'd actually have for being only level 45.

Luke got it. Really. Their whole society was afraid of leveling too high, so they learned their skills the hard way. It made sense to him. But his circumstances were different, and he wasn't interested in spending the next three decades learning everything the hard way. He had a bloodline custom-made to abuse the system, and by God, he was going to do so. It wouldn't matter if this inquisitor, Lath, had enough skills to be level 65 instead of 45 if Luke had actually been level 80.

And he could level up that high now. He just needed time.

Luke turned and ran. Despite the crazy skills Lath had, Luke was still faster than him. He needed to get out of the woods and onto a road to fully utilize that advantage, but he figured that was still a better plan than standing around to fight. Once they were safe again, he'd start asking System what those skills did.

Zea was waiting right where he'd left her, and he barely even slowed down as he scooped her up. She gave a frightened yelp, but Luke ignored her. He moved as fast as he could, barely managing to sidestep a tree before he crashed into it. "Shit," he said.

Another tree, another split-second dodge. "Shit," he said again.

The trees just kept coming, frustratingly thick and slowing him down. At the rate they were going, Lath was going to catch up in under a minute. "Shit. Shit, shit, shit, shit."

"What the fuck are you doing?!" Zea screeched.

"Inquisitor heard the explosion. He's right behind us!"

Zea started squirming, trying to get a look, but Luke needed her held tight against him. Weaving through the trees was hard enough at this speed; he was afraid he'd accidentally kill her if she poked her head up at the wrong second and beaned herself on a nice, thick tree branch.

[Peripheral Awareness] clocked something small, metal, and fast coming at him from over his left shoulder. Luke tried to duck out of the way, damn near tripped over a root poking up out of the ground, hopped a step to dodge that, and straightened back up. That was a pretty impressive display of coordination, if he did say so himself. His temporary smugness was immediately ruined when a second knife slammed into his shoulder.

He could feel the tip of the knife scratching against his skin, but it had gotten caught in the metal of the pauldron he was wearing and hadn't quite penetrated far enough to actually stick him. He worked his shoulder around in circles until it jiggled loose and fell into the dirt. Luke was thirty feet away by the time it hit the ground, and he didn't dare take the time to examine it for poison, not at the speed he was moving.

"Did it hit you?" Zea asked.

"No, got stuck in the metal. Armor was good for something after all."

It was still a bit of a sore point with him that by the time he'd gotten access to a decent set of armor, he was fighting someone who could cut through the steel easily. Sure, it helped with glancing blows, but he didn't trust the steel to protect him against any sort of direct strikes, and this was twice now a piece had gotten damaged by Lath. This time was even worse because the steel had been pushed in before the dagger punched through, and now he could feel it scraping against his shoulder.

"I have four binding straps on me," Zea said. "Here, set me down and see if you can get him with these."

He looked down and saw her holding some leather straps in her hand. Luke grimaced. The rest must have been in her bags, and he'd left those behind.

Four was better than zero though, and as long as he didn't waste them, they might be the difference between survival and death. He wasn't sure they'd be enough to tip the scales in his favor, but if he could tag Lath with all of them, that would slow the inquisitor down enough for them to make a clean getaway.

Lath was barely a few hundred feet behind them and gaining slowly. The only reason he hadn't caught up already was that Luke was more familiar with the forest than he was. Come to think of it, they weren't that far away from where he'd set up those tanning racks for that snakeskin. He'd almost forgotten about those.

"Not the time, dipshit," he muttered under his breath. He set Zea down behind a tree, snatched the binding straps out of her hand, and raced back toward Lath. He needed to drag that battle as far away from Zea as possible. Even if it was only a hundred feet or so, it would make it a lot harder for Lath to target her with all the trees in the way.

Luke tucked the leather away in a pocket as he ran. A second later, he whipped around a tree, mace already midswing, and struck at Lath. It wasn't that he honestly expected to hit the inquisitor. Luke's goal was just to push him off-balance and slap him with one of those binding straps. Even a miss might distract his target enough to sneak attack him.

Their fight quickly turned into a game of cat and mouse, except they were both the cats hunting each other around the trees. Luke's newly upgraded weapon skill helped him keep ahead of the inquisitor without having to resort to **[Life Surge]**, but it wasn't enough by itself. Whatever rank 3 **[Blade Master]** was, it was apparently strong enough to compete with rank 5 **[Mace Mastery]**.

Lath had his own bandolier of throwing knives, and Luke decided to play it patient. Eventually, there'd be no more knives left, and then he could get more aggressive, but for the moment, he stayed on defense and used the trees as cover to block thrown knives. There was no telling what kind of nasty poisons the inquisitor had dipped those blades in.

The knives ran low, and Luke saw his opening. He grabbed the first binding strap as he circled around a tree, using it to break line of sight with Lath and disguise the motion of him drawing his new weapon. As he came around the trunk, he flung the leather at Lath's neck, but the inquisitor's reflexes were too good. He parried the strap with his sword, and then something unexpected happened.

The leather stuck to the steel and started coiling around it like a snake. Luke saw the runes start to shimmer with magic, and suddenly Lath was pulled down to one side. Luke snapped another piece of leather into the air, again aimed for the man's neck. But again, Lath was too quick, and it ended up striking his arm instead. With two of them on one limb, the inquisitor staggered a single step to the side while he struggled to compensate for the increased weight.

The chance was too good to pass by. Luke came around the tree and struck at Lath's face. A solid contact would have been ideal, but failing that, he forced the inquisitor onto the back foot, and the man actually dropped his sword as he scrambled to recover. That had the unfortunate effect of freeing him from a lot of weight, which made it harder for Luke to take advantage, but did leave his opponent without a weapon.

Luke hadn't seen anything like **[Unarmed Martialist]** in Lath's skill list, but that didn't mean much. It could just as easily be tucked into one of those advanced skills, and the man moved smoothly enough that Luke wouldn't be surprised to find out he was correct. Still, losing a weapon gave Luke an advantage. Lath was only carrying the one sword and his collection of throwing knives, so he was effectively unarmed now.

That, combined with the two remaining binding straps Luke had in his pocket, might just be enough to win this thing. He just needed to get both of them on the inquisitor in the next few seconds before the first one died out. It wasn't going to be easy, but considering the handicap being lopsided in terms of weight Lath had going on now, Luke thought it was possible.

If he could get the man pressed up against a tree, even for a moment, that would limit Lath's ability to dodge. It would be the perfect opportunity to slap another set of weights on the inquisitor. Lath was already favoring his right side, keeping his body turned away from Luke like a fencer and with his empty hand raised to ward off incoming blows. His other arm wasn't exactly hanging limp, but it swung ponderously instead of moving with the quick, darting snaps that Luke had become accustomed to fighting against.

Luke moved forward and tried to probe the man for openings, to see whether Lath would block swings from his mace or try to dodge them. Even better, if he was lucky, Lath would try to grab the weapon by the handle, and Luke would be able to drag him into a grapple. His strength was almost twice as high. Unless Lath's skills helped there too, that would be a crushing victory for Luke.

And then Lath did something Luke hadn't expected. He made what was probably the best call he could make, given the situation. He turned and ran. Luke gawked incredulously for a second, then his brain caught up to his eyes, and he realized that Lath wasn't just fleeing from Luke—he was running directly toward Zea.

Luke scrambled to catch up to him.

Name	Luke Bennet	Zea Stenter
Level	41	34
XP	243138/254133	135941/144088
AP	125	82
Bloodline	SysAdmin III	None
Strength	61	7
Agility	70	27
Stamina	66	27
Perception	55	19
Skills	Mace Mastery (5)	Dagger Mastery (1)
	Sword Mastery (1)	Stealth (2)
	Unarmed Martialist (4)	Keen Instincts (1)
	Power Strike (2)	Lock Picking (1)
	Life Surge (2)	Disguise (2)
	Peripheral Awareness (2)	Deception (1)
	Tactical Foresight (1)	Bartering (2)
	Counter (3)	Streetwise (2)
	Twitch Reflexes (3)	Cooking (1)
	Stealth (1)	Mending (1)
	Survivalist (2)	First Aid (1)
	First Aid (1)	Thalian (3)
	Wood Carving (1)	Neyardic (3)
	Leatherworking (2)	Ostari (1)
	Butchering (4)	Mana Manipulation (3)
	Thalian (2)	Mana Sight (2)
	Ostari (1)	Metallurgy (1)
	Disguise (2)	Whitesmithing (1)
	Deception (1)	Goldsmithing (2)
	Detection (2)	Gem Cutting (1)
	Torturer (1)	Engraving (2)
	Analyze (BL)	Rune Forging (1)
	Remote Access (BL)	Painting (1)
	XP Mask (BL)	Arcano Dynamics (1)
		Sleight of Hand (1)
		Steady Hands (2)
		Cold Reading (1)
		Temperature Acclimation (2)
		Cadence (3)
		Bloodline Purification Ritual (2)
		Ghost Script (1)

CHAPTER 62

If Luke prioritized finesse and dexterity, he wasn't going to catch up to Lath before the inquisitor made contact with Zea. Despite having the lower agility stat, Lath's skills were too strong, and he effortlessly wove through the forest. Luke just couldn't compete, so he didn't try. He bulled ahead, tearing through branches and moving in as straight a line as possible.

It seemed counterintuitive. Breaking through the foliage should have slowed him down and left him battered and bruised, but Luke had started taking inspiration from heavy machinery back on his own world. At some point, it was just easier to bring an absolutely overwhelming amount of force to bear against a problem than to try to find an elegant solution. This was that point for Luke.

The cloak got ripped away almost immediately after it got snagged on something and proved weaker than the branch holding it. Wood exploded in every direction as he careened wildly through the forest, practically blinded and only taking a single step to one side or the other to avoid the trunks of trees. He caught a glimpse of Lath looking back over his shoulder at him, eyes wide.

Then Luke rammed into the man from behind. Lath darted to the side, trying to avoid being struck, but he lacked the room to make a clean dodge, and Luke bodied him into a tree trunk. Immediately, he slapped one of his two remaining restraining straps onto Lath's leg. Before he could get the other one, the inquisitor brought his good leg up into a backward kick that struck Luke right in the groin.

Luke let out a manly grunt that was not in any way a high-pitched squeal as he involuntarily hunched a bit. He spared a moment to mentally curse how useless **[Twitch Reflexes]** and **[Tactical Foresight]** were, then straightened himself back out and shoved harder. Lath got another kick in to Luke's knee before he was slammed into the tree. Luke hammered blows into his kidney with one fist while the other slapped the last restraining band around Lath's neck.

The inquisitor started glowing, at first softly, but within seconds to the point where light was pouring out of the neckline of his shirt and Luke could see the shadowy contours of the man's muscles through the fabric. He'd seen this happen before, when he'd met his very first human on Aros, and he knew what it meant.

For Lath though, the change took less than ten seconds before he brightened to full glow. Worse, the light hung around the inquisitor in some sort of golden aura, like that guy from those cartoons Curt used to watch when he went ultra saiyan or whatever it was called. If Lath started shooting energy blasts out of his hand, Luke was going to lose his shit.

Despite the enchanted leather straps weighing him down, Lath threw himself backward against Luke with enough force to send him stumbling. Luke staggered back two steps, planning on using his mace since there was enough space to bring it into play now, but before he got the chance, Lath spun in place and started laying blows into him.

That answered Luke's question about whether one of those advanced skills had an **[Unarmed Martialist]**-equivalent skill mixed into it. Even with his own skill at rank 4 and higher stats to back it up, Luke had a hard time just keeping up with the strikes. He blocked most of them, felt the force being delivered strain his weapon each time, and skipped back out of range for the attacks he couldn't deflect.

Lath pursued him, relentless, and Luke had no choice but to trigger **[Life Surge]** just to keep up. Somehow, he suspected that Lath's skill would work better and last longer, so if Luke wanted the fight to end in his favor, he needed something that would tip the odds in the next minute and a half. Once the enchantments started wearing off, it was going to be impossible to keep up with the inquisitor while he was glowing gold.

They crashed through the forest, no longer bothering to use the trees as cover. The wood wasn't strong enough to stand up to the battering they were giving each other, not with both of them juiced up on performance-enhancing skills. Luke focused on dragging the fight away from Zea, who had the good sense to scram. He wasn't sure exactly where she'd gotten off to, but thankfully she was nowhere near them.

There were plenty of nonhuman creatures living in the forest though, and with Luke showing no XP at all and Lath's own skills pushing his to a low level, it was perhaps inevitable that one of them was attracted to the noise of their battle and stupid enough to think it'd stumbled across an easy meal. It was some sort of weasel-looking thing that was six feet long and had eight legs coming out of its body instead of the normal four.

In a rare stroke of good fortune, it attacked Lath, who quickly moved to deal with it. Momentarily off-balance from crushing its skull with his heel, Lath couldn't reset his stance in time and took the full force of Luke's swing to his chest. The inquisitor was thrown through the air and crashed through the branches of at least four trees before he hit the ground and skidded across the dirt.

Luke was on him in a flash, leading with a jump that would drive both feet into Lath's stomach if it landed. If it didn't, and he didn't expect it would, he was fully prepared to bring his mace down on the skull of the inquisitor as he rolled out of the way. Perhaps sensing the trap, Lath did something Luke wasn't expecting. Still on his back, he brought his legs up to line his feet with Luke's, absorbed the shock of contact with expert timing in flexing and bending, and then pushed up and over.

Luke went into an uncontrolled tumble through the air for a second before he corrected himself and spun into a flip that saw him landing on his feet and facing Lath. The inquisitor was already closing the distance, and Luke saw with some surprise that he held a sword in his hand again. It took only a moment to realize that they were back near the clearing where Luke had left the bags behind.

Worse, the binding strap had fallen off the blade. That meant the one on Lath's arm was about to come off too. If that golden glow didn't disappear soon, Luke was going to find himself facing an unencumbered inquisitor wielding a poisoned sword.

Despite the incredible amount of damage they'd done, it had barely been a minute since the fight started. **[Life Surge]** was nowhere near giving out, and the skill Lath was using was going strong as well. They rampaged through the trees, Lath's fighting style shifting back to something closer to what he'd been using at the start, though with more weight behind the swings now that they weren't just designed to cut off Luke's options and set him up for a poisoned throwing knife.

Luke blocked or dodged each attack, but a new fear had presented itself. His weapon was becoming more and more damaged, and far faster than the blood silver could repair itself. His strength, especially with **[Life Surge]** running, was exceeding the tolerance the weapon could take. He didn't dare channel a **[Power Strike]** through it in this condition.

Then he saw something behind Lath, something that he didn't think the inquisitor had noticed. A carpet of red was rolling across the forest. Thousands upon thousands of ants were still searching for the intruder that had attacked their home, relentless despite the lack of pheromones to follow. A plan blossomed in Luke's mind, fully formed at birth.

He rushed forward, surprising Lath and accepting the long slash the inquisitor scored across his arm in exchange for getting in close.

[You have been afflicted by the following condition: Poison—Cobalt Scorpion Venom (46M).]

Fire burned inside Luke's blood, almost causing him to stumble to a halt in shock from the pain. Luke pushed through it, knowing that hesitating in that moment would mean his death. He dropped his mace and grabbed Lath with both hands. Then he heaved the inquisitor thirty feet through the air to crash into the middle of the swarming ants.

Adrevald Lath rolled to his feet immediately and leaped straight into the air to grab onto a tree branch, but there were already hundreds of ants clinging to him. Luke still didn't understand what exactly it was that made ants so scary. They were level 1, maybe 2. They had no stats and couldn't have more than a single skill. It didn't seem like they should be able to do more than tickle with their tiny ant pincers.

Lath felt otherwise. His face was twisted into a grimace of pain as he frantically swiped the ants off him and started stripping his clothes to shake them out. Out of curiosity, Luke picked a single ant to **[Analyze]**, something he should have done as soon as he'd gained the ability to see more of their status.

[Name: Crimson Ripper Ant]
[Level: 2]
[XP: 36/50]
[AP: 0]
[Strength: 0]
[Agility: 0]
[Stamina: 0]
[Perception: 1]
[Skills:]
[Swarm Bite (2)]

"System, what does **[Swarm Bite]** do?"

"The more times the same target is bitten, the more damage the bite does," System said. "Additionally, other creatures using the skill benefit from it."

"Ah," Luke said in sudden understanding. "So a thousand ants using **[Swarm Bite]** all at the same time are going to ramp that up into fuck-you ranges of pain pretty quickly."

"That is correct."

"Fuck. Well, good. Now, just to make sure . . ."

Despite the human landing in their midst, the ants didn't stop spreading in every direction. Fortunately, Luke's destination was still outside their radius.

He sprinted through the forest until he reached the bags they'd left behind, then tore open the one containing Zea's enchanting equipment. There were six more of the leather straps in there, and Luke took them all.

When he got back a few seconds later, he found that Lath had almost managed to find his way clear of the main swarm but still had ants crawling all over him. He must have jumped from the tree but missed grabbing onto a branch on the next one and fallen. He was back on his feet, maybe ten feet away from the leading edge of the crawling red carpet.

Without hesitation, Luke whipped the straps one after another at him. He tagged all four limbs in quick succession, paused a beat to aim the next one now that the inquisitor had been weighed down, and slapped that around the man's neck.

Now having nearly a ton of weight hanging off him, Lath slowed down considerably. His skin was red with bite marks and slaps from where he'd killed the ants crawling on him, but the golden light still hadn't died, and with a snarl, he took one step after another in Luke's direction. Neck muscles bulged against the strain, and with each step, his feet sunk an inch or two into the dirt, but he kept going.

Luke considered the last strap for a second, then with a shrug, tossed it into Lath's face. It was long enough to go all the way around the man's skull, and while that weight still wasn't enough to drag Lath down, it was one more thing to slow him.

Luke cast around, found a nice branch overhead about as thick as his thigh, and jumped up to grab onto it. With a heave, he snapped it at the base. A second snap about six feet down its length discarded a lot of the useless light growth. Then he lined it up like a spear and, using every bit of strength and agility he had, both pushed as high as possible with **[Life Surge]** still running, imbued a **[Power Strike]** into it, and hurled it at Lath.

The inquisitor was too weighed down to effectively dodge, and it struck him in the chest, throwing him backward to smash into a tree twenty feet behind him. Immediately, he slumped to the ground, and more ants swarmed him.

Something about the action seemed to have alerted them to Luke's presence as well, and he found thousands of the little red creatures skittering toward him, far faster than something with a 0 in its physical stats had any right to.

"Whoops, time to go. Good luck in there, asshole!" Luke called out.

Name	Luke Bennet	Zea Stenter
Level	41	34
XP	243781/254133	135941/144088
AP	125	82
Bloodline	SysAdmin III	None
Strength	61	7
Agility	70	27
Stamina	66	27
Perception	55	19
Skills	Mace Mastery (5)	Dagger Mastery (1)
	Sword Mastery (1)	Stealth (2)
	Unarmed Martialist (4)	Keen Instincts (1)
	Power Strike (2)	Lock Picking (1)
	Life Surge (2)	Disguise (2)
	Peripheral Awareness (2)	Deception (1)
	Tactical Foresight (1)	Bartering (2)
	Counter (3)	Streetwise (2)
	Twitch Reflexes (3)	Cooking (1)
	Stealth (1)	Mending (1)
	Survivalist (2)	First Aid (1)
	First Aid (1)	Thalian (3)
	Wood Carving (1)	Neyardic (3)
	Leatherworking (2)	Ostari (1)
	Butchering (4)	Mana Manipulation (3)
	Thalian (2)	Mana Sight (2)
	Ostari (1)	Metallurgy (1)
	Disguise (2)	Whitesmithing (1)
	Deception (1)	Goldsmithing (2)
	Detection (2)	Gem Cutting (1)
	Torturer (1)	Engraving (2)
	Analyze (BL)	Rune Forging (1)
	Remote Access (BL)	Painting (1)
	XP Mask (BL)	Arcano Dynamics (1)
		Sleight of Hand (1)
		Steady Hands (2)
		Cold Reading (1)
		Temperature Acclimation (2)
		Cadence (3)
		Bloodline Purification Ritual (2)
		Ghost Script (1)

CHAPTER 63

Luke found Zea without too much trouble, simply by turning off [XP Mask] for a few minutes. Between that returned sense and all the practice he'd gotten locating people by sight, sound, and smell, it wasn't difficult to pick her out from the other wildlife. Zea's relatively high level and lack of any sort of skills masking her XP made it particularly easy to find her once he got close enough.

He found her, eyes wide and back against a tree, holding her knife in one hand while her chest heaved. "Holy shit," she said, letting out a nervous laugh when he appeared. "I thought you were some sort of monster. Your XP is . . . a lot now."

"Oh, sorry. I turned off the skill to help me find you. Let me just . . . There we go."

Losing the ability to feel XP again after such a short respite was a blow. Luke had gotten used to functioning without it, but it was still nice to have it back. Not for the first time, he wondered if purifying his bloodline again would allow the skill to only hide his XP without blocking his perception of everyone else's.

"Did you kill the inquisitor?" she asked.

Luke shrugged and shook his head. "Knocked him into the ant swarm. Got a whole bunch of dings from when he landed and crushed a bunch of ants, but I don't see one for killing him in here, and my XP would have to jump up at least a little bit if he was dead."

"If he fell into the middle of thousands of ants, he's dead. It just might take a bit to stick. We should get out of here before they spread out any farther."

"Yeah. About that. It did kind of seem like they were coming right at me toward the end there. I'm not sure if I've picked up any of those pheromones or not."

"Fuuuuuuuuuuuuuccck," Zea said. "Okay, first, we're heading to water. Even with soap, you can't just scrub it away, but it'll help. We've got ten days until our boat leaves, and I've got enough AP to upgrade some enchanting skills. Maybe I can figure something out."

They headed directly away from the anthill in search of water. Luke dropped **[XP Mask]** again, not that too much of the local wildlife was interested in tangling with them. Given they both were high level now, plus the ants going ballistic thanks to Luke's bombing run on them, he supposed it made sense.

"It's quiet," Zea said as they walked.

"Yeah," Luke said. But he could remember the sounds of pain coming from Lath as he was covered with ants. That was a bad way to go. He scanned through his notifications again, trying to find one saying the inquisitor was dead. He should have done something more to make sure he'd finished the job instead of trusting the ants to kill him.

What exactly that something he should have done was, Luke didn't know. He certainly wasn't about to jump into the middle of the swarm to finish Lath off in hand-to-hand combat while they both got eaten alive. Maybe he could have found some big rocks to throw or something, although he would have had to do it quickly to stay ahead of the carpet of red ants crawling toward him.

Even that might not have been enough to finish Lath off. The man was obviously tough, as evidenced by the fact that he still wasn't dead half an hour after being thrown into the middle of the swarm. Luke couldn't even imagine how much pain he must be in to still be alive half an hour later. A small part of him almost hoped Lath had escaped, but only a really, really small part. Luke would have preferred to give him a quick death, but he'd still take a slow, agonizing death over the inquisitor being alive and pursuing them.

"Got that notification yet?" Zea asked.

Luke shook his head. "I almost think he had to have escaped. I don't know how. He could barely stand with all that weight on him. Even once the enchantments wore off, he would have been in so much pain . . ."

"Maybe he has a pain-suppression skill."

"Oh, shit. That's a thing, huh? Hey, System, did any of the skills that man had allow him to ignore pain?"

"Yes, Luke. The **[Zealot]** skill has a component of pain mitigation in it. At high enough ranks, the user wouldn't feel any pain at all while using it."

Luke and Zea shared an uneasy glance. "So, alive still, probably got away. Unbelievable. Okay, what do the rest of these skills do?"

They got a brief overview of Lath's skill list, with Zea asking the more insightful questions when she wanted something elaborated. In short, he had skills for using all manner of bladed weaponry, parrying, dodging, increasing his movement speed, filling himself with "righteous power" and ignoring pain, resisting any sort of mind-altering effects, one that made his blood poisonous somehow, sensory enhancement skills, skills for disguising himself, gathering information, blending in, operating at heightened capacity in total darkness, learning languages easily, increased agility in relation to various sleights of hand, increased potency of poisons and the ability to make his own unique ones, and extensive knowledge of the human body and how best to torture it. He was also apparently an amateur sailor and tracker.

"Fuck me, that's a lot," Zea said. "He has got to be near the top of the inquisitor hierarchy."

"Yeah, he certainly puts me to shame. What a monster." Luke wasn't thrilled that the one skill they shared between them was **[Torturer]**.

"A monster who's still alive and wants to kill us both."

"Well, there's always another anthill. I might not be able to match him right now, but we've got a week and a half before the ship leaves. I could put on twenty levels. Probably."

Considering how the XP per level kept going up, he couldn't honestly say for sure that he could do it, but he was willing to give it a try. He suspected Zea would be less enthused about the idea, and he was quickly proven correct.

"I don't want more XP, and if I make the bombs using **[Ghost Script]**, that's exactly what will happen. It takes me almost six hours and about three gold a piece to make them the hard way."

"I get it," Luke said. "Maybe make some more of those restraining straps? Or . . . I don't know, maybe not. He got wise to them pretty quick. I only got the last handful on him because he was distracted by the ants. Good thing his pain-resistance skill wasn't maxed out, I guess."

"Yeah. I'll keep thinking on it. Might be time to spend some AP, get some new options."

"Is this the same stream we were next to before?" Luke asked as they stepped out from behind some trees and he spotted the water.

"No idea. Does it matter?"

"Not really. Just curious. Guess it's time to go for a dip."

Zea didn't let him back out for over an hour. He used practically the entire bar of soap scrubbing himself until he felt like his skin should be raw. It wasn't, of course. He had far too much stamina for any amount of scrubbing to actually hurt him, but it felt like it should be.

He kept **[XP Mask]** going over both of them while he was trying to scrub off pheromone stink, just in case Lath had recovered from his ant ordeal and was back on their trail. It wouldn't do a lot to hide them, but every little bit helped.

His clothes were soaked, sudsed, and scrubbed just as much as his body. Even his boots got soaked, which Luke grumbled about but couldn't refute the logic of. He helped wring everything out when they were done and laid it out in a sunny spot to dry while he kept working on himself. Eventually, Zea pronounced his efforts good enough and insisted that he carry her in a jump over the stream to keep her from getting wet swimming it.

"Slightly damp clothes, check. Boots too soggy to wear, check. Armor that's probably going to start rusting now that it's been submerged in a river for half an hour, check. Gone through an entire bar of soap in one bath, check."

"Could be worse," Zea said bluntly. "At least you're not the other guy. He needs a lot more than a bath in a cold stream right now."

"Fair enough," Luke said. "Where are we going now?"

"I don't know. We're not going to convince a freight ship to leave early, so we've got ten days to spend, and it might be better if we stay out of the city. There's definitely a few dozen mercs left, and unless you got a notification you forgot to tell me about?" Zea glanced over at Luke, who just shook his head. "Then we've got to assume the inquisitor is going to take another pass at us. Let's give it a few days, then sneak into the city in the middle of the night, board the ship, and wait out the rest of our time there. As long as **[XP Mask]** can keep us both hidden, it shouldn't be hard to stow away. Even if they do find us, we're paying to be there. Just . . . we'll be there a few days early."

"Okay, that all sounds good, but what do we do in the meantime?"

"Set up a camp somewhere. Hunt some food. Enjoy a bit of downtime while I work on making some new surprises."

"Oh! That reminds me. System, can you point the way to that camp I made a few days ago?" Luke asked.

"Of course. It is approximately six miles to your southeast," System supplied.

"Thanks. Hopefully the wild animals didn't get into stuff."

"What's this camp?" Zea asked, confused.

"When I was out hunting for your moose, I found some other stuff, so I set up a little camp. You'll see when we get there."

As long as the snakeskin was still there, he'd be happy. Last time he'd checked, it was fine, but it only took one random animal deciding it wanted to destroy something to ruin it. Luke had known that when he'd set up the rack, but he hadn't been willing to babysit it the whole time, so he'd taken the risk that his labor would be for nothing. It would hardly be the first time something he'd been working on was destroyed midprocess.

"Speaking of moose, you can stop looking for those," Zea said. "I may have bought a few prongs to replace the ones I lost."

"Oh. Okay then. Ah, how are we doing for money?"

"About a hundred twenty left."

Luke blinked. "Gold?"

"Yes, of course gold," she said. "I told you that amaril hide was worth a lot."

"Yeah, right. Just . . . didn't expect it to be that much."

The snake hide was still intact when they reached his old camp, thankfully. Zea eyed it up on the rack, then shook her head and walked past it without a word. Luke chuckled and gave it a once-over. Everything looked good on it, and while it wasn't ideal that she knew about it now, he still had the time to make it into her present.

He frowned.

He'd been planning on spending AP to upgrade **[Leatherworking]** to rank 4, but now he only had exactly enough to learn **[XP Cycle]**, and he needed another 10000 XP to level again. The only reason he hadn't spent the AP already was that he wanted to hold on to it for emergency combat skill upgrades in case Lath attacked.

He also hadn't ever gotten the supplies from town he'd need to do a good job. His previous attempts at creating leather goods hadn't been . . . bad, necessarily, but they weren't high-quality, and he lacked the proper tools to do it right. There was no way he could make a case for her enchanting equipment with his current level of skills and equipment.

"Well, damn," he said, scratching his head. He'd just have to save it for later. It probably wouldn't take up too much space in his bags. He eyed up the length of the hide doubtfully.

"Damn," he said again.

Name	Luke Bennet	Zea Stenter
Level	41	34
XP	243781/254133	135941/144088
AP	125	82
Bloodline	SysAdmin III	None
Strength	61	7
Agility	70	27
Stamina	66	27
Perception	55	19
Skills	Mace Mastery (5)	Dagger Mastery (1)
	Sword Mastery (1)	Stealth (2)
	Unarmed Martialist (4)	Keen Instincts (1)
	Power Strike (2)	Lock Picking (1)
	Life Surge (2)	Disguise (2)
	Peripheral Awareness (2)	Deception (1)
	Tactical Foresight (1)	Bartering (2)
	Counter (3)	Streetwise (2)
	Twitch Reflexes (3)	Cooking (1)
	Stealth (1)	Mending (1)
	Survivalist (2)	First Aid (1)
	First Aid (1)	Thalian (3)
	Wood Carving (1)	Neyardic (3)
	Leatherworking (2)	Ostari (1)
	Butchering (4)	Mana Manipulation (3)
	Thalian (2)	Mana Sight (2)
	Ostari (1)	Metallurgy (1)
	Disguise (2)	Whitesmithing (1)
	Deception (1)	Goldsmithing (2)
	Detection (2)	Gem Cutting (1)
	Torturer (1)	Engraving (2)
	Analyze (BL)	Rune Forging (1)
	Remote Access (BL)	Painting (1)
	XP Mask (BL)	Arcano Dynamics (1)
		Sleight of Hand (1)
		Steady Hands (2)
		Cold Reading (1)
		Temperature Acclimation (2)
		Cadence (3)
		Bloodline Purification Ritual (2)
		Ghost Script (1)

CHAPTER 64

Pain.

Endless, agonizing pain.

[Zealot] had kept Lath from feeling any true pain for decades. Even losing a limb barely slowed him down, not that he'd suffered from that in years. He was too strong, too quick, and too smart to ever be seriously injured in a fight.

Then that apostate had crossed paths with his apprentice, thanks to that incompetent buffoon Gnox. She'd gotten herself killed, and Lath had inherited the problem. The job had been troublesome. He'd been too personally invested, made mistakes in the name of vengeance.

Now he was paying for it.

For the first second or two, **[Zealot]** shielded him from the agony of being swarmed by ants, but they quickly overpowered the pain mitigation the skill gave him. He'd barely made it out of the main swarm and still had hundreds of them biting him. The pain got worse with each second, but Lath knew he could escape. He just had to fight through it, retreat from the swarm, and kill off the ones still crawling on him.

The apostate had ended that plan before he could even get started, had forced Lath back into the middle of the swarm with those leather straps that made his limbs feel so heavy. They dragged him down, and there was nothing Lath could do but lay there and scream as the ants devoured him alive.

They were inside him, under his skin and in his veins, burrowing deep, eating him from the inside out, and Lath had no more strength to scream.

Time passed, and he floated along its river, his senses obliterated by the unending onslaught. A second could have passed, or it could have been a year. He had no way to tell. Then there was something new.

The queen. He could smell her. She wanted Lath, had commands for him. Her will must be done. He knew it, by the thousands of ants crawling through his body, their tiny forms replacing blood and sinew, their connection to their queen now his connection too.

Lath climbed to his feet, his body stiff and unfamiliar. That wasn't important. The only thing that mattered was that the queen wanted the creature that had attacked her hive killed. The pheromone trail was clear, but the attacker moved too quickly for her ants to keep up. There had been barriers, water specifically, that had slowed down her soldiers' pursuit. Lath would not be hindered in such a way.

He strode through the carpet of ants, his body still covered in them and more hidden under his skin. They were no longer his enemy, not now that he was part of the hive. With each step, he grew more confident in moving his body. The damage didn't slow him down anymore, nor did the encroaching darkness.

The pheromones stood out clearly to him, and he followed at a steady pace, eager to catch up to the vanguard of ants chasing after the being who'd dared to attack the hive.

They moved around a lot over the next few days. Luke thought it was overkill, but Zea insisted that no amount of washing would completely wipe away the pheromones the ants had hit him with. Everywhere he went, he was leaving a trail they'd follow.

It seemed like bullshit to him. Luke would be the first person to admit he'd failed science class, and that was before even taking into account system fuckery on Aros. Maybe their version of ants was different, beyond the obvious system-granted skill. Or maybe people were just wrong about how the pheromones worked. Neither would have surprised him, but Luke hadn't really been steered wrong by following Zea's advice yet, so they spent a lot of time traveling and hopping rivers, and he quickly ran through their entire supply of soap.

That, more than anything, was what convinced him that Zea believed what she was saying. She didn't like being dirty and had complained incessantly during their monthlong trip through the wilderness. There was no way she'd make him use up all their soap if she didn't think it was necessary. So, as much as it annoyed him, Luke diligently followed her instructions.

"One week left until our ship is scheduled to leave," Zea said while they were both hunched near the fire. Luke was committing some form of war crimes on the meat in the pan while Zea watched sadly. "You need to pull that back from the heat and flip it."

"Got it," he said, following her instructions. The meat tore as he tried to flip it, leaving behind a charred layer of black on the metal. "Huh, I don't think that's right."

"Obviously not," Zea told him. "I do not know how you manage to do this. I watched you do every step. Everything you did looked right, but somehow, you have a burnt mess that needs to be scraped out of the pan.

They cleaned it out, and she took over cooking while Luke watched. As far as he could tell, he'd done everything she had. He'd held the pan he same distance from their little campfire, he'd shaken it when needed, had put in the same seasonings from their supply, but when it came time for Zea to flip hers, it was deliciously seared instead of a charred black mess.

"I don't get it," he said.

"Me neither. As much as we've been practicing, and I've watched you cook every time, you should have gotten the **[Cooking]** skill already. I'm starting to think the gods have cursed you."

"Wait, is that a real thing?"

"Being cursed? Yes."

"No, no. I knew that. I got cursed by some goblins once. I meant is it a thing that the gods will hand down curses? I thought they weren't supposed to interfere."

Zea shrugged. "If it is, it's not something that shows up on your status. But I'm out of other possible explanations at this point. It's either an off-worlder thing, or it's the gods cursing you to never create a decent meal. If you want to cook for yourself, it's time to give up and spend the 1 AP on the skill."

"Never!" Luke declared. **[Cooking]** wasn't something he needed, and he was hell-bent on mastering at least one skill for real. **[Torturer]** didn't count, and he had no desire to ever advance that past rank 1 anyway. If he was feeling generous, he could say that he'd picked up **[Wood Carving]** on his own, but despite all the time he spent making little things with that skill, it had never gained a rank. It was the same with his language skills. He'd used **[Thalian]** for months now, and it hadn't gone up on its own. **[Ostari]** wasn't moving either, though in that case it had barely been a few weeks.

"If you're going to be stubborn about it, then you can eat your own cooking. This steak will be just for me," Zea told him.

"That's so cruel," Luke said sadly. "I can't believe someone I think so highly of would stoop so low."

"It's 1 AP," Zea said. "You've spent more on stupider things."

"Well, yeah, but it's the principle of the matter. Besides, right now I've got exactly enough to buy **[XP Cycle]**. If I spend that 1 AP on **[Cooking]**, then I'll need to gain another level."

Zea scowled at him. "Fine, I will cook for you, for now. But it's awful suspicious. A cynical person might think you set it up that way on purpose."

"Good thing you're not a cynical person," he told her with a cheeky grin.

Something broke through the undergrowth a few hundred feet to the north, and Luke's head snapped around instantly to home in on the sound. He held up a hand to Zea, scooped up his mace from the ground next to him, and rose to his feet. "Probably a wild animal or monster," he said softly, barely audible over the crackling of the fire. "I'll be right back."

Without [XP Mask] running, most of the local wildlife had avoided the pair, but they'd still fended off a few predators that had been overconfident in their abilities, which Luke hadn't complained about. They'd both gotten some free XP from that, though Zea was considerably more reluctant to participate now than she had been in the past. Luke was expecting this to be more of the same, but since he'd never gotten the kill notification for Lath, every time he heard something out of the ordinary, his heart skipped a beat.

They were fifty or sixty miles away from Sicanti, and at least thirty away from where they'd last encountered the inquisitor, but it wasn't impossible that he'd catch up to them again. Luke wasn't expecting him to, not unless the inquisitor had packed a few more ranks onto his [Tracking] skill. Or learned to smell pheromones, assuming the twenty or so baths he'd taken in the last few days had left anything to follow.

The sound of branches creaking and snapping came through the woods, and this time Luke was a lot closer. He caught a flash of movement through the trees and immediately changed direction. Whatever it was, it smelled odd. He couldn't quite put his finger on it, but it was familiar, like a scent he knew hidden under a perfume he didn't.

Something staggered out from between the trees and paused to turn its head and look directly at Luke. It was man shaped but resembled a piece of upright chewed meat more than it did a person. Most of its skin was gone, and what was left was more like a stringy collection of flayed strips glued to the meat of the body.

Even that meat didn't look like muscle. It took Luke a moment to realize exactly what he was seeing. Thousands and thousands of ants had taken the place of the muscles, all of them crawling all over one another and under the leftover skin that hadn't been torn away. Where its stomach should have been, there was nothing but a cavernous void of loose flesh and a visible spine. Somehow, the body still moved despite huge chunks of it having been destroyed.

It still had both eyes and most of its hair, but its nose and ears were gone. Luke could see ants crawling under the skin of its face, visible as they crossed the hole left where the nose used to be. Lines of them marched across the thing's cheeks, going in and out of the various holes that had been chewed through its skin.

"Holy shit," Luke beathed out. He'd seen a lot of gross shit since he'd been dropped onto Aros, but this took the cake. "This was not what I pictured when Zea told me about zombie ants."

Despite everything, the thing standing in front of him was unmistakably the corpse of Adrevald Lath, somehow still upright and moving around like some sort of giant flesh mecha being piloted by thousands of little red ants. Luke didn't see how it was even possible for it to stand up, let alone stagger through the woods. He supposed it confirmed Zea's theory about the phero-mones still leaving a trail for the ants to follow, at least.

What he didn't understand was why he'd never gotten a kill notification for an obviously extremely dead inquisitor. Had the ants somehow stolen his kill? Or was the XP divided into so many pieces that he'd gotten less than a single point? He felt like the system would still notify him even if his share was 0 XP, but he could see why it might not.

The corpse turned to face Luke fully, its movements awkward and jerky, like it couldn't properly control its body. Then it slipped forward impossibly fast, a bolt of red lightning heading directly at him.

Name	Luke Bennet	Zea Stenter
Level	41	34
XP	245561/254133	138478/144088
AP	125	82
Bloodline	SysAdmin III	None
Strength	61	7
Agility	70	27
Stamina	66	27
Perception	55	19
Skills	Mace Mastery (5)	Dagger Mastery (1)
	Sword Mastery (1)	Stealth (2)
	Unarmed Martialist (4)	Keen Instincts (1)
	Power Strike (2)	Lock Picking (1)
	Life Surge (2)	Disguise (2)
	Peripheral Awareness (2)	Deception (1)
	Tactical Foresight (1)	Bartering (2)
	Counter (3)	Streetwise (2)
	Twitch Reflexes (3)	Cooking (1)
	Stealth (1)	Mending (1)
	Survivalist (2)	First Aid (1)
	First Aid (1)	Thalian (3)
	Wood Carving (1)	Neyardic (3)
	Leatherworking (2)	Ostari (1)
	Butchering (4)	Mana Manipulation (3)
	Thalian (2)	Mana Sight (2)
	Ostari (1)	Metallurgy (1)
	Disguise (2)	Whitesmithing (1)
	Deception (1)	Goldsmithing (2)
	Detection (2)	Gem Cutting (1)
	Torturer (1)	Engraving (2)
	Analyze (BL)	Rune Forging (1)
	Remote Access (BL)	Painting (1)
	XP Mask (BL)	Arcano Dynamics (1)
		Sleight of Hand (1)
		Steady Hands (2)
		Cold Reading (1)
		Temperature Acclimation (2)
		Cadence (3)
		Bloodline Purification Ritual (2)
		Ghost Script (1)

CHAPTER 65

The corpse's movements were all speed, no grace. It lurched forward faster than Luke could blink, arms outstretched and ants streaming through the air as they were blown off the main host. Luke leaped backward a full fifteen feet, but the corpse followed him. When Luke landed, it was just as close as it had been at the start.

That half a second in the air had given him the time he needed to bring his mace around, and he was more than ready for its odd, limping approach when he landed. Forged blood silver whipped around in an arc between the corpse's arms and smacked into the underside of its chest cavity, right into the hole where Lath's stomach used to be.

The real Lath would have blocked that with ease. Whatever this creature was, it didn't have his skill or his finesse. What it did keep was Lath's raw stats, judging by how fast it was moving. Luke didn't want to get into an arm wrestling contest to find out if it still had Lath's strength too.

Despite how fragile the body looked now that it was more than half-gone, it still had weight to it. That didn't stop Luke from knocking it off its feet and sending hundreds of ants spraying off in an upward arc as the body flew backward, including a handful that landed on Luke and immediately started biting him.

His free hand was a blur as he crushed each and every one of those ants before they could gain any momentum. System's explanation of their stacking biting skill had been pretty basic and lacked such information like how long it took for the bite count to reset or even if it ever did at all, but no matter how Luke sliced it, it wasn't smart to let them bite more than he had to.

Lath's corpse was back on him with all the speed Luke had come to expect from the man while he was still alive but none of the precision. There was no intricate weaving of limbs and flashing steel, no clever footwork to force Luke into an awkward position, no signature look of superiority on Lath's face. There was only unyielding, merciless momentum, a forward push completely lacking in subtlety that was easy to see coming and easy to dodge around.

The corpse adjusted its path instantly as Luke flitted around it. He casually smacked it a few more times, and each hit knocked loose dozens or even hundreds of ants. The fight quickly turned into a cycle of Luke keeping away from Lath's mobile corpse while killing ants by the score. He was sure he didn't get all of them considering that they were in the middle of a forest, but having 55 perception made him pretty damn good at spotting them after they were detached from the host.

"Might want to start packing up the camp," Luke yelled to Zea. He was confident that the Lath corpse monster was fully focused on him, but on the off chance that they did need to make a run for it, he wouldn't want to have to leave anything behind.

"What's going on?" she yelled back.

"Dead body of that inquisitor stuffed full of ants. It's really fucking creepy but not super threatening," he said as he sidestepped the corpse's lunge and knocked it across the back of the head. Despite the condition of the body, it was remarkably resilient. More system bullshit, he was sure. It seemed like the ants had taken over the body, losing access to all of Lath's skills in the process but retaining his high base stats.

The corpse stumbled forward, and before it could spin to attack again, Luke brought his mace down on its back and drove it straight into the ground. It bounced once and lurched back upright after leaving a baseball-sized knot of ants on the ground.

Luke couldn't spare the time to study them, but he was pretty sure there was something weird about those ants. They were a different shade of red than the regular ones, almost a grayish brown instead of the vibrant red he was used to seeing. Their exoskeleton shells were broken open, and a thin netting of some gray stringy stuff connected them all together. Luke wasn't sure what he was looking at, but he went out of his way to stomp on it and crush as many of them as possible.

Notifications were coming up by the hundreds as he killed the ants all over Lath's body, all of which Luke ignored as a matter of course. He knew what they were going to say, and it was far easier to read the after-action notification that told him exactly how many ants he'd killed, what their level ranges were, and how much XP he'd gained from it.

He did make a mental note to go back through the individual notifications and find the ones for the weird-colored ones, but that was a task for later. Lath wasn't a quarter as dangerous now as he'd been a few days ago, but his corpse was just as fast and strong as always. Worse, it was shedding ants with every wild swing and jerky lunge it made. Luke wasn't sure how the whole pheromone thing worked exactly, but he was sure he was covered in it again, which made it important to make sure he killed as many of those ants as possible.

Probably. Maybe it didn't make a difference. He didn't really know, but better safe than sorry.

"You've got this under control?" Zea yelled from their campfire a few hundred feet away.

"Yeah, I think so," he yelled back.

"Give me a few minutes. I'll get you something to kill all the ants at once."

Luke liked the sound of that. A nice bomb to drop on Lath would go a long way toward wiping them all out, and it was no problem to keep up their homicidal game of tag for another few minutes. Luke even took a more heavily defensive stance since he was confident Zea's enchanted bomb would finish the ants off, and the more he smacked Lath's body around, the more he spread them around.

That wasn't to say he got lazy about it. Luke fully understood that even the shambling, ant-infested corpse of the inquisitor could kill him if he wasn't careful, but it wasn't a hard fight. The body moved fast, but without any intelligence behind it, its attacks were telegraphed well in advance.

Luke killed time leading it around trees and trying to trip it up in the undergrowth. That last part was less than successful, since the corpse still retained Lath's raw strength and it had no trouble breaking through anything its feet got caught on. If anything, it was just spreading more ants around, so Luke quickly abandoned that tactic.

"Got it," Zea called out from a hundred feet away. "Coming your way. You've got ten seconds before it blows."

Something went spinning through the trees. Luke snagged it out of the air, then shot Zea an incredulous glance. "Is this my cup?"

It was the little steel cup he'd gotten with the cooking equipment back in Kazos, now covered with flowing lines of light in various shapes. "It was what I had handy!" Zea yelled back. "Five seconds! Four . . . Three . . . Two . . ."

Luke hurled it directly at Lath's corpse. It made no attempt to dodge, and just as the cup struck, it exploded in a roar of fire and light. Luke stumbled backward, momentarily dazed from being so close to the explosion and the ringing of another few thousand kill notifications in his ears. He blinked away the bright spots, then examined what was left of Lath.

The body was still in one piece, more or less. It looked about the same as it had when Luke had first seen it, minus the ants and with a little extra fire damage. Without them crawling all over and inside the corpse, it was kind of deflated, and it was singed black now. There hadn't been a notification for the kill.

That made sense, of course. Lath was very obviously already dead. It was still something to ask System about when he got the chance, but for right now, he needed to have words with Zea. He stomped over and said, "Why the hell did you use my cup?!"

"It was what I had to work with," she said hotly. "There wasn't time to hack up a block of wood to be the perfect size."

"The hell there wasn't! You're so buying me a new one."

Zea rolled her eyes. "It's our money. I'm not sure how you expect me to replace it out of our joint funds."

"Not the point!" Luke said, jabbing a finger in her direction. "Replacing my cup is your responsibility now."

"Ugh. Whatever. Let's just get out of here. Time for you to find a new river to bathe in."

"Fuuuuucccckk. We don't even have any soap left," he protested.

"Still. Better than nothing."

"Goddamn it," Luke muttered under his breath. Then, louder, "Fine, let's get going."

They'd been walking for about ten minutes when Luke remembered he was going to check his notifications for those grayish-brown ants. After a few seconds of searching, he frowned and said, "System, why do all my kill notifications say regular ants? What about those weird-looking ones."

"As I told you, zombified ants don't grant XP. They are an extension of a living ant queen's skills, not living beings," System responded.

"Oh, I guess that makes sense," he said.

"I told you those were a thing," Zea said.

"I should have hit one of them with **[Analyze]**," he said. On the other hand, he'd been distracted with dodging a zombie inquisitor that was doing its best to murder him, and who'd been gradually getting better the longer they fought. At first, Luke hadn't been sure, but now that he looked back on it, he could tell that its coordination had gone up a little bit between their opening exchanges and when he hurled the bomb cup into its chest.

"Oh, there was another thing I was going to ask! System, is it possible to get 0 XP from a kill if it's split between enough other people?"

"Technically, yes," System said. "Each XP is the smallest possible portion of divine essence. It can't be divided any further, but the system does keep track of the fractions of XP you've earned when working in a group and makes adjustments to try to keep that number balanced by alternating who is awarded the single leftover XP in the event that a kill does not split evenly."

"Thought so," Luke said. "So that explains why I never got a kill notification when Lath died. I was sharing his XP with ten thousand ants and didn't earn a big enough fraction of a single point."

"That is not correct," System said.

"Wait, it's not? Why? What's supposed to happen?"

"You would still receive a kill notification in the event that you slay another creature with XP, even if the amount was for 0."

"That can't be right," Luke said. "Lath was dead. Like, in a real bad way. Did I miss the notification for the kill in all the ant messages?"

"You received no kill notifications for the human known as Adrevald Lath," System informed him.

"But he's dead," Luke protested. "And I fought him. Why wouldn't I get the kill notification?"

"I am not able to speculate on what scenarios would cause you to not get a notification that you believe you should," System said. "I am only able to confirm you did not receive one for this particular individual."

Luke and Zea shared an uneasy glance. "But that means . . . he's not dead?" Zea asked.

"There is no fucking way that guy was still alive. He had thousands of ants burrowing through his body. Half his skin was gone."

"You didn't get a notification this time either?"

Luke shook his head.

"Maybe we should go back and check on that body," she said.

Lath drew in his first breath and had his first clear thought in days. The pheromone-induced fog of the ant queen's desires had finally cleared away, destroyed when he'd been bathed in fire and the ants infesting his body had been slaughtered. **[Zealot]** was keeping him alive, but it had been a near thing. He needed food to fuel the skill if he was going to recover. At this point, he couldn't afford to be picky.

He grabbed a random piece of foliage and stuffed it into his mouth, then mashed it up with what was left of his teeth. Another leaf soon followed it.

Name	Luke Bennet	Zea Stenter
Level	41	34
XP	251850/254133	143782/144088
AP	125	82
Bloodline	SysAdmin III	None
Strength	61	7
Agility	70	27
Stamina	66	27
Perception	55	19
Skills	Mace Mastery (5)	Dagger Mastery (1)
	Sword Mastery (1)	Stealth (2)
	Unarmed Martialist (4)	Keen Instincts (1)
	Power Strike (2)	Lock Picking (1)
	Life Surge (2)	Disguise (2)
	Peripheral Awareness (2)	Deception (1)
	Tactical Foresight (1)	Bartering (2)
	Counter (3)	Streetwise (2)
	Twitch Reflexes (3)	Cooking (1)
	Stealth (1)	Mending (1)
	Survivalist (2)	First Aid (1)
	First Aid (1)	Thalian (3)
	Wood Carving (1)	Neyardic (3)
	Leatherworking (2)	Ostari (1)
	Butchering (4)	Mana Manipulation (3)
	Thalian (2)	Mana Sight (2)
	Ostari (1)	Metallurgy (1)
	Disguise (2)	Whitesmithing (1)
	Deception (1)	Goldsmithing (2)
	Detection (2)	Gem Cutting (1)
	Torturer (1)	Engraving (2)
	Analyze (BL)	Rune Forging (1)
	Remote Access (BL)	Painting (1)
	XP Mask (BL)	Arcano Dynamics (1)
		Sleight of Hand (1)
		Steady Hands (2)
		Cold Reading (1)
		Temperature Acclimation (2)
		Cadence (3)
		Bloodline Purification Ritual (2)
		Ghost Script (1)

CHAPTER 66

Luke looked around the woods again. It all kind of looked the same to him, and he'd seen a lot of miles of trees and brush over the last few months of his life, but he was positive he was in the right spot. They'd buried the remains of their campfire but hadn't made a lot of effort otherwise to hide their presence. There'd been no reason to, not when they'd assumed that Lath was already dead.

There was no sign of the body now. What he did find was a trail like something had been dragged across the ground leading to their old fire. More specifically, it led past that to where Luke had discarded the remains of his attempt at cooking, remains that were no longer there. It wasn't hard to put two and two together to get four.

"Son of a bitch," he whispered. "How is he still alive?"

It had to be impossible. There was no way. Half the man's body had been devoured by ants. Some other animal must have come by and eaten both the corpse and the food scraps. And dragged the body around before eating it. And left no footprints anywhere. Right. That was what happened.

It wasn't like it made any less sense than the idea that Lath had somehow dragged himself back out of the afterlife and across the ground. Either way, he needed to get back to Zea. Fortunately, what would have been a three-hour walk back on Earth was only a ten-minute jog now. **[Survivalist]** even helped point out his own trail to follow.

He found Zea pacing back and forth next to a stream. "Well?" she demanded.

Luke shook his head. "Gone. The food scraps we left behind disappeared too."

"Some sort of healing skill like yours," she said. "It's got to be divine intervention keeping him alive. The gods are fucking with us."

"Maybe," Luke agreed. "System, can you confirm anything like that?"

"I am not able to confirm whether any member of the Pantheon has overridden the system," the apparition answered.

"Does it really matter either way?" Luke asked. "The important part is that Lath is still alive. We fucked up. He was a lot easier to put down when the ants were all over him. He's going to heal back up now and be a threat again."

"It'll take time," Zea said. "Maybe too much time. We should go back to Sicanti and see if we can convince the ship to sail early. It was going to set sail in six days anyway."

"Why were they waiting so long to begin with?" Luke asked.

"Something about some cargo coming in by a land route. The captain wasn't thrilled about the delay, but he said he couldn't leave without it. Fingers crossed it comes in a few days early and we can get going right away. Or else get our money back and find a different ship leaving sooner."

They didn't sleep that night. Luke kept **[XP Mask]** going on both of them since Zea was only a few hundred XP away from leveling. Luke was still needed another 2000 or so, but they didn't go out of their way to look for extra monsters to kill.

"What are you going to do with the AP?" Luke asked.

"I still want to bump up some of my enchanting-adjacent skills, like I've been planning. I've just been waiting for us to get on the ship in case some emergency comes up first. I was thinking I might put a few points into raw stats too. Maybe just a few in strength, no more than 5 or 10."

"You could bump up your perception a bit too," Luke said.

Zea shuddered and shook her head. "Nope. It's already high enough. I do not know how you can live with yours as high as it is. Even with mine at 19, I hear so much stuff all the time. And the smells. Ugh. Who knew there were so many nasty, stinky things in cities?"

"I knew," Luke muttered. His perception had been higher back when he'd first set foot in Valtira than hers was right now.

"What about you? You're sitting on a lot of AP right now too."

"I'm still keeping that 125 banked for **[XP Cycle]**, but I want to wait in case some other emergency comes up. System said we had years left before we need it, right, System?"

"My current estimate is between four and five years before symptoms of XP madness become visible to others," System said.

"What about for me?" Zea asked.

"Ten years would be a conservative estimate. You might go as far as fifteen."

"And that's just until people start noticing," she told Luke. "You might want to take **[XP Cycle]** now. There's always going to be another excuse to put it off, something else to spend the AP on."

"That's true, but since we just lost track of Lath again, I'd still feel more comfortable waiting until we were out of the area. You don't think he'd follow us across the ocean, do you?"

Zea thought about that for a second before shrugging. "It wouldn't surprise me either way. I suspect that even if he does, unless he knows which port we're going to and beats us there, he's going to have trouble tracking us down."

Their conversation was interrupted when Luke heard something heading toward them. It was big and heavy, so he was confident it wasn't Lath. Whatever it was, it had crossed their path by sheer happenstance, and as it moved around, Luke became convinced that it wasn't even coming for them directly. They could likely just sit still for a few minutes and let it wander away.

Of course, they wouldn't get any XP if they did that, so they changed their course to intercept it. A minute later, Luke paused. "Uh . . . Maybe we'll just leave this one alone," he told Zea.

"Why? It's not that strong," she asked.

"Well, no . . . It's not that. It's . . ."

[Name: Goliath Mouse]
[Level: 9]
[XP: 2578/2881]
[AP: 0]
[Strength: 9]
[Agility: 14]
[Stamina: 7]
[Perception: 14]
[Skills:]
[Size Shift (3)]
[Trap Breaker (1)]

"It's just a mouse. It's not hurting anyone," Luke said.

It might have only been a mouse, but it was also six feet tall at the ass end. It had to weigh a few hundred pounds too, with a tail that trailed another seven or eight feet behind it. It was almost cute, if he ignored the fact that it could look him in the eyes without tilting its head.

The mouse was watching them while it casually sniffed around the forest floor. Luke wasn't sure exactly what it was looking for, but it wasn't making any aggressive moves toward them. It had barely even acknowledged their presence.

"That is unexpectedly softhearted of you," Zea said.

"Well, uh, you know."

"Considering how many things I've personally seen you slaughter, I wouldn't have thought you'd hesitate."

"This is different," Luke said. "If it attacks us, I'll put it down right away, but it's not making a move in our direction. Honestly, I'm kind of surprised. Seems like everything on this planet attacks on sight. It's nice to see a bit of wildlife that's not trying to take a chunk out of me."

"Mm-hmm. Well, if you're sure."

They left the mouse behind to find more aggressive prey. Luke knew Zea didn't see much difference, but she didn't give him any grief over his choice, and that was enough. Besides, she only needed a few hundred XP, and they had miles to go. He had no doubt something would attack them before they reached Sicanti.

[Zealot] did a lot of things for Lath. It dampened pain. He could use it to strengthen himself with holy light. It would heal minor wounds rapidly. Twice during his life, it allowed him to commune with Hestoc himself. But this was too much, even for [Zealot] to deal with.

He should be dead three times over. Somehow, he could still think and move, though not very well in either case. Lath clawed his way across the forest floor, his nose leading him to something that, under normal circumstances, he'd consider inedible. He scarfed it down, scarcely attempting to chew the meat. Considering how few of his teeth were left, he wasn't sure he could have chewed it.

Lath's gut had been torn open and half his organs eaten by the ants. The food had nowhere to go, but that didn't matter. It was gone before it made it down his throat, the energy from it absorbed and broken down. Lath was just a little bit closer to whole.

He dragged himself upright and balanced precariously on legs that had been decimated. The muscle was gone, consumed by the ants as they'd eaten him alive, and he was essentially balanced on the bones. He shouldn't have been able to move at all.

Somehow, he did. It was impossible, but he took a step, then another. Hestoc be praised.

The plants he'd eaten had provided matter, but they weren't filling. The scorched-black meat was closer, but not what he needed. Lath quickly found a wild rabbit, a weak little thing that was only level 2. He killed it and ate it raw, fur, bones, and all.

The meat turned into reconstructed mass for his body. Now he could move faster, better. He felt some of his old coordination coming back, but it was far from enough. Lath needed more.

For the next few hours, he roamed the forest, seeking out and eating anything he could find. Occasionally, he noted boot prints, undoubtedly made by the apostate who'd defeated him. Each time, he considered turning to follow them. But no, he was still too weak. He couldn't waste the miracle Hestoc had granted him.

It was the middle of the night when Lath hit the mother lode. A goliath mouse crouched in front of him, its whiskers twitching as it watched him. He lunged, and it leaped to flee. It was too slow to escape, even as weakened as Lath was now, and he pounced on it. His hands found its face and grabbed hold, then twisted to snap his neck.

Lath devoured the corpse steadily, one bite after another as he shoved the meat down his gullet. He didn't stop, barely even made a token attempt at chewing despite the new teeth that had grown in. It wasn't until he'd consumed half of it that he got a notification from the system.

[Your species has changed from Zombie Thrall to Revenant.]

Lath paused at that, confused. "No," he growled. "This is a miracle of the gods. I'm not . . . I'm not that thing."

Undead weren't tolerated, not here and not back in Valtira. No civilized land allowed them to exist, lest their numbers grow and become a plague that wiped out whole cities. It was impossible that he was no longer human. Impossible.

He didn't realize he'd started shoving more handfuls of meat ripped right off the monster's flank into his mouth until he'd already swallowed another five or six times. He had to force himself to pause again, to fight against every instinct that demanded that he consume the corpse. He knew he needed the meat, needed to regain his strength and reform his body.

Did it matter what mechanism Hestoc had used to save him? Lath was still alive, still able to complete his holy mission. The goliath mouse was providing the fuel he needed for his body to rebuild his muscles, to regrow the lost skin. His organs were thick bulbs in his chest cavity, rapidly swelling back to full size and settling into place.

What did it matter if the system mistook him for an undead? He could still avenge his apprentice and destroy the apostate. He could, and he would. Lath finished his feast and backtracked to the last place he'd seen human footprints. They were heading toward Sicanti, and he would meet them there.

Name	Luke Bennet	Zea Stenter
Level	41	34
XP	251850/254133	143782/144088
AP	125	82
Bloodline	SysAdmin III	None
Strength	61	7
Agility	70	27
Stamina	66	27
Perception	55	19
Skills	Mace Mastery (5)	Dagger Mastery (1)
	Sword Mastery (1)	Stealth (2)
	Unarmed Martialist (4)	Keen Instincts (1)
	Power Strike (2)	Lock Picking (1)
	Life Surge (2)	Disguise (2)
	Peripheral Awareness (2)	Deception (1)
	Tactical Foresight (1)	Bartering (2)
	Counter (3)	Streetwise (2)
	Twitch Reflexes (3)	Cooking (1)
	Stealth (1)	Mending (1)
	Survivalist (2)	First Aid (1)
	First Aid (1)	Thalian (3)
	Wood Carving (1)	Neyardic (3)
	Leatherworking (2)	Ostari (1)
	Butchering (4)	Mana Manipulation (3)
	Thalian (2)	Mana Sight (2)
	Ostari (1)	Metallurgy (1)
	Disguise (2)	Whitesmithing (1)
	Deception (1)	Goldsmithing (2)
	Detection (2)	Gem Cutting (1)
	Torturer (1)	Engraving (2)
	Analyze (BL)	Rune Forging (1)
	Remote Access (BL)	Painting (1)
	XP Mask (BL)	Arcano Dynamics (1)
		Sleight of Hand (1)
		Steady Hands (2)
		Cold Reading (1)
		Temperature Acclimation (2)
		Cadence (3)
		Bloodline Purification Ritual (2)
		Ghost Script (1)

CHAPTER 67

True to Luke's prediction, they were attacked just before dawn by a cloud of some bat-like monsters with wingspans wide enough to give him a hug. They lacked noses or ears like normal bats, instead having kind of rubbery beaks and what looked more like slicked-back insect antennae on their heads. They also didn't appear too keen to live off bugs either, judging by how willing they were to attack creatures larger than themselves.

They flew like bats though, and that cemented the impression in Luke's mind. He tossed off an **[Analyze]** or three to make sure there was nothing truly dangerous in there, determined that most of the monsters were below level 10, and got to work swatting them out of the air.

[Name: Night Piercer]
[Level: 9]
[XP: 2455/2881]
[AP: 0]
[Strength: 3]
[Agility: 13]
[Stamina: 6]
[Perception: 20]
[Skills:]
[Razor Wing (2)]
[Paralyzing Shriek (1)]
[Trick Flight (2)]

The hardest part of the fight was not killing them when he smacked them with his mace. Zea was the one hunting for XP this time, and her best weapon was her razor-prong whip, which was still only partially completed. She'd told him it would stretch out to twenty feet when it was done, but right now it barely reached seven.

It was a weird defensive position, one where Luke actually stood behind Zea and kept any of the night piercers from coming at her from the back or sides while she focused on slashing the ones coming straight at her with her shortened whip. Occasionally, one of them would emit what sounded to him like a high-pitched whine that sent a shiver down his spine but otherwise did nothing.

After about five minutes of circling around their attempted prey, the night piercers that were still alive gave up and flew off. Luke judged that they'd killed a third or so of the flock, which to him proved that they were smarter than the average monster. It was rare that anything ever bothered to retreat when it was overpowered.

[You have slain 4 creatures between levels 8 and 10. 314 XP awarded.]

[You have assisted in slaying 12 creatures between levels 7 and 12. 519 XP awarded.]

"That should be enough for you, right?" he asked.

"Yep, just hit 35," she said. "Between the ones we split and the nine of them I killed on my own, it was more than enough. I have 117 AP to spend. Way more than anyone should need, and somehow not even half of what I'd have to get in order to upgrade **[Bloodline Purification Ritual]** again."

"I don't think we should need to do that ritual a third time," Luke said. "At this point, I just need to grind out another 600 AP and I can do anything short of resetting someone's XP back to 0. And actually, System, was there a reason we can't do that? I mean, **[XP Cycle]** already pulls XP out of you. We just need to stop it before it sends new XP back, right? That should be an even easier skill to make."

"It would be a slightly different process, since **[XP Cycle]** maintains your status. Resetting XP to 0 in a target would also need to include an update to the user's status to remove all skills and stats, reevaluate the target's natural physical condition to assign new base stats, and update their register to show the changes."

Luke would be lying if he said he'd understood all of that, but it sounded like System knew exactly what the proposed skill would need to do. "Can you build that skill for us and let me know what the AP cost on it will be?"

"Certainly. One moment."

System didn't usually follow along after Luke for extended distances, but he must have felt his presence was still needed until he delivered his answer, which was taking a bit longer than Luke had expected. They reached the edge of the forest and gazed across the farmland that surrounded Sicanti while System worked.

Their trip had taken them on a long loop around the wilderness, and instead of approaching from the west, the city was north of them. Luke could see the ocean off to his right, beyond the fields and down a rocky slope miles long.

"I have finished creating the skill you've requested," System said. "**[XP Reset]** costs 50 AP. It will reset your XP to 0, remove all skills, and adjust your stats back to your unaugmented physical baseline. You can use it on a willing target when combined with **[Remote Access]**, or an unwilling target if you purchase **[Inflict Status]**."

"Really? Isn't **[Inflict Status]** for, you know, inflicting statuses?" Luke asked.

"It is, but it contains the matrix for what are considered hostile status alterations, which **[XP Reset]** works with."

"Wait, why don't I need that for **[Stat Assignment]** then?" Luke asked. "That's hostile."

"The AP is returned to the target in that case," System explained. "Nothing stops them from simply reassigning their AP back into their stats the same way, and because it transfers at such a slow rate, the combat applications are minimal."

"That's probably why it transfers so slowly," Zea told him. "Didn't it seem weird to you that the skill had an artificial limitation on it? You can spend the AP and instantly gain 10 strength, but to take it away, you have to wait a few minutes?"

"I guess I didn't think about it," Luke said. "The whole system has tons of weird shit like that. Like, why is it that **[XP Mask]** has an on-and-off switch now? It didn't when I got it. I didn't have to spend more AP to rank it up. Just purifying my bloodline changed it. I kind of stopped questioning it after a while."

"Did you ever start questioning it in the first place?" Zea asked.

"Ahem, that's not really relevant to this conversation," he said seriously. "So, moving on. I just need to grind out 250 AP for **[Inflict Status]** and **[XP Reset]**, and I'm untouchable. Anything that comes at me will find itself at level 1 again."

"You could reset me right now," Zea said, her voice barely a whisper. "I could start over without all the slave skills. It would be easy to push me back up to level 10 or 15 and let me do my build from scratch."

"I . . . I could," Luke said, frowning. "Do you want me to?"

Zea was silent as she thought about it. Finally, she gave a helpless sigh and said, "I don't know."

The return to the city was a lot more subdued after that. Luke understood Zea's desires. This was essentially what he'd promised her in exchange for her help, and he was now in a position to deliver on it. He could reset her to level 1 right now, help her level up to 10 in a day or two, and send her on her way. She'd be able to take a ship back south, and they'd never see each other again.

It wasn't quite that simple in practice. There was still the slave mark to deal with, and going back to Valtira probably wasn't a great idea, but it turned a trip to the other side of the ocean into a far greater commitment now that he could give her what she wanted without having to go another step.

"We should still have a few days left before you have to make a decision," he said.

"What about Lath? We can't just forget that he's still after us."

"You could get on a boat heading back south and leave him to me. I'm the apostate anyway."

"I'm sure we're both apostates in the eyes of the church by this point," she said.

"There are places where the church doesn't know who you are. Maybe a town or city with lots of dwifkin so you don't stand out so bad?"

Zea gave a helpless little laugh. "Are you going to escort me there? I don't think you understand how dangerous long-distance travel is for normal people. You look at a level 20 monster and weigh whether it's worth the time to harvest the XP. Most people see a level 20 monster and are terrified that they're going to die. Hell, most people see a level 10 monster and are afraid for their lives."

Luke hadn't considered that. Very few things could threaten him anymore, and it had only taken a few months to get to his current level. Admittedly, there'd been some cheating with the whole anthill-bombing strategy, but even that was possible for other people to replicate. It wasn't like Zea was the only enchanter in the whole world. Their society was rooted in a fear of dying, which was understandable, but considering the kind of hardships they faced, he thought he'd rather be stronger and die sooner than huddle together in fear.

Then again, he wasn't faced with that choice. He could keep leveling forever, and the stronger he got, the more tools he gained to defeat the restrictions the system placed on normal people. How could he judge everyone else as cowards when his situation was completely different? It was easy to say that he'd get stronger and damn the consequences when he'd never planned on sticking around long enough to face those consequences.

From the beginning, even before he'd known about XP madness, Luke hadn't been planning on sticking around on Aros. Almost as soon as he'd learned that having too much XP was a problem, System had handed him a way to deal with it. Maybe civilization would be better off if everyone leveled up to higher numbers and accepted that they'd have shorter life spans, but who was he to make that call?

"Five days before our ship is supposed to leave," Zea said.

"What are you thinking?" Luke asked.

"I have enough AP to become a master enchanter right now but not enough time. The things I could make for us with the right supply of materials and a few months to work on them . . . And then afterward we could sell the rest, you could reset me, and I'd be set for the rest of my life."

"But it doesn't work because I'm still going across the ocean in a week."

"Exactly," she said. "I need more time to take advantage of being high level, but we just don't have it."

"Well . . . We could cancel our trip and stay here for a few months? We just blow up anthills for a week and let Lath catch up to us. I'll crush him when I'm level 60. Once you're ready, I'll reset you, we boost you back up to level 10 or 15 or whatever, and then you take a ship back south."

"I . . . That would set you back by a long time," she said.

"I know."

"Are you sure . . . ?"

Luke shrugged. "Your happiness is important to me." Even if it meant they went their separate ways. Zea should get something for all the misery she'd gone through trying to help him.

"I'll think about it," she said. "We've still got some time. Let's see what things look like in town before we make any decisions. For all we know, there's going to be a whole army of inquisitors we have to sneak past just to get to the harbor."

"Doesn't seem likely," Luke said. "Like you said, if there were a lot of them, why was Lath out here by himself hunting for us? Why did he hire a band of mercenaries?"

"You're probably right, but let's still see for ourselves what our options are before we start making changes to our plans. We've still got plenty of time before the ship is scheduled to set sail. Even if they did get their inventory in early, I guarantee it'll be a day or two at minimum before they're organized enough to go once we get there."

"Unless they already went and left us behind," Luke muttered.

Zea scowled at the thought. "With the gold I already paid them? They wouldn't dare. They'd get in so much trouble with the harbor authorities."

"I guess we'll find out soon."

Name	Luke Bennet	Zea Stenter
Level	41	35
XP	252683/254133	145001/157276
AP	125	117
Bloodline	SysAdmin III	None
Strength	61	7
Agility	70	27
Stamina	66	27
Perception	55	19
Skills	Mace Mastery (5)	Dagger Mastery (1)
	Sword Mastery (1)	Stealth (2)
	Unarmed Martialist (4)	Keen Instincts (1)
	Power Strike (2)	Lock Picking (1)
	Life Surge (2)	Disguise (2)
	Peripheral Awareness (2)	Deception (1)
	Tactical Foresight (1)	Bartering (2)
	Counter (3)	Streetwise (2)
	Twitch Reflexes (3)	Cooking (1)
	Stealth (1)	Mending (1)
	Survivalist (2)	First Aid (1)
	First Aid (1)	Thalian (3)
	Wood Carving (1)	Neyardic (3)
	Leatherworking (2)	Ostari (1)
	Butchering (4)	Mana Manipulation (3)
	Thalian (2)	Mana Sight (2)
	Ostari (1)	Metallurgy (1)
	Disguise (2)	Whitesmithing (1)
	Deception (1)	Goldsmithing (2)
	Detection (2)	Gem Cutting (1)
	Torturer (1)	Engraving (2)
	Analyze (BL)	Rune Forging (1)
	Remote Access (BL)	Painting (1)
	XP Mask (BL)	Arcano Dynamics (1)
		Sleight of Hand (1)
		Steady Hands (2)
		Cold Reading (1)
		Temperature Acclimation (2)
		Cadence (3)
		Bloodline Purification Ritual (2)
		Ghost Script (1)

CHAPTER 68

Their timing couldn't have been worse. The sun had only been up for a few hours when Luke had caught sight of Sicanti, leaving them to decide whether to waste an entire day while they waited for night or risk someone spotting Zea and reporting back to the church.

After their discussion at the edge of the farmlands, they decided to retreat back into the wilderness south of town. The foothills had plenty of places for them to camp, and they ended up at the back end of a dry little ravine that was overgrown with trees leaning out into the open air above it to form a sort of living roof. Luke didn't think for a second it would keep them dry if the weather took a turn for the worse, but they'd both been soaked by the rain so many times now that it had ceased to be anything more than an annoyance.

Besides, they were only going to be there for about fourteen hours, just long enough for the sun to go down so that Zea could sneak through Sicanti to the harbor without being seen. In the meantime, Zea got to work on finishing her razor-prong whip. This was made easier by her spending AP on both **[Rune Forging]** and **[Arcano Dynamics]**. She paused after upgrading both skills to review her newfound knowledge, then shook her head and said, "I still don't think I could get that pheromone-blocking enchantment working."

"You want to upgrade to rank 3?" Luke asked.

"Not really, but I kind of feel like we should. Otherwise an entire colony of ants might follow us back to the city. It would probably take weeks or even months, but it could happen after we're gone. I don't want that on my conscience, you know?"

"Yeah, I get you. How's your AP looking?"

"82, down from 117 after those two upgrades. It'll be another 75 to upgrade them both again."

"Not like you can't afford it," Luke said. "Besides, we're short on time right now. Upgrading your skills would let you work faster."

"It would almost completely tap me out. Maybe if I don't take rank 3 **[Arcano Dynamics]**, I can use the 25 AP to bump up **[Engraving]** instead."

It ended up being 8 and then 15 AP to bring **[Engraving]** up to rank 4, plus another 50 for rank 3 of **[Rune Forging]**, leaving her with 9 AP remaining. Zea grumbled about it, which Luke rolled his eyes at. A few months ago, she hadn't even spent 9 AP on her stats, and now she was concerned that her banked supply was getting low. Transitioning back to level 1 with no stats or skills was going to be hard for her.

"Alright! Good news is that I finally know where I was going wrong, so I'm going to enchant the pheromone blocker right now. Then you can follow our trail backward and clean it up while I work on other stuff."

"I guess I can do that," Luke said.

Zea gave him a sharp glance. "You got something better to do?"

"Well, no. I mean, I thought I should stay nearby incase zombie Lath shows up, you know?"

"If he does, it'll be because he followed our trail. You can meet him out there." Zea paused. "You want me to make you some stuff just in case you end up fighting him again?"

"Nah, I'll be fine. Zombie Lath isn't half as strong as inquisitor Lath was. If I do run into him again, I'll make sure I destroy the body this time so the ants can't get him back upright. Not to mention . . . fuck that guy and all, but still, no one should be a living puppet to a bunch of zombified ants."

Zea shuddered. "Okay, give me half an hour to do this."

Her movements had been slow and deliberate before, very precise and very careful. Zea didn't make a lot of mistakes, and when she did, it was punctuated with a lot of swearing about the wasted material. Now, her hand moved fluidly across a piece of scrap metal she pulled out of her bag. It was more like writing than engraving, except the act was accompanied by the sound of metal screaming from the stylus she used being dragged across its surface. It was a smooth, constant whine, one that would have been annoying even without his greatly enhanced perception.

Luke settled down with a grimace and waited for Zea to finish.

"What's the eastern continent like?" Luke asked System.

He was walking through the forest, holding what looked kind of like an upside-down empty coffee can if someone had stabbed a bunch of holes in the bottom. Air flowed into the can, pulled in by a circle of runes inscribed inside the bottom lip, and the enchantments did something with that air before pushing it back out through the holes.

"Could you be more specific?" System asked. "I'm afraid the eastern continent is a rather large place."

"Okay, walk me through the route we'll need to take to get to the God Machine. We get on a boat in Sicanti, spend weeks or months or whatever floating around on the ocean, hopefully don't get eaten by any sea monsters, and then we land. What's the place we're going to look like?"

"The most likely port city connected to Sicanti is Naldrin. The locals there speak a language called Eledarn natively. Additionally, more than half of them are fluent in what they know as Consortium Standard, a sort of trade language commonly used between the various clans that hold supremacy over some thirty-six regions lining the coast."

"So that'll be the better language to learn once we get there," Luke said. "What about the places that aren't on the coast?"

"Largely uninhabited by what you would consider civilized species," System told him. "The closest comparison would be the large stretch of unsettled forestlands between the southern and northern countries on this continent, though there are far fewer forests on the eastern continent."

"You mean more stuff like those giant-squirrel trees?" Luke asked. He stopped walking and frowned down at the can. The runes on it were starting to dim. He gave it a gentle smack on the side, which did absolutely nothing to brighten them up again. "This thing didn't last long. It's only been a few miles."

"Not exactly, though there are species that form similar small societies in their appropriate habitats. There are far too many examples to list."

"How about just the ones near Naldrin?" Luke suggested.

"Very well. Directly east is an open plain that has been claimed by a form of snow hare for almost a hundred years now. Attempts to rout them have repeatedly met with disasters, and the clansmen in Naldrin have given up doing anything beyond preventing the snow hares from spreading any farther west. South of them is the hunting grounds of an intelligent species of falcon known for their incredible flight speeds and territorial nature. They are less of an overt threat due to their inability to cooperate with one another but can be significantly more dangerous to travelers who catch their eyes."

"Okay, but not, like, a threat to me, right? I'm pretty high level already."

"It would be hard to say," System said. "Depending on which route you take, you may encounter creatures upward of level 60, and the eastern continent is home to several species with so much raw power that they challenge humans who are 20 or even 30 levels above them."

"Really?" Luke paused and looked over at System. "If the monsters are that strong, how are there any people still alive?"

"Their culture is very different than the ones around here. It is not uncommon for a town to have someone close to level 50 to protect it, and that person understands that their tenure will by necessity be short. They expect to be slain, either in combat or by one of the people they are sworn to protect, and have made peace with that."

That was all kinds of fucked up, but Luke got it. If the monsters were stronger, the people didn't have any choice but to grow to match them. The only other option was to be wiped out. Maybe it wouldn't happen immediately, but eventually something would wander through, and that would be the end of that. If anything, the surprising part was that it hadn't happened on the western continent too.

"Why is everything a higher level on the other side of the world?" he asked.

"I am not able to speculate," System said.

Luke shrugged. He'd already gotten more than he'd expected out of System, and for far less of a headache than usual. There was definitely a qualitative increase in the kind of information System would give him that had come with purifying his bloodline. It was almost enough to make him want to shoot for another round, but the 500 AP price tag on it was a huge hurdle by itself, never mind however much the supplies might cost or the support skills Zea would need to upgrade. It wasn't necessarily out of reach, but it would have to be something they made a priority if they were going to go for it.

At this point, he wasn't even sure she was going to get on the boat with him, let alone cross the ocean and pick up another 15 or so levels. And honestly, he didn't much need her help anymore. 250 AP, just another 3 levels, and he'd be able to inflict a status reset on anyone and anything. Reducing something to level 1 would be more than enough to overcome any monster or churchman that got in his way.

He was only 1500 XP away from leveling again now. He could have that XP before he got on the ship if he could talk Zea into a few more bombing runs. Since she wanted her XP reset anyway, it wouldn't be a hard sell. He'd need another three levels after that to afford **[XP Cycle]**, but there were enough anthills in the wilderness that he didn't think it'd be a problem to clear out ten or twelve if needed.

"I think this thing is dead," he said, holding the can up to System. All the runes had gone out. "Maybe Zea can recharge it?"

"I am not able to answer that question," System told him.

Of course he couldn't. Luke didn't have any skills related to enchanting things, so System wouldn't give him an answer. He hadn't expected that particular restriction to change, though it would have been convenient if it had.

"Okay, well, only one way to find out. I think we went about ten miles, didn't we? That should be good enough anyway. I'm going to head back to the camp."

"You will need to adjust your course slightly if you wish to go directly back," System said, pointing over Luke's shoulder.

He shrugged and turned that way. "Thanks."

"You are quite welcome."

"I wonder if zombie Lath is still coming after us."

"I am afraid I do not understand your logic in naming him such," System said.

"Well, because of all the zombie ants controlling him."

"But you destroyed those ants," System pointed out.

"I mean, yeah, but you can't tell me that guy got up and walked away on his own. More ants had to come and take him back over. I kind of want to find him just to put him out of his misery."

"In point of fact, his [Zealot] skill could allow him to recover mobility without outside assistance."

Luke paused to think about that. "Creepy. But hey, good on you for volunteering some information. I like that you're doing that now."

"Of course," System said. "The purer your bloodline becomes, the more assistance I will be able to offer you."

"Yeah, well, the next step up is a big one. Don't expect us to hit it any time soon."

"As you say."

"So, you're saying Lath isn't a zombie anymore?" Luke asked.

"I am not able to confirm or deny that. I merely questioned your logic in assuming so, as I was not able to see anything to definitively confirm that based on your own interactions with him."

"Huh, well, good to know I guess." If Lath wasn't a zombie, he'd be a lot harder to kill. Luke might need Zea's help after all. Her enchanted doodads had been the tipping point in every confrontation between them and the inquisitor.

Luke started walking faster.

If Lath wasn't a zombie, he'd probably be a lot faster and a lot smarter. He might be on their trail even now, and blocking out pheromones wouldn't do shit to stop him. There was no way Zea was going to win against him alone.

Luke started running.

Name	Luke Bennet	Zea Stenter
Level	41	35
XP	252683/254133	145001/157276
AP	125	9
Bloodline	SysAdmin III	None
Strength	61	7
Agility	70	27
Stamina	66	27
Perception	55	19
Skills	Mace Mastery (5)	Dagger Mastery (1)
	Sword Mastery (1)	Stealth (2)
	Unarmed Martialist (4)	Keen Instincts (1)
	Power Strike (2)	Lock Picking (1)
	Life Surge (2)	Disguise (2)
	Peripheral Awareness (2)	Deception (1)
	Tactical Foresight (1)	Bartering (2)
	Counter (3)	Streetwise (2)
	Twitch Reflexes (3)	Cooking (1)
	Stealth (1)	Mending (1)
	Survivalist (2)	First Aid (1)
	First Aid (1)	Thalian (3)
	Wood Carving (1)	Neyardic (3)
	Leatherworking (2)	Ostari (1)
	Butchering (4)	Mana Manipulation (3)
	Thalian (2)	Mana Sight (2)
	Ostari (1)	Metallurgy (1)
	Disguise (2)	Whitesmithing (1)
	Deception (1)	Goldsmithing (2)
	Detection (2)	Gem Cutting (1)
	Torturer (1)	Engraving (4)
	Analyze (BL)	Rune Forging (3)
	Remote Access (BL)	Painting (1)
	XP Mask (BL)	Arcano Dynamics (2)
		Sleight of Hand (1)
		Steady Hands (2)
		Cold Reading (1)
		Temperature Acclimation (2)
		Cadence (3)
		Bloodline Purification Ritual (2)
		Ghost Script (1)

CHAPTER 69

"Everything alright there?" Zea asked as Luke barged back into their camp. He looked a little wild in the eyes, but whatever he saw must have reassured him since he quickly calmed down. "Sorry, System pointed out to me a little bit ago that we had no evidence that Lath is still being controlled by zombie ants. He could have crawled away to recover under his own power and might have been tracking us."

"Oh, I see. So you got a little spooked and came running back to me for safety and security," she said.

"Yeah, that's exactly it. I was worried he might find us separate and that I wouldn't have you around to protect me."

"A perfectly valid concern," she said, struggling to keep her face straight. "But as you can see, we've had no visitors while you were away."

"Good thing. Otherwise I might have to get jealous," he said with a grin.

Men, especially young men, were walking balls of hormones. It was a good thing Luke was cute and that they were both very, very flexible. That shirt he was wearing wasn't hurting things either with the way it sat on his shoulders.

The looming specter of danger was a bucket of cold water on her, and she shook herself out of her daydream before it could even get started. As much as she liked Luke and enjoyed spending her nights with him, she'd spent a lot of time lately considering whether she wanted to keep traveling with him.

She wasn't in love with him. Maybe if their situation was different, if they'd had a chance to really get to know each other before running for their lives, she might have grown into that. But that wasn't what had happened, and they were more like war buddies who liked to fuck than a couple in a committed relationship.

Zea had avoided voicing that thought for a while now, mostly because she suspected Luke might not feel the same way. He was fiercely protective of her, as evidenced by how quickly he'd come charging to her rescue from a theoretical threat, which would have been cute except for the fact that if he'd been right, she would have needed to be rescued.

That right there was the problem. Zea only needed Luke to stay safe because she was getting drawn into his fights. She'd survived for over two decades under level 10, though admittedly she hadn't exactly been thriving. That was still better than fighting the church or any of the many, many monsters that had crossed their path since they'd left the safety of civilization.

Things just kept escalating. This new shit with the anthills was going to blow up in their faces at some point, but Luke wouldn't let go of the idea. Even after seeing what had happened to Lath with their last bombing run, she had no doubt he'd be more than happy to go right back to killing them. He just didn't seem to grasp the potential consequences, for himself or for the rest of the area.

"So I was thinking, after we get things set up, maybe we should drop a few more bombs on the anthills. If I can get like . . . six levels, maybe seven, I'll have enough AP to pick up **[XP Reset]** for you, **[XP Cycle]** for myself, and **[Inflict Status]** to clear away any future obstacles."

There it was, right on time. It was her own fault for not stomping down on this harder before he'd gotten a taste of exactly how much XP was sitting in those anthills and how quickly he could claim a chunk of it. Sending him out to wipe any pheromones off their trail had probably put the idea back in his head.

The worst part of it was she could see the logic. Without his unique bloodline skills, it was crazy. But for his situation, it was practically perfect. All he needed was the time and XP to pick up the relevant skills and he could solve any problems created by his actions with a wave of his hand.

Well, maybe not. They'd thought **[Stat Assignment]** was going to be their answer to Lath, only to find out when he actually went to take the skill that they'd failed to read the fine print. She wasn't willing to pile on any more XP until she knew for sure that Luke could clear it away.

"No," she said. "Not until we know that this is actually going to work. We've been running down a slope, and we're about to fly off the cliff. I know you don't get this. You aren't from this world; you haven't seen what XP madness looks like. It's not just dangerous to you. You could kill a lot of other people in the process. What happens when you get all these levels, the skill doesn't work like you think it will, again, and you end up going crazy next year?"

"I can buy **[XP Cycle]** right now," Luke said. "We can test that before going any further."

She shook her head. "That's a solution for you. It only works for me if I follow you around for the rest of my life. Even if I was willing to do that, what about when you go back to your own world? Or what if you die?"

"Well I'm sorry, but I just don't have the AP for both. That's why I wanted to hit the ants again. I can't test them to confirm they'll work like we think until I actually have them. All we can go on is System's word until then."

"My answer is still no. Look, I've risked a lot on this scheme already. You understand that I'm not going to live to see forty as it currently stands, right? I may not even make it to thirty, and there will definitely be symptoms well before then. If this idea of yours works, then that's great. Fantastic. But I've hit my limits on grinding out XP."

Luke started to say something, stopped himself, and sat there in silence while he thought it through. Finally, he said, "We're getting to that point where we go our separate ways, aren't we?"

"I think so, yeah. Not today, probably not even this month, but soon. I did my part and helped you purify your bloodline. I need some time to get things set up, but once we get across the ocean and I take care of things financially, I think I'm going to ask you to reset me to level 1. Maybe help me get back up to 10 if we can do it quickly and easily."

"I get it," Luke said. "Good to know what you want to do in the near future too. We can plan for that."

Zea hadn't been expecting him to take the news poorly, but she figured it would hurt him a bit too. He'd gotten some ideas in his head that she was going to keep going with him to the very end, though he hadn't exactly expressed them out loud. It was better to nip those in the bud now rather than let him keep thinking that. As much as she liked him, she was already tired of this lifestyle.

She needed a place to live that was far, far away from where she'd grown up. Without regular maintenance to suppress it, the slave rune tattooed behind her ear would start broadcasting her position. Being on another continent was a great way to let that run itself out of power. No one who cared to track that magic would be able to reach her before the rune faded and broke on its own. In the meantime, she'd have plenty of opportunity to milk her enchanting skills for all they were worth before the reset.

And who knew, she might end up liking life on the eastern continent. She really didn't know much about it. She'd have to sit down and bash her head against the wall by having a conversation with System. Maybe she could find a place that was perfect for her there. It wasn't like she had a lot to come back to at home as a runaway slave, and the church had no doubt killed or imprisoned everyone she might have considered a friend back in Valtira.

Fuck those Hestocian assholes anyway. Other than Lath himself, who had followed them from Valtira, she hadn't heard a peep from the local church. Even Lath had used mercenaries to help him, which told her that the two churches probably weren't on the friendliest terms. Sicanti wasn't so bad, except for how cold it was all the time. It was supposed to be the warm time of the year! She couldn't even imagine what a winter would look like up here.

They didn't talk much that day. Luke was . . . Well, she didn't know if processing his feelings was the right thing to call it, but he was doing a lot of thinking about something. He spent a lot of time fidgeting and staring out into the trees but not a lot of time meeting her eyes. That was fine by her. She had plenty of work to do anyway, and upgrading **[Rune Forging]** by two ranks had opened her mind to a thousand new possibilities. She knew runes now that she hadn't even considered might exist.

It was going to be her ticket to wealth, as long as she had the time and resources to properly leverage it. It was also a way for her to help keep Luke safe. Money-making enchantments could come later. She was working on a few things for him first.

Just because she wasn't planning on going all the way to the other side of the world with him didn't mean she wasn't invested in him making the trip safely. He wanted armor, but even after only a week or two, the stuff he was wearing had been damaged and he'd been forced to do patchwork repairs. Neither of them were qualified to truly fix it, and it was only a matter of time before the armor was rendered useless.

She'd make him something better anyway. She just needed a little more time to finish it.

As dusk fell, the revenant of Adrevald Lath stepped out of the tree line and stared out across the hundreds of acres of farmland that surrounded Sicanti. Somewhere in there was his prey. Finding them was only a matter of time. Before that, he needed a disguise. **[Infiltrator]** could work with very little, but walking through the city naked without being noticed was beyond even his considerable abilities.

Lath stole up to the nearest farmhouse, confirmed it was empty, and broke the lock on the shutters. Ideally, he'd find a nice set of clothes, some farmer's churchgoing outfit, but it wasn't the end of the world if he had to settle for something shabbier. Unfortunately, it appeared that the owner of the home he'd broken into was a rather rotund man. Lath could have fit two of himself in the shirts he found.

It was better than nothing, and while he wasn't a tailor, he could do basic stitching. He sliced a chunk of material a foot wide out of it and stitched it back up into something approximately his size. It was still too long, but that didn't matter. The pants, on the other hand, were a more difficult task. It might have been easier to cut new trousers from cloth and sew them to shape than to alter the ones he'd found. Lath settled for pinning the excess material and holding them up with a length of rope he stole from the farmer's storeroom.

There were no shoes, but Lath did find a voluminous cloak to steal as well. Whoever this farmer was, he had to be huge. It was to the farmer's good luck that he was working late tonight, as his size would be no protection against Lath if he should come home too early. Even as Lath finished his work, he heard the sound of someone walking up the path.

Flexing the fingers on one hand, Lath turned toward the noise. Perhaps the farmer wasn't so lucky after all.

Name	Luke Bennet	Zea Stenter
Level	41	35
XP	252683/254133	145001/157276
AP	125	9
Bloodline	SysAdmin III	None
Strength	61	7
Agility	70	27
Stamina	66	27
Perception	55	19
Skills	Mace Mastery (5)	Dagger Mastery (1)
	Sword Mastery (1)	Stealth (2)
	Unarmed Martialist (4)	Keen Instincts (1)
	Power Strike (2)	Lock Picking (1)
	Life Surge (2)	Disguise (2)
	Peripheral Awareness (2)	Deception (1)
	Tactical Foresight (1)	Bartering (2)
	Counter (3)	Streetwise (2)
	Twitch Reflexes (3)	Cooking (1)
	Stealth (1)	Mending (1)
	Survivalist (2)	First Aid (1)
	First Aid (1)	Thalian (3)
	Wood Carving (1)	Neyardic (3)
	Leatherworking (2)	Ostari (1)
	Butchering (4)	Mana Manipulation (3)
	Thalian (2)	Mana Sight (2)
	Ostari (1)	Metallurgy (1)
	Disguise (2)	Whitesmithing (1)
	Deception (1)	Goldsmithing (2)
	Detection (2)	Gem Cutting (1)
	Torturer (1)	Engraving (4)
	Analyze (BL)	Rune Forging (3)
	Remote Access (BL)	Painting (1)
	XP Mask (BL)	Arcano Dynamics (2)
		Sleight of Hand (1)
		Steady Hands (2)
		Cold Reading (1)
		Temperature Acclimation (2)
		Cadence (3)
		Bloodline Purification Ritual (2)
		Ghost Script (1)

CHAPTER 70

It was far too easy for the people of Aros to see in the dark, even on a moon-less night, which this wasn't. Thus, the goal wasn't to avoid being seen by hiding in the darkness. It was merely that despite everyone having stats to see better in the dark and reduce their need for sleep, most people weren't out and about at night. Fewer people on the streets meant fewer people seeing them.

Luke led them on a roundabout path through Sicanti, ducking through side streets and taking odd turns whenever he sensed people nearby. Sometimes it wasn't possible to avoid someone seeing them, but in those instances, he did his best to keep himself between the observer and Zea. Hopefully they wouldn't be able to make out enough detail in the dark to tell that she was a dwifkin.

They added an extra hour to the trip with all the ducking and weaving around the people were who still out and about, but both agreed it was worth it. The most important part of the plan was getting to the harbor and onto the ship unseen. If they could manage that, they could just hide out in their cabin while they waited for the ship to set sail. With **[XP Mask]** shielding them from casual detection, the only possible hitch was a gossiping sailor tipping someone off that *The Averast* had a pair of interesting passengers.

"Which ship is the one we're riding on?" Luke asked once the harbor came into view. He knew it was one of the bigger ones, but he didn't see the one he was looking for. The cynical part of his mind immediately jumped to the idea that it had set sail already, leaving Luke and Zea behind and stealing the deposit she'd paid.

"Uh . . . It's . . ." Zea trailed off. "Not here?"

"Well. Shit. That's what I was afraid you were going to say."

"Maybe it got moved to a different dock," Zea said. "Come on, let's walk the length."

"Is that something that happens often?" Luke asked. He was more than ready to admit he knew basically nothing about *his* world's shipping processes, let alone how it worked on Aros.

"Eh, sometimes if there's a lot of cargo to take on from a warehouse on the far side of the harbor, the ship might redock. Usually it's easier to just load the freight on a wagon and move it over to wherever the ship is currently berthed. Less paperwork that way. Cheaper too."

Considering the average laborer was stronger than a world-record holder back on Earth, Luke supposed it wouldn't be much of an issue if they had to carry something an extra mile. He spared a second to wonder how the average beast of burden measured up. He'd seen horses, so they were still in use on Aros, but it seemed like a decently leveled human would probably beat a horse in speed and strength.

How would a horse even level up in this world? They were herbivores, more inclined to run from trouble than stand and fight. Did they get XP from eating grass or hay somehow? Luke couldn't recall a time he'd gotten any XP for beating up a tree, but maybe he just hadn't killed it all the way.

"No way that'd work. Farmers would be done after a few years of harvesting crops," he muttered.

"What?" Zea said, glancing back at him.

"Just wondering how horses level up," he said.

"Uh . . . What the fuck does that have to do with anything?"

"Never mind," Luke said.

"Focus up," she told him. "We're not fucking around out here. If we can't find our ship and get aboard tonight, we're screwed."

They caught a lucky break, and Luke spotted it ten minutes later at the north end of the harbor. "There," he said, pointing at a dark shape riding high in the water. "That looks right."

Zea studied it and said, "Crap. It's been seized by the church."

"How can you tell?"

She pointed at the waterline. "See how high it's sitting? The cargo was unloaded. It's in the dock with the templar guards patrolling it, and there's not a single sailor in sight over there."

Now that she mentioned it, he did notice that every person on the dock near *The Averast* was armored, and that none of them were working. Even this late at night, dockworkers were still scrambling around at reduced numbers, but not over near *The Averast*. The people over there just stood in place or walked a circuit around the area.

"What are the odds it's a coincidence?" Luke asked.

"Slim to fucking none. Someone told the church we bought passage on this ship, so they grabbed it. Probably trumped up some charge about consorting with apostates and threw at least the captain in a cell. They might have taken the whole crew in, but I think if they did, the docks would be a lot emptier right now. Ships would be fleeing before someone started looking too closely at them."

"So we need a new ride, and we're out fifteen gold," Luke said.

"Looks like it," Zea said, not taking her eyes off the ship. Her lips were thinned into a hard grimace, and she was unconsciously clutching at her money purse. Luke had his suspicions about which part she was more upset over.

"So the new mission is to find another boat that's leaving, preferably in the next day or two, buy passage, and get the hell out of here before anyone catches up to us," Luke said. "Yeah, that sounds easy. On the off chance that doesn't work, maybe we should start looking into my ant-genocide backup plan again."

"Humph. We'll see."

They wandered back down the docks, away from *The Averast* and its templar guards. "Where are we going?" Luke asked.

"I don't know," Zea said with a heavy sigh. "Chances are bad that we can find another ship willing to take us if they know they risk running up against the church. It's going to be hard to even look at this point. Anyone might turn us in, and the church will be watching the docks too. Shit, there's nowhere else to go."

"This can't be the only city on this entire continent that has connections across the ocean," Luke said. "If we're burned here, we'll just have to find another one."

"If there are, I don't know where they're at," Zea said. "Maybe System can tell us. But fuck. It would be a long, long walk. If it's any farther north, I can't come with you. The cold is already bad enough here, and it's not even winter yet."

"We'll figure it out. What do we do right now? Back out of the city?"

"I don't know. Maybe." Zea looked out across the harbor. "There has got to be a ship somewhere here that we can buy passage on. Or . . . stow away? **[XP Mask]** would keep them from sensing us. As long as we stayed quiet, they might not realize we're there until we're a week out of port. At that point, we can just drop some gold into the captain's palms, and we're good."

"That might work, but how do we know which ships are going where we need them to go?" Luke asked. "It's not like they're advertising."

"Oh, they are. Just go to any tavern right off the docks and there will be plenty of sailors more than happy to bitch and moan, often quite loudly, about how long their next trip to this or that place is going to be, how hard it is for them to go weeks or months without fresh booze and fresh whores, about what kinds of monsters they have to fight off on the trip."

"Great. Except . . ."

"Yeah," Zea said. "Except I'm too conspicuous, and you have no idea which questions to ask or whom to talk to. The last thing we need is to light off a signal fire that we're back in the city. We don't even know whom we're up against, not really. The church obviously isn't throwing its full weight behind Lath, or he wouldn't have needed to hire those mercenaries. Plus we have no idea where Lath himself is or what condition he's in, or whether those mercenaries are going to stay bought after everything that's happened."

Luke still had the 125 AP he was holding on to for **[XP Cycle]**. If he needed to, he could pump some ranks into skills like **[Disguise]** and **[Deception]** to help him blend in. He'd also need to bump up **[Ostari]**, probably all the way to rank 3 if he was going to pass as a native. It might be enough to let him walk into a tavern and make casual conversation with the sailors drinking there.

There were risks to that, of course. Zea would have to wait somewhere else. She was right that she was too conspicuous. He hadn't seen a single dwifkin in Sicanti besides her. It was almost exclusively human, with a bare smattering of other species, but none of those were of the short variety. Every hour they spent not on board a ship was another hour that they risked being discovered by an observer.

Deliberately seeking out people and questioning them about their ships' destinations, just hoping to find one that was going in the right direction, could also lead church agents back to them. Maybe he could just lurk near a tavern and put his high perception to work. If they got lucky, they might just overhear useful information. There was no telling how long that might take, if it worked at all, but he supposed they weren't on a time limit anymore, not if they didn't need to worry about following *The Averast*'s schedule.

[Detection] pinged his brain and pulled him out of his musings. Somebody was watching them, and the skill directed Luke's eyes right to him. A man stood on the deck of a ship, leaning on the railing and staring right at Zea. He noticed Luke noticing him immediately and gave him a nod. Cautiously, Luke returned the nod.

"Guy standing on the deck of that ship over there is looking at us," Luke said under his breath, so quietly that Zea wouldn't have heard it standing right next to him before she'd put points into perception. "He's not making any effort to hide it, and when I noticed him, he acknowledged it and kept on looking."

"Shit. That's probably a bad thing," Zea said. Her eyes narrowed as she inspected the man and the ship she was standing on. "Why does that look so familiar?"

"They all look the same to me. What do you want to do?"

"We should probably get the hell out of here before that guy makes . . . a . . . God damn it. That's the ship that tall bitch with the tits owns."

"The who with the what?" Luke asked, certain he must have somehow misheard her.

"The one who wanted sixty gold for passage across the ocean. Why is she still even here? She said she was leaving days ago when I tried to negotiate with her."

"So you're saying that ship is going across the ocean," Luke said. "And that for a price that's well within our means, we could get on it right now, salvage this clusterfuck of a plan, and put Sicanti behind us?"

"No," Zea protested. "Absolutely not. Not for sixty! That's robbery."

"Who gives a fuck?!" Luke hissed. "Give me a month or two and I will be able to literally conjure up all the gold you could ever use."

The man on the ship noticed they'd stopped walking while they talked. He straightened up, waved a hand near the railing to catch Luke's attention, then made a beckoning gesture.

"Looks like he wants to talk to us," Luke said. "You think it's a trap?"

"Probably not," Zea said reluctantly. "But . . . Fuck! So much money."

"You'll survive. Let's go see what he wants. Best case, we find our ticket out of here. Worst case, you get the satisfaction of watching me do way more than sixty gold in damage to that ship when we fight our way out."

"Well, I would like to see that. Try to knock over the mast or something if we have to fight. Those are a bitch to replace."

"I will keep that in mind," Luke said dutifully.

The two of them turned toward the ship and started walking.

Name	Luke Bennet	Zea Stenter
Level	41	35
XP	252683/254133	145001/157276
AP	125	9
Bloodline	SysAdmin III	None
Strength	61	7
Agility	70	27
Stamina	66	27
Perception	55	19
Skills	Mace Mastery (5)	Dagger Mastery (1)
	Sword Mastery (1)	Stealth (2)
	Unarmed Martialist (4)	Keen Instincts (1)
	Power Strike (2)	Lock Picking (1)
	Life Surge (2)	Disguise (2)
	Peripheral Awareness (2)	Deception (1)
	Tactical Foresight (1)	Bartering (2)
	Counter (3)	Streetwise (2)
	Twitch Reflexes (3)	Cooking (1)
	Stealth (1)	Mending (1)
	Survivalist (2)	First Aid (1)
	First Aid (1)	Thalian (3)
	Wood Carving (1)	Neyardic (3)
	Leatherworking (2)	Ostari (1)
	Butchering (4)	Mana Manipulation (3)
	Thalian (2)	Mana Sight (2)
	Ostari (1)	Metallurgy (1)
	Disguise (2)	Whitesmithing (1)
	Deception (1)	Goldsmithing (2)
	Detection (2)	Gem Cutting (1)
	Torturer (1)	Engraving (4)
	Analyze (BL)	Rune Forging (3)
	Remote Access (BL)	Painting (1)
	XP Mask (BL)	Arcano Dynamics (2)
		Sleight of Hand (1)
		Steady Hands (2)
		Cold Reading (1)
		Temperature Acclimation (2)
		Cadence (3)
		Bloodline Purification Ritual (2)
		Ghost Script (1)

CHAPTER 71

While the ship was much smaller than *The Averast*, once Luke was actually on it, it seemed plenty big. Still, to go out into open water, to cross the entire ocean in it . . . It felt like the entire cargo hold would have nothing but food and water in it. Maybe he was overestimating how long it would take to make the trip, or maybe there was a supply stop halfway.

They were met on deck by the captain, who was wearing much the same outfit as Luke remembered from the first time, complete with a truly prodigious amount of cleavage that had made it into Zea's description. Idly, he wondered how much of the captain's face Zea could even see without taking a step or two back.

"I was wondering if I'd see you two again," the captain said with a smirk.

"Why's that?" Zea asked.

"Well, you got poor Belikaron arrested on charges of heresy, so I knew you weren't going to be completing your trip across the ocean with him," the captain told them. "But I had a suspicion you weren't going to just give up. So I delayed a few extra days and set some men to watching for you to come strolling back into the harbor."

Luke shifted uneasily. The explanation sounded sketchy as fuck to him, but Zea was taking it calmly, so he resisted the urge to grab the handle of his mace. Listening to her heartbeat remain steady helped calm him too. That didn't stop him from tossing out an **[Analyze]** on the captain, just to refresh his memory and make sure there hadn't been any changes.

[Name: The Captain]
[Level: 17]
[XP: 16287/18255]

[AP: 1]
[Strength: 10]
[Agility: 21]
[Stamina: 9]
[Perception: 23]
[Skills:]
[Sword Mastery (3)]
[Dagger Mastery (2)]
[Crossbow Mastery (3)]
[Reflexive Aim (2)]
[Ambidexterity (2)]
[Stealth (3)]
[Bartering (4)]
[Intimidating Presence (3)]
[Deception (2)]
[Intuition (4)]
[Gardening (1)]
[Embroidery (2)]
[Cooking (2)]
[Tailoring (1)]
[Navigation (4)]
[Painting (3)]
[Calligraphy (1)]
[Ostari (3)]
[Thalian (3)]
[Consortium Standard (3)]
[Sailing (5)]

The stats were similar to what he remembered, and it was nice to get a look at her skills. There was nothing there that he'd consider all that dangerous to him, but it was obvious that she took her job as ship captain seriously. Even her name just said the Captain, strangely enough.

"Let me guess," Zea said. "You've still got room for two passengers."

"And I can leave immediately," the Captain said. "In less than two hours, the tide comes in and *The Silk Lady* can set sail. In fact, we will set sail, now that you're here. Whether you choose to board with us or not will be up to you. I've already delayed departure by a few days to wait you out; now that you've heard the offer, you can either take it or not."

"Sixty is robbery! It's twice what passage on *The Averast* cost."

"Oh, that does remind me. The price has gone up. It's now sixty each."

"What! Absolutely not. Why would we pay double on your already over-inflated price?!"

The Captain leaned forward and stared Zea in the eye. "Bitch tax," she said.

Luke couldn't help himself. He started laughing, which prompted both women to turn and regard him. "I was wondering if you heard that," he said by way of explanation.

He quieted himself under Zea's baleful glare and gestured for them to continue. "One hundred twenty gold," the Captain said. "Payable in full, right now. We leave in two hours. I'm not sticking around to wait for a bunch of templars to swarm the docks and drag *The Silk Lady* over to the church's private berths. You're either in, or you're on your own. Make a decision."

"We get a cabin," Zea said. "For that much money, I'm not sleeping in a hammock with the crew."

"Agreed, but you'll get the same meal portions as everybody else. No one gets extra rations on my ship, not even me."

"Give us a minute," Zea said. She grabbed Luke and dragged him over to the railing. "What do you think?"

"I think she's bending us over a barrel and fucking us on the price, which is the part you're sore about," Luke said. "She's got a predatory streak in her, if what she said about waiting and watching for us is true. She's probably making a ton of money off us."

"That's exactly what's happening," Zea said. "But I'm afraid she might just be our only option if we want to leave Sicanti by water."

"On the other hand, think of how much of a risk it is to her. The last ship that agreed to take us on ended up impounded. We may have gotten that captain killed just by shaking hands with him."

"You think we should do something about that?" Zea asked.

Luke shrugged. The altruistic part of him wasn't happy that an innocent man had been imprisoned by the church, but the practical part refused to accept the blame for that. He'd done nothing wrong, and he wasn't going to let his conscience get weighed down because a bunch of other shit heels were trying to isolate him by imprisoning and torturing anyone he so much as exchanged pleasantries with.

As far as rescuing the captain went, that wasn't even worth considering. Maybe if it was a bunch of level 20 to 25 templars, he could just run roughshod over them, but if there was even one inquisitor like Lath in that building, it was going to be a completely different story. Luke didn't think for a second there would be just one inquisitor there, or that there wouldn't be other problems he couldn't even begin to guess at.

"It's bullshit what happened to him, but I don't see how we can change it. Not from here at least. Maybe once we get to where we're going," Luke said. He was getting quite the list of things to fix once he finally had full access to the system at the God Machine's console.

"You know we're going to be basically broke if we do this, right? This is an insane amount of money. We could live for the rest of our lives in relative comfort for what she's asking. Sixty was already a rip-off."

"So what?" Luke said. "Let her have her big payday. That money isn't going to mean anything to us where we're going."

The whining sound that came out of Zea's mouth was probably inaudible to ordinary humans. Certainly, Luke at least wouldn't have known what it was if not for the look on her face. With a sigh, he said, "You can have all the money that's left over, okay? Whenever you feel like you've gone far enough and it's time for us to part ways, you keep everything we have at that point."

That must have been the wrong thing to say. "You're such an idiot," she told him. "It's not about that at all."

She spun on her heel and jerked the neck-purse string over her head. "Fine," she told the Captain. "One twenty, and we are immediately escorted to our cabin, where we'll stay until we're out of the harbor."

"Count out the coins," the Captain said.

The first mate ran for a small wooden bowl from the Captain's quarters, and Zea counted out twelve stacks of ten, going slowly and with everyone agreeing on the number every step of the way. Her eyes glinted darkly as she watched the bowl fill and her purse empty. Finally, the task was done, and the Captain grinned and poured the bowl into a leather pouch of her own and announced, "Welcome aboard *The Silk Lady*. Grimly, if you could take them below."

"Aye, captain," the first mate said. "Follow me."

Grimly led them to a set of deep, rickety stairs that were probably more dangerous to walk on than it would have been to just jump straight down. Luke reminded himself that not everybody had the strength stat to just leap ten feet straight into the air and that, for them, the stairs were a necessity.

The cabin had a simple lock on it, one that Grimly opened with a key produced from his pocket. He pushed the door open and gestured for the pair to enter, where they found a simple wooden bunk built into one wall with a hammock hanging off a pair of hooks above it. A chest sat in the back corner opposite it, and what looked like a wooden box with an opening for a chamber pot to be placed within occupied the front corner.

"Welcome home," Grimly said with a sneer. "First-class accommodations."

"Thanks," Luke said dryly. He hoped the man wasn't expecting a tip, not after the outrageous price his captain had extracted from them. Zea would gouge their eyes out before she'd consider giving them a single copper more. She was already fit to burst over the whole thing, no doubt because she'd planned on haggling for a better deal until Luke had made it clear that he didn't care about the money.

He didn't think she would have gotten it anyway. The Captain knew she had every advantage, that if Luke and Zea wanted to get across the ocean, she was their only ticket. Considering the risk she was taking just having them on board, and the possible long-term consequences if and when *The Silk Lady* ever returned to Sicanti, Luke honestly wondered if the Captain hadn't undercharged them.

"Hey," Luke said as the first mate moved to leave. The man froze and looked over at him. "What's the captain's name?"

"The Captain," Grimly said, a definitive note in his voice. "She don't answer to nothing else."

"Pretentious cunt," Zea muttered under her beath, just loud enough to ensure that Grimly heard her say it.

The man snickered. "Go say it to her face, see what she does. It's always a fun show."

[Name: Grimly]
[Level: 14]
[XP: 9122/10332]
[AP: 0]
[Strength: 16]
[Agility: 13]
[Stamina: 14]
[Perception: 8]
[Skills:]
[Sword Mastery (1)]
[Bow Mastery (5)]
[Wind Reading (3)]
[Mounted Archery (3)]
[Quick Draw (2)]
[Horseback Riding (4)]
[Implacable Intent (3)]
[Intimidating Presence (2)]
[Taskmaster (1)]
[Stealth (2)]
[Disguise (5)]
[Akohean (3)]
[Ostari (2)]
[Thalian (1)]
[Consortium Standard (1)]
[First Aid (3)]
[Herb Lore (2)]
[Medicine (2)]

[Wood Carving (3)]
[Sailing (4)]

Grimly's skills told an interesting history. He obviously been born to a very different lifestyle than where he'd ended up. Many of his skills were impressively high rank, especially for someone who was only level 14. Luke also didn't recognize that language skill, **[Akohean]**. Wherever Grimly had come from, his current position as first mate was an odd choice. In the end, it wouldn't make a difference.

Luke seriously doubted anyone on the ship could make him or Zea do anything they didn't want to. Luke could kill everyone on board single-handedly, if it came to it. Zea could at least defend herself until he could step in, and he thought he might encourage her to invest some of her remaining AP into her stats and a combat skill or two, just to be safe.

"Got it. I'll keep that in mind. Thanks, Grimly."

The first mate left, closing the door behind him. Luke listened to his footsteps retreat back to the stairs and climb them back up to the deck. "What an odd guy," he said. "I wonder how he went from horseback fighting to sailing the open ocean."

"What the hell are you talking about?" Zea asked.

"His skill list," Luke said absently. "By the way, the Captain's name is literally listed as the Captain in her status. That's some impressive dedication to her persona there. We should probably talk about spending the rest of your AP soon. Some of these sailors could take you in a fight if I don't intervene right now."

"Why would they? We're paying customers. Fuck, they ought to be treating us like royalty."

"I doubt the Captain is doling out gold coins to everyone on her crew. Don't be surprised if they don't bend over backward to accommodate us," Luke told her.

"Yeah," Zea agreed with a sigh. "Wouldn't want things to be too easy. Well, at least we're finally getting away from that inquisitor. I can't imagine him chasing us down now."

"Jeez, why would you say something like that?" Luke asked. "It's like you're tempting fate to rub our noses in it."

Lath stepped onto the docks and peered around. He was following the dwifkin's scent more than anything else, and she'd definitely come to the harbor. He just needed to figure out where she was hiding. The scent trail went north toward the church, and he followed it doggedly.

Name	Luke Bennet	Zea Stenter
Level	41	35
XP	252683/254133	145001/157276
AP	125	9
Bloodline	SysAdmin III	None
Strength	61	7
Agility	70	27
Stamina	66	27
Perception	55	19
Skills	Mace Mastery (5)	Dagger Mastery (1)
	Sword Mastery (1)	Stealth (2)
	Unarmed Martialist (4)	Keen Instincts (1)
	Power Strike (2)	Lock Picking (1)
	Life Surge (2)	Disguise (2)
	Peripheral Awareness (2)	Deception (1)
	Tactical Foresight (1)	Bartering (2)
	Counter (3)	Streetwise (2)
	Twitch Reflexes (3)	Cooking (1)
	Stealth (1)	Mending (1)
	Survivalist (2)	First Aid (1)
	First Aid (1)	Thalian (3)
	Wood Carving (1)	Neyardic (3)
	Leatherworking (2)	Ostari (1)
	Butchering (4)	Mana Manipulation (3)
	Thalian (2)	Mana Sight (2)
	Ostari (1)	Metallurgy (1)
	Disguise (2)	Whitesmithing (1)
	Deception (1)	Goldsmithing (2)
	Detection (2)	Gem Cutting (1)
	Torturer (1)	Engraving (4)
	Analyze (BL)	Rune Forging (3)
	Remote Access (BL)	Painting (1)
	XP Mask (BL)	Arcano Dynamics (2)
		Sleight of Hand (1)
		Steady Hands (2)
		Cold Reading (1)
		Temperature Acclimation (2)
		Cadence (3)
		Bloodline Purification Ritual (2)
		Ghost Script (1)

CHAPTER 72

Luke spent the next hour or so using **[Analyze]** on every sailor on the ship. None of them were over level 20, and in fact only one of them was a higher level than the Captain herself. Even then, it was only just barely, and that guy's skill set was so obviously geared toward being a sailor and nothing else that Luke actually considered him one of the weakest people on the ship in terms of his odds of winning a fight.

He still wanted Zea to bump up her strength a little bit, but she waved his concerns away. She'd already set up her portable enchanting worktable and was busy etching runes on a thin metal cable about four feet long. Luke hadn't seen her working on that piece before, but he knew better than to ask. Her explanations had always confused him, and since she'd upgraded her enchanting skills, that had only gotten worse.

It took her a few minutes to get used to inscribing runes while they were on a ship, and Luke wasn't all that confident that she would be able to do any finely detailed work once they left the harbor, but for the moment, Zea was happily working away at whatever it was. He'd thought she wanted to finish up that razor-prong whip, but this new project didn't seem to have anything to do with that. Or maybe it did, and she just hadn't gotten this far with her first attempt.

Once he'd finished scouting everything out, he turned his thoughts toward the upcoming trip.

"System," Luke said softly.

"Yes, Luke."

"How long are we going to be on this boat?"

"My apologies, but I'm not able to answer that. There are too many variables to predict how long your voyage will take with any degree of accuracy."

"Give me a rough guess? Two weeks? Two months? Six?"

"Somewhere between two weeks and two months is probably the most likely scenario," System told him. "If the weather was perfect over the next two weeks with no complications, it is theoretically possible to reach the shores of the eastern continent. It would be far more reasonable to assume it may take up to three times that long under average conditions, or even longer, circumstances pending."

"What kind of circumstances?" Luke asked.

"Any sort of attack on the ship that resulted in damage could theoretically slow down the trip. As I said, there are too many variables to predict what dangers *The Silk Lady* will face, if any at all."

"So, most likely guess, with average weather, is between four and six weeks."

Either the continents were much closer together than Luke thought, or sailing was much faster on Aros than it had been back on Earth. He was sure his history classes said it took explorers months and months to sail across the Atlantic. He couldn't swear to how many months, but more than one or two, usually.

Those people didn't have the system and all its benefits to help them. Luke wasn't precisely sure what exactly those benefits were, but everything here seemed to get done faster and better than it should be without the benefits of machines and computers. He didn't see any reason to believe sailing would be any different.

"Something's happening," Luke said, noting the noise of metal clanging against metal.

"They're pulling up the anchor," Zea said absently, not looking up from her runes. Somehow her hands were still holding steady with the motion of the ship. "Tide must be coming in."

"It's hard to believe we're finally on our way," Luke said. "So much shit happened to trip us up. The church, multiple times. Those mercs, even the stupid squirrel druids."

"Hopefully the church doesn't send anyone else after us," Zea said. "It would be . . . bad . . . if we ended up in ship-to-ship combat with them. *The Silk Lady* is not designed for naval warfare. It's pure speed and nothing else."

"She," Luke said. "Aren't we supposed to call ships she or her when speaking of them?"

Zea shrugged. "Who cares?"

"I suppose I'll just do whatever the sailors do. No point in picking a fight with anyone over it. Let 'em call the ship whatever they want."

Zea grunted but otherwise ignored his rambling. Her nose was practically touching the chain now as she etched tiny lines into it. It looked like she'd run out of patience for conversation, so he set the key next to her and said, "I'm going to go up on deck and get a look around."

"Have fun," she said absently. "Try not to get in anyone's way."

The deck was busier than he'd expected, but Luke found a barrel propped up in a corner and took a seat on it while sailors scrambled around, tying off ropes and lines as they raised and lowered various sails. The Captain stood on a raised deck at the back of the ship behind him, occasionally snapping out orders.

There were truly a dizzying amount of sails and ropes, far more than it seemed like there should be. Luke was almost tempted to pick up a rank in **[Sailing]** just so he could make some sense out of what he was seeing. Maybe it would also tell him why more than one sailor gave him a nasty look as they went by. Then again, maybe it was just that they were working while he was watching. God knew he hadn't met a person yet who enjoyed having someone else stand around watching them work.

The Silk Lady got pointed toward the mouth of the harbor and started inching its way out. It seemed like it ought to go faster, but when he considered the wind was blowing in the wrong direction, he supposed he ought to be happy that it was moving at all. He had no clue how the complex arrangement of cloth and rope managed to turn the wind cutting across the deck into forward motion, but it did.

"Captain," one of the sailors said up on the deck behind Luke. "Someone is rowing a boat out to us. I don't recognize him."

"How many of these assholes do I need to bribe before they leave me alone?" the Captain snarled. "Let this one on board, but if he tries to get so much as a single bent copper out of my coffers, I'll string him up and slice his guts open to feed to the seagulls."

Lath had gone up and down the harbor, and he'd come to the conclusion that the dwifkin and her apostate lover had boarded one of the ships. Specifically, they'd boarded the ship that was even now slowly sailing away from the dock it had been moored to.

The ship was only about fifty yards out, and the winds weren't favorable for exiting the harbor. It was going to get there eventually but not fast enough to prevent him from catching up to it. He might even be able to do it just by diving into the water and swimming, but it would be faster to find a . . .

"Ah, there," he said to himself, spotting a small three-man fishing boat with a single sail.

Lath ran at full speed, weaving through the few remaining workers on the docks and arriving at his destination in seconds. He snapped the ropes holding the sailboat to the dock with his bare hands, tossed the excess length into the boat, and lightly leaped on board.

A man was snoozing up against the bow, his form obscured by a light blanket. He groaned and blinked blearily as the boat rocked from Lath's landing on it. Before he could say or do anything, Lath leaned in and raked his fingers across the man's throat. Blood spurted, and a kill notification popped up in front of him. Lath dismissed it and flicked the blood off his hand.

He didn't bother setting the sail. The wind would be just as against him as it was the ship he was pursuing, and there was already a pair of oars ready to be locked into place in the boat. They were sturdy, though not strong enough to handle the full force of his strength. He'd need to be careful not to break them as he rowed after the ship.

Using one oar to push away from the dock, Lath started rowing. He made good progress as he cut through the cold water and still night air, and by his judgment, he'd catch up with the ship well before it crossed over the mouth of the harbor and into open water where it could alter its direction to better capture the wind.

They saw him coming. That was no surprise, considering it was a clear night and there was nothing he could do to hide an entire boat. It didn't matter. Even if they decided to run, which it didn't look like they were doing, he'd still catch them. With each stroke of the oars, he got another foot closer to the ship. With each stroke, he got another foot closer to avenging his apprentice and completing his mission.

Soon, it would all be over.

There was a smell in the air, something familiar that Luke couldn't quite place. At first, he hadn't even realized it was there, not until he'd overheard one of the sailors talking to the Captain. That was when it clicked. It was that dead smell Lath's not-zombie body had. It was fainter now, subtly different in a way Luke lacked the knowledge to express, but he still recognized it.

He jumped to his feet, almost knocking a sailor over in his haste, and turned toward the rear deck. The sailor started cussing at him, but Luke ignored the man. With a twitch of his legs, he leaped up, twisted around a rope line in his way, and landed next to the wheel.

"This area's off-limits to you," the Captain said immediately. "Leave afore I have you tossed off."

"The man in that boat isn't some dock official come to collect some coins," Luke said. "He's an inquisitor after me. If you let him catch up, there'll be a fight. I can't guarantee your ship won't get damaged."

"Gods damn it. You've barely been on board for an hour! We even set sail early. How did they find you this fast?" the Captain snarled.

Luke shrugged. "Can your ship outrun him?"

"Out in open water? Maybe, if the winds favored us. Here, now, in the harbor? Not a chance."

Luke peered out into the night to see a small boat with the oars working furiously to propel it toward them. "Got anything to sink it? Maybe he's a bad swimmer."

The Captain scowled and shook her head. "I should have charged you even more."

"Well, win some, lose some. That's how it goes," Luke said.

"Why don't we just give the inquisitor what he wants?" the sailor who'd let the Captain know someone was coming asked.

"Oh, that would not end well for you at all," Luke said with a sad shake of his head. "I'm not going in without a fight. And I've fought that guy before. Shit gets messy. Little ship like this will be lucky to still be above the water by sunrise if I decide to start breaking things."

"Don't you dare threaten *The Silk Lady*," the Captain said.

"Relax. I don't want to sink your ship. I'm relying on you and your crew to get me where I need to go," Luke said. "I'm just telling your idiot over there why it would be a bad idea to try to sell me out, especially after we paid you so much money in the first place. If you can't outrun a guy in a rowboat, well, I guess I'll deal with him when he gets here."

Luke reached behind his back and pulled his mace off the harness. He hoped his words sounded more confident than he felt because he figured he had maybe three minutes before Lath caught up to them. If all else failed, he still had 125 AP he could spend. **[XP Cycle]** was important, but not getting captured or killed by a psychotic inquisitor trumped XP-madness concerns in the short term.

125 AP. What was the best way to spend that?

Name	Luke Bennet	Zea Stenter
Level	41	35
XP	252683/254133	145001/157276
AP	125	9
Bloodline	SysAdmin III	None
Strength	61	7
Agility	70	27
Stamina	66	27
Perception	55	19
Skills	Mace Mastery (5)	Dagger Mastery (1)
	Sword Mastery (1)	Stealth (2)
	Unarmed Martialist (4)	Keen Instincts (1)
	Power Strike (2)	Lock Picking (1)
	Life Surge (2)	Disguise (2)
	Peripheral Awareness (2)	Deception (1)
	Tactical Foresight (1)	Bartering (2)
	Counter (3)	Streetwise (2)
	Twitch Reflexes (3)	Cooking (1)
	Stealth (1)	Mending (1)
	Survivalist (2)	First Aid (1)
	First Aid (1)	Thalian (3)
	Wood Carving (1)	Neyardic (3)
	Leatherworking (2)	Ostari (1)
	Butchering (4)	Mana Manipulation (3)
	Thalian (2)	Mana Sight (2)
	Ostari (1)	Metallurgy (1)
	Disguise (2)	Whitesmithing (1)
	Deception (1)	Goldsmithing (2)
	Detection (2)	Gem Cutting (1)
	Torturer (1)	Engraving (4)
	Analyze (BL)	Rune Forging (3)
	Remote Access (BL)	Painting (1)
	XP Mask (BL)	Arcano Dynamics (2)
		Sleight of Hand (1)
		Steady Hands (2)
		Cold Reading (1)
		Temperature Acclimation (2)
		Cadence (3)
		Bloodline Purification Ritual (2)
		Ghost Script (1)

CHAPTER 73

The simplest place to put AP was into stats. He had more than enough to drop 30 into every stat and just completely overpower Lath in terms of raw capabilities. Of course, that didn't guarantee a victory. It had been a painful lesson that had been beaten into him repeatedly, but he was finally figuring out that just having a higher strength stat didn't guarantee victory, especially when he was fighting against someone with skills that were way more advanced than Luke's. Given the nature of Lath's advanced merged skills, Luke felt it was fair to compare it to fighting someone with a rank 8 weapon skill and similar movement and dodging skills.

125 AP wasn't going to be nearly enough to bridge that gap in their skills. He could upgrade **[Power Strike]** to rank 3, and under other circumstances, he would have seriously considered that. With this particular fight being one where he had to worry about collateral damage, he didn't think he'd be relying heavily on that skill. It was going to be hard enough not to break the ship as it was.

If he had another 125 AP, he'd buy **[Inflict Status]** and **[XP Reset]** right now. That would have been problem solved, but Zea had been stubborn about attacking anymore anthills. That option wasn't available to him.

He didn't have the 250 needed for rank 3 **[Life Surge]**, but rank 2 **[Tactical Foresight]** was exactly 125 AP. That was an option, and probably a better one than a **[Power Strike]** upgrade.

[Mace Mastery] and **[Counter]** were both already maxed out, and **[Peripheral Awareness]** wasn't going to help him if he upgraded it here. That was more for handling large groups coming at him from every angle anyway.

[Unarmed Martialist] technically had one more rank available for 50 AP, but he didn't plan on fighting without a weapon, and he'd already absorbed all the lessons on footwork and positioning it could give.

His only real options were the upgrade to **[Tactical Foresight]** for all his AP or a raw-stat bumps. That was a tough call. Maybe a bit more information would help him make his decision.

Luke walked up to stand next to the Captain and watched the boat get closer. Despite being powered by nothing but oars, it was steadily gaining on them. He reached out with **[Analyze]** to target the man rowing.

> **[Error: Unable to detect user profile. Generating temporary profile.]**
> **[Temporary profile failed to generate. Target is not a viable user.]**
> **[Submitting error report . . . Error report failed to submit.]**
> **[Flagging error for administrative review.]**

Luke's brow furrowed as he read the messages. He couldn't recall something like that ever happening, and it sounded suspiciously like Pantheon fuckery. That last line was especially ominous, since it seemed to be saying that the God Machine's system was going to be letting the gods know something had fucked up.

In theory, that wouldn't make a difference. They were gods. They obviously already knew about him, since Hestoc had sent his flunkies to the valley to kill Luke, and then the church had come after him as soon as he'd reached Valtira. It didn't seem likely to Luke that the gods had lost track of him over the last month or two.

Why exactly none of them had reached down through the clouds and squished him like an ant under their divine thumb was a mystery he still hadn't figured out the answer to. And he didn't believe for a second it was their Covenant bullshit. Something else prevented them from coming down and dealing with him personally.

That was a problem for another day, one he might never find the answer to. Right now, he needed to deal with the problem right in front of him. "Can you tell what level he is?" he asked the Captain.

She shook her head, setting a pair of hoop earrings to jiggling. "Don't feel a damn thing from him. Kind of like you that way. Handy skill, that. Don't suppose you'd care to share what you're using to hide yourself completely?"

"No," Luke said. "You wouldn't be able to take it anyway. That inquisitor is using **[Infiltrator]** though. Rank 5." At least, that was what he vaguely remembered from when he could actually look at Lath's status.

The Captain let out a low whistle. "You don't see many people with advanced skills at max rank. He's dangerous, huh?"

"Yep."

"You can beat him though? Preferably without damaging my ship."

"Probably not," Luke said, his eyes not leaving the rowboat.

The Captain turned to face him fully. "The fuck is that supposed to mean? If you can't beat him, why the hell shouldn't I just throw you overboard now and let him have you?"

"I'd kill every single person on this ship before you budged me an inch in a direction I don't want to go," Luke said evenly. "You've been paid a hell of a lot of money. You knew we were apostates; this is the risk you took when you accepted that gold. I'll do my best to keep this ship intact because I need you to fulfill your half of the deal, but don't expect me to pretend to give a shit about you or anyone else on this tub on a personal level."

Before the Captain could say anything, the man rowing the boat stood up. He was clearly Lath, but not the Lath Luke remembered from their first two fights. He looked closer to the state he'd been in when he'd come back as a mobile anthill, but Luke's bloodline skills didn't work on him now. Something had obviously changed, and that scared Luke. Lath was the most dangerous opponent he'd ever met, and now was not a good time to be dealing with unknowns.

"He's about to jump," Luke said. "Get your people below."

The Captain gave him one last withering glance, then spun in place and started bellowing orders. Before anyone could even start to move, Lath leaped at *The Silk Lady*. He left the rowboat cracked in half behind him, both sides pushed underwater and immediately starting to sink. Lath flew through the air with explosive force, no weapon visible on his person.

That was good. It probably meant Luke didn't need to worry about his **[Blade Master]** skill or any of his poisonous concoctions. That could only help tilt the fight in Luke's favor. Maybe he'd get lucky and not have to spend any of that AP. On the other hand, this really wasn't the time to be holding back. He already knew how hard Lath was to fight normally.

He bought **[Tactical Foresight]** rank 2.

The skill immediately latched on to his brain and ran everything he knew about the inquisitor through it. Almost instinctively, he started making calculations about where Lath would land—crashing through the railing right in front of Luke—to what his first move would be—either a lunge for the throat that flowed into barehanded grappling or a kick with the torque of his full body behind it to disguise the motion of drawing a hidden weapon from beneath that enormous cloak he was wearing—to how well Lath would be able to dodge a hard strike to the chest if Luke struck right when he landed—pretty damn well, likely by dropping straight down and attacking Luke's ankles.

He had almost a full second to get used to the skill communicating with his brain before Lath crashed through the wooden rails, ducked Luke's mace by dropping straight down, and swept a leg out to smack at Luke's ankles.

Lath was every bit as fast as Luke remembered and even more aggressive than usual. But now, it was easy to predict the paths of the inquisitor's wild blows. Luke worked his mace around, perhaps for the first time really fully utilizing his rank 5 **[Mace Mastery]** since he'd maxed it out. Lath came at him, his limbs flashing out to strike a dozen times in the first second of combat, and Luke both predicted and parried every one of them.

He gave ground as Lath pushed forward, easily dropping backward to the main deck. It was clear of sailors except for three who'd been up in the rigging when the Captain had given the order. All three watched the battle start, slack-jawed with astonishment. They were far enough out of the way that Luke didn't think he needed to worry about them interfering, not unless the fight brought down one of the ship's three masts.

Lath landed right in front of Luke. He hit so hard that one foot cracked through the wood planks that made up the deck. He recovered his balance in an instant, but not before Luke struck him across the face with a **[Power Strike]**–infused mace. Skin tore to reveal muscle and bone underneath, but if Lath felt the pain at all, he didn't show it.

Then they were fighting again, Luke playing it defensively in hopes of minimizing the damage *The Silk Lady* took. The worst of it was trying to dance around all the ropes still hanging loosely. The ship's crew hadn't finished setting everything up yet, and there were plenty of spots where something or another hadn't been tied down properly.

It actually put a bit of a time limit on the fight. Without anyone to steer or a crew to complete their preparations, the ship was already turning with the wind. It wouldn't happen in the next minute or two, but eventually they'd run up against the seawall Sicanti had constructed to protect the harbor.

As he settled into the rhythm of Lath's new fighting style, Luke started letting **[Counter]** guide him into striking back. Those attacks rarely hit; Lath was simply too good to leave himself vulnerable, and despite all Luke's skills working in harmony, he wasn't on the level of the inquisitor.

They were fighting at a stalemate now despite Lath's lack of a weapon. It wasn't quite the same as their original fights, but there were plenty of similarities. Luke had fought this fight before, but he was better prepared now. He blocked or dodged Lath's attacks, struck back when he could do so without compromising his own defenses, and did his best to keep the inquisitor from inflicting too much damage on their arena.

That wasn't to say they didn't break anything. At one point, Lath seized a loose line, gave it a tug, and sent one of the men up in the rigging falling thirty feet to land on the deck. He didn't accomplish anything useful with the action; it just seemed to Luke to be a feeble attempt at distracting him, or maybe it had been done out of sheer frustration. The unintelligible snarls coming out of Lath's mouth were getting louder and more frequent the longer the fight went on.

Then Lath made a mistake. It was a small thing, just a misstep around a loose rope that caused it to roll under his foot. He corrected his balance so fast that no one with human levels of perception would have even noticed it. One of those cameras that took a thousand pictures a second could have picked it up.

And so could Luke. In that frozen hundredth of a second where Lath was vulnerable, Luke struck. His body flared with energy as he triggered [**Life Surge**], and he brought his mace around to smack against the same place he'd hit before. The metal struck the side of Lath's face, again infused with [**Power Strike**], and Lath couldn't dodge or move with the blow this time, not while he was busy sliding his foot back to the wooden deck.

Lath went flying away, his whole body spinning from the force until he crashed into the wall that separated the Captain's personal quarters from the main deck. Wood gave way, and Lath crashed through it. Luke was sure the fight was over for half a second. He'd seen the inquisitor's head spin all the way around in a full circle, far beyond the tolerance of any human's neck.

But there was no ding. And in that same second, Lath regained his feet. Head flopping loosely, he leaped forward to continue his relentless attack.

Name	Luke Bennet	Zea Stenter
Level	41	35
XP	252683/254133	145001/157276
AP	0	9
Bloodline	SysAdmin III	None
Strength	61	7
Agility	70	27
Stamina	66	27
Perception	55	19
Skills	Mace Mastery (5)	Dagger Mastery (1)
	Sword Mastery (1)	Stealth (2)
	Unarmed Martialist (4)	Keen Instincts (1)
	Power Strike (2)	Lock Picking (1)
	Life Surge (2)	Disguise (2)
	Peripheral Awareness (2)	Deception (1)
	Tactical Foresight (2)	Bartering (2)
	Counter (3)	Streetwise (2)
	Twitch Reflexes (3)	Cooking (1)
	Stealth (1)	Mending (1)
	Survivalist (2)	First Aid (1)
	First Aid (1)	Thalian (3)
	Wood Carving (1)	Neyardic (3)
	Leatherworking (2)	Ostari (1)
	Butchering (4)	Mana Manipulation (3)
	Thalian (2)	Mana Sight (2)
	Ostari (1)	Metallurgy (1)
	Disguise (2)	Whitesmithing (1)
	Deception (1)	Goldsmithing (2)
	Detection (2)	Gem Cutting (1)
	Torturer (1)	Engraving (4)
	Analyze (BL)	Rune Forging (3)
	Remote Access (BL)	Painting (1)
	XP Mask (BL)	Arcano Dynamics (2)
		Sleight of Hand (1)
		Steady Hands (2)
		Cold Reading (1)
		Temperature Acclimation (2)
		Cadence (3)
		Bloodline Purification Ritual (2)
		Ghost Script (1)

CHAPTER 74

Zea wasn't paying much attention to what was going on around her. The sailors were doing their jobs, Luke had fucked off to somewhere else and left her to her work, and she was entirely focused on compensating for the gentle rocking of the ship as she carved tiny runes into the steel. Unlike an enchantment forged with **[Ghost Script]**, the real thing couldn't be altered once she'd started. She had to do it all perfectly from front to finish, or she had to start over if she made a mistake. Worse, she would lose the material she was engraving the runes on.

Thankfully, her rank upgrades in **[Engraving]** and **[Rune Forging]** were more than up to the task, and she was so close to being done. Another ten minutes of work, then the final mana sealing to empower it, and it would last at least a year. Then again, Luke got into a lot of fights. Even if he used it multiple times a week, it would still hold for six months. Of course, he'd really only need it fighting opponents above level 30, which happened a lot nowadays. It might only run for three months if it had to keep him safe against powerhouse fighters.

She stared down at the chain. "Shit."

It wasn't a waste, but it probably wouldn't last as long as she'd initially expected it to. There was practically no risk of the enchantment fading away before he burned through the mana she was pouring into it. Hopefully, it'd come in handy.

Just as she was finishing it up, she heard a lot of people jumping down into the hallway and running past her door. Curious, she poked her head out and said, "What's going on?"

"Some guy attacked the boat. Your friend is fighting him up top," a sailor said as he ran by, barely even slowing.

Zea cast a horrified look at the stairs. She didn't need to climb them to know what she'd see. Luke and that inquisitor would be dancing around each other, each moving so fast that it was all but impossible to even keep track of where they were, let alone individual attacks. She'd seen that show already, and it was as impressive as it was scary.

Out on the water, on a fragile ship made of wood and nails and tar, all it would take was one bad block or one missed swing, and *The Silk Lady* could end up crippled beyond repair. Zea could easily picture the two combatants smashing through floor after floor until they crashed into the bilge, then breaking through that and continuing their fight in the water while the ship slowly sunk below the waves with her and everyone else still on it.

If there was ever a time that Luke needed her help, it was right now. He was *not good* at finesse. All the tools, all the strategies, those had been the result of her work. She snatched up the chain, pushed past the remaining few sailors, and made her way to where the Captain was standing at the base of the stairs.

"They're fighting," the tall woman said, giving Zea a look as she hustled over. The Captain had to have a bit of ostol blood in her, with that coloring and her overall size, but maybe a few generations back.

"He needs my help," Zea said, making to walk around the Captain and jump the first five steps. A few months ago, she wouldn't have had enough agility or strength to even consider that. Now, the thought of making a jump over the head of the average human wasn't particularly daunting.

The Captain caught her shoulder before she could move. "Can you? Those two . . . They're both monsters."

"I'm not sure," Zea said. She held up the chain. "I need to get this to him."

"What does it do?"

"Takes damage and spread it across the entire body to mitigate it, kind of like wearing armor."

The Captain gave her a sharp look. "Does it only work on people?"

Zea had designed it for Luke specifically, but now that she thought about it, there was no reason it couldn't be used on an inanimate object. It didn't actually interact with whoever was wearing it other than to coat their entire form in protective magic. She could tie it around a weapon to make it more durable, but there wasn't really much point in that. It was easier to just inscribe durability runes directly into the weapon itself.

"No," Zea said. "You could use it on something else too."

"Something as big as the ship?"

Zea started to say that of course it couldn't, that the ship was far too big, but when she stopped and thought about it, that wasn't necessarily true. It would be either a far weaker shield, something that only transferred a fraction of the strain instead of all of it, or it would only work for a few hits instead of thousands, but it would technically work.

"I see. You're concerned about damage from the fight."

"Of course I am. Either of them could sink us."

"It could work, but I didn't make this chain long enough to really wrap around something bigger than a human," Zea said. "And the enchantment won't activate until the ends touch. If it's going to protect the ship, it'll need to go around a piece of it, not just some random rope."

The Captain eyed up the chain and said, "The wheel or the baluster. It's not going to fit around any of the masts."

"The wheel would be better. That's got a stronger connection," Zea said. "Someone will need to get it up there."

From what Luke had told her, Zea knew she had the highest agility and stamina on the ship, though not the highest perception. She trusted Luke to intercept any attacks Lath might send her way. Plus, she knew how the enchantment worked. There was no question of somebody screwing up and failing to activate it as long as she was the one who did it. That just left one final detail.

"Eighty gold," Zea said.

The Captain's eyes bulged. "What!"

"I'll sell you this chain, including installation on your ship, for eighty gold."

"That's your enemy tearing through my ship! Looking for you! Why should I pay you to fix it?!"

Zea shrugged. "I'm sure we can swim back to land afterward and find a new ship somewhere else." At that moment, wood burst overhead down the hall, and a foot stuck down through the hole. It disappeared as quickly as it had arrived, and Zea turned back to the Captain. "Well?"

"Twenty-five."

"Eighty."

"Forty."

"Eighty," Zea said again, enunciating the syllables. "This isn't a negotiation."

"That's way too high!"

"Bitch tax," Zea told her.

The big maybe-ostal woman looked ready to draw the dagger tucked through her belt and go for blood, but she managed to calm herself down with an act of will. "Eighty," she agreed, "minus the cost of any repairs."

"Any repairs to damages after the enchantment is activated," Zea said.

"Deal," the Captain said through gritted teeth.

Without another word, Zea leaped up the stairs. It only took two jumps to reach the deck, where she found Luke and something that looked like Lath, except with its head flopping around at an unnatural angle, busy trading blows. Fortunately, they were near the stern, which left Zea a clean trail to reach the captain's deck and attach the chain.

Luke flinched back as Lath's nails dug long, painful furrows down his arm. The man had grown bolder in the last thirty seconds after Luke had literally broken his neck and he'd realized it wasn't going to slow him down. Defense was a thing of the past, and even with **[Life Surge]** singing in his veins, it was all Luke could do to keep Lath from tearing him apart.

One of the smaller masts was damaged from where Lath had slammed into it on a missed attempt at a tackle. The horizontal piece of wood near the bottom—Luke wanted to say it was called a boom—was broken six feet from the end. Lath had ripped it off and tried to club Luke down with it, but the mace had been the stronger of those weapons, and the splintered remains of the boom were now floating in the harbor.

Blow after blow rained down on Luke. He blocked and dodged what he could, but each hit was causing environmental damage. A trail of broken deck wood followed them like footprints across the deck as they fought, mostly from Luke setting his feet to take an attack. Lath didn't seem to care if he was struck and went tumbling away as often as not.

Mentally, Luke was cursing both Zea and the Captain. He'd overheard their entire conversation, and he was sure Lath had as well. As soon as she came up those stairs, the inquisitor was going to go after her. All Luke could do was try to drag the fight away from the stairs leading down to the crew quarters and hope that Lath didn't get the bright idea to bust straight through the deck.

So far, the ghoulish inquisitor had been focused entirely on Luke. Whatever was going on with him, he wasn't human anymore. A normal person would have died from the broken neck. Lath had kept right on going. Luke had also broken almost every rib in the man's body to the point where four of them were now jutting out through torn flesh. Lath didn't care. Hell, he wasn't even pretending to breathe anymore.

Zea scrambled up the stairs into view, and Luke kicked it up another notch to keep Lath distracted. As long as the inquisitor was focused solely on him, Zea would be safe. Hopefully she'd finish doing whatever she needed to do quickly and get back belowdecks, where at least the rule seemed to be out of sight, out of mind.

It didn't work. Lath noticed her right away, and the sly grin pasted on his flopping face gave away what he was thinking. In a flash, he'd pivoted and was halfway across the deck. Luke leaped, and here his superior stats gave him the advantage. He caught up to Lath halfway to Zea and crashed down on the man with a mace strike that sent the inquisitor careening off course into the big central mast.

There was a resounding crack when Lath hit, but he bounced back to his feet without even slowing down and resumed his attempt to reach Zea. Luke pummeled him again, this time with a **[Power Strike]** angled to blow the inquisitor right over the side of the deck and into the water. Whatever had happened to Lath, he was still cunning, and attacks that could throw him off the ship were the one thing he still reacted to.

Lath twisted nimbly, avoiding the first attack and taking a follow-up kick as Luke flew by that sent him skidding down into the deck. Luke landed, his own heels hanging over the edge above the water, and it was only a mixture of intense core strength and a free hand grabbing at the broken railing nearby that allowed him to pull himself fully back onto the deck.

"Ha!" Zea called. "Ship should feel a bit sturdier now. Let him have it at full power!"

Luke pushed down harder than normal, felt the wood of the ship resist the pressure, and grinned. Lath came flying at him, scrambling on all fours and seemingly ready to throw both of them into the water. Luke leaned in to meet the attack and, both hands clenched on the handle of his mace, unleashed an attack infused with **[Power Strike]** and with the full weight of his **[Life Surge]**-enhanced stats behind it.

Lath went flying backward, struck the mast, careened off to skid across the deck, and crashed into the crank that the anchor chain was coiled around. There was probably a proper name for that too; everything on the ship seemed to have one, but Luke couldn't recall hearing any of the sailors say it. Either way, it was sturdy enough on its own and, with Zea's latest bit of enchantment reinforcing it, was barely dented from Lath slamming into it.

Luke charged forward, able to move at full speed without worrying about damaging the deck for the first time since the fight had started. He needed to finish this before the magic wore off. If that meant dismembering Lath and throwing him overboard piece by piece, then that was what he would do.

Name	Luke Bennet	Zea Stenter
Level	41	35
XP	252683/254133	145001/157276
AP	0	9
Bloodline	SysAdmin III	None
Strength	61	7
Agility	70	27
Stamina	66	27
Perception	55	19
Skills	Mace Mastery (5)	Dagger Mastery (1)
	Sword Mastery (1)	Stealth (2)
	Unarmed Martialist (4)	Keen Instincts (1)
	Power Strike (2)	Lock Picking (1)
	Life Surge (2)	Disguise (2)
	Peripheral Awareness (2)	Deception (1)
	Tactical Foresight (2)	Bartering (2)
	Counter (3)	Streetwise (2)
	Twitch Reflexes (3)	Cooking (1)
	Stealth (1)	Mending (1)
	Survivalist (2)	First Aid (1)
	First Aid (1)	Thalian (3)
	Wood Carving (1)	Neyardic (3)
	Leatherworking (2)	Ostari (1)
	Butchering (4)	Mana Manipulation (3)
	Thalian (2)	Mana Sight (2)
	Ostari (1)	Metallurgy (1)
	Disguise (2)	Whitesmithing (1)
	Deception (1)	Goldsmithing (2)
	Detection (2)	Gem Cutting (1)
	Torturer (1)	Engraving (4)
	Analyze (BL)	Rune Forging (3)
	Remote Access (BL)	Painting (1)
	XP Mask (BL)	Arcano Dynamics (2)
		Sleight of Hand (1)
		Steady Hands (2)
		Cold Reading (1)
		Temperature Acclimation (2)
		Cadence (3)
		Bloodline Purification Ritual (2)
		Ghost Script (1)

CHAPTER 75

The chain was set to protect the ship as fully as possible rather than do the bare minimum, which meant it wasn't going to last more than a few minutes at the rate Luke was hammering on it. Zea winced each time the echo of another impact reverberated through the wood and the mana in the chain dimmed just a little bit more.

They were going at it hard now. Luke had been holding back before; she just hadn't realized it until she saw him cut loose. Both figures were blurs that ranged up and down the length of the ship, leaving behind shimmering flashes of mana as the shield absorbed some of the energy they pushed into the wood just by running across it.

Something flashed across her vision, so close that, for a fraction of a second, she couldn't see anything else. Then it was gone, leaving nothing but a faint stink behind. Luke stood in its place. "Get back below deck," he said. "Whatever Lath transformed himself into doesn't seem to have enough brains to focus on anything but what's right in front of it."

Before Zea could reply, Luke was gone again. She got a brief glimpse of him twenty feet away on the main deck with his mace whipping out to the side to smack Lath's hand away, then the pair disappeared behind the mast again. There was another loud crack, though this time it didn't sound like wood, and a quick glance at the enchanted chain showed that it hadn't lost any more mana.

Whatever it was, it was on the other side of the ship, and she had a clear opening to get below deck. Zea ran for the stairs and dove straight down.

* * *

Something was burrowing into Lath's brain, something that had taken over his arms and legs and was quickly eroding his ability to think. He'd been pushed to hunt down the apostates as soon as he was able to stand again, and that hunger only prodded him on the closer he got. Seeing the apostate with his own eyes had driven that thing in his head completely insane, and Lath couldn't have stopped himself from attacking even if he wanted to.

Not that he wanted to.

He wasn't fighting with his usual tactics though. Being a revenant gave him certain advantages, advantages like complete pain nullification and no loss of strength, speed, or coordination from injuries. Lath was still getting used to that, but it didn't matter. The revenant brain demanded he fulfill his purpose, that he destroy the man in front of him. It was his reason for still walking upright, the reason he'd held his body together as one coherent whole.

There was nothing left for him now except to finish the job. The apostate had to die. His little half-sized friend had to die. The heretical crew all had to die. Lath would tear each and every one of them apart with his bare hands, then break this ship and let it sink to the bottom of the harbor as a warning to those who would commit heresy and as a tribute to the gods.

Except this man would. Not. Die. He was too fast, too strong, and he was predicting Lath's every move. No matter how hard or how fast Lath struck, the apostate always had that red-and-silver mace in place to deflect an attack or had his feet lined up to dodge and weave out of the way. The thing in Lath's brain burned away his reason and left him with nothing but rage and violence.

All pretenses at defending himself abandoned, Lath threw himself on the apostate. He accepted the hits, barely even felt them connect really, and kept up his assault. Blood flew as he finally scored a solid enough hit to break the apostate's skin.

Then the tiny apostate had appeared. He'd smelled her somewhere, but with the big one right in front of him, Lath hadn't been able to focus enough to find her. She was weak, an easy target, and killing her would hurt the big one. It would be one apostate dead and one reeling in anguish, his focus broken and his life ready to be reaped.

Lath disengaged and moved to attack, only to find the big apostate still keeping pace with him and preventing him from reaching his goal. He was batted aside, almost thrown off the ship even. Some small sliver of intelligence left in his brain understood that if that happened, he wouldn't be able to catch back up. The apostates would escape.

As long as Lath stayed on the ship, he could keep fighting. He clawed his way toward the woman, only to meet with more resistance that flung him halfway across the deck. There were a few uninterrupted seconds he spent to reorient himself, something he desperately needed after the increased power of the last hit he'd taken.

The apostate got in front of him again, and the burning rage took over. Lath slipped through the wide-swinging mace, coming up under the apostate's arm, and connected with an uppercut right on the man's chin. The apostate went flying backward and up to slam into the foremast. Lath started to follow, but something slipped through the haze.

It was a flicker of movement, the tiny apostate diving back to safety. Lath's original plan wormed its way back to the surface of his mind, and he sprinted across the deck, taking it in four great, bounding steps that ended with him jumping down the hole to crash through a set of stairs.

The apostate was there, as was the heretic captain of the ship. Both would die.

Some part of Lath's skills were still helping him, even if the man appeared to have lost his mind. Luke had stupidly left himself open when he decided to unload on the inquisitor, and he'd paid the price for that. He gave it even odds whether his jaw was broken, even with **[Life Surge]** working overtime to repair the damage.

When he dropped back down a moment later, Lath was nowhere in sight. That was bad, if only because it meant Lath wasn't still focusing on him, and if Lath wasn't in Luke's face, that probably meant he was going after Zea again. Luke could hear the deck straining against the downward pressure of the inquisitor's footsteps, and he knew exactly which way they were heading. He got around the mast just in time to see the man leap literally headfirst down the hole leading below deck.

Never before had Luke wished he had one of those skills that gave a brief burst of movement speed. He'd looked into them, and they were not cheap, but right then and there, he wished he'd dumped the AP into getting at least rank 1. His raw stats had always been enough to keep him ahead of whatever he was racing against before, but he was afraid this would finally be the exception.

Luke ran for the entrance and had a brief moment to see the creature Lath had turned into land in front of Zea and the Captain, and then his skills all aligned. **[Tactical Foresight]** told him exactly how Lath was going to attack, and **[Unarmed Martialist]** worked to get his limbs coordinated to stop it. **[Mace Mastery]** had the weapon practically spinning across his fingers to bring it around at the right angle, and **[Counter]** was already lining up how to respond to what he was predicting Lath would do.

Luke crashed into Lath feetfirst and drove the man to the floor. Lath rolled immediately, exactly the way Luke had predicted, and Luke went with the momentum. He spun a complete circuit in the air that arced his mace around to smash into the back of Lath's skull, shattering bone and spraying brains and blood down the hall. Both women flinched away, but Luke wasn't done.

Even the head shot wasn't enough to put Lath down. Luke left the mace embedded in the back of the monster's skull, landed with both feet planted on Lath's shoulder blades, grabbed the inquisitor's arms, and pulled. [**Power Strike**] surged down into Luke's hands, and with a wet, tearing sound, both arms ripped free. Luke hurled them up behind him and onto the deck.

Still alive and thrashing, Lath managed to spin himself around now that Luke was no longer holding him in place with his arms. The mace smacked against the floor and fell out of the back of Lath's skull when he rolled, but they both ignored that. Luke got hold of Lath's shirt and heaved, tossing the inquisitor back up onto the deck.

"Gonna be hard to swim without any arms," Luke told him.

Lath didn't seem to care. He rolled to his feet and came back at Luke with a series of lightning-fast kicks. Luke had to let a few of them land to get a good grip on Lath again, but once he had it, he spun in place once and hurled the inquisitor over the edge of the boat.

Somehow, impossibly, Lath got a foot hooked in the railing just as he was going over it. Zea's enchantment worked against them then. Thanks to the magical reinforcements, the wood held, and Lath managed to roll back onto the deck and to his feet. He was already in the air when Luke caught a flash of red and silver out of the corner of his eye.

Someone, probably Zea, had tossed his mace back up onto the deck. It wasn't a very good throw, and there was a real possibility of the mace tumbling overboard if Luke didn't go after it, but there were good intentions behind it. Luke turned his back on Lath and sprinted for the weapon. He went into a roll as he snatched it up and came back to his feet just in time to lash out behind him and catch Lath with a solid smack to his ribs.

The inquisitor stumbled backward. Without his arms to help balance, he struggled to keep fighting, but Luke could see it was only the means that was missing, not the will. If he let Lath escape, there was every possibility the man would somehow come back from even this. There was no blood coming out of the stumps. His brains were exposed to the open air, and his ribs were basically powder after all the hits he'd taken. Whatever Lath was, he wasn't human anymore.

Luke tripped him, planted a foot in Lath's groin, and used both hands to tear off a leg. He tossed it overboard, then repeated the process with the other leg. The whole time, Lath struggled, not to escape, but to curl up on himself and bite at Luke's foot. It would have been an impressive display of flexibility for Lath to get his mouth down there if not for the fact that his teeth were gnashing the whole time.

"Maybe it's just that your ribs aren't in the way anymore," Luke said. "There was a rumor back when I was in school about a guy who had a rib or two taken out so he could . . . You know what, never mind."

With no limbs left to move him around, Lath was an easy target. **[Life Surge]** had worn off, but Luke still pummeled the inquisitor's face until everything above the neck was nothing but an empty broken egg of bone. Then he worked over the chest until it too was nothing but pulp. No matter how much Luke hammered Lath, he still didn't get the kill notification."

"Why won't you die?" Luke asked as he channeled one final **[Power Strike]**. His mace arced down in a golf swing that struck the bloody scraps of flesh in the flank, and Lath's remains went flying over the side of the ship to splash into the water.

Luke stood there, chest heaving, and stared down at the bloodstained hole he'd battered into the deck right below Lath as he'd beaten the body into mush. There was no way Lath could still be alive, not after all of that.

"System, tell me he's dead," Luke said.

"My apologies, but it appears that man was disconnected from the God Machine before he reached you. It's like he's never existed at all. I can extrapolate that whatever XP he had was returned to be recycled well before your fight with him, but only by noting an unexplained source of XP that matches what I would expect to see from someone of his level. Any records the system had of Adrevald Lath are gone."

"So I guess we'll never know if I actually killed him," Luke said. "But he's got to be dead. And I didn't even get any XP. What bullshit."

Name	Luke Bennet	Zea Stenter
Level	41	35
XP	252683/254133	145001/157276
AP	0	9
Bloodline	SysAdmin III	None
Strength	61	7
Agility	70	27
Stamina	66	27
Perception	55	19
Skills	Mace Mastery (5)	Dagger Mastery (1)
	Sword Mastery (1)	Stealth (2)
	Unarmed Martialist (4)	Keen Instincts (1)
	Power Strike (2)	Lock Picking (1)
	Life Surge (2)	Disguise (2)
	Peripheral Awareness (2)	Deception (1)
	Tactical Foresight (2)	Bartering (2)
	Counter (3)	Streetwise (2)
	Twitch Reflexes (3)	Cooking (1)
	Stealth (1)	Mending (1)
	Survivalist (2)	First Aid (1)
	First Aid (1)	Thalian (3)
	Wood Carving (1)	Neyardic (3)
	Leatherworking (2)	Ostari (1)
	Butchering (4)	Mana Manipulation (3)
	Thalian (2)	Mana Sight (2)
	Ostari (1)	Metallurgy (1)
	Disguise (2)	Whitesmithing (1)
	Deception (1)	Goldsmithing (2)
	Detection (2)	Gem Cutting (1)
	Torturer (1)	Engraving (4)
	Analyze (BL)	Rune Forging (3)
	Remote Access (BL)	Painting (1)
	XP Mask (BL)	Arcano Dynamics (2)
		Sleight of Hand (1)
		Steady Hands (2)
		Cold Reading (1)
		Temperature Acclimation (2)
		Cadence (3)
		Bloodline Purification Ritual (2)
		Ghost Script (1)

CHAPTER 76

Zixin appeared in the nothingness that surrounded her brother's domain. She could have manifested herself right in front of him of course, but that would be rude. There were niceties to abide by. Sometimes, observing those customs was the only thing that kept the Pantheon from fracturing.

For a minute, she thought that Hestoc would ignore her. He couldn't pretend he hadn't noticed her presence, not after she'd seen him watching her, but he could decline to invite her in. If he knew what was good for him, he would remember his manners. It would not be the first time she'd had to discipline her younger siblings, and with all the endless eons left to them, it surely wouldn't be the last.

The doorway opened, and Zixin willed herself through it to find Hestoc glowering down at the world of Aros. "What do you want?" he asked without looking at her.

"The God Machine flagged an error for administrative review," she said.

Hestoc started swearing. "That fucking tattletale. Of course it did. Piece of shit system never did work right."

"You've been meddling," Zixin said, her voice turning cold as the grave.

"Well it didn't leave me much choice, did it?! Somehow it got a cell off planet and found the progenitor's bloodline. What was I supposed to do, let the key walk himself up to the prison and unleash the end of the universe?"

"You were supposed to alert the rest of us. The Pantheon moves as one regarding all matters on Aros. It always has. The prison must be maintained at all costs."

"There wasn't time. If I got the humans there fast enough, they could have removed the threat, just like they did with that girl a few hundred years ago."

"Mm-hmm." Zixin peered down at the world's past and watched a squad of templars slaughter the elementals that guarded the exit out of the valley that housed the doorway. They'd done nothing but make it easier for the boy to escape. "How's that worked out for you so far?"

"If you've come to mock me, you might as well leave. I'm handling this. Don't worry about it," Hestoc said shortly.

"By cutting off a piece of yourself and keeping that servant of yours alive well past when he should have flowed to my domain? By making the prisoner stronger when you left that shard of your divinity behind after the vessel died?"

Hestoc spun to confront her, but Zixin talked right over him. "No, little brother, you aren't handling things. You've bungled this spectacularly. In a matter of months, you've managed to let the key walk himself halfway around the world and grow in strength until he can handle all but the direst of threats, and worst of all, permanently weakened yourself. This is pretty far away from handled."

"Barely a fingernail's worth!" Hestoc protested. "It's hardly permanent. It's a few centuries to regrow at most."

"And we're all still regrowing the power we invested in the God Machine twelve thousand years ago!" Zixin roared. "This isn't just your project! It involves all of us. You broke protocol trying to cover your fuckup, and now it's going to cost us all to fix it, you most of all."

Hestoc gave her a pained look, but he nodded. "You're going to . . ."

"Yes," she said shortly. "We don't have much other choice, do we? Maybe three months ago, there were other options, but at this point, the key has meddled with the system far too much. Did you see some of those skills he has available now?"

"Yes," Hestoc said. "The ones previous keys designed. That level-resetting one is a problem. At least the system does a piss-poor job of designing skills on its own. Its inflated the AP cost on all those bloodline skills significantly. That's slowing him down."

"For now," Zixin said.

"It does give us more time to work."

Hestoc's bluster was gone now. He had to have known just how badly he'd messed up as soon as Zixin appeared just outside his domain. She'd decide his punishment later, once the current crisis was averted. As much as she hated to do it, she had to open the portal and bring in something else from off-world. It would make an immeasurable amount of work for her with all the collateral damage, but it was necessary.

She'd wait until she was done cleaning everything up to assign Hestoc his punishment. That way he could sweat about it for a while, and she'd come down on him when she was in her most foul mood over the whole thing. Otherwise she'd be too softhearted, and he wouldn't learn anything.

"Did you see this new skill the system developed?" Hestoc asked, pointing toward the net of their merged divinity that governed how the prisoner's cells would be contained on Aros. "Look, here."

"Yes, I saw. **[XP Cycle]**. What about it?"

"It might be a worthwhile addition to add permanently. I'm still working on the logistics of it, but—"

"Absolutely not," Zixin said. "The system would break trying to handle the load if every living creature on Aros was constantly cycling XP through the God Machine instead of just at death."

"Perhaps if we were to reinforce it though."

"What? Spend more of our essence? Give the machine an even bigger chunk of divinity to play with? Why would we do that?"

Sometimes that boy could be so stupid. He was an idealistic fool, always wanted to muck around with the mortals living on the planet, as if they mattered in the slightest. Their purpose was to shift the prisoner's cells around, to keep it from reforming the hive. That was it. They were doing that just fine. What did it matter if they killed themselves off before the end of their natural lives, so long as they fulfilled their purpose?

"I just thought, if people lived longer, there might be more of them. They'd be better prepared to handle stronger threats, and the more of them there are, the more the prisoner gets divided up."

"True, but unnecessary. The God Machine is functioning perfectly fine as it is. There are more than enough redundancies built into it, and it has plenty of ways to alert the Pantheon well before anything gets out of balance enough to give the prisoner the opportunity to escape."

At least, it did as long as the key didn't walk right up to the physical manifestation of the machine and let the prisoner out.

Hestoc wasn't happy, but then again, he never looked happy when she denied one of his asinine requests. The system was his pet project, his last-ditch idea to save the last six remaining gods from assimilation into the hive. No one else cared about the God Machine, as long as it remained functional. The rest of the Pantheon devoted their time to regaining the divine essence they'd spent building the prison.

Not Hestoc. No, he was always trying to tweak it, to make little changes or sneak things in. At least once a century, Zixin had to come down and remind him of his place. He was but the architect of civilization, not the master of the world.

"There will be no changes. The Pantheon will gather immediately, and we will break the seal. The flood will be unleashed, the God Machine will be protected, and the key will be removed, just like every key that came before him," she said. "I will expect your presence shortly to participate in the breaking of the seal."

"It's going to cause a lot of damage to the eastern continent," Hestoc warned, as if she didn't already know that. He forgot who he was speaking to.

"Such is the price of your failure. That is why you will be donating the lion's share of essence to the ritual."

His face twisted into an ugly scowl, and he said, "Now see here. I'll contribute my share and not one shred more, the same as everyone else. If the Pantheon stands as one, then let all of us bear the burdens equally."

"We would, had you alerted us to the problem immediately. Instead, you broke the Covenant and meddled. Consider it a part of your punishment."

Before Hestoc could reply, Zixin willed herself back to her own domain. She stared down at the soul of Adrevald Lath with its little splinter of divinity that was so much bigger than the mortal soul itself was. It was a bit hypocritical, but she'd managed to snag Hestoc's fingernail before it had been absorbed into the God Machine. The prisoner wouldn't be feasting on that.

By all rights, she should have returned the splinter to her brother. But then, he'd already thought it was lost anyway. What he didn't know wouldn't hurt him, and besides, she'd be the one doing all the cleanup work after the flood killed thousands and thousands of mortals. She'd earned herself a reward.

She consumed Hestoc's essence and, not for the first time, considered eating her siblings. But no, the power she gained would not match their combined might as a Pantheon, and right now, they needed that full might. This little snack wouldn't hurt though. It was barely a nibble.

The soul was discarded. At this point, it had been so thoroughly mutilated by Hesoc's attentions that it was easier to just recycle it than spin it back out into a new person to be reborn. The pain that soul went through was as indescribable as it was delicious to her. It was rare that she got to destroy a soul anymore, and she savored the experience.

Then it was time to get to work. Zixin reached out to her brothers and sisters, and soon, all six of them were gathered. They all knew why they were here, though only Dar looked excited by the prospect. He would. His followers would fight against the flood and perhaps even find some measure of victory. Hestoc and Nuvari both gave her sour looks, knowing that their domains would be damaged in the coming months. But cities could be rebuilt, and trees could be planted anew. They'd survive.

Luos of the light and Ramira of dreams were less interested, here more as a courtesy in the service of the Pantheon than out of any personal desire. Their interactions with Aros were more ethereal, and other than the loss of some inconsequential worshippers on one completely unimportant planet, noted only for its status as the home of the God Machine, the flood wouldn't inconvenience them at all.

"You know why we are here," Zixin began, shooting a pointed look at Hestoc. "The seal must be broken and the flood unleashed. All of us will contribute. Hestoc will be the primary in this ritual and contribute fifty percent of the needed divinity. The rest of us will each contribute ten."

That drew some surprised looks, but they all knew by now that it was his fault the situation had gotten so out of hand, and none of them objected. Each took their place, and with Hestoc as the primary donor, he led them in merging their powers.

The seal broke, the portal opened, and somewhere deep out in the wilds of the eastern continent, the first demon fell into the world of Aros. It was swiftly followed by another, and as the portal widened, the trickle became a mighty river. They came in all sizes and shapes, no two quite the same but all united in their hunger for mortal flesh. The demons spread out in every direction, and the world of Aros suffered under their touch.

They would kill anything and everything they came across. And when they finally spread far enough to reach the key, they would kill him too. He would never get near the prison. It was only a matter of time until this problem was resolved, and then the mortals of Aros that survived the flood could begin rebuilding. The God Machine would move sluggishly for a few decades, and everything would be set aright. This was the last key. With his death, the bloodline would be extinguished.

Zixin watched the demons pour into the world, and she smiled. There would be a lot of deaths, and that meant a lot of work for her, but it was worth it. They were about to wipe out the final threat to their plans, after all.

Name	Luke Bennet	Zea Stenter
Level	41	35
XP	252683/254133	145001/157276
AP	0	9
Bloodline	SysAdmin III	None
Strength	61	7
Agility	70	27
Stamina	66	27
Perception	55	19
Skills	Mace Mastery (5)	Dagger Mastery (1)
	Sword Mastery (1)	Stealth (2)
	Unarmed Martialist (4)	Keen Instincts (1)
	Power Strike (2)	Lock Picking (1)
	Life Surge (2)	Disguise (2)
	Peripheral Awareness (2)	Deception (1)
	Tactical Foresight (2)	Bartering (2)
	Counter (3)	Streetwise (2)
	Twitch Reflexes (3)	Cooking (1)
	Stealth (1)	Mending (1)
	Survivalist (2)	First Aid (1)
	First Aid (1)	Thalian (3)
	Wood Carving (1)	Neyardic (3)
	Leatherworking (2)	Ostari (1)
	Butchering (4)	Mana Manipulation (3)
	Thalian (2)	Mana Sight (2)
	Ostari (1)	Metallurgy (1)
	Disguise (2)	Whitesmithing (1)
	Deception (1)	Goldsmithing (2)
	Detection (2)	Gem Cutting (1)
	Torturer (1)	Engraving (4)
	Analyze (BL)	Rune Forging (3)
	Remote Access (BL)	Painting (1)
	XP Mask (BL)	Arcano Dynamics (2)
		Sleight of Hand (1)
		Steady Hands (2)
		Cold Reading (1)
		Temperature Acclimation (2)
		Cadence (3)
		Bloodline Purification Ritual (2)
		Ghost Script (1)

ABOUT THE AUTHOR

EmergencyComplaints grew up reading fantasy and tried his hand at writing his first novel on an old MS-DOS text editor program when he was seven years old. That story didn't pan out; maximum character limits were a thing back then. Undeterred, he kept writing on other platforms, reading full-time, devouring JRPGs, and playing *D&D*, and he is now the author of the God Machine and Ascendant series. Check out his most recent work on Royal Road.

DISCOVER
STORIES UNBOUND

PodiumAudio.com

www.ingramcontent.com/pod-product-compliance
Lightning Source LLC
Chambersburg PA
CBHW030919120726
47906CB00002B/394